Knights Templar
Villeneuve du Temple

la Ville

la Seine

N

S

Paris (A.D. 1244)

The Crown Rose

THE CROWN ROSE
Fiona Avery

THE HEALER
Michael Blumlein, MD

GALILEO'S CHILDREN: TALES OF SCIENCE VS. SUPERSTITION
edited by Gardner Dozois

THE PRODIGAL TROLL
Charles Coleman Finlay

PARADOX: BOOK ONE OF THE NULAPEIRON SEQUENCE
John Meaney

HERE, THERE & EVERYWHERE
Chris Roberson

STAR OF GYPSIES
Robert Silverberg

THE RESURRECTED MAN
Sean Williams

FIONA AVERY

Published 2005 by PYR™, an imprint of Prometheus Books

Inquiries should be addressed to
PYR
59 John Glenn Drive
Amherst, New York 14228–2197
VOICE: 716–691–0133, ext. 207
FAX: 716–564–2711
WWW.PROMETHEUSBOOKS.COM

09 08 07 06 05   5 4 3 2 1

Library of Congress Cataloging-in-Publication Data

Avery, Fiona.
     The crown rose / Fiona Avery.
         p. cm.
     Includes bibliographical references.
     ISBN 1–59102–312–2 (hardcover : alk. paper)
     1. Isabelle, Princess of France, 1225–1270—Fiction. 2. France—History—Louis IX, 1226–1270—Fiction. 3. Kings and rulers—Succession—Fiction. 4. Immortalism—Fiction. 5. Princesses—Fiction. I. Title.

PS3601.V467C76 2005
813'.6—dc22

                                                                                                2005002209

Printed in Canada on acid-free paper

For Joe

My Compass Star

Acknowledgments

Angela, Ben, Benedict, Christos, Christy, Erin, Jim, Joe, John, Julia, Leah, Lou, Marva, Renae, Russell, Suzanne, Terry, Tippi

If I have prophetic powers, and understand all mysteries and knowledge, and if I have all faith, so as to remove mountains, but do not have love, I am nothing.

(I Corinthians 13:1–3)

Part One
B O O K   O F
VOWS

Preface

The women in my family were all queens. My great-grandmother was Eleanor of Aquitaine, queen of both France and England. Her daughter Eleanor, my grandmother, was queen of Castile. My mother Blanche was queen of France, and daughter of Castile.

I, Isabelle, failed them in this honor.

I am not a queen. I sit alone nights, without husband or family. I read. I have read books by poets, and the works on philosophy, science, reason, religion, literature. At one time or another my eyes have glanced the pages of nearly every book ever written. My mother Blanche never had time to read, or sew, or hunt. She signed treaties, held feasts, knighted sons, went to battle. She loved words, but she could never just sit and read.

Now, I am old, and as I sit beside the fireplace, I think about how my mother and I once seemed nothing alike. It is an odd thing, then, that today I should feel so very much like her. We argued constantly about what was right. We fought so much that we never saw we were talking about two sides of the same coin.

There were times when I didn't think she understood, but I see now that she always understood and had come to the same conclusions I have, long before I knew they existed. She had a wisdom I didn't want to learn, and a life I never sought. In straying from her life, my own became just like it. Though I fought against it, I too have stumbled upon the same unique fate that awaited all my ancestral line.

Though I was never a queen, I was destined to do great things. I would make changes that lasted forever, and influence the very world with my own imprint.

I was never a queen, but I was always a leader.

Editor's Note

The preceding letter was recently found along with the complete, original text of the manuscript *L'Histoire d'Isabelle*, first assumed penned by court chronicler Sir Jean Beaumont. But the recent discovery of this letter validates the theory that this is not a *biography* of Isabelle's life but rather a memoir. *L'Histoire d'Isabelle* means the story *she* told, in her own words. Why she chose to conceal that fact in the way the work is written is still a mystery.

It is one mystery among many that surround this royal family. King Louis and his sister Isabelle were canonized as saints after their deaths. But why Isabelle and Louis, of all the monarchs living in 1245, including the emperor of the Holy Roman Empire and the emperor of Jerusalem? Why this royal brother and his sister? What could possibly have touched their lives and immortalized their names?

Perhaps we finally have the answer, by Isabelle's own hand.

Foreword

12, *février, l'an de notre Seigneur* 1244

An overwhelming sense of time lay across the heavy stones of the tower. The first time she had come here, there was a road that answered only to *Him*; once departed, there were no roads that could take her back to this place if she came alone. Now the road was open to anyone who chose to brave the forest.

The rain polished the tower's dark stones and slipped down the mortar with searching fingers of running water. The tower's peak disappeared into the twilight mist that curled about the top of the forest. The passage of time was recorded in every stone; the convergence of dormant centuries overwhelmed the lumbering vehicle of her thoughts. She could sense it but not express it; it was as elusive as an odor; pungent, pervasive, and defying analysis.

Isabelle walked to the great oak door, afraid to open it. Afraid to look inside.

"I did this." She was as heedless of her voice as she was of her hair matted against her head and her skirts heavy with rainwater.

Her wet hand touched the oak door. It was cold, barren, and slick. She pushed.

Beyond the door, the tower was dark and deserted. She passed silently through the empty parlor, a trace of rainwater trailing behind her.

She climbed the weathered stone stairs, winding ever higher inside the massive tower. She climbed until she reached the Great Room at the top of the stairs and then stepped inside. The room was dark and nearly empty.

In one corner, across from the window, there was a withered rose in a pale glass vase. The sight of it made Isabelle's heart tighten. She knelt beside the vase, feeling the itch of damp skirts clinging to her legs.

The rose petals were wilted and brown. She was afraid to even breathe, for fear of scattering them. And she knew . . .

This rose had been left. For her. Alone.

She reached out to touch a wilted petal. It fell from the rose to the floor.

"Oh." She spoke as if she'd caused it pain. The scent from the decaying rose reached her, faint and elusive, then faded altogether. She cried and couldn't bear to look anymore. After a moment, she stood and walked over to the window.

Isabelle watched the western sky as the sun went to sleep beneath the trees of the ancient Western Wood. In the distance, silent geese were flying south. The shadows of the tower closed around her.

Her gaze fell to the grounds at the base of the tower. Despite overwhelming heartache, she spoke. "I can do this. I can build a wall, make dormitories and even a sewing hut. I promised, and I will . . ."

She sighed. "I will . . . when it doesn't hurt so much." The thought of the work ahead, building a convent with her bare hands, almost overwhelmed her. Yet that was the reason she owned this land, and had endured the cost it had exacted of her. The dream was all that remained. There was so much to do, so many things that must be started before anything could conceivably begin to begin.

As she turned and headed for the door, something caught her attention in the dark corner. Resting one hand on the door frame, she paused to look back. The rose sat in its pale vase. And it was in full bloom. Red as wine. Vibrant . . .

And alive.

Isabelle gasped, remembering the touch of the petals on her hand. She looked down and rubbed her fingers absently together.

"Where do I start?"

Greater things are believed of those who are absent.

Tacitus, *Histories* (A.D. 104–109)

1

26, *mai, l'an de notre Seigneur* 1234

Young Isabelle crept into Louis' room before dawn. The wooden floor was cold under her slippered feet, and the air was clammy against her white nightgown. A dressing gown of heavier fabric hung over her flat, girlish chest. She was only nine years old. Louis, asleep under the covers, was twenty.

She shuffled over to his large, ornate bed and crawled under the warm covers next to him. He stirred at the contact, but before he was fully awake, Isabelle cupped her icy little hand near his ear and whispered, "Why are you going away today? I want you to stay here!"

Louis, eyes still closed and one side of his face smashed against his pillow, smiled and said nothing. Little Isabelle took her fingers and brushed the curly, yellow strands of her brother's hair from his face. "*Maman* won't let me go with you today; she says I am too young to travel. Please let me go with you. You are the king. Make her change her mind, Louis."

Since he could no longer pretend, Louis rolled over and grasped his only sister with one arm. He placed the other one beneath his yellow locks of hair and stared up at her. Her eyes, like his, were a deep blue. Isabelle and Louis shared many of the same traits, and her eyes met his with an inquisitive, pleading stare.

"*Maman* is queen regent, Little Rose." Louis spoke with a voice still waking. It was lower and more gravelly than usual. "I can't go against her wise judgment on the frailty of little girls on long voyages. She has more experience than I do in these matters."

"Then please stay."

"I cannot stay, either."

Isabelle frowned. "But I am your favorite! Marry me!"

Louis laughed. "I don't think the Church would look too kindly on that, Little Rose. It's that prickly issue called *consanguine marriages* we'd be guilty of. They'd never allow it. But the thought is appreciated." He looked deep into her little girl's eyes. "I promise no one will ever take your place in my heart."

"You are mine, Louis," she said. It was the voice of an adult, reaching far past her youth. He knew how much his sister idolized him, and it touched him deeply.

"And I will always be yours," he assured her, though she seemed unconvinced. "I will be back, and things will not be different."

In the hallway, voices approached and footsteps shuffled across the cold, bare floors. As Isabelle looked back over her shoulder, baby-fine, golden locks spilled out of her nightcap and over her little shoulders. *One day*, Louis thought, *she will win a man's heart with that beauty and understand the entire affair that marriage is. But not today, not at nine years old.* Louis knew that he was her sanctuary, sheltering her small frame when the world turned about her and left her alone in confusion. He hugged her close.

The door opened and their mother Queen Blanche stood in the doorway with several attendants. "*Bon Dieu*, Isabelle! My heart stopped when I saw you were away from your bed, *cherie*! What are you doing in here pestering the king? This is not allowed. I can't make these exceptions."

"It's fine," Louis said. "She was saying good-bye to me."

Blanche threw up her hands. "I don't run a royal household, I run a menagerie!"

Louis rubbed Isabelle's back with the flat of his palm. "Well, our little monkey from the Orient is here with me. No need to worry now."

He could tell Blanche did not approve of his leniency. It was important to be patient with the younger siblings. They were confused and easily left out. He remembered being nine years old once, feeling insignificant among the large and looming rituals that were a part of palace life, and he wanted it easier for his brothers. And for Isabelle.

The servants began lighting the braziers around them in the Great Room. The fireplace crackled merrily as the smell of woodsmoke filled the air, closely followed by the scent of smoking sausages and sides of meat that hung high inside the chimney on little hooks. Isabelle knew the smell well.

Blanche stood perplexed at the foot of the bed. Her Castilian features were most prominent when she was still in her dressing gown, with her long, raven hair hanging down in a thick braid. Her eyes were brown and shimmering, and they had a lovely almond shape. Unlike Isabelle's or Louis' pale skin, her skin was olive hued, rich against the white of her nightgown.

"I expect you to hurry then. We leave at midmorning today." She seemed harsh, but under the surliness was the rough affection Louis had known all his life. He loved her for it.

"Of course, Mother," he replied. "I'm just getting out of bed now."

The queen and her entourage left the Great Room to Louis and his sister. Isabelle hopped out of bed and warmed herself at the brazier, which had wheels like an iron wheelbarrow and could be pushed to wherever heat was needed. While Louis slipped out of the covers and dressed himself in his undergarments, Isabelle regarded his naked, thin body with no special curiosity.

"Water for your ears and face?" she offered, going over to a nearby stand with the pitcher and basin.

"Not today. They're going to bathe me."

Isabelle was jealous. "You get a bath?"

✤ ✤ ✤

After his bath, Louis was dressed in splendid silks and rare cottons, and capped with a leather hat. By the time he was finished, his great four-poster bed had been turned back into a dais where the royal family could sit and attend to matters at court in the Great Room. The royal throne was actually assigned double duty as the royal bed for King Louis. It was a very comfortable dais by day, with many pillows propped up against the wall to form a seat from what had been a bed the night before.

As was the custom, four long tables were placed in the middle of the room, then four pans of charcoal were slipped under the tables to warm royal feet.

Isabelle was dressed in plain clothing, as was appropriate around the house when there was no special occasion. This depressed her even more. While they tightened the gown around her chest, she watched several servants adjusting an ermine cloak on Louis' shoulders. It just wasn't fair.

Suddenly Robert's voice echoed through the chamber behind Louis. "You look almost worth marrying!"

Much to the chagrin of Isabelle's handmaidens, Isabelle stretched away from tucking fingers to look at her brother Robert, who was also wearing fine clothing. Isabelle truly adored him: his looks and his might! And today she thought Robert looked even more dashing than usual.

Robert had their mother's hair, so black it had a purple-blue sheen in the sun, and a wet beard smoothed down in a duke's cut over pale, smooth skin. His eyes were a light gray under dark, rich eyebrows. And the deep purple overcoat he wore offset his eyes like an orchid to ice.

Louis turned at his tailor's behest and faced Robert, letting the tailor tuck the last of his garments together. The king smiled at his younger brother. They were only two years apart, and there was a joyous rivalry between them. Robert looked over Louis' outfit and whistled.

"Right down to the shoes, Your Highness!" He grinned, and then leaned in close. "But in the end, I'll be the one she longs for, and it'll only break her heart when she sees what she *could* have had." Robert tugged at his jacket collar in a distinguished manner.

Louis only shook his head and blushed. He never joked about women, and Robert knew it. Though Isabelle didn't understand the jest, today was a day Robert had obviously longed for: the chance to tease his older brother about lovemaking, the one thing King Louis couldn't handle in outright conversation. Robert had already handled lovemaking numerous times.

Isabelle's third brother, Alphonse, and Queen Blanche entered shortly after this exchange. Isabelle could hear them arguing down the hall. Alphonse was a small man with an emaciated build and hair that was somewhere between blond and brown. His eyes were almond shaped like his mother's but green-gray hazel. They were kept behind the latest technological development: pince-nez spectacles. His one saving grace was a keen intellect. He was especially accurate with numbers, and Blanche had placed him as head of the family coffers.

Isabelle rarely paid much attention to Alphonse. She didn't understand his rapid arguments with Blanche about finances. Blanche heard none of his arguments either, as usual. That's why she'd placed him in his position, so she wouldn't have to worry about it.

"Mother, it would be inappropriate to pay that much for a tent when we can—"

"Oh, enough already, Alphonse! This is a king's wedding, and I spare no expense for Louis. So *forget* the coffers!"

Alphonse stopped walking, at a loss, as the rest of the family stared at him. Robert was grinning as he poured water from a clay pitcher into a bronze cup and then took a big gulp. It was time for breakfast bread.

Blanche seated herself at the foot of one of the main tables. Louis sat at the head. The youngest children sat nearest to Blanche, where she could keep an eye on them. Robert sat next to Isabelle, then Alphonse across from Robert. Their places had long been established as children and had not changed. Charles, the youngest, was unaccounted for—again.

"Where is Charles? That boy is never present!" Blanche called to the table of servants across from them. "Go and find the boy! He can't go without breakfast! And I won't have him missing Mass again!"

But Charles could not be found. That was Charles' main trait: absence. His worse trait was that he was a peculiarly angry little boy, known for kicking and biting. Isabelle hated him. The two had had to be separated in the nursery when she was four years old, because she'd wake up with Charles biting at her arms.

After breakfast, Isabelle sat through the family sermons and marveled at the quiet grace of the tower's inner chapel. Mass was her favorite part of the day, and she pondered the wondrous rituals every morning, listening to the chants, smelling the incense, and hearing the Latin wash over her. She wanted to learn Latin one day, because she knew Latin was the very voice of God, the tongue of saints, and if she mastered it, she believed it would allow her to speak directly to God.

After Mass, distinguished royal guests arrived at the *palais*. The German emperor Frederick and his royal entourage were joining the Parade of Royals to Provence. They would be present at the marriage of France's great king to the noblewoman Margaret.

Isabelle paid little attention to all this until the royals lingered and mingled together, talking and laughing. They spoke French and then German, speaking pleasantly while the children who had come with them ran around in circles. Then they pushed two little red-haired boys over to Isabelle, who cringed with shyness. One of them held an offering of friendship: a flowerpot.

"Go on, Henry," the German queen said, standing firmly behind the older red-haired boy.

"No, I don't like her," he said. Isabelle's little mouth fell open in shock. Henry handed the flowerpot to his younger brother, also red-haired, then walked away.

Much to the giggles of all women present, the younger brother knelt on one knee before Isabelle. "I give thee this present as a token of Germany's affection for France's Little Rose."

Isabelle looked into this little boy's eyes. She had no idea what he meant. Neither did he, she realized. She took the flowerpot he offered, then ran to the corner of the room without saying a word.

Blanche called after her, "Princess Isabelle, you must say *merci*!"

She looked up from the dazzling little thorny bush in the flowerpot. "Thank you," she murmured.

Charles had finally appeared after Mass, and had started a game of tag with the young German prince Henry. Henry was Frederick Barbarossa's grandson—a big boy, a bully of sorts—and it wasn't long before Charles and he were roughhousing all over the Great Room floor.

"*Ow!* You can't pinch me! I'm to be king someday!" Henry shouted. The families turned to see Charles underneath the German prince, pinching the latter as hard as he could on the arm in order to get the stocky princeling off his chest.

Knowing that Charles was a mean boy and had no qualms about snagging in a blow below the belt, Blanche rushed over to stop him from an assault that could diminish the odds of any future German heirs.

Isabelle watched it all from behind the white robes of her governess, Neci, a kind woman with much patience. She hid behind Neci's long brown hair and heard that the other little boy who'd given her the rosebush in the flowerpot was named Conrad. Like Henry, he was pale and large, but unlike his brothers, he was also gentle and quiet.

She thought perhaps it was because he had a bit of a stutter. Henry and Conrad were introduced *again* to Isabelle, who shrank back only to be dragged to the front by Neci. Henry was talking about how many toys he had, while Conrad stood staring at Isabelle's gown. Isabelle wasn't listening to them, because she was looking around at all of the adults, who had gotten strangely still.

The women were staring at Isabelle, occasionally making remarks about the two red-haired boys in front of her. They were . . . watching her . . . for some reason. They had never paid any interest before. Isabelle turned her face to Neci's robes and buried it. She felt Neci's hand on the back of her head and suddenly, she was soothed and everything melted away into comfort.

Neci had that way about her. Nothing could harm Isabelle if Neci was near. She could hear the adults laughing, and saying things she didn't understand.

"She was talking marriage just this morning with Louis," Blanche said, and the others laughed.

"Come, Mother, or we'll be late," Louis insisted, and it seemed he was trying to push attention away from his little sister. His voice seemed strained.

"Well, it was good to see the three of them together. Instructive." The German queen, with her strange accent, was speaking to Blanche on the way out the door. "Come, children!"

Isabelle did not turn around to say good-bye, even though Henry and Conrad both said good-bye to her and bowed before running off to join the group. Then there was blessed silence.

Isabelle didn't go down to the carriages. Nor was she missed, for the excitement of the impending journey shut out all other peripherals.

Isabelle was such a peripheral.

She stared down from the tall tower, her little frame upon Louis' bed, her knees bent and legs tucked under. As Neci stood nearby, she held onto his pillow, because she could smell him on it: a sweet cinnamon smell that she loved. The window distorted the carriages and the horses, making them swell slightly.

"Good-bye, Louis," she said.

Isabelle pointed to the two red-haired boys getting into a wagon. "Why do *they* get to go with *their* parents?"

"Because they're German and their parents decided it was fine for them to travel," Neci replied. The governess sat on the dais behind Isabelle, holding the yellow-budded rosebush from Germany in her hands.

"I miss Louis already." Isabelle tried not to cry. She held onto his pillow and bit her lip.

"I will keep you company, Little Rose. You will not miss your brother for long," Neci replied.

"How do you know that?" Isabelle asked, looking back at the rose-bush in Neci's brown hands.

Neci seemed sad. "Because it is what I was told once when I was very young."

✤ ✤ ✤

Despite her assurance, Isabelle found that Neci was wrong. Every day without Louis was terribly long. There was no Robert for company to fall back on, either. Isabelle passed her days close to Neci, for want of affection. Neci gave her plenty, and sometimes Isabelle sensed a deep sadness within Neci that only a child could discern.

Isabelle missed Louis at bedtime most of all. He would often tell her the story of Montlheri. It was a special bedtime legend about her very own family. It centered around the three attendants who had been with Queen Blanche since the early days of her reign. According to the story they had mysteriously appeared to Blanche when Isabelle's father was killed during the Crusades.

Blanche was in the town of Montlheri when the news came that her husband had been killed. She was trapped in the city without an armed escort. *L'Ordre de la Rose*, three sisters who went by the name "of the Rose," came to her aid on that day. Without them, Louis said, the whole family would certainly have been killed by the barons.

And from that day forward, Neci, Norea, and Sofia pledged their lives to Blanche's service. Even now that Isabelle was older, the Order of the Rose helped Blanche maintain control over the powerful southern barons.

Neci, Sofia, and Norea all looked strikingly alike, only their temperaments were far different. Of the three, Neci was the most approachable.

Sofia had always intimidated Isabelle. She was silent and stern, and her dark stare was penetrating. Isabelle had fibbed a few times at dinner, and it was always Sofia's painful stare that made Isabelle confess her sins immediately.

Norea was never around very much. She always seemed to be Queen Blanche's errand girl. Whenever the queen mother had a letter to be sent, she often left the delivery in Norea's capable hands.

Louis called the three sisters guardian angels of the royal line. But they had a name of their own.

The Order of the Rose.

✤ ✤ ✤

Neci watched over Isabelle day and night, and was never far from the girl at any given point. She was an admirable governess: kind and constant, never raising her voice and always allowing Isabelle to follow her compulsions. Many of which took place out-of-doors.

The day after Louis had departed, they had planted the Crown Rose, the little rosebush given to Isabelle by Conrad. Isabelle spent her afternoons picking flowers out in the courtyard behind the great tower of the *palais*. This day, like the others, was warm and sunny, and the little wilting bouquet of wildflowers and daisies and marigolds was a pleasant distraction from her loneliness.

She found the buzz of black and fuzzy bumblebees prowling the garden hedge soothing, and the smell of honeysuckle wafting on the air turned the world into a sweeter place. Isabelle stood by the patch of daisies and swung back and forth, deliberating on which daisy would be added to her little fist of flowers.

The sound of conversation was carried on the wind, as many servants were also outside in the pleasant hours, going about the washing or sewing, or tending *le jardin*. Courtiers strolled idly about the yard. The sun was hot but the air cool, a benefit of the months of change.

As Isabelle leaned over to pick another daisy, she heard a sound and looked up. A giant black bloodhound was prowling the inner keep. It slavered and chewed at its own jowls, and blood and froth formed on its muzzle. Its eyes were red with pain and hatred.

The growling mass of fur and muscle stood only a few feet away from her. She froze with terror, unable to cry out in fear. The eyes of this hound were bloodshot, red-rimmed, and leaking. She had heard her brother say a word once: "rabid." The young girl could see the need for blood in the beast's wild eyes.

She felt the hair on the nape of her neck stand straight up. She couldn't move, could only stare at this feral, demonic hound, who crouched down for the killing leap.

Then its eyes slid past her face, and she realized it was staring just over her right shoulder. It cringed, its muscles contracting involuntarily, and it looked past her with such hatred and anger that Isabelle wondered what it was looking at.

Fighting her own fear, she turned and looked behind her. Neci was standing next to a tall, thin man whose hand was extended, index finger raised slightly. His dark eyes were staring directly into the hound's eyes behind her.

The stranger spoke only one word: *"Go!"* But that one word held the *power* of the *world*. Isabelle turned to look at the hound.

The dog was scampering away even before it had time to take its eyes off the man behind her. It turned tail and fled. Then it was completely gone from view. Isabelle stared after it, breathing fast, her heart beating hard against her ribcage.

She heard the sound of hurried footfalls and realized that Neci had approached and was calling her name.

". . . Isabelle?" Neci knelt down to look at the girl before her. Isabelle looked down at Neci.

"Yes?" Her breathing was easing up now, and she realized her knees were weak.

"You need to go into the house now, Little Rose. It is getting late, and it's not safe outside."

Isabelle frowned, but given the circumstances, she no longer wanted to stay outside anyway. The dog had frightened her. It was the kind of fright that consumes the world, its taste sharp at the back of the throat. Isabelle never forgot the first time she experienced that fear.

But she was *safe*. The dog had fled. The man had made the dog leave. Isabelle turned and looked behind her.

He was gone.

"Who was that?" Isabelle asked.

"Who?" Neci asked.

Isabelle pointed to where He had been standing a few moments earlier. "The man. He stopped the dog."

"You should run inside, Little Rose. Wash your hands for dinner. They're covered in soil." Neci stood and patted Isabelle on the back.

"But he was there . . ." The little girl trailed off in wonder.

"Dinner," Neci urged.

Isabelle walked with weak legs toward the door of the family tower. For a moment she was afraid that the dog was right behind her, stalking her, ready to jump on her back and knock her down to the ground. She wanted to speed up and run to the door and slam it shut behind her.

But then she remembered the man, and suddenly she knew that there would be no dog. She was *safe*, and he had made certain of it before leaving. Even if the dog came back, she *knew* he would be there to stop it. Isabelle didn't wonder why or how. She *believed*.

✢ ✢ ✢

The morning after the dog attack, they sat at the table eating bread and drinking water. As Isabelle sat beside Neci, picking at some bread, she asked, "Why is your hair wet every morning?"

"Because I wash it at dawn."

"Why?"

"It's a part of my oath," Neci replied.

"Knights take oaths, too." Isabelle had just finished reading about King Arthur's court with her tutors the week before.

"*Oui*, they do."

"But what is the oath?" Isabelle asked.

"To protect the king and his family," Neci replied, and Isabelle was uncertain whether or not she meant the knight's oath or her own.

"You protect the king?"

"I do, little one."

"Does that man also protect the king?" Isabelle asked again, for the sixth time since yesterday.

"What man?" Neci asked innocently.

"The *man*! The man who made the dog go away!"

"There was no man, Little Rose. Say no more on it."

"*Non*, Neci. Don't lie. You were with him!"

Neci leaned down, her wet dark hair sloping a bit against her face. "Isabelle, do you love me true?" Neci asked quietly.

Suddenly things seemed very serious. Isabelle replied in a low voice, "Yes."

"Then you will not speak of the man again. Ever. It is our secret, do you understand?"

Isabelle only nodded and swallowed. Neci's voice was serious, but still kind.

"Can you keep secrets?" Neci asked.

"*Oui*, I can keep secrets." Isabelle looked back at Neci, who leaned in with a smile spreading across her long cheeks, turning the corners of her eyes into small crow's-feet of delight.

"Then as your reward, I'll show you another secret. All right?"

Suddenly all was forgotten. "Yes! I'm very good at secrets, I keep many for Louis!"

"Hand me that rosemary needle over there from your bread," Neci said. Isabelle picked the rosemary off her bread and handed it to Neci, who put it in the palm of her hand and closed her fingers around it tightly.

When she opened her slender fingers again, inside, resting on her palm, was a tiny flower no larger than a pea. It was a pale lavender color and so delicate that Isabelle feared her breath would blow it out of Neci's hand.

Isabelle was stunned. "How did you do that?"

"A little divine inspiration," Neci said. "Perhaps one day, if you're very good, you will learn how to do it too."

And despite much prodding, that is all Neci would say about the incident. Isabelle desperately wanted to make flowers from leaves, but Neci would not show her how. Isabelle was always curious about Neci and her two sisters from that day on. She also grew very fond of Neci and carried her secrets faithfully in her young heart.

In the weeks that followed, Isabelle passed the time by reading as she sat by the window in the Great Room. Sometimes Neci would read aloud to her, as she stared at the road that led to the castle, in the hope that Louis would come charging up the center of it on his horse. Coming back home. Coming back to his Little Rose.

Then one day, she heard trumpets, and the thunder of hooves, and as she rushed down the long stairway, she knew that the wait was over.

She ran down the road to the castle gates as the large party paraded past. Finally, Isabelle spotted Louis. Isabelle fought her way through the legs of all the hangers-on, the courtiers who were at every public— and certainly tried to be at any private—gathering, in an effort to reach her brother Louis.

Isabelle had always been afraid of the hangers-on, fearing the way their eyes drank her in, and the yawning hunger they seemed to show through needy arms with grasping fingers. She strove to wriggle through them, and fought against them to reach her brother on the other side of the throng.

His blond hair, like hers, was shining in the sunlight. He had a smile so bright, it made her heart quiver. She ran up to him before he could dismount his horse.

He hopped down to greet his Little Rose and was pushed back by the force of her impact. Isabelle held him tightly about the waist, and a small tear rolled down one cheek. She didn't want to cry, but it had escaped. She had missed Louis—in fact everyone—but Louis the most. Now at last the stretch of eternity seemed over.

A voice from behind broke the tender moment. "Who is this, my dear?"

Isabelle turned and saw a woman with dark brown hair and blue eyes looking down at her.

"This is the Crown Rose of France, my little sister, Isabelle," he replied to the woman. Then he added, "Isabelle, this is my bride, Margaret."

"How do you do?" Isabelle said, and forced a smile.

"Very well, *merci*. Pleased to meet you." The grasp of the woman's gloved hand was soft and dainty as they shook hands. Isabelle felt odd, not sure what it all meant. The smile was nothing more than a formality. It was not unkind, but under the circumstances, there was no way it could ever be genuine.

Margaret took Louis' arm in her own and quietly pushed past Isabelle toward the castle walls. "Your Majesty, you must show me everything here that has meaning to you. Tell me all about your favorites. I want to know them so that I may better know you. . . ."

And then the royal couple were out of earshot. Isabelle stood alone in the road and watched them enter the castle. *But I am his favorite*, she thought as she watched Margaret doting on Louis. Her cheeks were hot, and another tear rolled down her cheek. *Louis? Why don't you tell her? Louis?* . . .

All that we do is done with an eye to something else.

Aristotle, *Nicomachean Ethics* (350 B.C.)

2

1, *mars, l'an de notre Seigneur* 1237

There was something warm and magical about the *palais de la Cité* during the reign of King Louis. Visitors commented on how the *palais* was always lit, even on dark nights, as if an inner light shone from the depths of the castle and into the night. Peace reigned no matter the argument. King Louis was often sought out to mediate disputes for other countries, because his presence, his castle, and his lands were hospitable to resolutions.

No one asked why; no one ventured a guess as to the nexus of the grace that favored the halls and its inhabitants. The children who grew within the walls of the *palais* grew to be straight as yew, firm in opinion, and kind in mercy.

In the year of 1237, when Isabelle turned the bright age of twelve, she was finally an adult of full stature and could attend court.

In appearance, she seemed a young woman of resolute character, good breeding, modesty, and piety.

But in her heart, she constantly fought to rein in her emotions, which were tempestuous and passionate. Her disposition was out of place against the cool cerebral qualities of the queen mother. Of all her brothers, only Robert understood her impulses.

But Robert often scandalized the family, and the queen mother began to insist in consistently more serious tones that he become serious about his duties, marry, and settle down to rule Artois, the province he would receive upon knighthood.

"If he ever achieves it," Louis would often joke, much to Isabelle's dismay. The thought weighed heavily on her.

"There's very little real passion in the royal court, isn't there?" Isabelle asked Neci as they walked the open courtyard halls of the *palais*.

"What do you mean?" Neci asked.

"People in my family never seem to get excited or angry. Haven't you noticed it?"

Neci walked silently for a little bit, and it seemed to Isabelle that something restrained her from answering directly.

"Is that why you read so much?" Neci said at last. "To stay out of the world as it truly is?"

"I like my books," Isabelle said. "They have passion, even if it's arguing geometric theory. But it's clear to me that *Maman* thinks passion is best discarded in favor of courtly manners. I am supposed to be judicious, wise, and contemplative. This is how Louis is, and how *Maman* expects us all to be."

"And so you're lost in a disposition that doesn't suit you?" Neci asked.

Isabelle thought about this. Three years earlier, Isabelle had learned to suppress her feelings for Louis when he brought Margaret home as his bride. She'd practiced containment over these last three years as Margaret and Louis became fast friends. Louis now studied his lessons and went gaming exclusively with Margaret, leaving his brothers behind. Louis' new favoritism often angered Robert. But Isabelle had realized the day that Louis brought Margaret home just how well the blessed art of detachment helped where matters of the heart were concerned.

She had somewhat replaced her passion for Louis with a passionate friendship with Robert. They were known for heated debates over dinner that often resulted in heavy nudges and tickle fights. Robert would resort to physicality when he was out-argued, much to the chagrin of the other family members.

"Well, it's like how Robert and I are often ostracized for our unruly behavior," Isabelle pointed out. "I see nothing wrong with our horseplay."

"You do tend to upset the entire table when you're rolling around on the ground being tickled into submission." Neci's eyes cast a playful glance.

"Isabelle!" someone called out. It was Margaret, from the other side of the courtyard.

Isabelle froze.

"Come walk with me," Margaret insisted.

Isabelle looked at Neci with pleading eyes, hoping to get out of this one. Neci shook her head.

"Sofia has some things I must attend to."

"No, don't leave me to the simpering one." Isabelle groaned. "She latches on to me every time Louis is at court, like a desperate courtier dying to hang on to anyone who'll give her the time of day. The woman can't occupy her own time. Stay. I much prefer your company."

"As I prefer yours, Little Rose, but I have to run an errand for Sofia."

Isabelle sighed as Neci left. She loved Neci fiercely. More than Margaret, who was already fast approaching from the other side of the courtyard. Isabelle's expression melted into a mask of detachment.

"Hello, 'Belle." Margaret embraced Isabelle and pulled her along as if she were no more than a stuffed doll.

"Hello."

"Come, walk with me." As if Isabelle had a choice.

In the beginning, Isabelle was jealous that Louis and his bride had become fast friends. It was even an annoyance to the queen mother. The two young royals were practically inseparable. Over the past three years, their studies together had created a firm companionship. Now, Isabelle wished that Louis was a "companion" more often so that Margaret wouldn't run about the castle looking for someone to cling to. That "someone" was often Isabelle, because she was the only other person who was around on court afternoons.

That Louis and Margaret had become best friends was not as tiresome to Isabelle as the fact that they had consummated their marriage. The "great act" (as Isabelle and Robert would often call it with a great deal of snickering) had happened six months earlier. Isabelle had not particularly wanted the details, but seeing as Margaret had no shame about telling the pope every detail of their nightly activities, she also had to fill everyone else in about her exclamations of joy.

To make matters even worse, since that day of consummation, the two lovers had become disgustingly affectionate with one another in plain view of the rest of the family, and neither could be out of the other's sight for more than a few hours without an overt display of agony, usually enacted over dinner.

For all of that, Louis was always busy with matters of state. Isabelle had grown up accustomed to this. Louis had always been king, even though he gained his true majority in 1235 and ruled single-handedly now. He had added responsibilities as an adult, compared to the responsibilities he'd had when he was just a boy and still in minority under *Maman*'s shadow.

"Why doesn't the queen allow me to sit by my husband when he is at court? Doesn't she realize that *I* am also a queen and have the right to be seated next to my husband?" Margaret began most conversations with a complaint.

Isabelle checked the compulsion to sigh heavily and stared past the hedges to the herb garden, where a great rosemary bush loomed over the sprigs of basil. Perhaps Margaret just needed to release her frustrations, and then the conversation could turn to some topic more tasteful.

Margaret noticed Isabelle staring off into *le jardin*. "Are you ill today?"

Isabelle grew irate. "I'm fine, and my mother rules the house more like a king than queen. When my father died, it took every trick she had to keep us alive. She has never wavered from that desire to sustain us. So you mustn't think her actions have anything to do with you. It's just how *Maman* is."

Margaret grumbled. "I have half a mind to write to my father and complain."

"You could," Isabelle offered.

"No, then you would find me cruel against your own mother. You can say it. Keep me humble, Sister. I am simply in a fit of frustration."

Isabelle shrugged, and they continued on in silence. She had no sympathy for Margaret. It was a spoiled girl's notion that a woman could have everything. After all, she had the ear and arm of Louis at any time during the day. What more could she want? Not even Isabelle had that privilege anymore.

"What did you mean about *Maman* keeping you alive?" Margaret asked.

Louis never told Margaret the story of Montlheri? It gave her a satisfied little smile inside to know that one small thing between her and Louis had not been shared.

"My father died when I was still in the cradle," Isabelle began. "I never knew him. Louis was eleven when he died. Too young to rule as a man. *Maman* was regent. I suppose in a time of peace that would have been acceptable, but the barons were rebellious, and they gave my mother great grief. They wanted their own leader on the throne, and there were many battles. My mother won. If she'd lost, we'd all be dead."

Margaret only nodded. Isabelle felt it fair to speak so bluntly. Perhaps it would give the girl a little respect for her family. She seemed to lack it.

"Louis never told me this." Margaret had found a new complaint.

"No, it's just that it's not his way to brag about these things." Isabelle thought about Neci and her sisters. They had come to the family's rescue in the city of Montlheri, had saved Blanche from certain death when Isabelle's father died. Without the Order of the Rose, there would be no royal family today.

She wished Neci were here now, to save Isabelle from what would be certain death if the conversation continued in this vein. Whenever Neci was around, for some wondrous reason, nothing was onerous, not even Margaret.

There was a disturbance at the far end of the courtyard, and the noise caught Margaret's attention. She was now tugging on Isabelle's sleeve and pointing.

"Look, 'Belle!" Again, the ridiculous nickname. "Something's wrong."

Isabelle looked in the direction she pointed, and certainly there was something amiss. She couldn't see very well over the assembled masses at the other end of the courtyard. A quarrel, perhaps? An impatient courtier waiting to see the king? It was receiving hours inside the Great Room.

Margaret was taller than Isabelle by a head. "It's a *frère*!" she exclaimed. Indeed, a monk in humble brown robes came shuffling up the garden path to the family tower where the great court was held.

It was a rare sight; the Franciscan monks did not come to court often. The more usual visitors were the parish priests or even bishops. Why this *frère* was here was anyone's guess.

"Let's go see what he wants," Isabelle said.

The two women quickened their pace to catch up. Margaret ran on ahead as they passed an open doorway where Isabelle heard Neci's voice. Isabelle stopped just past the door on the other side.

"But she told me to go to this monastery and see for myself," Neci was saying.

"I have already been there. There is nothing to see." A man was speaking, his tone unfamiliar.

"Well, what do I tell Sofia?" Neci asked.

"Tell her—"

"Isabelle! Come on!" Margaret called out from the tower, and Isabelle jumped. She hastened to catch up, in case Neci heard the call and stuck her head out of the room to see what was going on. Isabelle did not want to be caught eavesdropping!

The *frère* had been let in without much introduction, and he preceded the two women by a good length, so that by the time they caught up, his plea was already in session. Nobles and courtiers parted before Isabelle and Margaret as they made their way quietly to the side of the Great Room to listen.

"Please, I beg you to avenge this crime against God, Your Majesty! You alone understand the grave injustice that has been wrought! You are so pious and kind." The monk was shaking.

Louis and his mother sat with the most perplexed and concerned faces. "Good *frère*, We don't understand why anyone would break into your abbey to steal the Nail. No one has ever done such a thing in civilized lands. Can you recount exactly what happened for Us?"

"Yes, Your Majesty," the *frère* began. "Brother Michel and I came downstairs for morning gruel. Brother Stephan makes the gruel on Thursdays and it's not quite . . . well, I don't mean to complain but . . . it's not so easy on the digestive humors. Brother Guy makes a much heartier and tastier gruel."

"Yes, but the Nail?" Louis prompted.

"Oh, *oui*, I'm getting to that . . . ," the *frère* continued. "The Holy Nail—the!—the very iron that touched the hand of Christ on the crucifix!—was stolen well before dawn or even morning Mass. It is our most sacred relic, Majesty!"

"*Oui*, it is most grave," Louis replied.

"We all noticed that Brother Claude was not present at breakfast. I thought perhaps he was feeling ill. So I offered to check his dormitory. He wasn't there."

The *frère* was folding his tassels over and over in his hands as he recounted. "We set out to look for him, worried that maybe he was stuck out in the courtyard garden or fell down or . . . You see, Brother Claude is not a young man, and he has hip troubles and—well, he *had* hip troubles." The poor monk looked so sad. "You see, we finally found Brother Claude, strangled on the floor of the chapel. His body lay over the altar in a most horrible display." The poor monk choked up and could not continue.

Louis dismissed the entire court, save for immediate family and the queen's personal guard, the Order of the Rose. When the room was empty of strangers, he softened and spoke again to the monk.

"We feel for your terrible loss, good brother Thomas," Louis said. "We will look into this matter on your behalf. The murder of Brother Claude will not go unanswered. And We will now offer a reward for the Holy Nail's return. Clearly, an act of violence such as this must have been done by one who commends greed above faith. Your thief intends to sell this relic."

"He would not sell to Your Majesty. He would surely know that you will catch him and kill him."

"Naturally. Which is why We shall provide the funds to the claim, not the means. Our name will not be mentioned. Our good relatives in Portugal, kin through the queen mother's sister, Queen Urraca of Castile, will send out an announcement that the royal family of Portugal is seeking a holy relic for their lands."

Louis leaned in carefully with a gleam in his eyes. "They owe Us a royal favor as it is. Once they have the Nail in possession, and We are reasonably sure that the man or woman who sells the Nail is the culprit, he will be punished. Meanwhile, We will hunt the culprit with Our own bloodhounds. Rest assured, We will not relent until the Lord is avenged."

Brother Thomas bent down on his knees and kissed the hem of Louis' ermine cape. He kissed it repeatedly, and tears rolled down his cheeks as he blessed his king, who put a hand on the man's shoulder and dismissed him gently.

"Leave it in Our authority, Brother, and you will be appeased."

With that, Brother Thomas backed out of the room, bowing low until he was out of sight. When the great doors had closed behind him, Blanche motioned to Neci and Sofia, and the three left the room hastily. Isabelle followed them out, deep in thought.

Thefts happened every day. Possibly every hour. There were as many rogues as there were common men in the streets. There was always some news at the royal court about the latest burglary, theft, or pillage. Looting was a favorite pastime in many unruly baronies and counties. But Isabelle had never heard of thievery in a House of God—not outside of war anyway. And it wasn't just the House of God that was sacred and meant to be undisturbed, but the very object that was stolen.

Holy relics were the foundation of the Western world. Isabelle could not imagine a world without them. They were, each one, a conduit to Heaven, a presence of divinity, a brush against something greater than humanity. No country was without its honorific relic, no king without his most cherished saint; and certainly no individual turned down a chance to pilgrimage to see one of these sacred objects.

While playing on the road as a child, Isabelle had often seen people walking in such haggard conditions—their backs burned by the sun, their eyes squinting with permanent wrinkles—and always they looked so exhausted. But there was another look about them: a look of hard intent.

When Isabelle had asked her mother why the travelers were on the road, and where they were going, Blanche had told her, "On pilgrimage."

There had been a tone of reverence in Blanche's reply, as mother and daughter watched the pilgrims stagger down the road, out of sight. Something about their determination had always impressed Isabelle, from the time she was very small. She saw something in their eyes that she understood—the same glitter she caught in her own eyes whenever she caught her reflection in a pool of water or mirror or a window.

✦ ✦ ✦

Neci and Sofia walked with Blanche to the Queen's Chambers and were speaking in hushed tones. Isabelle walked behind, completely unnoticed as usual. A peripheral.

She was already curious about Neci's previous "errand," and when she saw her join up with the other two in the hallway, she stayed behind them until they got to Queen Blanche's room and closed the door.

Isabelle stood in the middle of the stairway, wondering. Should she go and listen in? Did the Bible ever say that listening to conversations behind closed doors was a sin? Isabelle couldn't remember having read it. Still, it wasn't exactly appropriate for her to eavesdrop.

But they wouldn't expect her to listen in. She was still ignored, despite being considered an adult in all royal happenings. No one had really started to treat her like an adult yet. But as Isabelle became more aware of the events and subtleties around her, she realized how life at court, in the Great Room, was performed as if the family lived on stage. The surprise was, there was also a *back stage*.

And it's much *more interesting*, Isabelle decided as she casually walked toward the closed door.

"This is a matter that the Order of the Rose must get involved in, Your Majesty." Neci was insistent.

"I don't know . . . ," Blanche said reluctantly; then there was a pause. A long one. Something was said that Isabelle couldn't quite make out.

Then, someone sighed. It was Blanche. Isabelle recognized the way it made her feel. "Very well, then. But you must use the utmost caution."

"You will not lose us over something like this, Majesty." Isabelle's mouth opened in awe. That was Sofia's voice. She had only heard Sofia speak twice in her whole lifetime. The elder sister went on. "Our own . . . contacts . . . will know where the Holy Nail may be found. We must make certain the true Nail is found, not a counterfeit. It requires precision."

Neci spoke next. "The situation is more dangerous than you suspect, Majesty. But we do not think it wise to inform the king of this."

"Very well," Blanche acquiesced. "I will leave it in your hands."

A rustling came from inside the room toward the door. Isabelle hurried into another room across the hall. She hid behind a large tapestry near the door and peeked out from behind it. The sisters walked down the hall together, past the door.

"Should I still go to the monastery? He said he's been there and found nothing of consequence."

"Why did he go?" Sofia was cold but irate. "I told him to stay out of this."

"He is getting restless," Neci replied as they passed out of earshot.

Isabelle waited, and then peeked around the corner. Blanche had already closed the door to her sitting room. Isabelle tiptoed out of the side room, leaving the protective tapestry behind.

Who was "he"? she wondered. The assassin and thief? She shook her head. Dear, sweet Neci didn't consort with those types . . . did she? She wasn't sure. Who *was* that man Isabelle had overheard earlier, the one in the room talking to Neci so secretively?

Maybe if she kept following Neci she'd find out. But she'd need a good excuse to get out of the *palais*, especially if Neci was headed to town.

"This is certainly an ill omen," Margaret said to her husband. She was sitting on Louis' lap, his arm about her waist.

"I'm thinking of assigning the Knights Templar to it."

"I think that's wise," Margaret said, then quickly moved to the queen's customary seat beside Louis as Isabelle walked purposefully into the Great Room. Isabelle had the fleeting idea that the rumpled seat beneath her sister-in-law was still warm from Blanche.

Didn't even wait until the seat had cooled, did you, Margaret? It made her chuckle, despite herself.

Louis heard the chuckle and looked at Isabelle approaching. "What amuses you?"

"Nothing," she said, and came up to Louis. She took his large hand in her small one and held it coyly.

"Can I address you on another matter, Brother?"

"You need not even ask—you know that."

"I'd like to make weekly trips to the Latin Quarter for more books. And I'd like to start today."

Louis frowned. "Why? We have plenty of books here."

"I've read them all. I want to see what's in the *Petit Pont* library in the Latin Quarter."

"It isn't really safe for a princess."

"I'll take an escort, if it makes you feel better, but I don't really need one." She pulled on their intertwined fingers. "Louis, they have copies of the *disputatio*, and Leonardo da Pisa's *Liber Abaci*! I want to see Arabic symbols, how they're used in equations. It's going to change everything, you know. Geometry, music, astronomy!"

Louis grinned. "Very well! Stop drowning me in things I don't study—you're making the king feel stupid!"

"Thank you, Louis," she said.

"You know, this is the first time I've seen you smile in . . ." A look passed between them. "Well, in a long time." She smiled and walked away as he looked to his wife.

"Books. She never comes to me asking about men; it's always books. You notice that?"

Margaret smiled. "She's not ready yet."

"I know." He was serious, and her smile faded. "I'm not sure what's going to happen when Mother tells her about Conrad."

Margaret looked out the door. "I don't like him. He's a German. They're so . . ." She couldn't find the right word.

"Mother knows best for us," he said. "She gave you to me, didn't she?"

✤ ✤ ✤

Isabelle hurried to her room at the top of the tower. *Not much time to catch up now, if Neci's already gone!* she thought.

At the age of eleven, she had volunteered for the chilly honor of living in the uppermost tower, because it meant the most amount of privacy. Not that she was particularly bashful, but the constant exposure to Margaret in the Ladies' Quarters annoyed her. She needed quiet in order to read or write, and the attic at the top of the tower allowed for a modest amount of solitude.

On the tall, curving stairway, she heard voices coming from the servants' room. She didn't think anything of it until she heard Neci's voice.

"The way in which he was killed is very indicative. The Hungarian Master always strangles his victims, and he leaves them lying in sacrilegious displays. The monk was resting over the altar—a clear warning to his enemies."

Next came Sofia's voice. "Then he must be stopped and the disaster averted."

The sisters came suddenly out the door, and Isabelle hurried past. She could almost feel them watching her ascend the stairs. Her ears felt hot.

Isabelle stopped and listened once she had rounded the corner. When it was silent again, she crept back down the stairs, and looked to see if anyone was about. She felt terribly naughty doing this, but she liked the excited way it made her feel.

Why would anyone want to steal the Holy Nail, and who was this "Hungarian Master" the sisters were referring to? Isabelle was determined to find out.

Isabelle stopped on the walkway outside. Below, Neci was walking through the courtyard alone. *Perfect*, Isabelle thought and raced down the stairs to follow her.

As she walked the path from the *palais* into the winding road of the *île de la Cité* behind Neci, she kept a good distance between them so that Neci couldn't easily spot her. Isabelle began to fantasize about someday being as impressive as Neci. Learning how to go after assassins and thieves. She'd follow Neci, find the secret location of the Holy Nail, and get to the stables just in time to go after the thief!

She fancied herself on a horse, riding over foreign country, chasing down the thief, who would be stealing glances over his shoulder in terror. She'd close in on him, ready to snatch the rusted, blunt Nail with its square plain head from his grubby hands.

She snorted lightly as she realized she was wearing armor in this fantasy. A product, she was certain, from growing up the only girl in a household of men.

She continued down rue Saint-Jacques to the bridge called *Petit Pont*. The *Petit Pont* crossed the Seine river and passed into the Latin Quarter, home of the *université*. She had broken her promise to Louis by not taking an escort, but she couldn't exactly follow Neci with one. With all the people crammed together in the street today, she began to wonder if not having an escort was particularly wise.

She looked across the bridge to the city beyond. It was broad daylight, and several people were walking around completely unconcerned. There were many nobles, and she didn't feel out of place.

"Louis is being overprotective yet again," she muttered beneath her breath as she pulled up her skirt and continued on her way. She looked around for Neci, spotted her white robe just a few people ahead, and chased after her.

Despite her intentions, Isabelle found herself distracted by the sights of the urban landscape. She had always loved walking among the people of Paris and admiring their ways. Even the bridge, *Petit Pont*, was bustling with daily activities. A man could be born, live a full life, and die without ever leaving *Grand* or *Petit Pont*. Both bridges held housing and shops on their firm structures. They'd been made by the Brothers of the Bridge long before Isabelle's time, and the bridges were just as alive as the men and women who lived and worked there.

Isabelle continued to follow Neci, who was weaving in and out of the stalls that served as shops, each with little windows fashioned from paper, parchment, or cloth that was oiled with a special white wax to keep the rain out.

Isabelle passed a cordwainer making new boots for fall harvesting. Attached to his shop was a smaller stall for the cobbler, who seemed to have more business repairing shoes and boots. The smell of tanning leather came to her, and she brushed her nose, which tickled at the strange odors.

"*Rags!*" came the cry from down the street. "Rags here! Drop 'em in the basket!"

The rag-catcher was a sorry sight, and he blocked Isabelle's view of Neci. Rag-catchers made possible the paper that Isabelle's brother Alphonse insisted on using instead of the more expensive parchment. Rag-catchers spent all day collecting scraps of material that they'd take to the *papiers*. It would then be tossed into boiling water and softened into pulp. Paper was cheap, and Alphonse preferred its texture for his quill pen.

As Isabelle looked around the rag-catcher to spot Neci, she tossed in a handkerchief. She thought how the handkerchief would make its way as paper to Alphonse's desk and he wouldn't even know it. The thought made her smile, and she kept going, even with the gasping stare of the rag-catcher behind her. Such a fine handkerchief was a rare commodity.

Once safely across the *Petit Pont*, Isabelle followed Neci down rue Saint-Jacques.

Where is she going? Isabelle wondered.

Heading for rue des Écoles? That's l'université . . .

Then a woman bumped into her as she passed. When she looked next, Neci was gone. Isabelle looked around at all the shops and side

streets, but she had completely lost the Sister of the Rose in the confusion of the marketplace.

"Buy a bushel, *mademoiselle*!" a shopkeeper yelled to her. Isabelle
came into town rarely, and never without an escort, so she was pleased
to realize that she wasn't recognized for who and what she was.

"Bats! Bats to cure most ills!" another man called out. She most
definitely didn't want a bat, so she darted to one side of the road and
moved on. She looked helplessly for Neci, but the Sister was long gone.

In another moment, Isabelle found herself standing at the cross-
roads of rue Garande.

If I've lost Neci, I may as well get my books, she thought. Then she
looked up at a rapping sound.

The steady and unyielding sound was a hammer tapping in roofing
tacks. Isabelle stopped and looked up at a shop with a barren roof on
which tiles were being laid. Most of the roofs were thatch, but every
now and then a workman would get enough money to tile the roof of
his establishment. The sign on the building read "Goldsmith," and
with all the bellows, furnaces, and heat of that trade that could ignite
a thatched roof, it was a very wise man who used tiles.

The man had his back to her, patiently tapping in every little
shingle. It was slow, deliberate work, and it made her wonder in
amazement. How could anyone stand doing that all day long? It
looked backbreaking.

The man turned, and she saw he was old and frail, yet there he was,
tapping away all day at those tiny little squares of damnation. Torture
couldn't be worse.

He glanced around and wiped his brow, looking terribly thirsty. She
could see he was looking for someone who could help him. Then, as if
he felt her staring, the old man looked down at her. Their eyes met.

Embarrassed at being discovered, Isabelle made a quick dash down
the street. It was wrong to gawk at such things, she told herself as she
hurried on to *Petit Pont* library.

It is no profit to have learned well, if you neglect to do well.

Publilius Syrus, *Moral Sayings* (c. 100 B.C.)

3

he *Petit Pont* library was a crowded, hushed stone building, filled wall to wall with tomes. Upon Isabelle's unannounced arrival, the entire staff stood and bowed deeply to welcome her.

Such a display always made her feel uncomfortable. *It's not as if I'm as important as Louis or even Robert. Why do they bother with such formalities?*

The question answered itself. Because men have always done it, since the first days of kings and queens. They bowed out of formality, for tradition, and not for her.

That thought made her feel better.

A young man with brown hair and darker robes came up to her, extending a hand in offer of friendship. "Princess Isabelle, this is a most wonderful—if unexpected—visit. We are so pleased to see you here."

Isabelle cleared her throat self-consciously. "I am sorry I didn't give advance notice. I didn't realize it was customary."

The young man smiled. "*Au contraire*, Her Highness may do whatever she wishes. We are merely honored that she wishes to grace us with her presence."

"Oh." Isabelle glanced around the room, preoccupied, still annoyed at having lost Neci in the crowd. This bothered her as she stood before these people, who waited for her to ask for books to borrow. She felt like a Pharisee.

The man stood straighter and adjusted his robes a bit. "Allow me to introduce myself. My name is *Frère* Pierre de Maricourt."

A voice came from behind. "But we all refer to our good Brother as Petrus Peregrinus." Isabelle turned to find another man who had just entered the room from a side chamber. He was prematurely gray around the temples and had a long, delicate face.

He bowed and then extended a hand. "*Frère* Roger Bacon, Your Highness. I am most pleased to make your acquaintance."

Isabelle took his hand and smiled. "I love your work, *monsieur*."

He looked up at her with absolute adoration. "Her Highness has read my work?"

Isabelle started to reply, then paused.

Just behind Bacon's shoulder, the open door of the library could be seen facing the street. Isabelle saw something white pass by the door.

Neci's white robe!

"*Monsieur*, I've read as much as I could of your work—all that we have in the castle library. I'm afraid I've run out of books and have come to arrange the borrowing of others. But . . .

"Do you have a tower here? With a window?" Isabelle asked.

If Bacon found this a peculiar request, he said nothing about it. "This way." He indicated for her to follow him.

Many cries of happy alarm echoed in the library as the two made their way to a staircase. A royal coming to officially tour the library was good news.

"Please tell me whatever it is you wish to study," Brother Bacon said as they continued up the stairs. The next floor had a small window that gazed down on the streets below. "I have many tomes on astronomy, optics, catoptrics, geology, the cosmos, geometry, zoology, mechanics, alchemy. . . ."

Isabelle stared out the window and looked hard for any sign of Neci, but couldn't find any white-robed figure walking through the Latin Quarter.

"I was sure she was here," she said beneath her breath.

"Excuse me?" *Frère* Bacon asked behind her. He was looking over a whole bookshelf of hand-crafted tomes.

Isabelle didn't turn around, couldn't take her eyes off the streets below, just in case! "I was just thinking I'd like some books on . . ." *Was that Neci there? No, just a white tablecloth.* "On mechanics."

"All right, just a minute. Those books are over here." He walked to the other side of the room.

Isabelle realized he didn't sound very happy with her. And the more she looked out on the street, the more she realized Neci was *not* there. The white that had caught her attention was only a tablecloth being shaken out on the opposite side of the street. There was a linen merchant there, just across from the library. Isabelle sighed. She gave up entirely on the idea of ever finding Neci at this point.

"*Oui*, mechanics," she said, and went over to where *Frère* Bacon was standing.

Isabelle took three books she wanted the most, and thanked Roger Bacon and Petrus Peregrinus. She was introduced to many others that day, Guillaume de St. Cloud, Albertus Magnus, and many students whose names escaped memory. By the end of her visit, she had forgotten about her failure with Neci. There were books in her hand. New books. Full of new possibilities.

She moved hastily through the streets in the dwindling afternoon light, the canvas-tied books tucked safely beneath her arm. As she approached rue Garande, she heard the same tapping that had drawn her attention before. She slowed and watched the same old and exhausted man still tapping shingles into place. He'd made little headway, it seemed, since earlier in the afternoon. Again she felt a pang of sympathy for him. Why wasn't anyone helping him? He was too old to be doing that kind of labor.

She didn't stop this time, and he didn't turn around to look at her. By this hour, he was clearly lost in the routine of tapping that consumed minutes and hours without notice.

She walked past, unhappy with the thought. These were the kinds of things Louis never saw in the sheltered happiness of life at court.

Well, that wasn't exactly fair. On many occasions Louis had walked along the streets of Paris and fed the poor. He'd been doing it on Easter and Lent since he was twelve years old. Still, there was a great difference between feeding the poor and taking note of the conditions of his subjects. There was something to be said for the power of quiet observation; anonymity in a crowd will show the truth of a country's subjects.

She realized she was speaking like a haughty Roman politician.

Syrus would be proud of me, she snickered to herself. As if she'd had any experience in politics or city affairs! *I'm neither monarch nor philosopher, why should I endeavor to act like one? It's pride before a fall*, she thought. Looking down at her books, she trudged back to the *palais de la Cité*.

❖ ❖ ❖

That night, Isabelle read her books from *Petit Pont* by candlelight. She went through several candles before she finally fell asleep with the book against her chest, one hand absently resting on the canvas cover.

She woke the next morning, panicked by the fact that she'd fallen asleep with one of the university's books. She might have damaged the thing in her carelessness. Thankfully, the book was not creased in any way. She frowned, angry at herself, and carefully put the book down on the floor beside her nightstand.

Isabelle put on her undergarments, feeling more tired than usual. Even though the sky hung outside her window as a clear, blue invitation to come out and frolic, she was cranky and sluggish. She heard the rattling of the servants' utensils and their garden instruments as they went about their morning chores in the courtyard below.

She washed her face, and her fingers paused over her cheeks as she realized . . . she'd had a dream last night! The old man on the roof, tapping away at his shingles, and then falling—falling off his roof and landing—landing at Isabelle's feet, his body sprawled out and his neck broken, lifeless eyes staring up at her. She cried for help, but no one stopped.

This is why I'm so surly today. She glared out the window at the bright blue sky. Once again it beckoned her to play.

Almost without realizing she was doing it, she came to a decision. *If he can't play*, she thought, *neither can I.*

The old man tapped more shingles on the roof. At this rate he realized it would take him the rest of this week and most of the next to finish. He was used to it, though. Things were never easy anymore, and he'd learned to appreciate the slow moments for what they were. It was the beating sun that caused him the most distress. If his children were here, he could have asked for a drink, but they were all gone. They had families of their own to tend. And he'd lost his wife Beatrice to a fever two years earlier. So he was all alone now.

He continued tapping until he heard someone calling from the street. He ignored it, thinking someone was calling out to another person.

But the voice persisted. "You there, on the roof!"

He sat back, put one gnarled hand on his thigh, and looked down. A woman stood on the street below, dressed in men's clothing, her long golden hair pulled back into a knot at her neck, though loose strands of the curly locks were hanging down her back.

"I've come to help you with your roof, sir."

His wrinkled eyes widened in surprise. He suddenly remembered her. It took a while for him to see the face without all the fancy dressing that went with it yesterday, but now he was sure of it. This woman was the one he'd caught staring at him from the street yesterday.

"I have it all under control, thank you," he said.

"You're tired, sir." She was already climbing the ladder.

What in God's name does this girl think she's doing? If she fell to her death or wounded herself it would be his fault and her family would probably have him hanged.

"No! Don't come up here! I'm liable to get in trouble if you do that. I don't need help." He was afraid, but she didn't stop. It seemed she expected this kind of reply.

"If no one else will help you build your roof, then you will teach me how to nail these on." She took a few shingles and walked gingerly over the surface of the roof. It sloped very gently and had no peak.

"What's your name, sir?" she asked.

"Jacques."

"Mine is Isabelle. I'm sorry I didn't stop yesterday. This has been bothering me since then. I didn't sleep well last night because of it. I stopped and rudely stared at you but didn't even offer to help. You should not have to roof your entire building alone."

The girl looked a lot like his beloved Beatrice when she was young. But this girl's hair was a blaze of gold. Real gold too, which he'd handled a lot, being the *Petit Pont*'s best goldsmith. The sun caught strands of her hair and set it on fire.

She was looking at him, at the lines of his craggy face and the sweat beading up on his forehead. Her stare told him that she was gentle, and honest. And that she felt true sorrow for him. It almost offended him. He was not one to be the subject of pity, but the earnestness in her face meant she felt sorrow about his predicament, not his age or status.

He would not let her work very long, or very hard, but if it would help her conscience to help him, then he would let her.

Besides, everyone should learn a useful skill. One day the girl might need to patch her own roof. Certainly knowing how would mean she could inspect the work of any builders she or her family might hire. And in a way, it pleased him to know that he could pass on this knowledge, the way he had done with his own children. It was something good old Jacques could give this noblewoman that no noble birth could provide her. That made him happy.

So he held the roofing hammer out to her, and she took it in her soft hands. He looked at those hands and knew they would be well blistered by the end of the day.

Isabelle had no idea what toil it was to put on a roof, but she soon learned. By midday her back ached fiercely and her hands were raw and sore. The man had tried to stop her from continuing after just one hour, but she wouldn't give the hammer back. She knew he was afraid to wrestle it from her, lest she trip and fall off the roof during what she anticipated would be a titanic struggle.

He complained, but his strength was returning by the end of the day. Perhaps it was a direct transfer. While she toiled, he recovered. At one point, he even descended the ladder and brought them a huge bucket of water with two cups. But Isabelle did not stop to take a drink, for she knew it would be an opportunity for him to yank the hammer away.

He drank a considerable amount of the water out of the bucket, and Isabelle smiled to herself to see that. It meant he was actually enjoying himself despite his need to personally finish the roof. As sunset lingered on the horizon, Isabelle was just finishing the very last roof tiles. She had made good time, for a beginner.

The blisters on her hands had popped open and were seeping. Not a wonderful feeling, but better than the old man's hands breaking like this. Hers would heal quickly. His might infect, and that could be disastrous. For her, stinging hands meant the gentle turning of pages in books. That was an easier burden to live with.

"*Mademoiselle*," he said, looking over the edge of the roof. She looked up. "I think maybe you should take a look." He pointed with the cup still in his hand.

She turned slowly, her back twinging unhappily. Gathered in the street were about one hundred people, from peasants to merchants, nobles to guards. They were all staring at the roof.

More precisely, at her.

She almost fell off the roof when she realized one hundred people were staring at her. Steadying herself with one hand, she gently laid down the hammer in front of her and gazed around at everyone.

Jacques was chuckling and drinking some more from his cup. "It appears that you've created the afternoon entertainment on *Petit Pont*. I don't think I've ever seen this many people gathered for anything."

Isabelle looked over at him. She was shocked, and seeing all these people with nothing better to do than stare at her from the street made her realize once again why she had come and torn open her hands to help him.

She called down, "Go home if you're not going to help."

Some chuckles, a few murmurs around the crowd, but that was it. No one really moved.

Disgusted, Isabelle turned back to Jacques. "I think we're finished, *non?*"

He looked around and nodded. "*Oui*, we are finished. *Now* will you have a drink?"

Isabelle rubbed her hands tenderly. They smarted with every movement of her dirty fingers. "I . . ." She started to decline, but he looked at her with such an expression of sincerity that she could not refuse. "All right."

"You did something wondrous, young un'. I shouldn't've let you. If I weren't such an old man, I'd've hauled you off a long time ago. It's not right for me to let you ruin your pretty hands like that."

"It isn't right for you to build this roof by yourself," she replied, her anger showing.

Their conversation was interrupted, first by sounds from the crowd, and then by the call of a royal guardsman. *"Make way! Her Majesty the Queen Mother approacheth!"*

Isabelle sighed. This was most unfortunate, but she should have realized that it would come. Jacques dropped his cup and sputtered, "The queen!"

"Yes," Isabelle groaned. "My mother."

The poor old man sucked in a breath of air and choked on it. He was coughing as Queen Blanche walked through those gathered, who were now on their knees.

Isabelle stared down at her mother. She realized wearing men's clothing was not going to go over well with her at all.

"From the description, I thought it was you, Isabelle," the queen mother said. "Now, come down. We should go." Blanche would not admonish her daughter in public, but all the same it felt degrading to be ordered like a child. Isabelle wanted Blanche to understand. She wanted everyone to understand what she had done.

"I will of course come with you, Mother," she said. *"After* I have said my mind to those assembled."

Blanche raised her eyebrow but was silent.

Isabelle held up her bleeding and blistered palms. "This work I have done for a man without family. But he is a subject of my own family. He was a stranger to me, not a nobleman, not even a friend. I learned to call him Jacques only today. Because he is a part of my royal family, as all of you are, I came to him when he was in need of help." She looked around at the upturned faces. "And not one of you gave him any of your own." Some faces fell to look at their shoes as Isabelle continued. "You have walked past here two days in a row, and only lingered to see a woman in man's dress, doing man's work. Now you see that I am a princess. A princess who was not too lofty to do the work of a builder. I am here to teach you a lesson: Learn to help your neighbors. Paris will be stronger for it."

With that, Isabelle stepped down the ladder, taking one last look at Jacques. She smiled at him, and he smiled back. It was a moment she never forgot. It was worth the three weeks of stinging palms that would follow.

To her surprise, Blanche did not speak on the way back. Isabelle watched her face, but it was impassive. She wondered what Blanche was thinking. Louis fed the poor and helped the sick from time to time. Shouldn't Isabelle endeavor to do the same?

Perhaps, though, this was slightly more . . . eccentric. *Mother might be angry that I worked so gruesome a task. But didn't the martyrs walk on their hands and knees to pilgrimage and ruin their skin on the way? Why is this any different?* No, Mother could not be upset about this. If she was, then she was wrong.

At the stables, Blanche dismounted without a word to anyone. She left her horse in the care of Philippe, the stablemaster. Isabelle did the same, and they walked to the castle. Blanche reached the Great Room doors and opened them without a glance back. Inside, Isabelle could see the throngs of courtiers curiously looking out at the Queen Mother and her daughter.

Isabelle was uncertain what to do. Was she to follow Mother into the Great Room? Perhaps Louis was the one angry with her. And if so, then she most definitely did not want to be reprimanded by her brother in front of the hungry eyes of the hangers-on.

Would Louis have stopped to help that man? she wondered. *Probably not.*

Blanche glanced back over her shoulder, her dark eyes meeting Isabelle's blue ones. "Go and change."

It was not harsh, nor admonishing. Her tone was . . . soft. Honestly, wonderfully, maternally soft. Isabelle stood, transfixed, unable to move.

Blanche did not stay, only continued into the Great Room without another word.

Isabelle stood for a long time, a smile slowly appearing on her lips. She felt different after this painful ordeal. She had not been chastised or punished. But she hadn't been praised either. The moment was so fragile, Isabelle was afraid perhaps she had imagined it.

Mother would *have corrected me. She's not ambivalent about these things.*

The very still, small voice of Isabelle's thoughts barely whispered, *I did the right thing and she knows it.*

Then the girl, now a woman, ran up the stairs to her attic room. She changed into her regular attire and tended the wounds on her palms. For the next three weeks her hands would be wrapped in gauze strips. But every time they winced or stung, Isabelle would not gasp. Instead she would smile a secret little smile, remembering the day on the roof and keeping it with her always.

When I was a child, I spake as a child, I understood as a child, I thought as a child: but when I became a man, I put away childish things.

I Corinthians 13:11

4

27, mars, l'an de notre Seigneur 1237

Word reached Louis that not only had the Holy Nail been brought to the royal family in Portugal, but that *eleven other* Holy Nails had managed to find their way to King Sancho II as well. All claimed authenticity, all looked measurably alike, and every owner's eyes twinkled with the thought of receiving the reward of one thousand *gros tournois* for "its" return.

Robert watched as Louis put the letter down and sighed. He had been reading it over breakfast bread in the Great Room with hope that had now been dashed.

Beside him, Margaret looked at her husband from her new place at the meal table: between Robert and Louis, arranged so that she might sit next to him during family meals. This made the table lopsided on one side, with three members now, facing two, but Margaret had insisted.

"What is it?" she asked.

"God despises us, I fear."

Robert had rarely heard his brother this dejected. It unnerved him. *A king shouldn't let that kind of concern loose, even in front of family*, he thought.

"No, Louis, . . . the only person in this room God despises is Charles," Isabelle said, only to be kicked in the shin with great force by her younger brother. She yelped in pain and rubbed her leg as Robert grinned at his younger sister. She often made good jokes at the table, but no one else seemed to appreciate them.

"That will be enough presumption on your part concerning the Lord's intentions, children," Queen Blanche said. "I will send Norea to determine which of these is the Nail, and that will be that."

After breakfast, Robert sauntered up the stairs, thumbs tucked into his sword belt, while his mind chewed on the letter from Sancho. Charles came racing down the stairs with a wooden sword. The boy was slashing and whacking at everything, but when he saw Robert, he bolted past like a scared rat, then continued on his way down the staircase.

Robert watched him absently until he was around the corner. Why hadn't his mother just shipped the brat off to Germany to study among the brutes? Charles was never happy here, never spoke to anyone, and as far as anyone could tell, spent all his waking hours in the palace yard, away from the castle.

The child was an extra burden in a household already weighed down. *And what's worse*, Robert knew, *the boy realizes it.*

If I were king, I'd set a better example for him. For all of us. But Robert didn't really want to be king. Robert just wanted to be important.

He reached his room and turned the latch of the door. Once inside, he realized he was not alone. There was a woman in here with him. He'd had lots of women—it was one thing that made him feel important when he was particularly out of sorts. But this was an unexpected visitor.

"Hello, Your Highness," Neci said.

For a moment, he had a flight of fancy that she was here for some particularly physical reason. Instead of being stirred by the thought, it made him nervous. The sisters had always made him a little nervous. But he'd never let it show. "What are you doing in my room?"

Neci chuckled and shook a long finger at him. "You rogue! Nothing like that."

Robert smiled his deliciously wide grin. "A man can hope, you know."

Neci turned serious. "I have come on behalf of my sisters. We have found a way to retrieve the Holy Nail, but we need your help."

This was both welcome and unwelcome news. "Louis just received word—" he started, then realized. "But you probably know all about that."

Neci nodded.

Robert sat on the edge of his bed. "What do you need me for?"

Neci took a breath, then said, "I know who has the Nail."

Robert's eyes narrowed with a sense of huntsman eagerness, but Neci kept going before he could speak. "He will get away from us if we don't act quickly. Créteil is where we can find him."

His eyebrows went up. "We?"

"Yes, I can lead you to him."

Robert shook his head. "*Non*, it's too dangerous for you."

"Robert, I was fending off barons while your mother was still spanking your behind. I understand the nature of danger." Neci crossed her arms. "My question is, do you?"

"You don't need to taunt me into going with you. I'm crazy enough for it. But I don't like the idea of you going with me. It isn't safe."

There was truth to the sentiment, but that wasn't the only reason that Robert wanted to go alone. The sisters had arrived when he was nine years old; young enough to be mystified by their presence, but old enough to note their mysterious actions.

The sisters had not aged one bit since the day they had appeared on the doorstep at Montlheri and asked to help Blanche. The entire town had stood behind them, ready to escort his brother and mother to Paris. An entire town of bodyguards.

In the years that had passed, Robert had grown from a young child of nine into a man of eighteen. The sisters were still exactly the same. They had no age spots, no silver in their hair, no indication of age at all. Even Blanche had aged gracefully, but not the sisters. It was unexplainable.

He had no plain reason to fear them, and in a certain respect he even loved them like family; but he liked to keep them at arm's distance, because something about them made him nervous. Though he'd never admit it, even under duress.

"Objections or no, I *am* coming with you—" Neci started when Isabelle bounded into the room through the open door.

"Robert?" she called, then abruptly stopped at seeing Neci and Robert talking seriously.

"Hello, Little Rose," he said to Isabelle, using her pet name.

"It seems I've come at a bad time."

"*Non*, we're finished," Neci said, casting a look at Robert, as if to say they'd finish later. Then she was gone, leaving Isabelle in the doorway, looking perplexed.

"What was that?" Isabelle asked.

"Oh, nothing." Robert looked down at his belt and adjusted it.

"What did she mean by 'I *am* coming with you'?" Isabelle stared at him. "Are you leaving?"

Robert looked up at her and was about to tell her to worry about other things, like her studies, but stopped. He realized that he wasn't looking at a little girl anymore. Isabelle had matured into a young woman. She hadn't asked with any modicum of childish concern. She had a *tone* about her voice now—a mature, womanly tone.

Isabelle blushed and looked around. "Why are you staring at me so?"

Robert felt like telling her what he saw, but realized that it might be the wrong thing to say, given the circumstances and her discomfort. He cleared his throat and then said, "It's nothing that concerns you. And I'm not going away, no."

She looked at him as if suspecting that he was lying. It didn't help that he *was* lying. Robert sighed and scratched his head behind his ear.

She stood resolutely in the doorway just staring at him until finally he said, "Can you keep a secret?"

Isabelle shut the door behind her. Robert told her about Neci being in the room when he came in. He told her about going after the thief who had the Holy Nail, and that he was somewhere in Créteil.

Isabelle listened and seemed to take it well—no hysterics—but then his younger sister was of a different type than many of the other women in the house. He liked that. He respected a woman who could be as resilient as any other member of the royal court. He liked Mother for that, and he assumed Isabelle got her resilience from Blanche.

"Let me go with you," Isabelle said. The request was so absurd it yanked Robert out of his thoughts. He laughed.

"That's ridiculous!"

"Why? If Neci is going—"

"And I already object to that." He was stern but kind. "I won't have two of you to worry about."

"I can ride, and I can look after myself. I'm in town nearly every day, and I never get in trouble. Let me go."

"*Non*, Isabelle. Not on my life. This is dangerous. And you're still too young."

She curled up on his bed and put her hands over her knees. "You and Louis were fighting against the barons at my age. Why can't I come along on this? It's less dangerous than fighting barons!"

"Because Mother would never allow it, for one thing. You know that."

"I'm tired of being sheltered like this."

"Isabelle, we do it because we love you. Listen to me. Did I not just confide something very important in you?"

She looked up at him. "I want to do more than just listen to other people's secrets."

"One day, you will. But not today." He kissed her flushed forehead. "Enjoy this time of your life. Trust me, it only happens for a little bit, and then it's over and you'll be wishing you could go back to it later."

She scowled. Knowing how stubborn she was, he could tell she wasn't enjoying it at all. "For me?" he added gently.

Scowling gave way to pouting. "It isn't fair," she said. "You make me loyal to you, despite my own best interests."

Robert grasped at Isabelle's golden hair. He knotted it up gently in his fingers and tugged twice, lightly, with a smile. "I'm just as loyal to you too, despite my own best interests at times. You know that."

She could not hold in the smile, though she tried.

"Now, tell me why you were so excited to see me." He stood and opened the door of the room, and they both walked into the hallway together.

✢ ✢ ✢

Louis paused as he dictated a letter to King Sancho II, choosing his words carefully. "I can't in good conscience ask you to accept any of the supposed Holy Nails." He was grave and his eyes heavy. "We're sending an emissary to look them over, but if she doesn't see our Nail, we will have to withdraw our offer until the genuine article appears."

As the scribe scratched these words on a piece of parchment, Louis looked up at Blanche. "It's hard, but I don't see what other choice we have."

Blanche nodded and sat forward on the Great Room dais. "You must do what you feel is right. Just remember, there are other matters at hand even more pressing than the Holy Nail."

"I cannot deal with this missing Nail *and* keep my eye on England, Mother," Louis said.

"That is why I am looking into it," Robert said as he entered. "As for England, things are quiet there for a while. King Henry has married Margaret's sister Eleanor. And in his court, he is surrounded by many French, all in peace. Things with England and France, for the time being, are fine."

"I would be more comfortable with that if Simon de Montfort and Hugh de la Marche were not among the men in England," Louis replied. "That traitor de la Marche will continue to whisper into Henry's ear, and in time we may have another war to worry about."

De la Marche and his conspiring wife were the troublemakers who had nearly cost Louis his life. When he was eleven and the rest of the family were children, the barons, led by Hugh de la Marche, marched on Louis and his family. The battles had been fierce, but Louis had commanded well. He'd had his own wise counsel, comprised of such stalwarts as Jean Beaumont, *Seigneur* Joinville, Pierre Raucliffe, and of course Queen Blanche. Their superior prowess as strategists had helped the boy-king win the war against the barons. Those knights still held counsel with Louis.

Hugh de la Marche had taken up residence in England after that decisive war, because he was sorely hated by the loyals of France. Louis had won the crown back from de la Marche, but he could not dispatch the villain personally before de la Marche and his wife fled to the sanctuary of England.

"Don't borrow trouble, Louis," Blanche said. "England will always be a threat, but for the time being we watch and wait. Hugh de la Marche was put in his place long ago, when we first came to power. Simon de Montfort is now England's advisor, and while I don't especially trust Simon, he has done very little to displease me. I believe he will keep an eye on de la Marche. It's Raymond of Toulouse in the south who worries me anyway."

"That willful cousin is—"

"My favorite cousin," she replied. "As for now, you cannot concern yourself with *every single* matter that arises. Let your brother take care of the Holy Nail while you worry about the rest."

"Very well," Louis said. "Of all the tragedies, this is the worst. It's the one that haunts me. By divine choice, I am the Lord's vessel, and I live with the consequences of that privilege every day. The Lord vests authority in me; He has graced me as no other man may be graced. It then becomes my direct responsibility to clear *any* blight on His name. If I do not serve Him well, then I have failed Him."

Louis held out a hand to Robert, who took it, and they embraced. "So I leave it to you, Brother. Because I know you will secure the Nail while other matters threaten not just us, but our people."

"I will not fail you," Robert said, his eyes serious.

Blanche smiled at her two sons. It was rare that Blanche ever smiled, but when she did, Louis could see why the dark woman was considered poisonously beautiful by her contemporaries. She had the most mysterious allure when she chose to wear it. Blanche's smile could fend off whole English armies.

✦ ✦ ✦

Isabelle made her way down the stone hallway to the spiral staircase. It was late afternoon, and she had gone to her attic room to get a book.

As she walked the stairs that wound up the side of the tower wall, she passed the level of the tower that held the small family chapel for Sunday Mass. There she found Neci at the altar, kneeling in prayer. Isabelle stopped on the stairs. She stood looking at the Sister of the Rose, whose eyes were closed and her hands folded gently before her face. Her lips were moving.

It looked like something Isabelle had seen before, but she couldn't place it.

This is what devotion looks like. It struck a deep chord within her. Isabelle stepped into the chapel. She wanted to talk to Neci alone, for a moment.

"What are you doing here?" Neci asked Isabelle. She seemed shocked to be discovered praying like this.

"I want to talk to you about Robert going away."

"He told you?"

"I'll not pretend I didn't hear you when I barged into Robert's room. I'm not used to my brothers having secret meetings in their bedchambers."

"No, I imagine not."

"He said you're going with him on this trip. I want you to make sure he comes back in one piece. He's . . . If something were to happen to him . . ."

Neci nodded, understanding. "I will watch over him."

"Do you remember that day when I was a little girl? The day you told me not to mention the man and the dog?"

"Yes, I do." Neci seemed vaguely worried.

"I know you are powerful. I know you and the Sisters can . . . do things. I want you to protect Robert. The way that man protected me. Will you do that?" Isabelle asked. She knelt down by Neci at the altar and stared into her eyes.

Without looking at her, Neci said, "I can do this for you. But you must not linger in our presence. You are right." She looked up at Isabelle. "There are strange forces at work in our lives that the common person would never understand. They can be misconstrued by the others, mistaken for something malign."

Isabelle took Neci's hands in her own, and Neci seemed surprised by her forwardness. "Ever since that day with the man, I have believed in miracles. And I have always believed in the goodness of you and your sisters, ever since you saved my family from death at Montlheri." Isabelle wanted to believe so badly that these women were the guardian angels of Louis' bedtime stories. Even if she had to *will it* with her own words.

Neci stared at her, and her eyes betrayed a gentle expression of awe. "I will never betray your trust."

"You have nothing to fear," Isabelle added. Then she crossed herself before Christ's image in the stained glass before standing.

"You have shown an understanding that the Order of the Rose has never encountered before," Neci said. "Especially from someone on the outside looking in."

"I've lived my life on the outside looking in," Isabelle said. "I suppose that's why."

⚜   ⚜   ⚜

Isabelle felt unable to grasp the words of Aristotle that night. Perhaps it was because she was painfully aware of how much had transpired today that was of substance, whereas the words printed neatly on the vellum page about the practice of philosophy fell flat.

She gave up trying to read or do anything except sit on her bed and look out the window. *Who is the Hungarian Master? Why must Robert go to Créteil?*

She was certain her mother, Blanche, knew quite a bit more about the Order of the Rose than anyone else, but she never spoke about the sisters to anyone. Not even Louis.

Still, the recent confrontation with Neci was too powerful to keep still. Neci had so much as admitted to being truly powerful. It was just too much. First Robert having to leave, and now this truth revealed. It made her soul weary just thinking about it. Who could she turn to?

Robert.

She could go to him before he left, and talk to him. He was radically different than the rest of her family, and he would talk to her about anything. Calm her.

It was late, but she rose, slipped on her dressing robe, and walked down to the Gentlemen's Quarters. When she reached Robert's room, she overheard Alphonse talking.

"I don't want to wait until I'm knighted to marry her—I love Joan!" Whenever Alphonse was irate, or agitated, or thoroughly filled with passion—a feat hard to achieve with his bony little body—his voice became supremely nasal.

Alphonse was interrupted by Robert, whose deep voice made his brother's voice sound like a tiny, raspy reed. "I'm rather distracted right now. Can we talk about this later?"

Isabelle took advantage of the silence to step inside the doorway, and both brothers turned around.

"Isabelle," Alphonse said.

"Hello." Isabelle didn't want to say why she was here in front of Alphonse, so she just stared at Robert after a quick smile to them both.

Taking the hint, Alphonse cleared his throat and walked out of the room. Once they were alone, Isabelle realized Robert was fingering some clothing. His good sword was out on the bed for cleaning. The rag and oil sat nearby.

"Robert, I know we talked about this earlier and it's set and everything but . . ." She wasn't quite sure how to begin, but the whole of the situation flooded into her.

"I don't want you to leave."

Robert nodded quietly and put a small bundle into an open saddlebag at his left side. "I won't be gone for very long."

"Please be careful, would you?"

Robert chuckled. Isabelle adored his chuckle more than anything else. She walked over to him. "I'm going to miss your laughter."

"You make it sound as if I'm not coming back."

"Are you coming back?"

"Of course I am. Just a quick jaunt to Créteil and back. When I come back, I'll have the Holy Nail in hand.

"Well, not *in* hand." He grinned. "In my *possession*. That sounded terribly wrong somehow. . . ."

Isabelle laughed, despite herself. "Robert, you shouldn't say those kinds of things!"

"It wasn't intentional, Little Rose, I assure you."

"I want to do something to ensure your safe return."

"What's that, Rose?"

"I will go to Notre Dame to pray."

Robert came around the side of his bed and planted a soft kiss on his sister's cheek, taking her in his large arms and squeezing her tightly in a warm embrace. He smelled of wild forest and tart berries. She loved the way he smelled, very different from the sweet cinnamon smell that Louis had. She held him tightly and kissed his neck once for good measure.

"Don't do anything foolish," she scolded.

"My very advice to you!" He picked up his saddlebags, put them beside the door, and sat to continue cleaning his sword.

She sat beside him then, and neither spoke of his journey, or of the perils that might lie ahead as he went after a thief and killer. He made many pleasant jokes, and they laughed. He promised not to seduce tavern maids and sow his oats on his travels, so that he would not come home with several bastard brats.

His way was so calm and pleasing, and Isabelle could really talk to him about anything. The day's entanglements slipped away from her. She smiled.

This was one of the highlights of her life, and she often forgot how well the two of them got along. She'd never had that kind of friendship with anyone else in her family, and because their duties often kept them apart, she would often neglect to come find time with Robert.

They stayed and talked through breakfast, and Isabelle even missed Mass for the first time. They finally descended the stairs for the midday meal. Then, she helped him carry his saddlebags down to the servants in the Great Room and made a promise that she would start finding time with him when he returned.

Making that promise somehow ensured that he would return. It protected against the possibility of his death. She would see him again; she was certain of it.

It is not strength, but art, obtains the prize,
And to be swift is less than to be wise.

Homer, the *Iliad* (ninth century B.C.)

5

The cathedral at Notre Dame, on the east side of the *île de la Cité*, was a work in progress. Even when Blanche had arrived in 1200 to marry King Louis VIII, the cathedral was just getting its start. The enormous structure loomed from the ground like Noah's ark, with its steep walls and squatting buttresses. Over the course of Isabelle's life, the cathedral would grow in every direction.

The man who thought of this design never lived to see it built, she thought. Then she wondered what it must be like to set one thing in motion—one thing you'd never know the outcome of and yet would be perfectly satisfied on your deathbed to know that you'd begun it. As she stared at the beautiful, looming structure, she could almost grasp how it felt to birth such an idea.

As she approached today, work had been halted for the benefit of Mass. But all the scaffolding was in place, as usual, with ramps inclined up the sides of the great structure, supported on poles.

Isabelle took a moment to marvel at the sheer size of the monumental cathedral. All of the tools had been left aside. Plumb lines, levels, axes, adzes, mallets, and chisels. She saw the windlass with its radiating spokes, like a wagon wheel without its outer edge.

There was even a great treadmill, large enough for six men to walk side by side. As the wheel turned under their weight, it pulled on a large rope that raised monolith stones up to the highest portions of the cathedral. It must have been tiring, exacting work. One misstep and a stone would come crashing down to the ground. Someone might even die.

All in the name of God, we do this, she realized. *We build mighty cathedrals as a show of our devotion. And we can't even live to see their completion.*

She entered the great dark doorway and walked between the hallowed walls. The ceiling arched high above her, difficult to make out in the gloom. The few ornate stained-glass windows in place let in only a trickle of light.

Isabelle had visited Notre Dame only a few times in the past, and the interior had undergone many changes since then. It was alive with change. In the process of becoming a complete structure, large interior stairways of stone led up but then dropped off into nothingness. They were the skeletal remains of scaffolding where men once finished interior work. It was not just strong stone, but art. Living, breathing art.

She was at peace in the silence of the great nave. For once she realized what true silence was. For here there were no edicts sounding down hallways, no footsteps of eager, spying dilettantes or starving noblemen who wanted the king's ear. There were no arguments between Blanche and Alphonse to interrupt her concentration. She heard only the sound of her own breathing as she closed her eyes to pray.

It was odd, but Isabelle did not feel diminished by this. She knelt before all the dark, hushed stones and felt something turn and align itself in her soul. She felt like a mariner who scouts the Compass Star, even though she hadn't considered the actual destination of her ship. There was a comfort in knowing where true north was, and today, that was all that mattered.

She prayed for Robert. She began by saying, "I believe in him, Lord. Please protect him."

She did not rise from prayer until sunset.

✢ ✢ ✢

Pierre Mauclerc smiled as he stood before King Louis in the Great Room. "The Templars are extremely busy right now, but they have allowed me to act as their emissary," he said. "I do some work for them, in . . . how do I put this delicately? . . . procuring reticent returns."

Louis stared down at Pierre from his dais. Beside him, Blanche sat as impassive as ever with Sofia standing directly behind. Even the chattering courtiers were silent as their king contemplated Pierre Mauclerc. The royal court had reluctantly called upon the Templars, much in need of assistance in reclaiming the Holy Nail. Louis couldn't decide if Pierre's arrival the morning after Robert's departure was a good sign or a bad sign, given his nature.

"You're a thug. You go and beat up whomever hasn't paid," Louis said.

"The Templars do allow some small leeway in my actions. You must understand, there are many in France and all over Europe and Jerusalem who would and who *have* taken advantage of the kindness of the Templars." Pierre smiled. "The Knights of the Order must abide by certain spiritual limitations in how they encourage the return of funds from traitors, thieves, and other scoundrels. As long as I get the money returned to them without incident, I don't have to abide by those limitations. Further, I am not directly a part of their sacred order."

Louis leaned forward on one arm. "Your relationship with the Templars is not the issue here. Can you help Us?"

Pierre walked casually to the window and looked out while he spoke. "The Templars have told me there is a man, an ancient sorcerer called 'The Old Man of the Mountain.' Some refer to him farther east as 'The Hungarian Master.'

"Legend has it he's the bastard son of an angel and a warlock. But you know legends." He turned and looked at Louis. "When I told the Knights Templar what had happened to your Holy Nail of France, they suspected him immediately. Several of his minions, thieves who are trained as assassins, have been attempting to steal relics all over the known world for years."

"Why? What good does it do them to steal relics?" Louis asked.

"We don't know exactly. The Templars are very eager to find out what it all means. They have employed me to follow the Nail, as it is not one of the greater relics."

Louis raised his eyebrow at the insinuation.

"Let me put it another way." Pierre shifted on one foot. "It isn't something like the Ark of the Covenant or the Crown of Thorns."

"The Ark of the—"

Mauclerc interrupted the king. "I can say no more. Will you accept my help or not?"

Louis sat back and sighed. He could not see Sofia's expression of supreme dislike as she stood behind him. In his heart, he matched the glare.

"I accept the help of the Templars. I will send a personal inquiry of my own to the grand master of the Templar Order in Paris. It shouldn't take long. But you may as well start on your journey anyway."

"Very well." Pierre Mauclerc refastened his cape to his chain mail. "Is there anything you wish me to take to your brother Robert?"

"How did you know that Robert—?"

"I'm afraid that is privileged information, Your Majesty, that I cannot even tell you. However, you can rest assured I have a very reliable source. Would you like me to take him word of anything?"

"I will send you with a message from Sofia." Louis didn't like this man at all. "I assume you know where to find him?"

"Créteil, by sunrise." Pierre bowed, turned, and then seemed to have another thought. "One more thing, Your Majesty. Where by chance is Princess Isabelle?"

"She's praying for Robert's safe return, and I'm afraid she cannot be disturbed. Good day."

When Pierre Mauclerc left the room, Louis let out a great sigh and turned to Blanche. "He has revolted me since the day I first met him."

"*Oui*, he is definitely a scoundrel of the worst type." She continued to weave on a small loom in her lap. "Ever since Isabelle was born he has been vying for a position of marriage. Even now, I can see it in his eyes."

"I wouldn't give my sister in marriage to such a man." Louis frowned heavily and wondered at the whole of Pierre's information, and at his alliance with the Knights Templar.

"I like the Knights Templar. They are honorable and wise," Blanche said. "But sometimes a man like Mauclerc can deceive even the most well-meaning people. Pierre might very well hide his more sinister side from the Templars. Even I have been fooled many a time by sweet-talking troublemakers."

"Ah, *oui*. That poet Thibault, you've told me."

"*Oui*, Thibault. Kind and gentle, and yet capable of such cruelty." Blanche yanked a thread. "Such men play the game well, and you really can't tell anything about them without the aid of others."

"If I find out about anything even remotely suspicious with Mauclerc, you can be assured I will alert the Templars of his misdoing. He's headed for a fall, that one."

"Naturally, I expect it of you," she replied. "That man was the product of an atrocious mother."

In Mauclerc's mind, Isabelle was only waiting for him to become a great and gallant figure before admitting her feelings for him. The chance to prove himself never seemed to turn up; so this time, Pierre was going to make it happen.

No sense letting opportunity pass by, he thought to himself and chuckled. *Besides, there's no reason why Prince Robert should get all the glory—he's already a prince and has nothing to prove. God granted him the privilege of royal birth. I have to earn my great honors.*

Without hesitation, Pierre opened Sofia's letter to Robert and read the contents. It stated that the assassin was leaving Créteil tomorrow and once gone would be hard to track. He was leaving France for a destination no one could discern.

This was the same basic information that the Knights Templar had told to Pierre, but Pierre decided to ensure that Prince Robert would not receive the letter. He would stop off at a local *bordel*, a house of ill repute, he knew along the way and pay a forger to replicate this serving woman's—*Sofia's*—signature and penmanship on another note. The new note would read, *"The man heads north to Calais."* That would send Robert away while Pierre searched Créteil.

Smiling and satisfied, Pierre spurred his horse to catch up with Prince Robert.

✤ ✤ ✤

Robert and Neci rode to reach Créteil. He stretched in the saddle. "We're stopping at the next village."

Neci nodded but said nothing. He wasn't sure if that unnerved him or annoyed him. He felt like a whimpering child asking to stop and rest.

"Are you tired?" she asked.

"Of course not," he said.

A village came into sight: six houses clustered together with one long building at the end. Luckily this village had a tavern. It was resting on the top of a gentle hill.

Robert dismounted. It felt so good to be back on solid ground. Neci hopped off her horse and stretched a little bit, then walked toward the tavern.

The tavern was quiet and dark. There were few patrons today: just three local farmers who sat by the fire to keep warm. The tavernkeeper walked over to Robert as Neci excused herself to the back room.

"*Oui*, I know the man you're looking for," the tavernkeeper said after Robert explained his mission. "He went east without paying the bill."

Robert nodded. "A thief, yes. *Merci*."

"I've always admired you, Prince Robert. You're a good man." The tavernkeeper smiled a rotted-tooth grin of true appreciation. It made Robert laugh.

✤ ✤ ✤

Pierre had just stabled his horse and was at the tavern door when he heard Robert's laugh. He hated it. Arranging his cloak over his chain mail, he walked into the tavern and approached the bar.

"Prince Robert!"

Robert turned, surprised to see Pierre Mauclerc standing there. "Yes, *Seigneur* Mauclerc?"

"I have been commissioned to bring you this letter from His Royal Majesty, King Louis." He handed Robert the letter. "It is by way of one of the Sisters."

"Ah, then this must be most important news." Robert tore at the note eagerly and opened it.

Pierre watched him impassively. Part of him worried that Robert would cry out "Forgery!" And then he would be executed on the spot. But Robert simply closed up the letter, folding it differently than it had originally been folded.

"Thank you, Pierre," he said.

"Would you like me to stand by as your man while you find this rogue?"

Robert looked at Pierre. "*Non*, I can handle it alone. Told you about the Nail, did they?"

Pierre nodded in response. "It's terrible."

"Yes, well, it'll be over tomorrow. *Merci*."

Pierre bowed and started toward the door.

"Not staying for a drink?" Robert asked.

"I can't. I'm on my way north," Pierre said. He was going east to Créteil, but why give any impression that might betray the forgery?

"Ah, well, it's cold out tonight. You shouldn't hurry home without even a stiff drink to keep you warm."

"Many things to do, Your Highness. I appreciate the offer." Pierre walked out the door and toward the stable. It was easy to fool princes, he mused, and smiled to himself.

Robert looked across the bar to the barkeep. He grabbed his cup of ale in one hand and downed the rest of its contents. Then he set the cup down, leaned way over, and spoke in a low voice, "That man is a terribly poor liar."

He looked up as Neci walked in from the back room.

"I saw Mauclerc," she said. "What did he want?"

Robert raised the note still in his hand. "You see this note?" he asked the tavernkeeper. "The woman who is supposed to have sent it always folds it a certain way. Always. This one is folded incorrectly."

Neci took the note and looked at it. She didn't have to stare long. "This was not written by Sofia. It's not her handwriting."

The barkeep's eyes widened with amazement.

"That's the problem with being second-born," Robert said. "Everyone assumes your older brother's always smarter than you are. As if you can't think strategically. As if you don't understand the hearts of men."

"Well, you were always a favorite in my eye, Prince Robert." The barkeep seemed a little unnerved, thinking perhaps Robert was going to cut loose here with his sword and hack the place up out of anger.

Instead, Robert smiled a bright toothy grin with a slick beard over it. That smile had won the hearts of many women in his time. "I always win the popular appeal," he said. "Now, I'm going to find out what he's really up to. Don't bother paying me back for the room. Keep it. Consider yourself well paid for telling me the thief was here two nights ago."

"Use the side door, sir," the barkeep urged. "He won't expect you there."

"Wise! Thank you." Robert quickly slid into the shadows out the side door, Neci beside him.

Once outside Neci asked, "Are you sure you want to apprehend him now?"

"I have no intention of doing anything to him right now. I'm going to let him take me right to the thief," Robert replied.

"What makes you think he would go there?"

"Well, . . ." Robert shrugged. "What other reason does he have for throwing me off the scent? The Templars may want the Nail for themselves."

"Why would they want it now? They could have had it long ago during the First Crusade."

"True," he mused. "I don't know. He works for the Templars, though. And I'm certain *they* know where he is. Although it's hard to imagine the *Templars* in foul play."

"Such an act is beneath them."

"Perhaps. Still, whatever the reason, he's our guide. Some things I just know, Neci. Trust me on this." Robert looked up as, in the distance, Pierre Mauclerc trotted off on horseback.

"To the east," Neci remarked. "Just as you'd said."

"Of course. I'm smart," Robert said.

"Very well, Smart Robert, let's go."

"*Non.*" Robert turned suddenly. Neci looked up at him, and he felt a twinge of protectiveness reaching out beyond his blustering façade. "I can follow him from here. You've been a great companion, and you showed me the way, as you promised. But now Pierre will lead me to the thief and I'll handle it."

"I'm not leaving. Now we should get going before we lose sight of him."

Robert knew it was useless to argue. He could have stood his ground and gone into high dudgeon if he thought it'd help. But he remembered many a debate between Blanche and the Order of the Rose, and when a Sister made up her mind to do something, not even the Queen Mother could supersede it. And that was saying a lot.

He glowered, then turned and marched to the stables, where they had been given fresh horses for the remainder of the trip. As he climbed back into the saddle, he felt his legs shake and tremble at the strain.

"I could have used a night's rest," he said.

"There isn't time, now. We have to move even faster than before." Neci nudged her new horse and it sped down the road.

Robert followed after her, not to be outclassed.

❖ ❖ ❖

When they reached the small town of Créteil, they couldn't spot Pierre Mauclerc or the horse he had been riding. Robert jumped down off his mount and looked at Neci.

"I'll ask at the inn," he said.

She nodded and held the reins of his horse.

Robert walked up a few steps and opened the door—and a man came flying out, tumbled right into him, and knocked him back against the ground. Robert's head hit the dry dirt, and he felt something crack painfully. For a moment he was seeing will-o'-the-wisps. Then he closed his eyes tightly.

Something moved over him, and he snapped his eyes open to see a man trying to get up above him. Robert grabbed the man by his arm and got up.

A voice came down from the inn's door. "And stay out! You lousy thief!"

The man tried to run, but his arm was held fast. Robert had hold of him—and not lightly either, for the prince's head smarted from the blow to the ground, and he was highly perturbed.

"What's the meaning of this?" Robert thundered.

The inn owner took a step back. Robert saw him looking over and realizing that a noble or royal had been pummeled.

"Oh, Your Highness. I didn't mean for—"

"Thief?" Robert pushed the man around a little bit, shaking him up. "What did you steal?"

The man was older, graying at the temples and very thin. He didn't look like he could take much jostling.

The innkeeper spoke up. "Oh, I'm so sorry, Good Lord, I didn't realize that I was going to throw him against your person. I have struck you indirectly—"

"No, don't worry. You did the right thing with a thief." Robert wondered if this was the man who had the Holy Nail. He looked at Neci, who had dismounted and walked over.

"It's not him," she said quietly.

"What did you steal?" Robert asked again. "Speak up!"

"I . . ." The thief seemed to slump against the strength of Robert's fist around his arm. "I was hungry, *mon seigneur*, and I asked for bread when I could not pay."

Robert didn't know how to react to such a confession. He couldn't be truly angry about it, because it was an act of desperation.

Neci looked at the innkeeper. "He asked only for bread?"

"*Oui*, he ate and then couldn't pay for it!" The innkeeper was shaking his finger. "I don't let scoundrels into my establishment. He should be whipped!"

Robert looked at the man in his hands. The poor thin thief was staring up at him. "Please, sir, I was hungry. I gave my bread to my wife and children this morning. We've hit a dry spell with the crops, and all our good grain went to the lord of this land. Forgive me. I am insane with hunger."

Robert softened his grasp on the man's arm. The thin man shrank away a little bit as Robert pulled out two *gros tournois* from his pocket. He held them out to the innkeeper.

"Here," he said. "This pays his tab and pays you for your troubles."

"Well, I . . ." He seemed to flush at the money handed to him. "Very well," he said, after a pause.

"Have you seen a brown-haired man, slight build, on a black horse come through?" Neci asked.

"*Non, madame.* No one at all like that came in here." He shook his head and then raised the two *tournois* in salute to Robert before walking back inside.

Robert sighed and rubbed his head.

"Are you all right?" Neci asked. She went over to him.

"Yes, I think so." He looked down at the little twig of a man and let him go.

Neci put her hand up to the back of Robert's head and felt around. He winced as she found the soft spot.

"Sir, you're looking for a man on a black horse?" the peasant asked. "He wears the symbol of a rooster on his shield?"

"Yes, that's him," Robert replied.

The peasant nodded. "He didn't stop at the inn. He rode straight to my farm and asked for my horse. When I didn't give it to him, he demanded it in the name of his family and left me with his black *destrier* in its place. Poor beast was worn tired and nearly fell over."

"Do you know where he went?" Neci's voice was urgent.

"He rode off. That direction." He pointed. "I can show you."

"Yes, please." Neci walked with him. Robert looked back at their horses tethered to the inn's post. He realized that when he turned his head, he no longer felt a sharp pain.

"What's your name?" Neci asked the peasant.

"Roger."

"Thank you for helping us, Roger."

"Thank you, actually, *madame*," he insisted humbly.

Robert followed after them until they reached a clearing. Roger pointed up to smoke that they could all see trailing up in a thin little line. He spoke again in a whisper.

"I think he's there. You can go on. I won't go up there."

"That's it," Neci said. "That's the one."

"That's Pierre . . . or . . ." Robert started to ask, then looked at her. She was shivering. As with the fact that his injury was no longer throbbing, giving him an enormous headache, he knew that this was another assurance. Neci had found something important. She didn't explain. She didn't need to.

Roger turned to leave when they all heard a scream from the top of the hill. Robert rushed headlong up the hill, his sword drawn. Neci followed behind him.

✤　✤　✤

Pierre looked up into the face of the madman whose hands were about his throat, and he remembered thinking that taking this man on alone was a good idea. Now he wasn't so sure.

The madman was strangling him and speaking in what sounded like Arabic. He smelled horrible, and his eyes were wild, the whites showing veins of pink. Pierre tried to push him off, but he couldn't muster enough strength. He scratched at the man's face, going for his eyes. Anything to get a breath of air!

With a cry, the man let go. Fighting to breathe, Pierre scrambled to get up as the other man reached into his belt and pulled out a sharp knife. Pierre staggered away, gasping, as the assassin reached for him, then grabbed him by his hair. Pierre howled and was pulled backward, the assassin's knife pressed into his neck below his ear.

The man cut into Pierre's neck. Pierre screamed.

Then Pierre felt a terrible jolt from behind. The knife fell to the ground, and Pierre was instantly released. He scrambled away from his assailant, holding onto the wound at his neck and feeling the warm blood trickle between his fingers.

When he turned, he saw Prince Robert. The prince had stuck the assassin through the back. The man wrenched free, and Robert advanced on him.

"Who are you, foreigner?" he bellowed. "Why do you attack a citizen of the *Cité*?"

"I curse you!" the man said in broken Latin.

"That's our thief," Neci declared. "Seize him."

"I am here to destroy the king of France. The pale king threatens my master! I destroy him by destroying his faith!"

Robert held up his sword. "You will tell me the name of the man who sent you. Tell me everything."

"I die first!" the assassin cried, then suddenly fell to the ground. Black liquid spilled out of his mouth. Robert shouted, dropped down, and saw the man spit out a hollow metal tooth. He could smell poison on the man's breath.

With his last breath, the assassin said, "I curse your family, your name. I curse you all." Then he died, his secret intact.

"Oh, no! No!" Robert was pained beyond belief and had nowhere to vent. Until he saw Pierre Mauclerc, hand to neck, covered in blood.

"You!" Robert thundered.

"I can explain!"

But Robert received neither the satisfaction of an explanation nor a solid punch when Pierre fainted from blood loss.

He turned. Neci was crouched over the stranger's body. She tugged at his coat and found a hidden pocket.

"It's here," she said.

✤ ✤ ✤

Louis held the letter from Robert in his hand. They had all waited for this moment. The rider had come at noon, at a full gallop. He had run into the Great Room without being presented and knelt before King Louis.

It was midday meal, and Isabelle and the rest of the family were gathered to eat. Louis seemed almost afraid to open the letter. He spoke softly after reading it.

"It appears that Robert saved the life of Pierre Mauclerc. He is bringing the Nail home. The thief killed himself without telling Robert anything. Robert says he'll tell us more when he gets home. But he is safe."

Isabelle breathed a great sigh of relief. Sofia said nothing.

"I thank our Lord that this problem is resolved." Blanche bowed her head reverently in a short, silent prayer, then looked up after a moment. "Because we still have Raymond of Toulouse and the southern barons to contend with. He's getting problematic, family or no."

"Yes," Louis said. "I must also thank the Templars personally for their help. Especially since it seems that Pierre was wounded." He rose from the table. "I should prepare a gift for them. I will rejoin you here for court after a bit."

Authority is never without hate.

Euripides, *Ion* (c. 421–408 B.C.)

6

15, mai, l'an de notre Seigneur 1237

The bells of Notre Dame were ringing on the *île de la Cité*, across the island from the *palais* of Louis and his family. The news of Robert's arrival into Paris had been heralded the night before. Robert was marching to Notre Dame in a solemn procession of priests, monks, and cardinals. The lord archbishop of France, Stephen Tempier, awaited the assembly at Notre Dame, where Robert would return the Holy Nail. Notre Dame was still being built, but its tower was a needle reaching to God.

Women and men swarmed behind Robert in a sea of bodies as his steed slowly pranced up the great avenue toward the church. The entourage contained every member of society, with many in tears.

The Nail rested on a red pillow held in Robert's hands. He delivered the sacred relic with great reverence to the archbishop, who took it and then said a prayer for Robert. Then the priest proceeded to reacquaint the holy relic with its rightful surroundings.

Many priests and cardinals delivered speeches over the Nail, in Latin, and it was bathed in the incense smoke from swinging censers. It was then sprinkled gently with holy water and patted dry with utmost care by small altar boys wearing white.

The archbishop blessed Robert and cleansed his soul of any impurities. After this, he gave the Lord's blessing to the entire congregation. The choir, a whole heavenly host of small boys, sang beautiful chorales, some written especially for today and never heard before.

When it was time, several hours later, the Nail was produced before the abbot of the monastery where it was originally kept. Brother Thomas was there, and when the procession was over and everyone was parting ways, he came up to Robert.

"I want to thank you, in God's name, but also in Brother Claude's name. I know he would want you to hear his thanks from Heaven, Lord rest his soul."

Thomas had taken Robert's hands in his own and then put his forehead on Robert's fingers. He stayed there for many minutes, in a posture of genuflection, and Robert realized that the man couldn't stand up because he was crying.

Robert was at a loss for what to say. He wanted to make a joke, or at the least use a nicety that would break the tension of the moment. But there were no words to break the silence. He simply stood there and stared at Thomas. At first he was uncomfortable, but as the moment passed, he felt more at ease.

It was truly the first moment a man had ever shown him devotion and loyalty—as a prince, and as a man to be feared and respected. He realized it, and his acceptance was both bitter and sweet.

It had been a long wait since the capture of the Nail at Créteil. He was happy that the festival and ceremony were over and he was home. Such was the way of holy relics, but it was not his way. The planning, praising, waiting, and formality of "the return" resulted in a well-orchestrated event that was weeks in the making. Only now could Robert get back to his normal life.

After the lengthy church service, Robert tucked his horse in its stall. As he fed the stallion warm oats with a flake of hay for good measure, Louis came to the stable.

"Robert, I want to thank you for what you did for the family," he said.

Robert's eyes were tired, but he smiled warmly. "I didn't know what to do exactly, but somehow it all worked out."

"I know exactly what you mean." A rare and understanding smile passed between them. "You saved my soul today. I owe you a great debt. Would you tell me how it happened?"

"Not too much to tell that wouldn't bore you. We traveled to Créteil. I asked a tavernkeep about this man and we found him. Then you made me wait weeks in the field while you planned all this fanfare."

"My apologies, Brother."

"He was a Saracen."

Louis nodded. "I should have known."

"A heathen's the only one who'd do this. It didn't make sense for any Christian to have attempted it."

"Sometimes a man's greed can betray his better judgments," Louis replied.

"What worries me is that we've never had a problem with the Moors or the Saracens before."

"I know. That worries me, too."

"And there's more you should know. I found him in the dark woods outside of Créteil. He was there with some kind of . . . pipe, or water pipe it looked like. Neci found it after the swordfight. I've only seen such things in the East."

Louis scowled. "Opium."

"Ah, drugged indeed. The man was crazed and dangerous. He had cut into Pierre"—Robert lingered on that with a scowl—"and I cut the heathen down before he could kill the man. He was completely willing to die, and he killed himself with poison. It was the first time I'd really seen anything that savage."

"I've never seen a fanatic like that. I hear the East is full of them. Crazed, drugged Saracens."

They started toward the castle, but Robert put his hand on his brother's arm. Louis turned and looked at him.

"That's not all. I wasn't going to tell you, but I want it out in the open, because it's been eating away at me."

"You can tell me anything."

"As this Saracen lay dying, he cursed our family, Louis."

"That's to be expected from a Saracen. They hate Christians. Probably the reason he was stealing our holy artifacts. To destroy them or to put some wicked spell on them."

"I don't think this was some old wives' curse. It gave me a chill to my very bones. I haven't been able to shake the man's image from my thoughts. I dream about it at night."

Louis put his hand on Robert's shoulder, giving it a firm squeeze and then a pat. "You've been through a lot on behalf of our family and the kingdom of Heaven. I'm sorry you had to go through it. But I've been thinking, and I believe that in enduring this, you've earned your knighthood. If you're willing to take the oath, I am willing to grant it."

Robert seemed stunned. "You mean that?"

"Yes. I want to formally commend you for this. With you taking care of this problem, I was able to do much here. I owe you a debt of immense gratitude, Brother, and I'm prepared to deliver it."

"I would be most honored. But Neci must also be honored. She's the one thing that kept me going."

"You know the Sisters can never have formal recognition. They prefer anonymity."

"I know, but I want to do something for her. Her faith and persistence were . . . I've never seen such devotion."

"Mother will think of something. She always has in the past. They are her handmaidens to reward as she sees fit."

"I suppose." Robert nodded. "I never thought you'd offer me a knightship, after all your joking."

"Nonsense. There is a time and a place for everything. Come, let's announce it." Louis opened the side garden gate by the castle wall. Robert realized that Louis couldn't grasp the ferocity of the Saracen's curse because he had no point of comparison. Perhaps Neci could convey it better to Queen Blanche, assuming she'd tell her at all.

Robert was not the sort to get sentimental or superstitious, but something about the curse had frightened him. What had his family done to earn this hatred? What would come of it? More attacks, directly related to his family and loved ones?

With that thought, he asked, "Where is Isabelle?"

Louis didn't answer right away, and when he did speak, there was some measure of anxiety in his voice. "She has just returned from Notre Dame. She went to the cathedral every day you were gone."

Robert's face split into a proud, happy, stupid grin. "She said she would, to pray for me."

Louis nodded, but his voice was not happy. "Yes."

"What is it?"

"We had a visit from Archbishop Stephen Tempier about Isabelle."

"Oh, no, what did she do? Read him Aristotle's *Disputations*? You know how opinionated she can be about things like that."

"*Non*, he was calling on us because he was impressed by her candor, her piety, and her modesty. He said that she had a natural gift for the divine and wondered why she wasn't married yet. . . ."

Robert groaned a bit. "I'll bet you some eggs Mother was none too pleased to hear that."

"That would be an understatement. She told the archbishop she's already made several arrangements with Emperor Frederick of Germany about marriage to his son Conrad. The priesthood asking after Isabelle was a rather unwelcome advance."

"Hmm. Don't worry about it. The Church isn't in Isabelle's nature. She's too impetuous."

"That's what I thought, until I spoke to her last week. I don't know what's come over her."

Robert opened the castle door. "She was incredibly upset that I was leaving, and my guess is, she needed to focus that worry. Now that I'm back, things should return to normal."

"Same old Robert. You still assume the sun and moon revolve around the Earth because you are standing on it."

"Don't they?"

✤   ✤   ✤

Robert chose not to mention the forgery or that he'd nearly killed Pierre Mauclerc for his part in it. He had taken Pierre to a nearby village shack, where a peasant woman had bound Pierre's wound.

Nor did Robert tell Louis about their conversation the next day, on a noble's honor. It was enough that Pierre's crime had nearly killed him. The Saracen assassin was far more efficient than he had anticipated.

Robert could not let such foolishness kill him. Neither could he in good conscience murder him in cold blood. He was a lord, and that demanded mercy.

Instead, Robert had shamed him by sparing his life.

He had also threatened Pierre Mauclerc with a solemn vow. If he ever did another foul thing against a member of his family, Pierre would find himself on the execution block. And Robert assured Mauclerc that his would-be scar would lengthen from two inches under his ear to all the way across his mangy neck.

Pierre had promised not to do such a thing ever again, and Robert figured he'd learned a valuable lesson, paid in a good deal of his own precious blood. Though Pierre's scar would be a constant reminder of his betrayal, Robert decided to keep an eye on him as long as he could.

With that ugly business now put to rest, he had one last matter to attend to: Neci.

If she was not to be honored, then he must convey his sentiments to her. He had spent these last weeks in her company, waiting to return home. He didn't understand her any more than he had when they started the journey, but he no longer feared her. And she no longer made him uncomfortable.

He finally found Neci *dans le jardin*, sitting near the yellow rose bush that she and Isabelle had planted years before. It was blooming bright yellow, tight heads of perfumed petals.

"Neci?"

"Hello, Robert." She turned to look at him. "What brings you to *le jardin?*"

"You, actually."

Neci raised an eyebrow as Robert sat down beside her on the stone bench.

"I'm going to be knighted," he said. "Louis has seen fit to give me my land and title because of our deed."

"I am pleased. You earned it."

"But that is what troubles me. You earned it as well, and yet we are doing nothing to commemorate your bravery."

Neci looked into Robert's eyes and saw such serious concern there, she smiled. "You really think that."

"I do. I don't know what I would have done without you there to spur me on. I told Louis as much. I know I . . ." He faltered and looked at his shoes, embarrassed at being so honest. "I know that I was brusque and didn't want you along, but now that it's over, I think I couldn't have done it without your perseverance."

"You could have done it all without me."

Robert looked back up at her.

"I was only there in case something changed at the last minute," Neci continued. "It didn't, and you alone succeeded. As for rewarding me, you don't need to. Not really. I don't protect your family for public endorsement. I protect your family because I'm quite fond of you and believe you are *all* quite worthy. I need nothing more than that."

"You're really quite an amazing woman," Robert replied. "It's a shame I can't do anything to show my appreciation."

Neci looked at him again, strangely.

"I mean," he quickly added, "like a feast or a holiday in your name."

"Oh!" Neci laughed. "I wouldn't want that. Robert, your gratitude is enough."

Their conversation was interrupted by approaching footsteps. Robert turned to see Norea approaching, also wearing the white robes with the red embroidered rose on the front.

"Well, hello there. We never see enough of you."

Norea smiled a mysterious little smile. She was more like Sofia: quiet and reserved.

Neci stood up, and the two sisters embraced each other. "Good to see you."

"And you," Norea replied. "Good afternoon, Prince Robert."

Robert stood then and bowed to them. "I see you two have matters to discuss, and I will leave you to it."

The two sisters watched him leave the courtyard garden and then strolled together toward the rosemary bush at the far end of the wall.

Arrangements were made within a month, and Robert's knighting ceremony was scheduled to take place on 22 *juin*. A summer solstice festival boded well. Even the men from the *université* were invited to attend, and they would be seated at Louis' table along with his favorites. Louis always had a large entourage around him at any public event. He enjoyed the verbal sparring that occurred when important men came together under one tent.

To his right at the long table would be seated the family tutor, the verse maker, the most esteemed brewer, the family's chaplain, and the blacksmith. The common folk thought the blacksmith was involved with diabolical spirits, but the royal family knew it was just his own. He had quite a temper.

To this entourage, Louis would add the men from the *université*: Albertus Magnus and his followers. Isabelle had become good friends with Albertus while visiting him on Wednesdays at *Petit Pont* library. She loved his entourage of scholars like brothers.

Large, colorful tents were placed outside in the warm, hay-heavy air, and tables were dragged from buildings across open plazas of the courtyards and set up inside the tents. Nearly enough tables and seats for three thousand guests.

The night before the grand ceremonies, all the prepared tents stood brightly in the moonlight, gold and red ribbons flagging off the sides. In the dark, under the solstice moon, the entire place was deserted. The ribbons flapped loudly in the breeze, like dry leaves tagging each other in the wind.

Robert walked among the empty tables, listening as the stillness settled before the rasping of ribbons in the air took off again. He wasn't supposed to be here, but rather in the family chapel or even Notre Dame, praying before the altar.

But he couldn't concentrate, and prayer had never been one of Robert's strong points. So he came here instead, and he stared at the tables and chairs assembled before him in neat rows, like soldiers on a battlefield. So many chairs assembled for his ceremony. Thousands of guests all lined up like battlements. He thought about what it meant to be a knight. It was something he'd always wanted. Tomorrow it would happen. Would people actually *honor* it? Or would he continue to be quietly mocked?

"This is a unique idea." Isabelle spoke behind him.

He turned and stared at his sister in the moonlight. She was outside in her nightclothes, heavy slippers over her feet, her thin nightclothes covered by her warmest cloak. Its hood was up.

"What are you doing here?"

"I saw you wandering and wondered why you weren't praying at the altar like you're supposed to."

"I am considering tomorrow carefully." His voice was gentle, and he let his gaze return to the empty tables and chairs.

"Shouldn't you be reciting your vow of knighthood or praying? That is the custom, *non?*"

"*Ouai*, it is. And I know my vows. I have known them since I was eight years old. I watched Louis learning them in the chapel at Poitou. I listened to the words carefully, wrote them down, and carried them with me for years. I have always known the words of a true knight. Here I am, thirteen years later, ready to finally recite them."

"I didn't know that."

"My dream, I suppose. We all have them."

"Yes." She said it as if she wondered about her own.

He sat on one of the large wooden tables, one knee drawn up. "There is only one problem."

"What?"

"I never bothered to learn how to dance for formal occasions. I fear I'm going to make a fool of myself tomorrow."

Isabelle smiled. There was a quiet moment between the two as the ribbons danced in the darkness like wood sprites. Then she held out her hand to her older brother.

He looked at it, then at her. She didn't waver. "Come. I'll teach you a few steps."

He took her hand. "Isn't it sacrilege for a knight to be dancing on the eve of his ascension?"

"Probably," she said.

He smiled and gently took her hand. They danced until dawn.

The worst things:
To be in bed and sleep not.
To want for one who comes not.
To try to please and please not.

Egyptian Proverb

7

Robert's solstice ceremony was beautiful. There were knights and ladies present as far as the eye could see. Minstrels played all day, and jousting tournaments and swordplay entertained the crowds. The sounds of clashing metal rang out like peals of church bells. Laughter, horses, merry conversation, and the sounds of crackling feast fires were heard at each tent and its surroundings. More torches were set as sunset came and went.

Gathered at one end of the tent were the *université* scholars, Albertus Magnus and his crew. The men of the *université* had attracted the attention of Louis and his usual band of attendants. Isabelle wandered over to listen to their discussion. Albertus Magnus was holding court when she came within earshot.

"Natural science is not simply receiving what one is told, but the investigation of causes of natural phenomena," he told the assembled men.

Mort, the blacksmith, replied, "Why would one bother to ask *why?* I know the hot iron goes bad after I count to one hundred. Knowing *why* doesn't make it stay good when I reach one hundred and one."

The other men chuckled.

"Ah, but you listen when someone casts your horoscope for the day, don't you?" Albertus asked. "I mean, even His Majesty chooses special dates according to the rotation of the heavens."

Paul, the quiet and reserved verse maker, spoke up. "Well, that's different!"

Bacon shook his head. "It's no different than applying *why* to everything you find. *Why* is a fundamental question. We were given minds to ask why. If we weren't meant to explore the world God created for us, we'd be as dumb as draft animals."

"I agree," Louis said, and the others stood a little taller in their clothes. "Without asking why, Prince Alphonse wouldn't have spectacles. They were developed in Italy because someone must have asked why he couldn't see, which led to the question 'How can I fix that?' The same can be said of the windmill, a recent invention that allows our lords in the fields to grind their grain without being near a fast stream. Someone had to wonder if there was a way to harness the wind to their advantage."

"Ah, wise, Your Majesty," Guillaume de St. Cloud concurred.

"Yes, I can accept all of that," Philippe the stablemaster groused. "Science puts shoes on my horses. But what about all this arcane lore like alchemy and astrology? Pardoning Your Majesty's use of astrology, but I see no good in it. In the Bible, it says that we have free will to choose our fate. Astrology says we're all fated to one course of action depending on the planets."

Grosseteste, Albertus' mentor, had finally arrived alongside the chaplain, and the men nodded to him. He was the senior member of the *université* and the most respected. "I have given this much thought, for your point is a valid one. So let me ask you this: If the moon can affect the tides, why then can it not do the same of human beings?"

Isabelle smiled and wandered over to get more wine. These were familiar conversations to her. She almost hadn't invited the men from the *université*, but she missed their company here at the *palais*, and this was a good excuse to see them all in good humor and to prove her friendship's merit to her brothers.

She put the wine cask down and looked up past the party, to the moonlit field glowing pale silver. The wheat grass moved in a gentle breeze, and among the stalks, a silhouette stood against the moon, staring in at the happy festivities.

Isabelle moved closer, past the edge of the table. Something about this silhouette looked so lonely.

Why does he not approach? she wondered.

A passerby on his way to a local tavern, perhaps. Or a lost traveler uncertain if he'd stumbled onto a faerie kingdom of revelers.

No, a traveler wouldn't linger like that. From the way he stood, she could tell that he had been standing for some time in the chilly night air and just . . . watching.

Why?

A flutter in the air caught her attention, like a stray bird making its way across the plain. It was one of the tent ribbons, loose and flying across the dark night sky.

The ribbon fluttered and spun to the moon's edge and then landed against the wheat grass by the man's figure. She watched him bend slowly and pick up the red silk ribbon. He examined it closely.

Now she could see the shape of his profile against the moon. He regarded the ribbon and fingered it gently, almost sadly, before putting it to his chest. Then he turned and walked into the moon and disappeared over the hill.

She wanted to run out after him and invite him in, but someone was tugging at her arm. She looked over to find a courtier smiling at her. He had crooked teeth and a red nose.

"Hello, sir."

"Princess Isabelle," he said. His breath smelled like liquor. "Would you do me the honor, could you just introduce me to your brother Robert, and your brother the king, just once? It's such a glorious occasion, and I want to congratulate your brother on his knighting."

Isabelle shifted uncomfortably and looked back out at the hill beyond. The plain was empty under the moonlight now. She turned back to the man. "I don't really get involved in introductions at court, I'm sorry," she replied. "Perhaps you can just go up to them yourself."

Their conversation was interrupted by trumpets sounding, and it was time for Robert to recite his holy vows before King Louis. Isabelle's place was at the center of the main tent, so she excused herself from the man and walked to the dais with her brothers.

Robert recited his vows with absolute perfection, punctuated with pride. His chest was puffed up proudly, and his beard, always glistening, was smooth and trim over his strong chin. His eyes were alive today, more than they had ever been before.

He was born for this, Isabelle thought with pride, and felt her heart swell inside her rib cage. When he received his knightly garments and strapped the new sword to his side, she felt as if she were there, in his place, receiving the highest honors.

Thousands of guests came to the large tables and sat for the evening meal. The conversation and delectable smells brought them all to the table as the night winds set in. Fires were built higher for warmth.

Isabelle was seated at her usual place at large family gatherings, which did not alter from where she sat at humble midday or morning meals: across from Charles, who was older now, but still surly.

Robert sat a space away, and the chair next to Isabelle was empty, though an extra place had been set there. She looked around nervously.

"Why's this chair here?" she asked, but no one paid attention. They were laughing and carrying on.

Where's Mother? she wondered. She looked around the tent, and her gaze rested upon a newcomer. He was at least six feet five. She had never seen a giant like this before. His hair was red like fire. Where her brother Charles' hair smoldered, this man's hair was bright as the tips of a flame.

Isabelle was shocked to see her mother walking next to the giant, smiling that familiar dark smile and doting on the giant with a kind of gentle amusement. She seemed to find the man quite entertaining.

The two approached the family table, and everyone stood.

"My dear children," Blanche said. "This is our very special guest come all the way from Germany. King Conrad is son to Emperor Frederick the Second." Queen Blanche indicated the empty seat by Isabelle. Conrad bowed and approached his seat.

Isabelle wondered why she suddenly felt like a sinking ship. Conrad took Isabelle's hand in his enormous grasp and kissed it lightly.

The giant spoke in halting French. "Princess Isabelle, I am honored to meet with you."

"Thank you," she managed. She felt horridly on display. She turned and realized the entire family was staring at the two of them.

Not a normal kind of staring either, but one of complete anticipation. Suddenly, she remembered being only nine years old and watching the entire family stare at her as she buried her head in Neci's robes the day that two red-haired German princes were presented to her as "friends." One was named Henry, the other *Conrad*.

With that, she realized why the empty chair had been placed next to her and why Conrad had traveled all the way from Germany for Robert's knighting ceremony, when he had never been present for anything else. She was also certain *this* was why he had been present as a child at Louis' marriage to Margaret.

She looked around at her family, and she felt eighty-five years old. The moment must have hit everyone in kind, because as Isabelle withered away beneath their gazes, they started to look away, or drink from their glasses.

Blanche destroyed the moment with an exclamation. "Let's begin the festivities, Louis! I am famished."

Why, Mother? Why?

Conrad was still holding her hand lightly in his own. As she curled forward, he gently let go of it and looked at her with those no-nonsense blue eyes. They were not sky blue, or ice blue; they were a simple, steel blue. Understated and genuine, without pretension.

The look in his eyes was not eager, nor anticipatory. She realized he was about as worried and concerned as she was. It couldn't really be what she was imagining. He could not be here for her hand, not yet. She wasn't ready.

Isabelle tried to push the thought to the very farthest corner of her mind, but it was too late. Throughout dinner, she would look over at Robert, sitting now one whole place away, and it felt like one whole country had come between them. She knew immediately that this stranger, no matter how short a time had passed between them, was not right for her.

It was not a first impression. It would not go away with time. This man could not be her . . . husband.

This isn't the right man! she wanted to cry out.

This man couldn't protect her from harm, not like the man she had seen as a child in the courtyard. Not like *Him*.

Conrad was speaking to her, and she attempted to focus on what he was saying. "I have a fondness for horses, Princess. In my country, we breed the Clydesdale and the Belgian Drafts. They are most magnificent creatures, standing at seventeen or eighteen hands high."

"I have always had a soft spot for horses myself, Conrad," Blanche said. Her words were slow and soft so he could translate them as she spoke, but she wasn't patronizing. "My late husband, the good King Louis, and I would go riding daily. It is something I love even to this day, though I admit I have not been on a horse in some time."

"You are, Majesty, extremely busy," Conrad replied.

"Yes, I have been rather detained in matters of state since Louis passed away. I would love to go hunting again sometime." It was a sincere sentiment. Odd that Isabelle had never heard it from her lips before now.

"Then let us go, Majesty, tomorrow. We can go out hunting, and if Princess Isabelle would come with us, perhaps she enjoys the horses too?"

Isabelle cleared her throat and pushed away her plate of food. She looked at her mother with the look of a woman tied to a stake.

Why? I would have told you what I wanted. If only you'd ever once asked me. I could have told you about Him.

Then she looked at Conrad and smiled, but it was distant despite her best efforts. "Of course, Your Majesty, I would enjoy hunting tomorrow. I have nothing else planned."

Conrad smiled. It was sincere and boyish. He was a truly good-natured fellow, which was something, at least. Isabelle spent the rest of the evening staring at her plate of food and wondering why *He* wasn't here to rescue her from a fate worse than a deadly hound.

✠ ✠ ✠

In the morning, Isabelle dressed in riding attire with gloves and a hat. She had not slept all night, tossing and turning in her bed.

She walked down the large stone staircase, and her boots felt like shackles against her ankles. The smell of bread wafted through the Great Room, and she could hear Robert's voice echoing from within.

"I'd love to stay, Mother, but it's imperative that I visit Artois immediately and give an inspection. My wife also awaits me. I plan to go after the midday meal." His words made Isabelle's heart sink. She stepped inside.

"So soon?" she asked.

Blanche turned to see Isabelle in the doorway.

"The dress is agreeable, but you look more drab than the gray collar, darling. Smile." It was an order.

Isabelle looked at Robert, too shocked even to hear her mother's words. "You're leaving? *Today?*"

"There's my Rose. I was wondering if the festivities would have made you too tired to go out today." Robert sat at the table, not answering her question.

"I'll be in the stables, children," Blanche said, turning to leave. "Breakfast will help your face, Isabelle. Eat some bread."

Isabelle sat. "Yes, Mother."

When Blanche was gone, she turned to Robert. "Why are you leaving us now? You can go next week. Why now?"

"I'd rather get an early start," he tried to explain. "You see, I learned something in that race for the Holy Nail. Perseverance will win every time. I don't want the locals thinking of their new lord and master as a sloth who'll get around to work whenever he wants to. I should get right to it."

"Don't go yet. I'll be unhappy without you. Please just . . . Don't go until Conrad is gone."

Robert looked at her apologetically. "I have to go, Isabelle. The trip's been arranged for weeks, and people are waiting for me."

"If this is your last day, then I want to share it with you. I saw so little of you at the ceremony last night. Didn't our time dancing mean anything to you?"

"Of course it did! What's that got to do with anything?"

"I won't go riding today." She crossed her arms over her chest.

"You have to go. Conrad's waiting for you as my people are waiting for me. Besides, Mother would be furious with you."

"But I don't care about Conrad. I care about you. Artois is leagues from Paris, and you'll be *gone* after I get back!"

"So come stay with me at Artois, then. You're under no obligations. I'm sure it can be arranged."

Isabelle's hot tears pricked her eyes, and she tried to keep them in. "I . . . I wasn't expecting you to leave so soon, Robert. I thought you'd give it a week at least—"

The cry came from down in the courtyard. "Isabelle, are you finished yet?" It was Blanche, impatient and slightly upset.

"Go, or she'll be mad. You don't want that."

"But Robert—"

"*Go!*" he commanded, and she stared at him, slack-jawed.

Then she left the room and didn't look back. She had prayed for him at Notre Dame, every day. Had taught him to dance on the eve of his ascension. She had believed in him, and now he didn't even bother to stay long enough for her to say a proper good-bye.

She loved Robert, as she'd once loved Louis, but now Robert was as unreachable. And she would not, *ever*, go to Conrad. The more her family pushed, the more she'd rebel.

Isabelle wanted to ride Hugo, the dapple gray mount, but much to Isabelle's horror Blanche insisted, in front of God and the stablemaster, that Isabelle would look more becoming on the palomino named Hal. It was blatantly obvious that Blanche was prettying her up as a package, ensuring proper presentation. Isabelle blushed to her boots and would not look anyone in the eye.

Isabelle knew the stablemaster, Philippe, personally. She had a few mounts here that she would take out and ride at least twice a week. In the past she had hunted game with her brothers. But today, she was absolutely mortified to be discussed in front of her longtime friend as if she were a pretty bobble meant to hang attractively from the mane of some wonderful stallion.

It was becoming unbearable. She was outraged. Isabelle wondered how her mother would like it if *she* were treated as such an object.

Conrad met them outside the stable, for which Isabelle was grateful. At least Philippe wouldn't see the man for whom Isabelle was being "prepared" so handsomely. She found she couldn't look Conrad or her mother in the eye.

The horseback ride through the meadows and wood was a very long one. Queen Blanche and Conrad did all of the talking. Isabelle listened to them cover a wide range of topics: art, music, literature, Germany, customs, clothing, science, Germany, mathematics, agriculture, Germany . . .

Isabelle realized that Blanche was trying to include her in the conversation, but Isabelle would not oblige.

This trip was not *her* idea. She had no reason to make conversation with this prince. She corrected herself . . . king. And why was he "King Conrad," after all? One could only rule after a parent died or abdicated. Why hadn't Blanche gone over his "credentials" yet? They should be all-important.

And hadn't Conrad had an older brother, Henry? Wasn't that the impetuous little red-haired boy who'd been fighting with Charles that day as young boys? And wouldn't *Henry* rule Germany? So why was Conrad now called king of Germany? Had Henry been promoted to nigh-emperor or something?

Isabelle decided to ask. "So, Conrad, how is your brother Henry these days?"

There was a pause as mortified and silent as the way Isabelle had felt in the stable. She looked up at her mother, whose face was completely puckered, as if utterly horrified by the question.

Conrad seemed to be at a loss for a moment. "He's . . . still in prison. Kind of you to ask after him."

"Oh." Isabelle said no more, but she felt vindicated despite the others' agony. Blanche quickly shifted the topic and discussed her daughter's love of religion and learning.

"Isabelle is unaccustomed to the ways of the world. I do not believe she meant any harm in the question. She studies the ways of the Holy Father quite fervently."

Conrad nodded and smiled at that. "It is definitely the more commendable pastime. It certainly leads to healthier activities." His words seemed friendly, but with a bitter undertone that betrayed a difficult life.

Isabelle felt slightly bad for him. Whatever had caused Henry to be imprisoned was certainly not a topic for discussion. She wondered what kind of man he was. Her mother was not pleased. But Isabelle didn't care. She hadn't slept a wink, hadn't gotten to say good-bye to Robert, and was supposed to acquiesce to a complete stranger whose brother was imprisoned by his own father.

Isabelle had no desire to become a part of the German landscape. If Emperor Frederick could throw his own flesh and blood into jail, then what would he do with a foreign bride?

8

14, novembre, l'an de notre Seigneur 1238

"Emperor Frederick demands a response to his inquiries regarding his son, King Conrad of Germany. Why must he remain engaged to Isabelle with no set date of marriage when you have plans to marry your son, Prince Alphonse, to Joan of Toulouse before harvest?" The messenger spoke and then banged his scepter flag down on the wooden floor of the court.

Blanche stared at him, her face an impassive mask of stone apathy. When she spoke, it was an imperial tone, laced with the slightest fringe of ire. "The Holy Roman emperor does not respect Our ability to discern the relationship between his son the king and Our *only* daughter, princess of France."

"He demands to know why you would not usher the marriage through as you have done for your third son. The marriage of a third son to a noblewoman is not so important an affair as the marriage of the king of Germany to a full-fledged princess of France." The messenger stared straight ahead, without looking at either Louis or Blanche, but at an indistinct point on the wall behind them.

"Tell His Majesty that this is precisely why the arrangement must be a natural one, and that I intend to nurture my daughter's relationship with his son, the king, to its fullest potential, to ensure that our countries will be allied not only in name, but in heart."

108

The messenger, without a reply, turned to relay the message, but Blanche was struck with another comment. "And"—she made the messenger turn around—"you will tell His Majesty that the king and queen mother of France wish the best not just for their countries, but first and foremost for the children and future rulers of those countries. That it is the contented relationship between man and woman that makes a full partnership under which a country may blossom."

The messenger bowed low before the queen mother and walked out backward, until he was well beyond the point of the door. Blanche had been sitting so upright at his approach that her back was nowhere near the pillows she usually lounged in.

Louis turned with a worried look. "I grow more concerned with this affair by the day. And less able to like our friends in Germany. How dare he put such pressure on Us?"

Blanche sighed. "I am doing something unheard-of. Isabelle should not be engaged to Conrad by any rights. She should be married, and they should be taking this three-year period in Germany, where Isabelle would be learning German and getting to know her new homeland. I am being too kind."

"Mother, I object—"

"No, Louis. It is how things are done." Blanche was bitter. He could see that the entire situation distressed her. "But I like to think that I know my own daughter, though she sees fit never to speak to me about matters of her heart. Still, a mother can only be so lenient until it taxes the patience of a nation."

"Would you like me to speak with her?"

"*Non*, it would only confuse the situation and prolong the agony. I give her another full year with Prince Conrad. They have only had five months together. Then I must promise her hand in marriage if she has made no overture herself."

Louis only nodded, his face grim. He could see well that Isabelle and Conrad were friendly but not amorous. He wondered why Isabelle was so reluctant to grow fond of anyone. It made him very sad to see his sister shutting herself away from the world like this, unable to feel real joy or trust anyone she ever met. What had possibly made her shrink away from the close bonds everyone else in the family seemed to share?

✢ ✢ ✢

The woods were dark as Neci made her way quietly through the underbrush. She was heading toward a beautiful, moss-covered ruin. Though the sun was shining, it did not reach the floor of the forest here. It was thick in the heart of the wood where the royals hunted.

Neci put her hand against the door frame of the ancient ruin but did not step inside. She knew he would be waiting for her inside and peered into the darkness.

"I'm here." The voice within was male; it spoke gently.

"I'm glad. I came with thoughts and questions." She stepped into the darkness, and it swallowed her white gown. "The emperor of Jerusalem has left his land and is coming here. He brings disastrous news."

"What has happened?"

Neci couldn't keep the disdain out of her voice. "He has squandered away the Crown of Thorns."

"We must restore it." The voice was measured in reply, dignified and quiet.

"I know, but how?"

"The king of France."

"Possibly," she ventured, and put a finger to her lips in thought. "But what if he doesn't consent?"

"He will," the voice replied. "Come to me again after the visit."

"What shall I tell Sofia?"

"She shouldn't speak to the queen mother about this matter; it will have worse influence than if she left it well alone."

"She won't like that." Neci sighed and looked out at the forest beyond the dark doorway.

"She must not, if the Crown is going to be ours." The voice said nothing more.

Early in the month of *juillet*, as preparations for Alphonse's wedding to Joan of Toulouse were nearing completion, Isabelle and Conrad had taken horses to the wood in order to have a picnic. It was Conrad's idea, and he had packed everything, including a little bouquet of flowers as a centerpiece.

Isabelle looked at Conrad. He was wearing comfortable attire, though there was always something out of place about his outfits, one decadent object that seemed to spoil the casual flow of the ensemble. Today it was a gold brooch with a sterling ruby the size of a *gros tournois* and glittering white shoes.

The brooch itself was so intricately decorated that it looked like lace that had been dipped in gold. It was so feminine against his russet brown velvet tunic with plain collar and cream trousers that it stuck out painfully as a sign of how foreign he was.

Isabelle had learned that every oddity Conrad wore was a special token of affection from someone important to him at home. The brooch was his mother's. A few weeks earlier, when he wore the black hat with the large batch of peacock's feathers, she learned it was a hand-me-down present from his great uncle. And peacocks, being rather rare, made it a valuable keepsake for him. In their months together, Isabelle had come to know a good deal about Conrad's family just by the show of gaudy objects that stuck to Conrad like ornate pins to a pincushion.

She'd also learned of his gentle disposition and how very unlike the rest of his family he was. Early in their friendship, she had apologized for her rude assumption on behalf of his brother, Henry. Conrad had told her that Henry was imprisoned for attempting to take the throne away. Henry had not been satisfied with just Germany, and he had been angry at his father's steel-fisted policies over his sons and land distribution. In the end, Henry greedily took to war against his own father and lost.

In the days that had passed between their first horseback ride and their latest, Conrad had painted a picture of his father's Holy Roman Empire that was cruel, capricious, and dangerous. It was a revolution waiting to happen. Conrad's own reticence as king of Germany was as heavy as Isabelle's growing feeling that she could never come to marry him.

But as they sat in the middle of a quiet glade and ate bread and cheese with slices of fruit, Isabelle realized that she genuinely enjoyed Conrad's company. He had become a dear friend. His German accent had greatly diminished, and her German had grown as well.

At first, she had been reluctant to even consider learning German, afraid that if she did, she would be immediately shipped off to Germany with Conrad. But Conrad had the most gentle way about him, and he was very pragmatic. He had always spoken to her in a direct fashion, from the very first day they had gone hunting together. And it was always in stilted French, which somehow made it seem all the more earnest.

She pointed at his pair of shoes that glittered like snow, and the points that actually curled up slightly at the toes. Shoes of this nature on a man as large as a giant were an amusing sight to Isabelle, and she had been heckling him all day about it.

"Faerie giant, get me some more wine, please. My cup is empty."

Conrad leaned over and grabbed the bottle in his huge hand. "You may scoff, but these shoes are very dear to me."

Isabelle laughed. "Does your family get you anything else but strange articles of clothing as a means of showing affection?"

He smiled. "I suppose it is our way."

"The ways of Germany are very backward." A silence passed between them.

"You don't wish to find out more about them, do you?"

Isabelle sighed and looked at him. Her eyes betrayed sympathy for his plight, stuck here miles from home trying to woo a woman who had no heart for marriage. She looked kindly at him as he stretched out, leaning back on one elbow to look up at her. His pale, lightly freckled face and red thatch of hair looked oddly out of place against his outfit today.

"Your Highness," she began.

"No, it is Conrad with you. No 'Highness.'"

"Conrad, then." She set her cup down beside her carefully. "You are such a dear friend, I don't want to hurt you. But I can't think of anywhere I would rather be than here in France with my family."

He nodded at her, his eyes very serious and wide. "I see in your eyes, a reluctance. I see we are very good, very . . . how do you say . . . deep? . . . friends? But it is nothing more. Your eyes, they focus away from me, to something distant.

"You may tell me the truth. I am first your friend, and only at the wishes of country and Father anything more. The engagement comes between us, and I see that. So please, forget this engagement and tell me . . . is it another you love?"

Isabelle was struck dumb. Did she really radiate that kind of needy affection, like Margaret? By the Heavens, she hadn't felt that kind of love for any man she'd known. And yet here he was thinking that she—

Isabelle broke into giggles at the absurdity of his concern. *Another man! Ha!* It was downright funny. The only man that could take such a place in her heart was a man she had never known, a glimpse from her past. A dream. Conrad looked at her, a smile spreading over his lips. His eyes squinted in the confusion a man can only have when probing the depths of a woman's soul.

"It's nothing like that!"

He seemed slightly relieved, but a bit confused. "Then, I am actually not pleasing to you?"

"Oh, please, let's not talk of this. It's depressing. You've spent so much time in my company, I feel obligated to keep you amused."

"I think what you feels, is the truth." She would not look at Conrad as he spoke. "And you feels that I am not one to love, and also a bit of guiltiness because your family wants us to love each other." He took his large finger and put it gently under her chin, raising it so that her eyes would meet his. "As my family does. And yet here we are, far from loving."

Isabelle had a very hard time meeting his gaze. She felt so horribly bad, as if she had led him astray. "I wanted to please my family, but . . . I *can't*!" Despite herself, her eyes welled up with tears.

Conrad nearly cried at seeing her anguish. His face curled into the saddest, most empathetic expression, and he quickly reached into his shirt and withdrew a red handkerchief decorated with gold brocade folk dancers. He held it out for her to use, and it dangled off one of his large index fingers in front of them.

Isabelle stared at the hanky, and her tears stopped coming. She realized what a genuine, honest gesture it was, despite how horribly ugly the hanky was. She took it from his gentle fingers and wiped her eyes with it, wondering which German relative now bore the brunt of her tears.

"I am sorry to have ruined your lovely picnic with this outburst."

"Isabelle. It is better that we be honest with one and the other. I am a little sad, but I honestly will tell you that it is the same for me, too. You see?"

Isabelle looked up at him, rather surprised.

"Yes, I also don't feel that . . . how do you say? . . . passion. Perhaps we were not meant to, but I understand now what you are expecting. I think maybe, if you loved me, I might then love you. But

I cannot spark a fire by myself. The most of importants is that I have come to know you well, and that we are friends."

Isabelle started crying again, but it was a wash of relief. She hadn't known that he felt the same way, and it would have been easier if she had. How wrong of her to think that he had been making advances because he *wanted* to. He was just as forced to this arrangement by his father.

Maybe their engagement was forced, but that was too strong a word for their blossoming friendship. There was a deep affection between them, and he was very kind with her and funny sometimes, too. Over the past year, she had grown rather fond of him, despite the situation.

She looked up at him. "I consider you one of my best friends, Conrad. Strange, isn't it? I've never actually just had a friend."

"It is an isolated life we both lead. I think that is why our parents thought we would be good for one another. They made good judgment, as far as judgment can go. We are good for each other, I think—just not as they meant it."

"Please don't be angry about it."

Conrad put a finger back up to her cheek and stroked it gently. "I cannot be angry with you. You are honest, and I see sometimes in you, that you are better than all of us. I can't say how, but there is something . . . mysterious about you. You are reaching for something unreachable. And I am too humble for your greatness. But you are my good, dear friend, and you always will be, no matter what great thing you do in life."

She hugged him then, and cried a little bit on his shoulder. He held her tight.

There was a rustling behind them, and Isabelle saw Neci come from the underbrush. Isabelle quickly withdrew from Conrad's shoulder in shock.

"Neci?!" she asked.

Neci looked away, flustered. "Oh! Oh my goodness! I didn't mean to disrupt your—"

"What are you doing out here?" Conrad asked with a smile.

"I am just out for a stroll." Neci's eyes searched for an exit. She looked like a startled deer.

Isabelle was puzzled. "Without a horse?"

"Why don't you come and sit down to picnic with us?" Conrad patted the blanket.

Neci seemed to have no choice but to accept his hospitality. "Very well, although I can't really stay long."

"Neither can we," Isabelle said.

Neci took a seat and glanced at Isabelle's puffy, red eyes. She seemed ready to say something about it, but closed her mouth instead and looked away.

"A nice arrangement, Conrad," Neci said.

"*Merci.*" He handed her some bread. "I didn't know you enjoyed nature as much as we do."

"Oh, yes." Neci seemed desperate to find words while her thoughts raced on about something else. "I hope I'm not interrupting."

"Not at all," Isabelle replied. "We were just talking about our families."

No one said another word as they quietly munched their bread and cheese. After a quarter of an hour had passed, Conrad cleaned up the picnic and they made their way back to the castle. Isabelle gave Neci her horse and rode behind Conrad on his monstrous steed. It was the last ride into the country that Isabelle would take with Conrad. Part of her was grateful, and a larger part was actually very sad about it.

✤ ✤ ✤

Neci came to the Great Room after dinner and knocked softly on the door. A servant opened it.

"I came to see His Majesty," Neci said.

"Come in, please."

Neci stepped in and saw a lovely picture displayed. The fire was going in the hearth, and near it, Margaret was rocking a lovely little baby to sleep in her arms. The queen wife looked up and smiled at Neci.

"Almost asleep," she whispered.

"I shall endeavor not to wake her then, Majesty," Neci replied.

Louis was reading over by a lit brazier on the far side of the room. He was sitting on the window seat that Isabelle occupied during court. When Neci spoke, he looked up from several rolls of vellum.

"Good evening," he said, and stood, going over to Neci. "It's not often that we have a visit from you here."

"I'm sorry to interrupt your personal moments, but I felt this matter was of great importance and you'd want to know immediately and privately."

Louis nodded at Neci. "What is it?" He gestured her over to the dais, now pulled out as a full bed, and the two sat down on the foot of it. They spoke in low tones.

"The Order of the Rose has good reason to believe that the emperor of Jerusalem has forsaken the most holy relic of our time," Neci said.

"Dear Lord in Heaven, what has the world become?" Louis rolled up his vellum and nearly swatted the bed with it, but held himself in restraint. Neither woman said a word at it.

He continued in a more reasonable, hushed tone. "What makes rulers of men act today as nothing more than scrounging, rutting dogs? There was a time, Neci, when we did not do these things. When we stood for valor, honor, and courage without bribery and blasphemy."

Louis stood up and paced, quietly adding, "My father said very little to me in this life—you know that, Neci. But he never allowed me to treat anyone or any precious thing in such a manner. It isn't proper for a king or a knight, and certainly not for an emperor."

The baby in Margaret's arms fussed a little. "Hush, Louis. You'll wake her."

Neci and Louis both regarded Margaret with a cold stare. The queen turned and rocked the baby in the corner with her head down.

"My father, Lord rest his soul," Louis continued, "still looks after me. I can't imagine what he would do to the emperor for such an act. I would ask him, but . . . ever since that day I told Mother about the falcon, he's never come back."

"Queen Blanche forbade you to speak of it," Neci remembered, but she wasn't reminding him.

"She never believed it. She never understood because she wasn't there. His favorite falcon came to me when he died, and sat on my windowsill, Neci." Louis rubbed at the sill before him, vacantly. "He came to me and tried to tell me something through that gesture. I was too young to understand. When I tried to tell Mother, to figure it out . . ." He stopped, painfully remembering.

"She punished you and sent you to your room for a fortnight. Louis, she was very distressed."

"I know things, Neci. I know them in the pit of my stomach like I knew about that bird. This . . . squandering by the emperor of Jerusalem. The Crown of Thorns, the holiest relic of our faith . . . What he has done is a mortal sin."

"I know," she said simply. "Because of what you did for the Holy Nail of France, I thought you would want to know the details."

"Yes, please," Louis said. "Go ahead."

"The emperor has sold the Crown of Thorns to a Venetian merchant because his kingdom has gone bankrupt. He sold this most holy of relics before embarking on a trip through Europe. He will be in France within a few months."

"Then I will confront him about it when he visits my court."

"No!" Neci surprised Louis, but she had plans of her own. "There is another way, Your Majesty, and we must turn this to our advantage."

"Tell me," he said.

✦ ✦ ✦

Conrad left the night before Alphonse and Joan's wedding. He said his quiet good-byes to all in the royal household. No one said a word to Isabelle, who stayed in her attic room all day and would not come out for meals.

The night passed in silence until dawn, and then Isabelle heard Blanche making her way up the stairs to Isabelle's room. Her skirts moved with the determined footfall of every step. By the time she reached Isabelle's room, the girl knew she was coming. Isabelle was standing, facing the door, ready to receive her mother.

"What happened to cause this?" Blanche asked quietly.

"Nothing ill or unexpected."

"I don't understand why he left when it was going so well."

"I'm surprised he didn't tell you why he left, himself. Why should I be the one to talk about his reasons?" Isabelle wouldn't bother to go into the details. In some ways she felt her own failings were private and not open for familial dispute.

"He told me that things did not work out, but that you were not to blame."

"That is correct."

Blanche's tone grew more stern. "I didn't ask if he was right or wrong; I am asking for an elaboration."

"Mother, I don't want to talk about it."

"You owe me an explanation. I house a guest here for nearly six months at our expense, I do not pressure you into an immediate arranged marriage, and you turn out your fiancé without seeking my permission."

"I did not turn him out; he left voluntarily," Isabelle said. "We did not quarrel or argue. We simply don't feel anything for one another, despite the friendship that has grown."

"What do you mean? How could you know?" Blanche had received a partial answer and yet all truth. This was a game Isabelle knew her mother was getting weary of.

"I know because it's my heart we're discussing. Just like it's Conrad's heart he's going to have to explain to his father when he gets home. I'm sorry it didn't work out, Mother. I truly am. I wanted to make you all happy and fall in love and be just like you and Father were. But I didn't feel for Conrad like you felt for Father."

Blanche swished over to the window and stared out at the countryside still gray with dawn. "Emperor Frederick is going to be very angry."

"Let him be angry. He's the one who imposed this ridiculous idea."

"No, child. I was in total agreement with him. You and Conrad seemed to have much in common, and I knew you would make a good match. I feel as if this is—"

"A direct insubordination to your parental authority," Isabelle finished, and Blanche looked at her with shock and dismay.

"It *isn't*," Isabelle said. "So don't think that. I know you choose wisely for us. You made a good choice for Louis, and Joan seems right for Alphonse. Sometimes things seem right on the surface, but underneath they are not. I know you did not formally announce the marriage because you were certain I'd be miserable." Isabelle saw Blanche's eyes soften at her words of praise. They were duly meant. "For that I am truly thankful, Mother. It is not your fault, so please, don't act as if my actions were blaming you."

"Then this . . . Conrad? Was he a brute? Distasteful? What was really wrong? Be honest, child." If Blanche or Isabelle were not to blame, then surely it must have been something that Conrad himself had done. Isabelle saw this shift in accusation and parried it.

"It's not Conrad's fault, either. He is the truest friend I've ever had." She lingered on this sudden thought, realizing that this was a truth stemming straight from her heart. "I suppose if he were more like Robert, if I felt for him like I feel for Robert, then maybe I could have loved him truly and married him. But instead, it is more like the cool love I share for Alphonse."

Isabelle remembered the man in the courtyard: the one who had turned the vicious dog away from her with a simple word. She saw that man once more, and realized what she wanted to say was that a man to marry should be just like Him. Someone who could be the lion and the lamb, whose force of personality was powerful and yet gentle. If there was a man like that at court, if Conrad had been like that man in temperament . . . but he wasn't. And Isabelle could not discuss that man with anyone. She'd promised Neci.

"I like Conrad, but he's not right for me," she said, still seeing *Him* in her mind's eye.

Blanche sighed. In some ways, Isabelle thought she might understand; in others Isabelle could tell she just plainly disapproved. In any case, Isabelle was clearly a mystery to her mother.

"It is just something that did not work out. Better for France and Germany, and better for both Conrad and me in the long run."

Blanche looked at Isabelle and then turned to go. "We had better hurry and get ready, or we'll miss the ceremony for Alphonse and Joan."

As Blanche passed the doorway, Isabelle realized aloud, "I'm sorry, Mother. I want something else, something more for my life."

Blanche hesitated a moment, said nothing, and then continued away.

I just don't know what that is yet, Isabelle thought. She looked out her attic window and thought about the day she was like a mariner, in Notre Dame, trying to find true north. She wanted the alignment of her Compass Star once again. Maybe she could find it in church. Isabelle grabbed her cloak and headed out of her room.

✤ ✤ ✤

Novembre's cold skies saw two of the world's brightest young royals married at the family chapel. Alphonse and Joan's marriage was small, but in many ways it was as splendid as Louis' marriage to Margaret.

Isabelle stood with her family and thought of the many marriages passing through her life. She remembered the quick and dirty marriage of Robert to Maud of Brabant. It had been a quiet ceremony held after the large feasting of his knighthood. He had asked Mother to keep the marriage quiet, since the knighting ceremony was so prominent and expensive. In truth, he didn't like Maud at all. How strange that Blanche had not chosen well for Robert, either.

But the marriage of Alphonse to Joan was a splendid and happy arrangement. Isabelle started to wonder if those few and lucky hangers-on now assembled behind the family were watching *her* rather than Joan. She could almost hear the gathered masses asking in one thought, *Why is the princess not married to the king of Germany? Why does she stand here before the altar and shame God?*

But she didn't feel like she had shamed God. Instead, she thought He might be proud of her. Instead of just taking what she was given, Isabelle had passed up monotony for something greater, something destined to come her way. She would know it when it came. It was like a slight pressure building with each passing day. And she tried hard not to be upset with herself in the interim.

Joan of Toulouse looked radiant. She was the one who had insisted on the marriage first and the knightship after. She did not mind marrying a humble prince without knightly vestments. They were deeply in love, and neither cared about status and title. They were as endeared to one another as Louis and Margaret. She even seemed a shadow of Margaret in her doting affections.

Maud was here next to Robert but not happy. They had come from Artois for the ceremony. She was hardly ever seen with the royal family, except at official functions. She lived with her father, the duke of Brabant. After their marriage, Maud had found Robert's incessant flirting with other women to be highly distasteful. The royal family was rather shocked at her display of disapproval, as Robert was the family's secret favorite. He could do no wrong. So in the beginning the family had firmly suggested Maud return to her father's estate at Brabant. Better to let the wound heal apart from Robert than to insist it stay deeply embedded where it wasn't wanted. Now they both lived in Artois though neither looked pleased about it. Isabelle pitied Robert's return home.

Isabelle stared at the altar and looked at the vision of God in the stained-glass artwork as the church choir sang in Latin, a language she now knew better than most of the clergy. She had already corrected a few of the psalmbooks.

Then, as if the light through the stained-glass windows shone down at her with the light of realization, she said quietly, "I will never marry."

Then she realized she was speaking aloud and looked around. No one had noticed. The Latin was too loud.

Margaret, Maud, now Joan. But never me.

She looked at all the noblemen assembled, awash in the glow of that special light. Nearly everyone in the near lands was here. But *He* wasn't here.

I won't see Him *ever again. Whoever he was, whatever he was doing that day, no one can live up to that. I was the object of a miracle that day. It affected my destiny in life. I can no longer contemplate such a union because my destiny lies somewhere greater. Neci knows about Him, and about this too, I suppose, but I can never reveal it to another living soul. Because I made a vow to Neci.*

How can any man live up to one as great as that?

But she knew the answer. No man ever could. But there was always God.

✦ ✦ ✦

Several days after the marriage, Isabelle grabbed her cloak and headed out the door of the *palais*. She wanted to speak to Bishop Maurice at the Episcopal Palace near Notre Dame. She wanted an outside opinion about her revelation. He had been her personal attending Father during the time she prayed for Robert's safe return. Father Maurice would talk to her, let her know if she was right or wrong.

Unfortunately, Joan managed to catch Isabelle on her way out to the courtyard. "Princess?"

Isabelle turned, a bit vexed at being unable to go about her intentions. "Yes?"

"I'm sorry, were you going somewhere?"

"To Notre Dame."

"May I accompany you?" Joan asked. "I've rarely been there and would like to see more."

Isabelle stopped and looked at the castle gate that led to the rest of the world beyond. She wanted to talk with Bishop Maurice alone, but it would be rude not to let Joan accompany her, since she had asked politely.

"Of course," she said, and they started walking.

"We haven't had much time to get to know one another, and I thought I should remedy that," Joan said.

Great, Isabelle thought. *Another Margaret.*

"I don't want to intrude, and I want to take things slowly. But it's always hard when a person has to fit into someone else's happy family. Do you agree?"

"Yes."

There was only the sound of feet walking along cobblestones for a while. Then, "I noticed the other day that you were reading Ptolemy."

Isabelle raised an eyebrow at this. "*Oui*, his treatise on astronomy and the positions of the planets is contrary to established theory."

"I've heard the same. He believes differently than Aristotle. The positions of the Earth and sun are reversed, right?"

"Something like that. Do you read?"

"I used to read quite a bit, before I met Alphonse and came here. I left my library back in Toulouse."

"That must have been difficult. I can't imagine being without my books."

"It was a little difficult. Perhaps I will write my family. I could probably send for the books in my library."

"Probably so," Isabelle said. "Do you write?"

"Latin, vernacular, some Greek."

"You write in Greek?"

"I studied it a bit. Why?"

"I can't write in Greek. Although I recently read up on the Arabic numerals. They use these ten digits to make up any number, and it's fast and easy. I showed it to Alphonse."

"Did he like it?"

"I think it's going to take a while for him."

Both of them chuckled. They walked on a little bit in silence before Joan offered, "You know, I could teach you what I know of Greek. I don't know much more than the basics."

"I would like that," Isabelle said.

"So would I."

They continued together to Notre Dame. Despite not being able to speak to Maurice that day, Isabelle looked forward to the Greek lessons with Joan with a sort of happy trepidation. She didn't want to be betrayed by another new member of the family, as she had by Margaret.

But Joan stayed true to her promise, and over the days that followed, Isabelle learned the Greek letters and the fundamentals of putting them together to form words—mostly verbs and nouns. On Saturdays, Joan would weave at her loom in her bedchamber while Isabelle spelled out Greek words and checked them with her amateur teacher.

She realized she rather liked Joan for being quiet and steady. The woman spent most of her time spinning wool, dyeing it, and then making rugs, clothes, tapestries, and other fine textiles on her loom. It was a hobby, but her love for it began to fill the couple's bedchamber with lovely tapestries and plush bedding.

Something else filled their bedchamber on Saturdays. Joan knew the great ballads of the Greeks, Romans, and even the ancient Gauls. Her singing at the loom was sweet, and Isabelle learned about many myths, from Toulouse to the Island of Calypso.

Isabelle soon found that Saturdays slid by and were becoming the highlights of her week, next to Sundays at Notre Dame and Wednesdays at *Petit Pont* talking with her Franciscan friends.

Love nothing but that which comes to you woven in the pattern of your destiny. For what could more aptly fit your needs?

Marcus Aurelius, *The Meditations* (A.D. 167)

9

Baldwin II ruled the Holy Lands of Jerusalem from the recently conquered city of Constantinople and claimed Christian dominion over all the Crusader states won by the recent Crusades. Though his seat of power was Constantinople, he was often referred to as the emperor of Jerusalem.

"He's begging for money," Blanche told Louis before the great and esteemed emperor of Jerusalem came before the French court.

All bowed low to His Royal Majesty, and the eye of every courtier and hanger-on in the palace was carefully watching the two rulers as they regarded one another. King Louis and Queen Mother Blanche stood and bowed in the emperor's presence, then took their seats again on the dais and waited to hear what the emperor had to say.

The emperor declared firmly, "I am glad to see my brother France and his mother the queen in good health. Congratulations on your thriving kingdom. Would that I could spend most of my time in the glory of your hallowed halls."

Louis nodded, but did not smile. "I would speak to His Majesty the emperor in private," the king said to his court.

There was a great deal of murmuring and surprise at this sudden declaration. But Isabelle, who was sitting at the window, rose and ushered everyone out, being the last to leave the room. As she closed the great doors, facing Louis, she saw him watch her until the doors hid her face from view.

Outside in the stone hallway, the courtiers moved off a little bit, but didn't stray too far. Isabelle knew they were hoping to overhear parts of the private conversation. Some went to the servants' kitchen for a bite to eat, but only because the kitchen was close to one of the courtroom walls. If Isabelle had peeked around the corner of the kitchen door she might have found fifteen noblewomen with their ears pressed against the wall behind the kitchen fireplace.

More respectful courtiers mingled in the courtyard sunlight, while they waited for the king to finish speaking with the emperor privately. It was *novembre*, and the frost was starting. The winter weather meant Isabelle could make fewer trips to the Latin Quarter to *Petit Pont*, or Notre Dame. She would soon be housebound and unable to go much of anywhere save for short trips to Notre Dame, on the *île de la Cité*.

In Notre Dame, Isabelle had made an ally, the Bishop Maurice of Sully. They had spent long hours talking about her situation with Conrad, about her love of her brothers and mother. Most especially, he had absolved Isabelle of any wrongdoing in the broken engagement. That had taken a great weight off her heart.

As Isabelle stood by the large double doors of the Great Room, she wished nothing more than to find peace and sanctity away from the courtiers of the *palais*. Notre Dame was safe. Safer now than even her attic room. Safe and quiet.

From behind the door, she heard Louis speaking: "If you do what I say, this *will be* a goodwill tour." This made her more curious, and she pressed herself up against the door, straining to hear all the words spoken in the room. "But if you don't, you can return home with your goodwill, but you will only keep your head temporarily. Because the people of Constantinople are going to want the money you have forsaken the Crown of Thorns for, not you. If you return without money worthy of such a pawn, you will be dead within a day of returning."

"How did you—?" That was the voice of the emperor, who sounded positively astonished. "How did you know I'd bartered the Crown of Thorns? That was a *private* transaction!"

"Nothing is private in the eyes of the Lord, Emperor. You can consider my source to be divine inspiration."

"I don't see why my giving up the Crown of Thorns means anything to you."

Oh, that was a bad thing to say to her brother the king, Isabelle knew. She cringed, waiting for Louis to strike. "Here is why it matters to me. Here is why it doesn't matter to you. I do not rule Constantinople; or the lands of Jerusalem; I do not parade my empty faith about as emperor of the Holiest Lands on Earth. But I rule France in God's name. I am God's vessel, for he picked my family to lead the common people to faith and good discipline. My role as a leader is to show by example. It is my duty to restore the old virtues, and to extol honor. He that sells the Crown of Thorns to a simple Venetian merchant has neither virtue nor honor—"

"That's outrageous!"

"And if it takes my intervention to set the Crown of Thorns in a land of dignity, so as not to abuse the face of God, then I will do so."

Louis' voice grew quiet, almost inaudible behind the closed doors. "And you *will* help me transfer that most holy of relics to a place where it will be safe and treasured. Or you will go back to Constantinople a destitute king who sold out his own people."

She heard no other distinct noises from behind the doors, just vague muttering. The Crown of Thorns, among the True Cross and one of the four Nails of the crucifixion, were all kept at the Crusader states near Jerusalem. The Crusaders had managed to hold the Holy City for a few generations, and all of the saintly relics of importance were said to be housed with the Christian rulers with the express belief they would be cherished and never removed.

After a few minutes, the door opened and the emperor rushed out, cheeks blazing red, with Prince Alphonse at his side. Princess Isabelle curt-sied low in the emperor's presence, but her thoughts were not so courteous.

"Follow me to the treasury room, August Majesty," Alphonse spoke. "We will rectify this terrible situation. You are in the good care of my brother, the king of France. Louis will see to it that you are well compensated for the Crown of Thorns. When the holy relic is deliv-ered safely to France, all will be well."

Isabelle tilted her head and watched them, and then she stood up from her deep curtsey.

Of all the sanctity and holiness, of all the holiest people—the emperor *of* JERUSALEM, she thought, *pawning off the Crown of Thorns!* Perhaps it was spending time at the cathedral of Notre Dame that made her so angry about this, or perhaps she had been raised by a family that respected the threshold for politics crossing into the sanctity of the Holy Church. Not long before this, a Saracen had stolen the Holy Nail, and it was Robert who had risked his life to retrieve it again. This Crown had been carelessly sold off, and yet another relic was in great peril. What was happening to the world?

She ground her teeth together as she walked into the Great Room.

Louis growled, "Shut down court today." He pointed menacingly at the chancellor, Jean Beaumont.

"Yes, Your Majesty." The old man was wise and bowed low while rushing out to suspend the day's events and reschedule. He made haste, and spoke in deference to a ferocious king.

Louis turned to Blanche. "What is his excuse, handing over the Crown of Thorns to a petty merchant like that! It's sacrilege!"

Isabelle winced as she walked over to the window. Blanche only shrugged, staying out of the line of Louis' temper. Such matters often infuriated him. He turned and saw Isabelle.

"Not now, Isabelle." He was curt. "I'm in the process of remedying a tragic mistake."

Isabelle hadn't said a word, hadn't even approached Louis. She glared at him. Blanche looked at Louis, and then Isabelle with soft eyes. Isabelle noticed this but knew her mother was forgiving Louis more than comforting her. Isabelle turned on her heel and walked out of the room. She closed the great doors behind her.

She was bitter. *Fine. Let Louis once again play the hero for the Church but continue to torch his own family. He's forsaken all of us ever since his marriage. I'm going to pray.*

Isabelle swished down the hall, her skirts briskly rustling as she strode out. She would go to Notre Dame to speak with her friend, Bishop Maurice, she decided as she passed Neci emerging from the kitchen.

"Is everything all right, Isabelle?"

"Fine," Isabelle shot back. "I'm going to Notre Dame." The growling in her voice was obvious.

"Oh, I'm heading out as well. Good day." The Sister of the Rose bustled off, seemingly lost in thought.

Isabelle wondered what was going on. Usually Neci would stop and talk to her, or at least ask why she was so surly. But the youngest of the mystic sisters was bustling off in such a hurry that she was already out of sight down the stairs.

What's she up to?

Isabelle had attempted to follow her through town once, and failed. She never had found out where Neci was going that day. Now, Neci had the same look in her eye. Of all three sisters she was the least able to hide her feelings. Something was going on, something secret. Isabelle, tired of being kept at the fringe of things, wanted to know what it was. Notre Dame could wait for a while.

When Neci had crossed the *Grand Pont* and reached the outer walls at the northern part of Paris, Isabelle was not far behind. She stayed back just enough so that she wouldn't be spotted, but Neci never seemed to be looking behind her. Isabelle had learned a thing or two since the last time she'd tried to follow Neci through town. She didn't lose her a second time, despite Neci winding into occasional shops and leaving through their back doors.

When Neci kept going right out of the town, Isabelle wondered what in the world was going on. Neci walked through the plains between the great city wall and the gaming forest. The very forest where Isabelle and Conrad had picnicked several months before.

Why?

She followed, but only after Neci had gotten far enough ahead to be a bright white spot on the horizon. Isabelle didn't want to have the Sister look back and see her following on the open plain. At least this way, she'd be as indefinite a blur on Neci's horizon as Neci was on hers.

The forest at the edge of the plain was starting to loom taller up ahead. Isabelle saw Neci enter the dark band of trees. Then she remembered Neci coming out of the underbrush the day of the picnic when Conrad and she were in the gaming wood.

What is she up to?

Isabelle raced along the plain to catch up. Once inside the dark forest, she followed Neci to a small stone ruin, the remains of an old Benedictine monastery. The darkness inside swallowed Neci as she entered.

Isabelle waited. *Should I go in after her?* She looked around at the length of the ruin and saw that it was only one room wide. *No, it's too small. She's in there, right inside the door, doing something. But what?*

Isabelle crouched down quietly in a bush just beyond the tree line. After what must have been an hour, Neci finally emerged and walked back the way she had come. Isabelle let her get far out of sight, and waited for a little bit. She didn't want Neci to return and find her snooping where she shouldn't be.

Neci didn't return, though, and Isabelle stared at the monastic ruin. It was very dark in there. Isabelle wished she had some sort of light source, a candle or torch. But Neci didn't have one either.

What was she doing in the dark without a torch?

A few imaginative notions gave Isabelle the shivers. Conjuring black spirits came to mind, but she knew that Neci wasn't bad. She hoped so, anyway.

I'm just going to have to go in there and find out.

Isabelle's hands were shaking as she stood and made her way to the edge of the monastery door.

Inside, there was only silence.

Isabelle hesitated. Stared. Swallowed hard. Then took a step into the pitch darkness.

She couldn't see anything. Not even her hand in front of her face. How was she to know what Neci was doing in here, if she couldn't even find her way through the darkness? She stood still, thinking.

Something whispered; something rustled. Isabelle froze. She wanted to turn and run into the light. But she couldn't move.

A voice spoke from out of the darkness. "What brings you here?"

Isabelle felt all the blood in her body rush to her feet, and the hair on the back of her neck stood straight up. She remembered this feeling; it was the same feeling she'd had as a little girl when the hound scared her.

"I came"—her body tingled with fear—"to find answers." Isabelle held her ground, reminding herself that whatever was speaking to her had not harmed Neci.

There was a pause of consideration. "You have questions?"

"What did Neci want?" Isabelle asked. She wasn't certain it was smart to ask it, but it was spoken.

"I can't tell you that. Neci's answers are for Neci only." The voice paused. "What are *your* questions?"

She wanted to ask this disembodied voice whether he spoke for good or evil. But it was such a kind and gentle tone that it seemed obvious. And Neci would not be fooled by evil voices. There was also something familiar about this voice that she couldn't put a finger on. Something so calming . . .

She tried to collect her thoughts. "You mean, I'm to ask you some-thing about myself?"

"If that is why you came here, then yes."

She couldn't very well tell him that she'd come to spy on Neci. Isabelle fidgeted in the darkness.

Was this a vision? The kind that saints and prophets were said to have?

She remembered Neci telling her as a very young girl that if she was very good, maybe one day she could turn a rosemary needle into a rosemary flower. The memory came back to her strongly.

And she remembered Neci pleading with her to keep the dog and the man who saved her a secret. She wondered if this voice, this spirit, could tell her about that moment. For it had bothered her most of her life, and seemed to crop up here and there whenever something impor-tant was about to happen. And she'd never told a soul until today.

"There was this time," she began, "when I was a very little girl, that a man saved me from a dog. I believe the dog was Evil, and I believe that the man was Good. No one knows this story," she con-fessed. The voice said nothing in reply.

"But I *know* it happened. Even though Neci, who was there, will not tell me who the man was. She was speaking to him that day. Every so often, I am reminded of this one moment. I shouldn't be alive today, because of that dog, but because this man saved my life . . . I have to wonder . . ."

Was he saving me for a greater destiny? she thought. But that was not the one question that truly burned within her.

She looked into the darkness, tried to pinpoint the source of the mysterious voice. She focused all her being into one question: "*Why?*"

She waited in the darkness for an answer.

"Your faith has made you strong. Because you adore this memory above all others, those who adore you come from below you. You now live above them. Your devotion to one perfect ideal will lead you to happiness. But you have yet to truly embrace and uncover it."

She felt the words rush over her, burn in her ears, and then after a long silence, she called to him again. But the voice was now silent, and she could sense that the presence was gone.

Isabelle stumbled out of the darkness and into the light. Though the light was dappled in the forest, it was like blinding sunlight after the darkness of the ruin. Isabelle held a hand up to her eyes, but it was a long time before she could truly see.

Isabelle came to the door of Maurice's room inside the Episcopal Palace and knocked softly. From inside she heard his gentle voice. "Come in."

He turned when she opened the door. Inside the room was a small bed with a straw mattress, no pillow, one blanket. A desk sat against a tiny window looking out at Notre Dame. And a small stool sat beneath the thin man, Maurice, who was about forty years old, but seemed to be sixty. He was wearing cleric's robes and a belt of straw tied around his waist.

"Hello, Father. I'm . . . back again," she confessed.

"Yes, it's good to see you. What can I help you with, Princess Isabelle?" He stood up and ushered her gently to the door, and she realized she should not be in a clergyman's room alone with him.

They walked along the hall of the Episcopal Palace. He was taking her outside.

"Father," she began quietly, "something's happened to me."

"What is it, child?"

"I don't know. I need to talk to you."

"Is it still about King Conrad?" he asked.

They had reached the large oak door of the rectory, and he pushed it open for her and gestured her out into the sunlight.

"No, it's something more . . . sensitive than that." She looked around to see if anyone else was within earshot before saying, "I've seen things my family wouldn't believe."

"Have you had a vision?" Maurice was serious and stared at her.

"I think I have," she whispered.

"Perhaps you would like to confide this vision in me?"

"Yes," she said, then paused. "I mean, no."

"Oh?"

They continued, making their way across the courtyard to the large steeple of the great cathedral.

"I really shouldn't tell anyone. It was rather personal. But it had to do with me and my future. And something else . . .

"Conrad once said, 'I cannot be angry with you. You are honest, and I see sometimes in you, that you are better than all of us. I can't say how, but there is something mysterious about you. You are reaching for something unreachable. And I am too humble for your greatness.'"

Maurice seemed to reflect at this, his eyebrows raised as he stared at the cold ground deep in thought.

"He believes in my future. And he wasn't angry that we didn't marry. He's the only one who understands, and now he's gone."

"What do you think he meant, child?"

"I don't know, really. I just know I never do what my family wants me to do."

"What do *you* want to do?"

The question reminded her of the voice in the darkness asking about *her* question. "I want to help people, Father. I want to do good work with my own two hands. I don't want to rely on a husband, or even be a partner in a good marriage. I haven't found one person in my life that could be as ideal as—" She grew quiet, but thought, *As the man who saved my life as a child. Not one person could ever match him.*

Maurice nodded quietly.

"And I know what I want to do, and it's something my family will never approve of." She took a deep breath.

"Yes?" Maurice asked

She told him about Jacques, and how she helped him to tack on his roof when no one else would. And she told him about how she taught Robert to dance on the eve of his knighthood. Then she hit him with her decision. "I want to be a member of the Church. Is that bad?"

Maurice smiled an old smile then. There was something mysterious and telling in his eyes, but Isabelle didn't know what it was, exactly.

"Child, before you jump into that decision, I would like you to come and visit me on a regular basis. I think we must start looking at you in a fresh, new light. Will you do this?"

"What days, Father?"

"Come any time you like. Try for once a week. We will meet in the nave of Notre Dame."

Isabelle nodded.

✣   ✣   ✣

While walking back to the *palais*, she thought about what it all meant. She would tell no one about meeting with Father Maurice. Just as she would never mention the voice that came to her in the dark monastic ruins that day. It was her little secret, and for some reason, it made her feel better.

She went to Maurice on Mondays. Their conversations grew lengthy and even slightly controversial. She grew to appreciate his candor, and he was not coy with her about what a life in cloth would be like if she chose to join a convent. She should consider other alternatives as well. He told her how the Church had once asked for her, but that Queen Blanche had said she was spoken for by Germany.

This insight, and the fact that she'd turned down Conrad, was starting to root itself in her soul. She was beginning to feel oddly in control for the first time in her life. Her destiny felt like a mast with a sail let down and tethered tight. There was a wind blowing, and it was now up to her to choose the direction of her future.

Isabelle had to know. She went back to the monastic ruins, but this time, she came with a torch in hand. When she reached the door, she lit the torch and looked inside. The room was completely empty, overgrown with ivy along the walls and floor, not one piece of stone or furniture inside. Empty, deserted, a simple ruin.

Isabelle looked around with a frown. Had it actually happened? It had seemed so real, but with the passing of time, she wondered if it had been her imagination. Should she doubt it? Was it wrong to doubt something that powerful?

Perhaps it was all the books she'd read on philosophy, or a natural trait passed down from a father she never knew, but Isabelle was a skeptic at heart. Something inside her wanted proof.

The monastic ruin had so far provided none. The old roof looked about to cave in, and was covered in wet green algae from the centuries of rains it had already withstood. It was empty and deserted in here. Only the vague memory of the voice remained.

Isabelle turned to go when her foot stepped on something uneven on the ground. She looked down.

One rose lay on the dirt.

Isabelle knelt down and picked up the rose. It was deep red and looked as if it had been snipped recently. There were no rosebushes around here, not even wild ones. Isabelle held onto the bud with trembling fingers.

Neci and I planted a rosebush that afternoon, in the courtyard, just before the hound came. Just before . . . the man.

The rose in her hand was beginning to slightly unfurl.

It is proof enough. I will never doubt again, she thought.

What is god, what is not god, what is between man and god, who shall say?

Euripides, *Helen* (412 B.C.)

10

18, août, l'an de notre Seigneur 1239

Louis solved the problem of the Crown of Thorns most admirably. He paid the pledge to Baldwin II the very day of the emperor's visit, then tracked down the pawned relic and purchased it from the Italian merchant himself. He received the blessing of the Holy Church of Rome for his actions and was highly praised throughout all of Europe. He had saved the face of the emperor of Jerusalem and recovered a valuable emblem of the Christian faith.

What he lost in the process was his sister. Isabelle placed herself on the roster of initiates to the Church the day that Louis left to collect the Crown of Thorns. She continued her religious training as the relic began its long journey from Venice to France. By the middle of the year, the Crown of Thorns had reached the small village of Villeneuve-l'Archevêque. Two Dominican brothers, James and Andrew, had brought the Crown in a chest all the way from Venice with the utmost care, employing a battery of troops from the Vatican itself. The chest was a silver box with a gold box inside, containing the Crown of Thorns.

Isabelle learned of the arrival of the relic while at Notre Dame with the Bishop Maurice. She was receiving Sacrament when messengers came in.

"King Louis is racing to Villeneuve-l'Archevêque in order to take the Crown of Thorns back to the *Cité*! Robert of Artois will meet him at the *Grand Pont*! They are bringing it here, to Notre Dame!"

"Very well." Bishop Maurice smiled. "We will be ready for him."

After the messenger had departed, Isabelle stood. "My family knows nothing of the vows I have taken with the Holy Church, Father."

"Do not fear, child," he said. "They will learn of your allegiance to Rome when they arrive. And under the circumstances of such a sacred day, they will understand the necessity of sacrificing their only daughter to the Church. The return of the Crown of Thorns will seal the unification of the royal family with the most holy ruler, God Himself."

Isabelle nodded sadly. She knew her family would be upset, despite the formalities of what looked best. This was not what they would have wanted, especially Robert. It would be bad tidings on one of his rare visits back home. But it was at church that she had always felt the most secure, even at family Mass, for as long as she remembered. Here she would be safe from political maneuverings and constant manipulations. She belonged here between man and God.

Maurice reassured her. "You have heard the voices, child. You are not a candidate for the secular life anymore. You are very special, able to hear the calling of God. If your family cannot see that, then I will take it upon myself to protect you from their ignorance."

The reliquary holding the sacred Crown of Thorns was on a litter carried by two men without special attire. They were nobles who had volunteered for the job. They walked barefoot, like penitents, while bearing the litter. Robert walked behind them, solemn and contemplative. Louis, the king, walked at the front.

From Villeneuve-l'Archevêque all the way to the *île de la Cité*, the precious burden was escorted by crowds. All were on foot, and the roads were thronged with people as far as one could stretch up to see.

Three days after Assumption, the relic, the king, his brother, and the barefoot penitents entered Paris. They reached a platform outside the walls of the city, at a place named La Guette, near the Abbey of Saint-Antoine. Everyone came to see the relic as it was placed here for the common people to look upon with wonder and awe.

Never was there a day in history when Paris was so thronged with onlookers. They came not just from France's countryside, but from England, Italy, Germany, and other far-reaching countries. All coming for the sake of the Crown of Thorns. Women and men alike, of all social ranks, came to the platform, and many cried upon seeing the beauty of it.

When it was time, the reliquary was put back on its litter and it was escorted, just as before, into the city amid the singing of hymns. A huge multitude of clerks, monks, prelates, and knights who had joined the throng of worshipers led the way.

They were going to Notre Dame.

In the Great Cathedral, Mass was held, after which the procession formed up once more to go to the *palais*, where the holy relic was placed in the family chapel—the Chapel of St. Nicholas.

When the brothers arrived with their litter and climbed the steps of the chapel, they found Bishop Maurice at the altar, waiting to receive the Crown of Thorns and bless it before putting it safely away.

They also found Isabelle. She was not dressed as a princess, but rather wore a plain cotton robe, her hair pulled back tightly. Everyone saw her, and their hearts froze. No woman would dress such a way for an occasion like this unless it meant—

Isabelle had joined the Church.

✢ ✢ ✢

Shortly after the ceremony, Robert thundered up the great stone stairs and marched into Isabelle's attic room without knocking.

"What is this I hear about you joining up with the Church?"

"Robert!" She stood, her tone just as forceful. "It's customary to say 'Hello, Isabelle! How are you doing today?' when you come into my room."

"Isabelle, I do not jest, today."

"Neither do I," she replied. "Why is it that whenever I make a decision about my life I'm suddenly treated as if I don't have a life to make a decision about? It's my life, isn't it?"

"Yes."

"Then what is the problem?" She was irate. She had reluctantly changed into courtly attire, but it was much more plain and dark than what she had once worn proudly before. She still lived among her family, but in her lofty attic room she was no longer really a part of them.

"This giving yourself to the Church . . . I don't understand at all. It's not that you aren't pious . . . I just don't understand how abstinence has anything to do with you!" He paused, turned in a fluster. "Why would you do something like this?"

"Because I have an obligation to God," she replied.

"You can spare me the platitudes. I changed your swaddling clothes a time or two, young lady."

Robert pressed to the heart of the matter. "I think it's because you're afraid."

"I'm not afraid. But I am disappointed, now that you bring it up. My family has never been there for me, but God always has. And I have an obligation to Him. Not you."

"That is absolute horse manure, and you know it. We've always been there for you. The marriage to Conrad is what you were afraid of. But you went overboard. None of us are ready to make commitments like those; that's why our parents do it for us."

"No, you don't understand. It has nothing to do with the marital bed. I'm going on fourteen now. When Mother was twelve, she was already a joint ruler. And yet my own family can't recognize me as an adult. I made a carefully considered decision, and I'm sticking to it."

Robert looked out the window, having no reply to that, as she continued.

"I know *myself* better than any of you do, and I know that I am not a queen. I have other ambitions."

"And you think that running away to the Church is going to be satisfying to you?" he asked, amused.

"It is not 'running away' to fulfill a pious obligation. If Louis decides he wants to go out among the poor and feed them, he's not chastised for it. Why am I? Yes, I want to commit my life to God, to do good work for my fellow countrymen. I want to feed the poor, help the sick, write books. What is so wrong with that?"

"Only that it has nothing to do with the Isabelle I know and love. It isn't the kind of goal my sister would set for herself."

"Perhaps it's *your* goal, and that's why you oppose this decision so much."

He snorted. "Hardly."

"I see it now. You think I'm being selfish. I'm somehow being childish about marriage to Conrad, and I should just do what I'm told." There was tense stillness before she hit him with the final insult. "You're no different than Mother."

"I am quite different than Mother! How dare you speak to me that way!"

Isabelle lowered her voice a little bit. "I spoke hastily, in anger. But you came to chastise me just as she did. I don't want to be chastised for my decision. I took a great deal of time and consideration with it. And I did wonder if I was escaping responsibility. But I decided that I want a responsibility of a higher nature."

"How could *you* want that?"

"That is the problem. You never asked me what I wanted. Not one of you."

"What do you want, then?" he asked, more softly now.

"To help people. Not by writing laws. To fight evil, not battles. I want to make an indelible mark somewhere outside of politics and marriage. What I *don't* want is to spend my life negotiating for it."

"You think the Holy Church is free from negotiation, dear sister? You don't think they're political? They have a long history of political offenses as base as any in our own royal past. It's child's folly to think the Church is pure."

"As a nun, I'm only obligated to works of public service. I don't get involved in the affairs of the Church proper."

"This just isn't like you, Isabelle."

"What do you know about what is and isn't like me? When's the last time we had a lengthy discussion since you left for Artois?" Her accusation hit him like a slap in the face. "I'm sorry, I didn't mean that."

"Yes, you did." He said it quietly, wounded. "You're angry with me. You're feeling neglected."

Isabelle took Robert by his arms. "I want to make my own life now, not wither in the shadows of my brothers. And the only partner who will let me come into my own, on my own, is God."

Robert looked at her and sighed.

"I want to be as impressive as Louis!" she said.

"You'll *never* be Louis."

"You and Louis are not cut from the same cloth. Although you are siblings, your dispositions differ greatly. Louis is cool-tempered, even, judicious. You are passionate, spirited, and independent.

"You spend so much time trying to emulate him you can't even see what you're really like!"

Isabelle stared at him, wondering how much he had thought about this during his life, and why it affected him so much.

"There's nothing wrong with wanting to be like Louis."

His voice was hard. "Don't you realize that every day I wake up and think I should be more like *dear Louis?* Heaven forbid that Louis die and the kingdom is left to his pathetic brother, Robert of Artois!"

Isabelle saw the raw core of Robert's heart, for what she realized was the first time. Carefully sealed from view, hidden behind his joviality and passion, were the same traits that so many people scorned in her. Isabelle felt her heart break at having pushed Robert to this admission. Robert had always meant so much to her.

He clenched his fist and rested it against the window, looking out at the landscape beyond. "I'm nothing like Louis. I'm just the unworthy Robert of Artois. And if you are closer to anyone in terms of temperament, it's me. Not Louis. We care about things too much."

He turned to her, his eyes heavy with the insight into his own soul. "You can never be like Louis if you're like me."

She nodded and spoke to him gently. "Our passion put to one side, what's done is done. I didn't ask for anyone's blessing. I am happy, and that's all that matters."

"How can you be happy in . . ." He pointed to her dark garments. "In that?"

She looked at him earnestly. "You say I'm just like you, but you don't trust me enough to believe what I say."

"I suppose because I feel an overwhelming need to protect you."

Isabelle smiled. "Well, I'm just fine. And may I point out that as of two years ago, I'm an adult and quite capable of making my own educated decisions."

"You're saying I no longer know what's best for you, Little Rose."

"This is what's best for me. Understand?"

There was a long pause before Robert finally answered. "I do. Well, I don't . . . but . . . I do."

Isabelle tried to hide her smile and failed miserably. Robert was positively adorable when talked into a corner. "Good," she replied. "I really need someone who will support me right now, particularly with Mother."

"I don't know if I'd go so far as to contradict Mother, but I'm not going to yell at you anymore about it."

Isabelle stifled a laugh at this. "Well, I suppose I'll have to take what I can get. So I'll have to take your surly reply as a feeble show of support."

He sounded quite beaten. "Very well." He looked out at the city beyond the castle window. "I need to go. I'm hunting with Louis this afternoon. We're meeting at the lodge." He turned to leave; then he stopped. "You could come with us. It'd be like old times."

Isabelle listened to the sadness under the attempt at a reunion. "I have some paperwork here; I have to attend to it."

"All right," Robert said, realizing the futility of his suggestion. He started away.

"Robert!" She made him stop, and their eyes met. "Did you really mean it when you said I'm more like you?"

"Of course I really meant that, Little Rose. Why?"

"Because I believe that is the highest compliment you have ever paid me."

He allowed a small smile, but his eyes were heavy. "I'll . . . see you at dinner."

Whatever God has brought about
Is to be borne with courage.

Sophocles, *Oedipus at Colonus* (401 B.C.)

11

13, novembre, l'an de notre Seigneur 1239

Though the wind was blustering and the clouds were rolling in like dark marbles across a slippery floor, Robert spurred his great black steed into the Western Wood. His hounds were only a few lengths ahead, hot on the scent of the fox that had run for cover in the dark and brooding trees.

The wood was dangerous and foreboding. The branches hung far over the meadow, as if outstretching long dark fingers to try to snatch up the heather plants that taunted it from just beyond the tree line. The wood waited like a riddle, too dangerous to answer, too dark to understand. The people had always left the Western Wood alone, and any king who sought to hunt game or try to clear hunting trails soon learned that the Western Wood had a will of its own and would never be claimed.

Robert knew the Western Wood was dangerous, and he knew the fox would probably be long gone by the time he managed to pick his way through the brambles and thorns. But surrender was not in his nature. As his horse's hooves landed in the dark soil just on the tree line of the forest, a crash of thunder came pealing from overhead, and rain spit from the sky.

He could still hear Louis calling him to come back. All the more reason why he couldn't turn the horse around. It was a brotherly jest.

As king, Louis was an iron ruler with a gentle fist. As brother, Louis would often turn a blind eye to Robert's recklessness. Louis never ordered Robert from doing what he was too cautious to do himself.

A branch snagged Robert's riding coat, speckled now with the first raindrops. Women had told him that he smelled rough and wild. He knew it was because his heart was rough and wild. For a few moments he thought his spirit alone could conquer the Western Wood.

I'll come back with something, he thought. *If not a fox, then at least a tale of adventure to tell at the Christmas feast.*

Adventure. The word rolled around his head like a loose bearing in a waterwheel, even as branches tore at his face and clothing, and his horse was repeatedly tripped by thistles and roots. He pulled the horse down to a more reasonable trot. The branches were dangerously low and close together. They raked at everything, leaving marks on his horse's flank and saddle, and even on Robert's cheeks.

It was as if nature had set a dangerous trap, and Robert had ventured into the mouth of it. Needles above, thistles below. His poor horse picked its way as carefully as possible between the two evils.

He could hear the hounds barking in the distance; they had cornered the fox beneath some craggy tree somewhere. He nudged his steed in the direction of their yapping, hoping to reach the tree by the time the fox was uncovered.

I'll kill it and return to Louis and the hunting party. I'll be the victor of the day, for a change.

He rather liked the idea of one-upping his brother in the field of courage. It was the only way one could overshadow the greatness of being a king, even if it was in play. For if there was one thing Robert had never wanted, it was to be king.

He trotted carefully now, letting the horse pick its way carefully through underbrush that held no pathway. *Not even game trails*, he thought.

He turned for a moment, and looked back. Blackness was beyond the sheets of falling rain; no sight of the tree line from this far into the wood. No sound of Louis and the hunting party. Nothing but wood all around now.

He turned back around in the saddle. The hounds were digging and pawing under a mighty fallen tree, old and rotting away under moss and lichen. The dogs were grunting and rooting, trying to hole out the fox they had cornered. He could hear the thunder rumbling angrily above the wood.

Looking up into the falling rain, he couldn't see the sky through the treetops, the branches were so tightly woven together.

The thunder was right overhead, so loud it vibrated within his chest. His horse grew restless beneath him. Robert laughed and attempted to calm the beast. His hand stretched out to stroke the long, arched neck. The creature from beneath the log finally came out.

It was not a fox.

Whether it was a bear, or a giant form of wolf or other predator, Robert couldn't be certain, for the creature scared his mount into rearing up and he was unhorsed. He landed with a sharp pain in his side, the breath knocked out of him. He heard a hound whining and yowling in pain as he struck the ground.

Pain tore through his side; something was moving straight through the soft flesh between his hip and ribs. Something sharp, then a splintering of bone and wood.

Then darkness took him away from the pain.

When he opened his eyes again, he found himself looking up into a face that was completely unfamiliar to him. More pain came as the man pressed a wadded-up piece of cloth against his open wound.

The world seemed to swim. He tried to speak, but the pain was too great. The strange man spoke to him then, with a quiet voice. "You've been impaled."

Robert looked down with great effort. His overcoat had been removed, and his undershirt was soaked in dark, clotted blood. The stranger had pushed his shirt up to his rib cage and then applied some sort of material to stanch the blood flow on his side. The sight of his hunting pike stuck through him like he was a festival pig made Robert reach for it.

"Don't move," the stranger said. "It's very dangerous right now!" His voice was soft but certain. Robert dug his fingertips into the dark soil on either side of his body. The world was spinning. The man's dark face and gentle words faded as shock took Robert away once again.

⚜ ⚜ ⚜

When Robert opened his eyes, he was in a dark place. As his sight slowly adjusted, he realized he was staring at an extremely tall cedar ceiling. He was lying flat on his back, on a soft cushion. Beyond that, he had no idea of his surroundings. He vaguely recalled someone having stood over him after he fell, and the pain—ah yes—there was still a great deal of pain on his left side, underneath his rib cage.

A mortal wound, he suspected. *What an undignified way to die.*

If he'd had the energy to snort, he would have. *Serves me right, I suppose, for trying to outdo Louis. Caution wins out again.*

There were faint noises to his immediate right, but he could not move his head to see what or who was making them. Then the face from before came back. The stranger looked like a tame lion. Perhaps it was the delirium from the fall, but that is how Robert first came to think of his savior. He had a lion's mane of hair, only it was a dark, satin brown. It did not wave or curl, but hung straight down to his shoulder blades. His eyes were brown and gentle.

"I see that you are awake."

Robert tried to speak, failed to produce sound, and licked his lips. The man held a wooden bowl to Robert's lips. "Here, drink this."

Robert sucked down a sweet-tasting, minty liquid that tasted of soft herbs and honey. Then he winced in pain at the small movement he'd made. The wound was excruciating.

"You've been impaled through the side. If I were to leave you like this, you would die within a week," the man told him. "I can help you, but you'll have to give me your permission."

Robert was confused. "You are royalty, Your Highness," the stranger continued. "I cannot do anything to your person without your permission, or it could be tantamount to treason. And I will need your word that you will never tell anyone what happened here."

Robert closed his eyes and nodded. The pain was overwhelming, and if this man could somehow help, he would allow it.

"Very well. Rest now," the man said. Robert felt the strange liquid having an effect on his thoughts. He was warm and fuzzy, like the times he spent drinking just enough mead to feel good without penalty. Thoughts swam together until he was lost in the darkness of sleep.

When next Robert woke, it was to the sound of a door crashing open. Then he heard a familiar call. "Lower your weapons and stand aside—in the name of His Majesty, King Louis!"

Robert sat up, without thinking, and his vision blurred. He lost his balance and fell against his elbow on the cushion he'd been lying on.

Robert tried to straighten himself on the bed, and this time, he succeeded. He realized that he was no longer in any pain whatsoever. It was amazing. He looked down at his bloodstained, ripped under-shirt and felt his side. No bandage, no hint of stiffness or soreness.

He didn't have much more time to examine his condition. He heard sounds of a struggle outside his little alcove. "Where is he?" Louis' voice sounded unusually passionate. The scuffling noise continued.

Robert stood, wobbled a bit, and then proceeded to hastily walk out of the alcove into the main room. There he saw an entourage of Louis' men as well as Sofia, who always accompanied Louis wherever he went. The poor stranger who had rescued him was being held against the wall by Louis himself.

Louis turned at the sound of Robert entering the room; his eyes widened when he saw the blood on his brother's shirt. The stranger also looked to Robert, his eyes heavy and pleading.

"Robert!" Louis sounded relieved and yet anxious at the same time.

"I'm fine, Louis. Please let go of him. He helped me, carried me here."

Louis turned and carefully removed his hands from the man's person. "Everyone, outside at once." As his entourage moved out, he was quick to apologize. "Forgive me. I thought—"

"My brother loves me," Robert said, interrupting Louis. "He never wanted anything to harm me. I'm sorry for this."

The stranger smoothed his surcoat and nodded. He said nothing.

Louis turned to Robert. "What happened to you?"

"You wouldn't *believe* what just—" Then Robert looked at the stranger, and remembered his promise. He changed his tactic.

"I actually *fell* off my horse." His usual jovial voice was still a little weak, but he bluffed through it. "It was an accident, and I cut myself on a very sharp branch—a vine I think. Hard, to be sure—I was knocked out by the impact. It's a harmless little scratch." He pointed at the stranger. "This good man found me and brought me here to recover."

Louis walked up to Robert and lifted his shirt. They looked down at the flesh beneath it and discovered to their shock that there was no wound at all. Robert ran his fingers over smooth, unscarred skin.

They traded a look, and Robert said, "Well done, isn't it? Good patchwork. Like I said, it was only a scratch."

Louis pulled Robert's shirt back down. "Then why is there so much blood on your shirt?"

Robert replied, "Oh, that . . ."

The man's voice was soft. "It's a pigment from the kind of root I used to take his scab away and heal the wound quickly. A salve that's bright red. It only looks like blood."

Louis looked questioningly at Robert, whose face was far too innocent to be true.

"I don't know what happened here, but I don't really believe Robert. What happened to him?" he asked the stranger.

The man did not reply.

"Louis, really," Robert said. "I am insulted that you don't take us at our word. That's what happened."

"He is telling you what happened, but he slept off a concussion as well," the stranger replied, then looked at Robert again. "Sir, you *gave* me your permission." He was gentle, but urgent.

Robert felt compelled to explain, though he didn't know how to start. He honestly didn't want this fellow to get into trouble for saving his life, so he tried to recount the events. "He did ask my permission to patch me up—and I gave it. I am better now. That should be all that matters, *non?*"

"What is your name?" Louis commanded rather than asked the man.

"Jean Adaret Benariel, Your Majesty." The stranger bowed low before King Louis.

"Why have I never heard of your family before?"

"My family were simple woodsmen. I am the last living descendant. I am told that there was a town to the south, but I hardly ever leave the wood and haven't seen many other people since my mother passed away." Jean's eyes flicked to Robert. "Not until your brother showed up in my woods, while I was out picking berries, Your Majesty. These woods are treacherous. One must be careful here. I had heard the royal family likes to hunt near these woods. I found your brother, and I felt an obligation to help him. I didn't know it would displease Your Majesty."

"And you used an herb? That was the redness on his shirt?"

Jean only nodded once, briefly.

Louis looked around the room at the high bookshelves filled with old tomes of philosophy, religious scripture, and poetry.

"There is no harm in whatever he used," Robert said. "It was benign."

He could tell Louis couldn't reason with it, that something just didn't sit well with the situation.

Finally, Louis put a firm hand behind Robert's neck and put his forehead to his younger sibling's. "I thought we'd lost you, Brother."

"Thank *him*." Robert grinned and then pulled away.

Louis turned to regard Jean Adaret Benariel. Something in the man's demeanor, his very nature, seemed so . . . gentle. It was persuasive. Robert realized how utterly ridiculous it was for Louis to be suspicious of him. The man seemed too kindly to inflict any harm on a stranger, nobleman or not.

"I am sorry to have offended. It is my love for my brother that sometimes outshines my own reason. Please, allow Us to make it up to you by inviting you to Our household."

Jean blinked a bit at Louis' statement, as if he didn't understand the formality.

"Will you come to the *palais de la Cité* with us, for Christmas celebrations?" Louis clarified.

Jean blushed at this and looked at the floor. "I would like to come to your castle, Your Majesty, but—"

"It is done." Robert didn't wait for Jean Adaret Benariel to finish. "For you are now a friend of Prince Robert of Artois, *Seigneur* Benariel. You saved me from harm's way."

"Anyone who would save my brother is one I would call brother as well." Louis held out his gloved hand to Jean, who looked at it a moment and then grasped it in friendship.

"Come then, let's be on our way!" Robert insisted, gaining in strength. "You will have a chance to see Paris in full holiday cheer."

Jean smiled, but seemed hesitant. "I thank you, Sir Robert. Most kind of you."

"In return for your kindness, you will be under my protection," Robert said. "Your land falls in the district of the *palais* anyway, so I will consider you my own sworn knight. In honor of saving my life, you are exempt from any taxation or tithe. It would be foolish of me to ask such a thing after being given the greatest gift possible. Will you accept?"

Jean seemed to hesitate again—his eyes cast a sidelong glance—but at last he said, "Very well."

"Good! Then we feast!" Louis unlatched the door and walked out into the dark forest with his brother Robert. The entourage was waiting for them out front. Upon seeing the brothers' good mood, a cheer went up.

Except from Sofia. She walked into the Tower of Benariel, barely noticed by the others.

Once outside the tower, Louis took Robert aside privately and said, "You will tell me if you have *any* ill effects from this . . . miracle herb."

"Naturally, Brother. Don't be so suspicious. Not all good deeds come sealed with the benediction of the Church. Miracles happen in the common world every day. Remember, our Christ was a simple commoner, himself."

"True. God works in mysterious ways. It was bold of me to assume the worst."

✦ ✦ ✦

In the tower, Sofia approached Jean Adaret Benariel. He held a silk banner—old, worn, and pale red now, the dye having long since rubbed out. It was a familiar piece of cloth. He'd had it ever since the night he'd watched Robert's knighting ceremony from the field.

Sofia spoke to Jean with familiarity. "You cannot come with the king. You were supposed to stay here."

"No, I must do as they ask. I tried not to go, but they were insistent. They already suspect me greatly and . . . I'm afraid if I don't go with them, it will look black against me."

Sofia sighed. "We meant you to stay out of harm, out of politic.

You are the most important of us, Jean. The youngest. This is most unfortunate. You should not have touched Robert."

"I had to help him, Sofia; you know that. If it is within my power to heal, I do it. I can't let someone die. It wouldn't be right. I promise you it will be well. I will be careful."

"I will be watching for your safety, Brother," she said, and left the tower.

Jean had wanted to tell her that he was finally invited to *belong*. But she wouldn't have understood. He put the faded red sash down on the mantel. Then Jean Adaret Benariel picked up his small bag and followed the others out the door of his lonely tower and into the realm of men.

> You win the victory when you yield to friends.
>
> Sophocles, *Ajax* (447 B.C.)

12

15, novembre, l'an de notre Seigneur 1239

Heading back from another wonderful trip to *Petit Pont* library, Isabelle let herself admire the smell of baking bread and tanning leather, and the sound of water mills on the shore of the *Petit Pont* beating the water with their wheel paddles as, inside their walls, they also beat the linen flax to remove the harsh bark and make linen pulp for boiling.

It was a beautiful day—sunny and bright, though a chill was in the air—and rain from the day before had washed the streets clean of their usual, fetid smell. A book was clasped firmly in Isabelle's hands as she walked along the cleaned cobblestone street and looked at merchant stalls open for business. Everyone was bustling with preholiday activities. Sheep and oxen plodded through the streets to the markets, and sacks of goods were trundled past on wheelbarrows.

The pleasant sounds were interrupted by a loud voice. A man was arguing with someone.

He was a brute of a man, maybe three feet wide and at least six feet tall, with straw for hair and a big nose. He was accosting a frail young woman of no more than sixteen years of age.

Where is her escort?

Isabelle waited to see what would happen, edging closer to the two.

"I paid, and I want to go now."

"I can't roll in the hay until this evening—"

"I said now, you stupid—"

"Desist, sir, or you will be punished for these actions." Isabelle's voice behind him took him utterly by surprise.

Then he sneered, looking at the noblewoman who had upbraided him.

"Oh, yeah? And on whose authority am I gonna get punished?" he asked.

Isabelle stood straight. Already a few people had stopped to watch, so she let the decree fly with as much pomp and ferocity as she could muster.

"By Her Majesty the Princess Isabelle of France."

The man instantly deflated, and the circle of onlookers spread out wide enough to move two carts within her space. An armed sentry over on the far wall looked at the parting crowd with curiosity.

Isabelle caught his attention and looked back at this pig-eyed thug with disgust. She didn't flinch, and he seemed to shrink down before her. *And to think, I once thought I might need an escort in this part of town.*

"I was just settling our arrangement," the man mumbled.

"I suggest you consider it settled and move on, or I'll signal that sentry to stick an arrow through your fat belly."

The man looked over at the sentry, who was watching the confrontation with hawk's eyes. He glared resentfully at Isabelle, shamed and thoroughly unable to strike back in any way.

Then he shambled off, pushing violently through the crowd, who now began to murmur in the background. Isabelle didn't have to hear them to know what they were saying. She'd been a legendary figure ever since Jacques' roof, and using that loud outburst against this thug had merely reinforced with the locals that she did indeed traverse this part of town and would not stand for any mischief in her presence.

The young woman was scurrying out of sight, and as Isabelle called out to her, she stopped in her tracks and turned with a resentful stare.

"Where are you going?" Isabelle asked.

"To do my work. If I don't get going, I'll be late and they'll release me."

"I'll walk with you."

"I'd rather you didn't."

Isabelle ignored the sentiment, in part because she used the same tactic to avoid people herself. She knew it well and casually brushed aside the girl's curt behavior. "What did that man want?"

"He was just trying to jump his place in line."

Isabelle didn't quite understand. "Where do you work?"

"I'm a seamstress."

This girl didn't look like a seamstress—she looked like a thief or worse. And men didn't jump their place in line for tailored leggings. What kind of life did she also lead among the shadows? Isabelle frowned. Whatever kind of life it was, she would bet good *tournois* that it wasn't savory.

"Born in the city?"

"No."

"Then you came from the country."

The girl stopped and pointed a dirty finger at Isabelle. "What's it matter to you? You got your happiness from telling that brute to leave me alone. Great. *Merci*. Now, leave me alone."

Now Isabelle was truly curious, if a bit offended. "Why do you speak to me in such a manner?"

"Because this isn't any of your business, and I don't like your pity."

"Who said anything about pity?" The girl stared ahead. Isabelle saw a lot of anger in her brown eyes—the same kind of anger that she was used to feeling about her own entrapments.

"What's your name?"

"Claire."

"Claire, then. I'm glad to meet you. Tell me how you came to the city."

They continued walking. "I want to be a merchant and do my own embroidering and seamstress work. I want to be among the *femmes seules*. I've been here eight months, and if I can manage it another four and a day, then I'm free. Do you understand that? I don't want to jeopardize my freedom by making a spectacle of myself."

"I didn't think I was compromising anything. I was saving your life back there, or at least defending your integrity."

"I don't have any integ—whatever you just said. I barely make ends meet as it is. I'm starving because I can't scrounge up two *tournois* a week. That's why I took up nights."

Isabelle suspected she knew what the girl meant by *taking up nights*: prostitution. "Listen, two *tournois* is not much to scrounge up. There are other alternatives to prostitu—"

This hit a nerve in Claire. "Oh well, maybe for you it isn't, but for me, I have to lay with two men a week to get two *tournois* to pay for my food and water. So don't tell me about how easy it is!" She was shouting and had stopped again.

"I didn't mean to insult you. I meant to offer help."

The girl was suspicious. "Why?"

"Because I think that I can help you easily. Two *tournois* a week, in exchange for you to come to the *palais* and mend some of my garments."

"I don't want your charity."

It was Isabelle's turn to raise her voice, and she did it with the same stern inflection her own mother used when she wanted to impose command. That voice now froze young Claire in her place. "Charity is a much larger scale. Two *tournois* would buy me a button, and you'd do well to remember that. In the meantime, I *expect* you to come to the *palais* and mend my garments. If I don't see you tomorrow afternoon, I will send for you. With armed escort."

✤ ✤ ✤

Claire came the next afternoon, and Isabelle set her to work mending clothes she had purposefully spent the evening ripping at the seams. While the girl sat on a small stool and mended the garments, she spoke of her home on a farm outside the city walls. Isabelle listened as she wrote a letter to King Conrad at her writing desk in the corner.

"They made us pay to grind our own grain that we rightfully earned and kept on our own lands at the lord's water mill." Claire scowled. She obviously needed to vent, and Isabelle let her carry on.

"I see." She put the quill in the pot and folded her hands on the writing desk.

"My father was to stand in line for five hours a day, just to get our grain ground, and was to pay one thirteenth of the grain as payment." Claire tied off a thread and bit it with her teeth.

"We didn't think much of it, until Father started to see free men coming up to the water mill, and getting to cut in line. Once he was the next one up, and a man came and cut in front of him, and he heard that this man only had to pay the miller one twenty-fourth the amount of grain. Father was absolutely furious. He stormed out of the line and announced that he would rather eat porridge than have his grain ground by the lord's mill—that it was a cheat."

Isabelle's brow knit. She didn't like what she was hearing. "Go on."

"He probably shouldn't have made such an outburst, because he made the other villagers mad about it, and they told us they'd stopped going to the lord's mill. Some of them had even started to mill their own grain with hand mills at home." Claire put the dress down in her lap. She stared at it and would not look at Isabelle.

"Go on," Isabelle said gently, trying to get Claire to let go of whatever pain was making her so volatile. She glanced down at her letter to Conrad, remembering how good he was to insist that she tell him exactly how she felt, even though tears had come of it.

Claire's voice was shaky now. "He thought it was a good idea to do the same thing. And we all milled the grain by hand for a while." She

wiped her eyes with the back of her hand, still looking down at the
gown in her lap. "I guess the lord started to notice that no one was
showing up at his mill, because he sent his troops out to frighten us
into submission. I suppose the miller had told him about my pa's outburst, because the men—"

She couldn't go on.

Her heart stinging from these confessions, Isabelle got up from her
writing chair and came to sit beside Claire on the floor. She held onto
Claire's hands. "I'm here. You can tell me everything."

"You—" Claire's mouth broke into a crying grimace, and her nose was
turning red. She sniffed heavily. "You won't do anything to me, will you?"

"I am here to protect you, as your royal family. Tell me what happened."

"The men came for Father. They took him outside and—I saw
him—" She was sobbing now, her hand reaching out as if she could
still see it right before her. "Dragged between horses and beaten,
flogged, and then they tore . . . him—a—apart."

Claire collapsed against Isabelle's shoulder and wept bitterly. Her
body shook until she could no longer cry. Isabelle felt the warm tears
seeping into her silk overcoat, as Claire trembled against her, too
humiliated to pull away after the storm of sobbing had passed.

"We will right this." Isabelle put her hand to Claire's hair and
stroked it gently. She spoke so softly. "We *will* right this."

When Louis and Robert finally arrived at the *palais*, Isabelle had been
pacing the Great Room for hours. Even Blanche had left her well
alone, seeing that something was terribly wrong. Every five minutes
she had asked the guards to see if Louis was on his way to the castle.
By the time he finally arrived, introducing Jean to those he met,
Isabelle approached him without any greeting or warmth.

"I want to see you. Now."

Louis walked with her, excusing himself from the group as Robert pointedly remarked, "That is my sister, Isabelle. Usually she is much nicer than this."

Then they were out of earshot. Isabelle took Louis into the Great Room. Louis made no pretense about his irritation. "Don't address me in that manner again, Isabelle, in front of a guest. I am still the king here."

"Then as king, you had better sit down and take some notes. I have been waiting for *two days* for you to return from your happy hunting spree—"

"That's because Robert was lost and wounded in the Western Wood! It took us two days to find him again!"

His words made Isabelle pause. That information was a shock, but she couldn't deal with it right now. She had been working up to this moment, and it couldn't slip away.

"Louis, I have just been informed of a most terrible crime; one that our own lords, our very vassals, have been committing against the peasantry."

"What crime?"

"They're forcing the peasants to grind their own grain at the lord's mill instead of by hand."

"What's wrong with that?" Louis asked, seemingly confused.

"What do you *mean*, what's wrong with it?" Isabelle shook for a moment. "A peasant should be allowed to grind his own grain by hand if he wishes."

"But the peasants are not grinding their grain by hand; the lords have been coming to complain that they are grinding grain at neighboring freeholds, where the grinding price is dirt cheap. They are showing disloyalty to their own lords by going and spending elsewhere."

"Oh, for Heaven's sake! That is the most pathetic thing I've ever heard. A peasant was tortured and killed because of this entire act of territorialism. So what if peasants go to get their grain ground else-where? They're paying peasant fees! Our lords are rich as it is and not lacking in grain and workers! Look at the fields! They don't lie fallow or unprofitable! It is greed talking in these men, Louis—nothing else."

"I disagree, and I have heard enough."

"You don't understand. I just took in a girl from the streets who was working as a prostitute to make ends meet because her father, her sole provider, was killed by his own lord over the matter of having his own millstone! They took this girl's father, dismembered him pub-licly, and then used his very millstone as a gravestone to give fair warning! Can't you see that this is wrong? Do you not go out among your own people and see these things for yourself?"

"I wash the feet of the poor every Easter—you know that. I hear their woes as well as you do. But I am the king of France and I—"

"Maybe you need to stop washing their feet and instead follow those poor feet on the very ground they walk for a year. Maybe you need to pay more attention to reality and less to the platitudes of ruler-ship! Christ sacrificed himself on the Cross, Louis. . . . That goes far-ther than simply washing the feet of the poor. As a *true* ruler of men, you need to do something that is equally uncomfortable."

She saw that this outburst hurt Louis gravely, and she immediately wished she could retract it. But it was too late. Some words when spoken can never be taken back. She left the room, angry at herself for resorting to a personal attack. Now, it would never be solved.

On her way out, she bumped into the new visitor, Jean Adaret Benariel. She brusquely apologized, and in a rushed mumble of words, left him standing in the hallway, looking after her.

That man travels the longest journey that undertakes it in search of a sincere friend.

Ali ibn Abi Talib, Sentences (seventh century)

13

25, décembre, l'an de notre Seigneur 1239

Pierre Mauclerc watched the festivities of the Christmas feast from a dark corner of the room. He was surprised he'd even been invited, considering Robert of Artois was here. He reflexively put his hand to his neck. The scar, inflicted two years before by the mad Saracen, was a twisted mass of tissue under his probing fingertips. But the scar was deeper than just skin.

He watched Robert kissing a young woman's neck while discreetly fondling her breast with one free hand. She was pretty, blonde haired and blue eyed. Nothing like Isabelle's golden hair and sapphire gaze, though. Still, he could see Robert's interest in her. He wondered if Robert had ever had the same kind of devotion to his sister that Pierre had for Isabelle.

Where was she tonight, anyway? She hadn't made her appearance yet. She wanted to tantalize the men, probably. Oh, yes, he'd heard about her joining the Church, but many women were given to the Church to provide husbands with absolutely pure and unadulterated brides on their honeymoons. He also knew that she'd given up on King Conrad of Germany. He knew why, too.

Isabelle was waiting for him.

He imagined leaving the feast and climbing the dark tower stairs by himself to the Ladies' Quarters. Finding Isabelle's room unlocked, letting himself in. Taking her in his arms and smelling the sweet smell of her gold hair. His hands would make their way down her sides to her hips, then to her thighs. She'd sigh with delight, even though she was pure as snow—she'd have been dreaming about this. Dreaming about him, no doubt.

But he was a patient man. Even though he was fifteen years her senior, he would wait. She'd come to him when she was ready. In the meantime, he had learned the value of patience. He could not afford to err as he had a few years ago. He had to keep his foothold or lose her forever.

Pierre stayed in his dark corner, and he waited with his eyes on the door, ready to approach Isabelle tonight and ask her once for a dance. Just one dance, with her in his arms. It would be enough to satiate him until the next feast.

Jean Adaret Benariel stood by the far wall of the Great Room, looking at the Christmas feast around him with awe. He had kept a low profile during the last few weeks, still lurking at the fringes of the lives of others. Tonight however it was clear that he was just a normal man, at a normal Christmas feast, enjoying normal activities.

It exhilarated him. He was almost edgy. They smiled at him—at *him*, not at someone nearby! People talked to him tonight. Over the course of the evening, Robert introduced him to many friends and courtiers. Tonight, he was no longer looking in on the world; he was a part of it.

It was intoxicating. Somewhat disturbing. But absolutely breathtaking. After a few hours, he started to feel fatigued. He wasn't ready to leave quite yet, but he needed some space. Somewhere cool to breathe open air and settle his emotions.

When Robert had started dancing with a blonde woman from a

neighboring fief, Jean saw that he would have some time to catch his breath while Robert was distracted by the beauty. Jean wondered what it would feel like to dance with a woman.

No, he reminded himself. *It will never be possible.* Then he slowly melted into the shadows of the far wall and made his way quietly to the door for some air.

At the door, a woman entered whom he immediately recognized. She didn't see him at first, but he saw her plainly. She was dressed in black. A horrible color for her face and golden, shimmering hair. She looked nervous, angry, somehow pinched. It was a look that didn't suit her delicate face and pointed chin. He found himself staring at her and wondering.

Because he remembered her. And remembering her made him smile.

She was looking around the room, uncomfortably, when she spotted him. Their eyes met across the darkness and through the festive merrymakers dancing and weaving between them. She saw *him*.

Does she recognize me?

He waited to see.

No, he didn't think so. She was abruptly accosted by a few women asking to be introduced to her brother Robert. Isabelle immediately tensed up and tried to explain that she did not do such introductions, but they were welcome to go up to Robert themselves and he would be most kind to them. He could see her mouth tense with pained courtesy as she attempted to get the hangers-on off her arms. He could relate to that expression, suddenly.

Jean had nearly forgotten about this one, but wondered if he would ever have the chance to meet her, now that he was a part of her world.

He ducked out the door for the quiet hallway outside, where the *décembre* wind coming in from the narrow, open windows would cool his restless thoughts.

✦　✦　✦

Isabelle took note of the stranger leaving the party through the oak doors. She hadn't missed his exit. It was his discomfort that first caught her attention. He looked as uncomfortable as she felt. But had she recognized him from somewhere?

Oh, yes, he was the man she'd bumped into in the hallway after shouting at Louis. She still felt horrible about that day, and that argument. She had behaved abominably, and there was no way to make up for it. Well, there was no way with Louis. But perhaps she should try again with this stranger.

He tugged at her conscience. In a fit of shame, she wondered if *she* was the main reason for his discomfort as he slipped out the door into the hallway beyond.

Nonsense, she said sternly to herself. *He probably just doesn't know anyone here. And I should take the opportunity to rectify my poor first impression.*

She disengaged herself from the two chattering courtiers who had latched onto her with needy eyes and hungry fingers, and once free of them, Isabelle slid out the large oak doors to the quiet hallway. She looked around and then noticed the stranger standing in the shadows by the window. His pose pulled at something within. She didn't understand what, though. Was it his height?

He probably stood a head taller than Robert, who was the tallest of her family and of all the men at court. But there was a presence about him that made him smaller, a brooding nature about the eyes that made him seem somehow approachable.

The quiet stone hallway was lit with small sconces. The window before him, like all the windows in all the *palais* halls, had no glass, and it was a snow-laced evening. The man was dressed in a brown silk surcoat that was so dark, it could have been mistaken for black, but the candlelight caught it and made it gleam a dark amber. His eyes were fixed on a point in the distance, someplace she could never see; perhaps a foreign land, a foreign love.

She wasn't certain how to begin a conversation with him. Perhaps he didn't speak her language, which would explain his discomfort. She stood outside the doorway for many moments, deciding what to do.

His eyes, still lost in a gaze out the window, didn't waver in their stare as he spoke the first words. "Good evening, Princess Isabelle. Retiring so soon?"

All the questions subsided as she formed an answer. "I am, sir."

He looked at her in earnest then, giving her face a full appraisal. "Are you ill?"

"No, sir. Nothing such as that."

"I see." He leaned against the window, his dark coat and breeches contrasting with the snow fields behind him. He regarded Isabelle with a relaxed manner. His mood had changed, in the space of one motion, and he was a different season than he had been mere seconds ago. All the fatigue, worry, and displacement in his gaze now gone. "Do you always come to your family's feasts late and leave early?"

She smiled. "Do you wish to find someone with whom you can relate?"

"I was unaware I was under your observance."

"Or I yours."

"I tend to be an observer more than a participant," he confessed. "You were among many subjects of interest at tonight's gathering."

Isabelle was not sure how to take that statement. On the one hand it could have been a compliment of courtly nature, but perhaps it was also an indication that he was regarding many different women and a purveyor, in which case she liked it not.

There was an awkward silence for a moment as Jean realized the reason for her reticence to speak further. His expression changed, his eyes grew soft, and he quickly added, "Among the others were your four brothers: Robert, Charles, Alphonse, and the king. I was seated at your brother Robert's table, as his guest."

Isabelle's mouth popped open as she realized what Jean had meant. He stepped over to her and offered his hand. She noticed that it was gloved.

"Excuse my manners," he said. "I am an awkward guest at anyone's establishment. Let alone a king's." As she took his gloved hand, he bowed slightly before her. "My name is Jean Adaret Benariel."

Isabelle's fingers felt the warmth of his palm beneath his leather glove, and something within her tingled with excitement. It was as if she were flustered or unnaturally excited by his touch, which was odd because she had never felt that way with the myriad other hands she'd held before. Even in the early days of her womanhood when there were a few lads she had admired briefly.

It was not that kind of feeling, though. Holding his hand, she felt as she did on horseback on a brisk, windy autumn day, while chasing a fox through a tangled wood. The thrill of something unexpected.

When she didn't return his greeting, Benariel stood up from his bow. Isabelle's eyes were glistening and unfocused, and her cheeks flushed with a kind of anticipatory fever. He noticed all of this and looked down at her hand sitting in his own. He pulled his hand away, as if he knew the effect his touch had on people.

She pulled back herself. Back from the forest of her imagination and into the room. "Is there something out the window that you found of interest?" she asked, indicating where he had been staring.

"Do you like the forest, Princess?" His eyes sparkled with the question, but she didn't understand it.

"I do," she replied courteously.

"I do, as well. Although there are sometimes wild animals in it that can be dangerous. Fearful hounds and other beasts that prowl on the helpless. It is, nevertheless, an enchanting place."

Isabelle thought his tone seemed odd, and she shifted the conversation. "I don't think I know you or your family, *Seigneur* Benariel."

"No, we . . ." He reflected briefly. "I, actually, live in the Western Wood."

"The Western Wood? Isn't that . . . ?"

"Well, it's not a groomed part of the king's forest, if that's what you mean," he replied.

"Yes, I didn't think anyone had gone in to claim it, because it was
. . . well, actually it's rumored to be . . . uhm . . ."

"Haunted?"

Isabelle laughed a little, embarrassed at what she was describing.
Her manner was as superstitious as a common housewife's. It had no
place in polite conversation about his home. "I'm sorry. . . . Forgive me."

Jean Adaret Benariel was staring with a twinkle in his dark eyes,
a wry smile on his lips. Something passed between them, and Isabelle
could not put her finger on what it was. She tried to discern what was
special about such a mundane conversation, but when she turned her
attention to it, it melted away like a sliver of ice on her hand. Certain
it must still remain, the more she felt for it the less it survived until
it was all but dissipated.

"You're alive!" Robert's voice echoed through the small hallway,
and the moment between them passed. Isabelle and Jean took two
steps back, as if they'd been caught in a lovers' embrace, although
nothing of the sort had happened. Still, it gave Robert a moment of
pause and a grin.

"I see you're making overtures to my lovely sister, Princess
Isabelle. No doubt she's trying to slink away to her devout little cell
and escape all this frivolity. I'm glad you . . . uh . . . caught her. She
needs some pleasure in her life."

Isabelle was shocked. She slapped Robert on the arm.

"Come back inside!" he insisted, laughing at her. "We're about to
play a game!"

Robert pulled Jean and Isabelle with him, one in each arm, back
into the Great Room.

Part Two
BOOK OF
INCARNATION

Friendship either finds or makes equals.

Publilius Syrus, *Moral Sayings* (c. 100 B.C.)

14

23, janvier, l'an de notre Seigneur 1240

I n the weeks that followed the Feast of Robert's Return, there was peace and prosperity in the lands of France. In terms of kindness and laughter, no kingdom outside France could rival the merriment of Blanche's sons, their wives, and her daughter. The kingdom thrived, even with the ill winds starting to blow from the southern baronies.

Word had come late in the fall that the southern baronies of France were uniting with one Raymond of Toulouse, a favorite cousin of Queen Blanche's, with whom she had often had frequent correspondence. The Church and the Catholic Inquisition had been hard on Raymond's family and the inhabitants of his lands in his father's day. Priests persecuted thousands of heretics, looking for "Albigensians" in what they called a crusade. The same Crusade that had killed Blanche's husband, King Louis VIII.

Raymond knew it had been a massacre for profit and had spent his life in silent preparation for revenge. Only now, after Church lands had been ransacked and seized by Raymond's roving army, had word of his intentions spread to Paris and the royal family.

Luckily, Blanche was suspicious of everyone, even favorite cousins. Louis had learned from his mother never to become distracted in the careful protection of his realm. Two years earlier, Louis had acquired the estate of *Castle Angers*, which he then began to renovate. Behind the architectural adornments, he was secretly fortifying the battlements.

Angers would not only stave off Raymond of Toulouse if necessary, it would protect France against Henry. The English king was
growing restless. The marriage of Henry to France's daughter of
Provence meant that his eye would soon turn to the acquisition of
other French lands.

Angers became a dual mission: Suppress Raymond of Toulouse and
keep out Henry, King of England.

This was no small feat, and Louis had personally allocated a huge
sum of his treasury to the Angers renovation. The timing could not
have been better. Soon after word arrived regarding Raymond of
Toulouse and his armies, a message came from Angers that the castle
was finally ready for the king to inspect.

Louis was torn between the two, but knew that the castle at
Angers was the more important. Diplomacy could prove to be a short-
term solution to the problem at hand, but the castle would be a defi-
nite long-term solution if diplomacy failed.

"I will save you some time and write to Raymond, inquiring about
his actions," Blanche said. "For he moves against the royal family when
he moves against the Church. Raymond's a fond cousin, and I hope he
will listen to reason."

On the day Louis prepared to leave for Angers, Jean Adaret Benariel
also said good-bye.

Jean found King Louis in the Great Room, rolling up a great map
of the Angers territory. He bowed low before his liege before speaking.
"I must take my leave of you, good Sire. But I wished to say that you
have been very kind to me, and I shall never forget that. I am thankful
for all that you have bestowed upon me. But I must return to my keep,
or it will wither away to nothingness."

Louis, understanding the upkeep of buildings, reluctantly nodded.

"Very well, *Seigneur* Benariel. But you are welcome here any time." Louis was very firm about this; it was nearly a command.

"I will endeavor to visit."

"Do not endeavor, my friend. Make it a habit. You are a blessed friend; you helped my brother Robert when We could not be there for him."

Jean stared at the floor in a blush.

Louis continued. "You were given to Us in friendship by God, and We wish to keep it that way. If you do not visit often, We will be hurt by your insolence." His tone was stern, but his eyes friendly and warm.

In the midst of politics and courtly pretense, Louis wanted to make sure that Benariel knew he was sincere. In the past few weeks he and Jean had spent many hours speaking of science, nature, philosophy, and religion. Louis was most impressed to find that Jean had a tremendous knowledge of biblical history and knew the verses of the Bible even better than he did. They'd had many lengthy discussions on religious scholars and even some saints that Louis had never heard of. Louis realized today how he was truly fond of Jean Adaret Benariel.

"I count your friendship as one of the most important gifts I have received in my entire life, Majesty," Jean said. Louis saw in the man's eyes that this was a compliment of the highest order. Especially coming from a man who seemed to be, in all but age and beauty, a monastic hermit.

Louis let him go.

When Benariel left the room, Louis called the guards to ask for his sister Isabelle. He had something in mind for her.

⚜　⚜　⚜

Jean was already on his steed and just starting to cross the open meadows past Paris when thundering hooves turned him back to look in the saddle.

Isabelle was charging down the road to catch up with him. She waved at him and when she was near enough, slowed her horse to a trot, then stopped.

"Greetings," he said. Isabelle thought he looked a bit surprised.

"*Monsieur. Seigneur* Benariel. I am to accompany you to your tower. If you will have me." Isabelle was a little breathless and pushed a stray lock of golden hair out of her eyes.

Jean's mouth curled up in tender amusement. "Is this by command of your brother, the king?"

"In part, and partly due to my own curiosity," she said, and nudged her mount into a comfortable walk as Jean came up alongside.

"I regret that during your stay we haven't had time to get acquainted. I have been rather busy at Notre Dame and not present in the household very often."

"I noticed that. Your family is good to spare you from secular authority."

"I don't know if they're good about it at all." Isabelle frowned. "At least, not when we speak of it among ourselves. The world sees one thing; the truth is sometimes quite different."

"Why did you join the Church?"

She'd been asked this question by many now, but never with the kind of gentle curiosity that Benariel showed.

"I want to do good things, make a difference somehow. That sounds very trite, doesn't it?"

"Trite to your ears, perhaps. Refreshing to mine."

"Well, I'm still waiting to actually do something benevolent."

"When I first came here, you were arguing with your brother, His Majesty."

"Yes, I was sorry to put such a bad foot forward. We were having a disagreement about the grain distribution among the peasants. I'm afraid I got too personal at the end and lost the argument to my own temper. I think nothing will be done about it now."

Jean rode on silently for a bit. "What of this girl from the street, the prostitute?"

"Claire."

"What of her?"

"She is my personal seamstress now. Really doing much better since I took her in."

"Then I think you've already done something good in the short time you've been a member of the clergy."

She chuckled. "Perhaps. But given the overwhelming difficulty of combating every social problem in existence one at a time, if I keep going at this pace, I will have to take one prostitute of Paris a day and put her to work on a different task."

"Then perhaps that is what you should do."

"That isn't very practical."

"You're an intelligent woman. Given the right amount of time on this train of thought, I'm certain you'll come up with a suitable alternative."

After that, they were silent. Isabelle found herself unable to come up with a refutation and had to acknowledge the sensibility of his words.

As they approached the Western Wood, Jean reined his horse to a stop. They shifted quietly in their saddles as they regarded the dark shadows of the forest.

"You really . . . live here?"

"Yes."

"It's so dreary."

He chuckled. "It's safe. I suppose it's a little dark, but I never minded it."

"What do you mean 'safe'?" she asked, but Jean was already moving forward.

"Come and see!"

Jean's mount entered the wood and was swallowed by the darkness. Isabelle hesitated, then followed behind.

The Western Wood was not just trees and shrubs. Large, thick vines and brambles prevented easy entrance. It had never been tamed, despite the attempts of Louis' predecessors. People stayed away from the wood. It was said to be a haunted place.

Jean and his horse slipped through a narrow crack in the brambles and thorny vines just wide enough for a horse to make it through with only soft touches from the protruding thorns. As Isabelle passed through the narrow opening, the same thorns now tugged viciously at her skirts. Then abruptly, to her surprise, they pricked free and she was on the other side of the barrier, in the deep and foreboding forest.

She looked around. The trees here grew at least twice as tall as in the tame forest just a few acres to the east. Long and covered in moss, the branches stretched far up into a canopy of radiant green that glowed like a natural stained-glass window. Every now and then a branch would give way and a shaft of sunlight would shine down, spreading against a tree trunk or dancing across the floor of the forest before being obscured by a passing cloud.

She looked back at Jean, who was staring at her. Always very quiet, he never gave much away on the surface, but his stare made her feel very much the object of interest. Despite her years on display at court, it was a place she was not used to occupying. There was an intensity in his eyes that was hard to meet, something deep in the darkness of his brown gaze that she didn't want to see.

Where can we be going? she wondered. All around them were only brambles, thorns, needles, ferns, and interlocking berry plants and bushes. They grew like wild tantrums, pitching fits on tree trunks and fallen logs.

Then she looked again, as if her vision had just cleared. She now saw a path before them: a plain dirt trail, even and smooth, that was three horses wide in width. Isabelle moved her horse onto the path. It was perfectly travel-worn and easy on the hooves of her mount.

"I don't understand." She frowned.

Jean looked as if waiting for her to explain.

"Everyone knows that this wood is impenetrable. If you can find a way into it, you'll be pricked alive trying to reach the heart of the forest. Wild beasts aside, the brambles and thorns alone would tear man or beast apart."

Perhaps he smiled; it was hard to tell. "Everyone knows this, hmm?"

"Well, many men have ventured here and found it impenetrable. It's been like that for centuries. My own ancestors wouldn't even set foot in here."

"How very brave of you then." He smiled.

"I—" Isabelle stopped short. That wasn't what she'd meant. "No, what I mean is . . ."

He was just watching her, his eyes widening slightly as she fumbled over words, gave up, and then asked, "Why is this road here?"

Benariel looked at the road and thought about it. "For travel, I suppose."

She shook her head and tried to clear her mind by closing her eyes. "You don't understand. There *is* no road in the Western Wood!"

"Are you so certain of everything, Princess?" He held out his gloved hand, gesturing for her to ride before him on the road.

She looked at him, vaguely and unaccountably annoyed, then nudged her white mare forward.

After riding for several more minutes in silence, Jean pulled his mount up beside hers.

"Here is where your brother fell," he said.

"He didn't mention a road."

"Given his condition, it isn't likely he would've remembered one."

Isabelle decided it was useless to argue. She looked at the spot where Jean Adaret Benariel had pointed. There was a large black tree trunk, jagged and torn, perhaps struck by lightning at one point. The ground around it was disturbed by spiky protrusions, as if large thorns adorned the roots of the tree. Around one spike she noticed a tall plant.

It resembled celery somewhat. A stout, round and hollow stem, purplish in color, divided into many branches that were covered in tiny white and greenish flowers in a globe shape. Beneath were pinnate leaves with coarsely toothed leaflets—three-lobed.

The giant plant grew five feet high before them, flowering out like a natural crown around the spike. Although it was completely out of place in the surroundings, Isabelle recognized it immediately from her studies.

"Water Hemlock." She looked at it with frightened awe.

"Not hemlock." Jean slid down from his mount and walked over to the plant. "This is where your brother fell, and where I came to him. It's called angelica. Hemlock is poisonous. But angelica is benevolent. We use it to make sovereign remedies. It grows by the sea, in swamps, by streams, in moist meadows, and by mountain brooks."

"Odd that any water-based plants would grow here at all," she said.

"Yes, rather," he agreed. "Do you know anything about angelica?"

Isabelle shook her head.

"Angelica is a storied herb, in more ways than one. Many tales surround it, describing its angelic nature, its healing powers, and its wonderful taste, as well as its potential hazards. The plant is said to bloom every year on the eighth of *mai*, the feast day of St. Michael the Archangel. They call it *Angelica archangelica* in Latin. So that is how it derived its name."

Isabelle nodded her head and admired the tall, striking plant. "Is this the herb you used to heal Robert? He told me you used an herb—"

"No, I didn't use this."

"Oh, I see."

She looked down at the spot where her brother had fallen. "I can't help but think that this is uncommon: a beautiful, delicate plant like this growing in such a desolate place."

"I suppose it is." She looked at him and thought she noted an odd sadness in his voice.

How like the plant he is, she thought. But Jean said nothing else, only mounted his horse.

His words were always simple and direct, like a child's faith, yet so much more lay beneath the surface. So much more he would not tell her.

"How did you come upon my brother? What would make you go out into such a storm?"

"I hunt here and forage for other food, much like your serving women go to market once a day. After trial and error, one learns a little bit about what can and cannot be eaten.

"I was caught out in the sudden squall just like your brother, and was making my way back from foraging when I heard a horse's frantic neighing. I followed the sound of it, and found him here.

"Your brother was wounded badly, impaled by his own pike, barely alive."

Isabelle was stunned. "He said it was just a scratch."

"He lied about it to protect me."

"But the wound was gone completely when he woke the next day! He said that you . . . healed him in such a manner as he had never seen."

Benariel looked away and did not reply.

"Why did you tell me the truth?" she asked.

"I don't know. I felt . . . as if I could trust you with it."

"Like you could trust Robert?" she asked.

"Yes, and no. There's more to you."

Isabelle blushed and looked down. "Louis was not pleasant that day. I am told he was rather rough with you."

"True."

"I'm sorry for that."

"It was his brother," Jean said quietly. "He loves Robert—that much is plain. And love can make us all do . . . unexpected things."

With that, he nudged his horse forward, and Isabelle followed him into the heart of the Western Wood.

In a philosophical dispute, he gains most who is defeated, since he learns most.

Epicurus, *Vatican Sayings* (third century B.C.)

15

At the Tower of Benariel, they stopped and put the horses outside at the standing post. Isabelle stared at the enormous structure. The tower stretched up into the trees and beyond, its peak lost in the mists above them. It had been built with simple gray stone, and it was very, *very* old, though still in good repair. She noticed that the tower had been expanded to include a side hall, which was newer and made with fresh stone.

"How old is this?" she asked Jean.

He looked up at it. "This tower has been in my family for longer than I can remember. It is nearly sacred in its antiquity."

"A thousand years?"

"Perhaps even more than that." Jean began walking to the large oak doors of the tower. "Come, I will show you the inside."

Isabelle started to follow, then glanced back, noticing something that she had not taken in before. In the center of the clearing, before the tower, was a rosebush: the most magnificent she had ever seen.

"Oh!" she exclaimed. "How did I miss this? It's beautiful."

He nodded. "It is a family heirloom. Did you know that wild roses have been bred for a thousand years, to create the variations we have now?"

"My brothers refer to me as the Crown Rose, a breed of rose in Paris. It is a bright, beautiful yellow, after my hair, and was brought to me when I was very young." She paused, remembering Conrad and

Henry as boys. And she remembered Louis saying nothing would be different. "The rose was named in honor of me."

His gloved hands lovingly grazed the rose petals, straying to one wine-colored bud in particular. "These roses are centuries old. They have grown here for at least a thousand years. They are very special to my family. Wild roses."

"The red is so truly deep. Almost a blood red . . ." She had seen it before, somewhere . . .

"Yes," he said. "It is something of a symbol for us."

Isabelle touched one petal of the rose, and it was warm, even in the cool air. "They're lovely." She looked across the splash of roses to his face, framed in red and thorns. "Thank you for sharing this with me."

"No, I must thank you, actually, for seeing what I sometimes take for granted, and forget to see." He motioned her toward the door to the tower.

"Has your family name always been Benariel?" she asked.

"Yes."

"Who were your parents?"

"They died a long time ago."

"When you were young?"

"When I was younger," he answered.

She stepped inside the door as he held it open for her. Inside, it was dark and unlit. Strangely, it smelled familiar to her.

"How lonely it must be here," she thought aloud.

He entered the tower behind her, stepping close enough to squeeze by between her frame and the door, and he let his gloved hand rest on her shoulder as he reached for something in the darkened room.

She stiffened at the contact. She wasn't used to the hand of a stranger. Her brothers were the only men who had ever really touched her so casually.

He seemed to notice her stiffening, glanced her way, and then looked back at what he was reaching for. But he didn't move his hand from her shoulder. His closeness aroused a strange compulsion. She felt something stirring quietly inside, like a little moth caught around a hot flame. She tried to break the sensation by speaking. "Why would you never leave this place?"

"I was advised against it," he replied.

He held a torch in his hand now. The flame danced over his features and hers. They couldn't look more different. In a way, he looked like Blanche, dark and brooding, only he was not Spanish like her mother was. His features were different, as if his family came from the East.

"Your family wanted you to stay here, alone?" she asked. "How cruel."

"It really isn't lonely. There's much in the forest and in the Tower of Benariel to keep me company."

He walked to a wall covered with plain iron sconces and lit them. The flames danced and guttered before blazing steadily. Each flame lit the room a little more and revealed why the tower had smelled so familiar to her. There was nothing against the walls except row after row, shelf after shelf, of her favorite, most prized possessions in the whole kingdom: books. Books everywhere. Books to the ceiling, books going up the sides of the spiral staircase that wound its way up the inner tower like a snake.

She could only gasp at the sight of so many books.

"These . . . books . . . ," she began in awe. "They're yours?"

"Yes," he replied.

"How did you acquire so *many*?"

"I know a few discreet individuals." He put the torch down and extinguished it. "Like yourself, I have a passion for reading."

"How did you know?"

"Your brother said so. Robert was fascinated by my book collection. We spent a good deal of time talking. He assumes, incorrectly, that he owes me some debt for his life."

She smiled. "That's my brother. Robert is reckless and daring, and quick to pledge himself."

"I see that in him."

Isabelle instinctively went to the bookshelf and reached for one, then pulled her hands back hastily and looked over at Jean. He was staring out the still-open doors of the tower. "May I?" she asked.

Her words stirred him from his reverie. "Yes, of course."

She picked up one of the books. *Poetics*.

She chose another, putting the first away. *Saint Augustine*.

Her fingers ran over the other books on the shelf before choosing one farther down the row. Jean walked over to her and looked down as she ran her hands over the thick canvas tomes. They were cool and rugged against her pale fingers.

"*On the Nature of Courtly Love?*" She read the title aloud, then blushed.

There was a great stillness in the air, but neither wanted to disturb or acknowledge it. Isabelle silently slid the book into the dark space where it had been resting. "Have you read them all?"

"Yes," he replied. "Even that one."

Isabelle looked down at her hands. "Oh."

Another long and uncomfortable pause. Then he asked, "Would you like to see more of the tower?"

"Yes, please." She wasn't sure what was upstairs, but it had to be better than this awkward silence. She realized that neither of them were natural conversationalists. That was more Robert's specialty, or Louis'.

She followed Jean Adaret Benariel up the long, winding staircase to the second floor, where several small rooms containing narrow beds reminded her of the rectory at Notre Dame. They were rather plain, without portraits or tapestries, but he didn't seem to need elaborate decor. In addition to the one small bed with a coverlet, each room contained a modest writing desk.

"Guest rooms?" she asked.

"For my multitudes of guests, yes," he said, and smiled. She believed it was the first time he'd made an attempt to be charming.

"Come," he said, and touched her once, gently, on her back. His touch made her tingle. Like his hand on her shoulder, there was a precision about his touch. It was deft. She felt a combination of being safe, protected, and understood.

They made their way out of the guest rooms and up the stairs. There was something powerful in his presence. His touch was indicative of a precision of living. A quality of mercy and refinement and yet he was utterly alone, living under the most Spartan conditions. She had never experienced such a combination of opposites before. She realized that whoever Jean Adaret Benariel was, he was certainly a master.

But a master of what?

The third floor was taken up almost entirely by a large suite, with a reasonably modest bed and more bookshelves all around. Some tapestries of passages from the Bible hung upon the walls. Nothing unusual.

A window beside the bed looked out over the trees to the plains beyond. In the distance, she could just see the long meadows at the edge of the forest. She looked out the window and thought about the reality that they were deep in the heart of the Western Wood. A place no one dared to venture, which had kept Jean Adaret Benariel and his family hidden for centuries. Now, he had no family, no contact with others of his kind.

She turned back to him. "Now that you are Louis' friend at court, you can have access to much more than this."

"I seek nothing more," he said, and didn't look at her. "I am happy here."

"Happier than you were with us?" She sounded hurt. Benariel said nothing in reply. "There's so much more you could see. Festivals, Mass, feasts, harvest and planting, Michaelmas—"

"Companionship?" he finished for her.

There was a stillness. Isabelle couldn't move. Now that he was inside, Jean took his gloves off, and she noticed a ring on his finger. It was in silver with a red inlay, and its design reminded her of the Templar cross.

"I have no need of companions, dear Princess. I have been alone for a very long time. After a while, it becomes something one prefers, something one is good at."

"You need not speak of being alone to me as if it were a foreign concept. I took the oath of the Church to ensure that my way of life was not interrupted. The priests, the holy Sisters, they are my friends, and in time they will become my family. But you have no friends, no *family*, nothing other than books and writing. There are finer things my brother is willing to help provide. I would take it as a very great favor if you would not dismiss his gift."

"What is his gift, exactly?" Jean asked.

"The gift of an extended family. Robert has brought you to our home, under our roof, and you are treated with the same respect that we give to one another. If you stay here, after what they've done, they will be hurt. I daresay insulted."

He looked at her again with that look in his eyes that she didn't want to translate. "And you?"

"Well, of course I'd be disappointed."

"Ah."

There was a moment where she almost said more, but stopped herself. When the moment had passed, he opened one of the drawers beside his bed and removed an old scroll. She saw that it was made of papyrus.

"Tell your brothers that I'm flattered by their demands. Tell them that I wish I could stay, but I can't. Please let them know I am touched that they'd send their only sister as an emissary to my heart."

She stared at Jean as he sat on the bed, wondering why he'd just said that. It had come out so cool and measured, as if he couldn't really care, and yet she knew better somehow. And there was the fact that she couldn't return to Louis without some assurance that Jean would be back. Yet he plainly had no intention of returning with her. Not only that, it seemed that he had so much as dismissed her. She was not accustomed to being dismissed and decided to stand her ground.

"I can't just go back," she said. "Not without an escort."

He looked up from his vellum. "Then I suppose you will have to stay here as my guest until you feel secure enough to travel the wood alone."

Isabelle felt her cheeks flush with indignation. She was used to having an escort whenever she wanted, used to having things at her command. And this lord was making it difficult for no discernible reason other than pure spite. She'd come on behalf of her brother, the king! Wasn't that enough?

"But Louis requires—"

"I have heard you out, but I have some things to attend to. You should prepare for dinner if you're staying."

Her mind was reeling. Why was he behaving like this? It was true that she'd only known him a little while, but his manner seemed completely at odds with what she had come to expect from him in the few short hours they'd been in each other's company. If he was going to be like this, then she wasn't sure she wanted to stay.

A little voice in her mind spoke up. *Staying will give you a chance to soften his resolve. He will bend if you apply enough pressure. Louis wouldn't have put you to this task if he thought you weren't capable. He's counting on you.*

Isabelle often wondered about that voice, where it stemmed from, who it really was; for it was too intelligent and wise to be the voice of her own soul. But perhaps she didn't give herself enough credit. She had seen more of life than the average princess.

She looked at Jean, who was still reading from his papyrus. His downcast gaze betrayed a certain pain, like he was hiding some inner turmoil.

"In any event, I certainly can't make the journey home tonight. It's too late. Who will show me to my room?"

He set the scroll down on his knee, gently. "I have no servants here. But you will find one of the guest rooms on the second floor to be quite accommodating. The last room at the end of the hall has been set for you."

Irked, Isabelle nodded and left the room.

I need to calm myself and consider what is happening, she told herself.

It's so frustrating! Part of her, the princess and child, was not finished throwing a temper tantrum.

Yes, it is frustrating, but necessary. He's not going to be swayed after a lifetime of privacy and comfort. Remember that this is his home and you are a surprise guest. You've behaved similarly on visits from your own family into your little attic room when they were unwelcome.

He obviously has no heed of royal decree. The princess inside snorted.

But that wasn't exactly fair, either. Louis didn't order his friends about, and neither should she, for that was misusing her authority.

I have acted poorly on behalf of my brother. She came to the room at the end of the hall, and the door was open. She looked inside.

The last room has been set for you.

She'd assumed he was speaking broadly, that the room was always ready for guests. She had anticipated that having to make the room comfortable would fall to her. But to her astonishment, torches were lit; a fire danced in the fireplace; and a wardrobe, crammed and popping full from inside, stood open with dresses, dressing gowns, robes, and jackets.

There was an open trunk at the foot of a great, carved four-poster bed containing hand-knit blankets, throws, pillows, and other bedding. The bed itself was made up with silk pillows and a warm cotton bedspread of wine-soaked russet. A little dressing table in the corner held a silver brush and comb, each with ivory handles. It was beautiful in here. Not at all like the other rooms on the floor. The room felt warm and inviting.

The window by the bed was frosted glass and had a latch to open individually paned windows. There was a fur rug on the floor before the bed, and pale tapestries hung on all the walls. Candles were lit in their holders on tables and at bedside.

Isabelle could not speak. She walked to the wardrobe and stroked the fabric of the dresses inside. All pale garments, or dazzling whites. No dark garments of the kind she was supposed to wear as a member of the cloth. But it wasn't as if she could or wanted to complain. These had been put here on her behalf.

By whom? she thought suddenly. *Benariel said there are no servants here to look after my needs.*

Her nose caught the scent of lily.

Lilies? Here?

She walked over to the opposite side of the bed and found a huge, brass, claw-footed tub filled with steaming hot water. It was a little milky, as if . . .

Isabelle dipped her hand into the hot water and put her fingers up to her nose.

Yes, lily. He's put lily in the water for a scented bath.

Isabelle realized how chapped and sore her skin was from the ride here. It was an all-day trip, and her riding dress was creased and dirty from the journey. Her body yearned for a long, hot soak.

Isabelle closed the door, undressed, and sat in the heavenly bath with her eyes lightly closed, allowing the pressing questions of the day to float before her and gently bob in consideration.

Something did not make sense in the way that Benariel had addressed her upstairs. She remembered Louis telling her how Benariel had expressed such pleasure at a royal friendship. Why would he then shun it? Louis was not the sort of man to mistake courtly gestures. He had been certain that Benariel meant what he said.

She remembered the painful look his gaze had held while he read over the old scroll. *What had he said, again?*

Tell your brothers . . . I wish I could stay, but I can't.

Why can't he? she wondered. *What force makes him stay here in seclusion against even his own wishes?*

There was something here—something she could not yet see but that she knew she must wait to find out. Time would loosen up the question and reveal the answer, just as the water was loosening her sore muscles from today's journey. She let the problem float away on the gentle lapping of lily-scented water.

For the time being.

Jean pored over the papyrus scroll that held the words he'd read so many times in his long life. Occasionally, his attention would move to the ring he wore on his finger; then he would pore over the words on the scroll again, trying to find some semblance of reason in the mystic words.

They were printed in fine, ancient ink—words that held the meaning of the world if one could only discern them ahead of their circumstances. Yet it was only in the heat of new circumstances that he realized what the words meant at all. Jean kept searching for any sign, any mention of a golden-haired woman, a princess, a prince fallen in hunting, a royal family or palace. . . .

He just needed one hint. One guiding phrase. But after an hour, he replaced the scroll carefully in the bedside drawer, knowing that the only words his father had written long ago told him nothing of how to proceed now that life had taken a strange turn of events.

Jean sighed in thought as he twisted the ring on his finger.

Few have greater riches than the joy
That comes to us in visions,
In dreams which nobody can take away.
Euripides, *Iphigenia in Tauris* (c. 412 B.C.)

16

hey spent four nights at the tower—passing whole days in conversation, speculation, and debates on theology, cosmology, and natural science—only gradually realizing that time was slipping by without mark. To her surprise, Isabelle found she didn't mind. She was enjoying herself too much with Jean Adaret Benariel. She had come here for Louis, but now her own interests had taken over.

Here she had found good conversation, good food, and, above all, good company. Even in the silences between conversation, Benariel was wonderful company, like no one she had ever had the privilege to know before. Not even her brothers were this well versed or surprisingly well educated. And yet Benariel did not flaunt his education. He was so quiet, so modest and unassuming, that only when she let herself get carried away with a thread of discussion would he mention something utterly obscure but blindingly apropos that would completely astonish her.

On the morning of the fifth day, she came down from her room and decided to turn left instead of right at the landing, to a part of the tower she had not yet visited. As she came into the long room, Isabelle gasped. The room was adorned with great tapestries, thin linens, and other fragments of Eastern origins. Ancient scrolls, carefully preserved, even covered the tables, chairs, and tiny niches.

I have found the library at Alexandria, she thought distantly as she heard Jean enter behind her.

"What *is* this?" she asked.

"The conservatory," he said simply. The glass roof was formed of colored tiles molded together with iron. In the center of the room, a small dogwood tree grew, twisting and gnarled as if it had been trained by an expert gardener's hands.

She walked over to one of the tapestries. "Is this Arabic?"

"Some are Arabic, some Hebrew, some Latin. They are very old family heirlooms."

Her voice was hushed in appreciation. "These are absolutely beautiful. How did your family acquire them?"

"I don't know, exactly. They have always been here. For as long as I can remember."

"Do you know what they say?"

"Yes. I am fluent in Hebrew and Arabic."

"This script is *ancient*." She wanted to run her hands over the lettering but stopped herself, as her barest touch would mar the hard work of the craftsmen. The writing on the scrolls, like the tapestries, contained passages from the Bible. Isabelle recognized several passages; however, she saw some she'd never read before.

"I was told they are very old," Jean said. "Come, there is more to see." He held his hand out before him, and Isabelle reluctantly followed him into the hallway.

"You have such a passion for the written word," he said.

"I have always appreciated writing. My brothers don't have the ability to sit through any work of real length. But I've devoured all the books written for the Crown and have read my way through most of the *Petit Pont* library."

"Ah, your brother was telling me about the *université*. He says you can't be kept away from the place."

"Well, I do what I want most of the time. It's futile to try and stop me."

Jean's eyebrow went up. "Is that a warning, Princess?"

"I won't be turned out until you return with me."

"I don't mean to disappoint your brothers, but . . . this is my home and I require seclusion and privacy."

He was hesitating. Now that she had come to know his manner-isms well, she was certain he was conflicted about staying here. Though he was trying to hide it.

"I'm not speaking for my brother, today. I think you value my request very little, if you won't heed it. Do you find me unworthy?"

"I don't think you unworthy. But I need more time to deliberate. There is much that hinges on my decision."

❖ ❖ ❖

Later, in her room, Isabelle considered recent nights. A few days ear-lier, Jean had been unwilling to even open discussion on his return. Today, she'd seen him soften slightly in his resolution. She decided there was something worthwhile in being so forward. But how long was she to stay here like this?

The tower was foreboding when she was alone. It was nothing she could even put a finger to, but somehow the walls seemed colder than the outer castle walls. Probably from a lack of direct sunlight in the forest. And silence permeated the entire estate. No servants bustling by in the morning hours, or lighting fires in the evening, even though the fireplace in her room was lit every morning when she woke and every evening when she went to bed.

Things here did not seem to abide by natural law, but they did it so discreetly that until Isabelle focused her entire attention, she failed to notice them. Her window looked down at the rose garden in the center of the courtyard. The roses were bobbing gently in the wind.

Isabelle realized from her bird's-eye perspective that the little topiary garden near the roses was planted in the form of a cross, with little side rivets at the tops and bottoms, and it reminded her of . . . something she'd seen recently.

His ring, she thought. His ring was also in the shape of a cross, only it had little *fleurs-di-lis* on either side of the crossed axes to accent it. She leaned her forehead against the cool glass and felt shivers down her spine.

Everything seems so strange here, she thought. *As if there is some kind of secret right under my feet. Something I'm not supposed to know, or am supposed to overlook. What did he mean when he said "There is much that hinges on my decision"?*

There was always something just under the surface of conversation; parts of rooms she had been shown that were left unmentioned. And what of those tapestries in the conservatory? She had appreciated their beauty more than anything else he'd shown her, and yet she was only allowed to spend a short amount of time there.

Why? She looked back. The scroll room was on this level and only a few hallways down. She hesitated only a moment, then threw on her dressing robe and slippers and shuffled out the door. It wouldn't be sneaking if she was looking at things hanging in plain view. She would hardly be rummaging through drawers or doing anything the least unseemly.

She crept down the hallway toward the conservatory. It was dark now in the room; only a pale shaft of moonlight was shining down through the glass ceiling. Isabelle walked silently around the circular room and took in each tapestry. Many held biblical verses with some extraneous verses she had never seen.

But there was one tapestry that was particularly intriguing: a painting of a bare woman, hands outstretched, grasping a clay jar above her head. Her face was tilted back so that only her chin, dainty and pointed, could be seen well, her long dark hair falling down covered the rest of her body. Behind her was painted a golden aura, made of delicate, gold illumination over the tapestry's cloth. Her feet were relaxed, and it looked as if she were floating up with her clay vessel, into the night sky.

Isabelle stared at her for a long time and felt drawn to the picture. She realized this was the first time she had ever seen a naked woman at the receiving end of heavenly light. She tilted her head and read the Hebrew inscription near the lower half.

I AM the Beloved. What is hidden from you I will proclaim to you. Seven powers of wrath, in seven forms: the first darkness, then desire, the third ignorance, the fourth the excitement of death; the fifth is the kingdom of the flesh, the sixth is the foolish wisdom of flesh, and the seventh is wrathful wisdom.

They asked the soul, "Whence do you come, slayer of men, or where are you going, conqueror of space?" The soul answered and said, "What binds me has been slain, and what surrounds me has been overcome, and my desire has been ended, and ignorance has died. In a world, I was released from a world, and in a type from a heavenly type, and from the fetter of oblivion which is transient. From this time on will I attain to the rest of time, of the season, of the Aeon, in silence."

Isabelle had no idea what it meant. *I AM the Beloved. . . . Well, there was the Beloved Disciple of Christ.* And the tapestry spoke of ignorance, darkness, and desire; so perhaps the naked woman was meant as a devout warning to avoid the world of the flesh. But it didn't look like a warning. It looked . . . beautiful.

The woman tugged at her imagination. She stared in fascination a while longer, before a yawn came and interrupted her quiet reverie.

I must sleep, she told herself, and quietly shuffled out the door. As she made her way to the guest bedroom again, she realized that of all the works of art she'd seen in Benariel's tower, she had not seen any family portraits. Such portraits were not uncommon in wealthy families, but Benariel had no record of his ancestors.

Later, as she lay in bed, she wondered at this. It would have been nice to know what his mother and father looked like. Or even the other men and women in his lineage. Were they all as thin and dark as Jean? Or did he take after one in particular with his chestnut hair and beautiful brown eyes? She considered this as she drifted to sleep.

In her dream, she was picking flowers. The hand of a child reached out and plucked a perfect daisy from a bush in front of her. She remembered this day, this place, and she turned, knowing that the dog would be there, just as it was that day when Louis was away from the castle to marry Margaret.

The dog's red eyes were filled with hatred and terrifying anger, and pain. . . .

Isabelle's hair stood up on the nape of her neck, and trembling, she dropped the flowers from her little fist. Her body would not move. She was frozen with fear. Even her eyes could not tear themselves away from this black, sleek hound and its slavering, bloodstained jowls. Thick ropes of foaming drool oozed out of its lips as it glowered at . . .

No, not at me. That's right. It stared past her, just like before, at . . . *at Him.*

Isabelle turned and saw the man behind her, talking to Neci in the garden. She knew him well from all the dreams before tonight. He really *was* there. Like a guardian angel, with his hand outstretched to the dog in a powerful, graceful gesture of banishment.

His lips moved, and the words struck Isabelle's ears with the sound of thunder. "Go!" *He spoke to the hound behind her, and she turned . . .*

Slowly . . .

Slowly . . . and the dog ran. In her mind she heard the dog scream, his crazed brain terrified by the word "Go!" *She blinked again, and the dog was gone from view. Forever banished from her sight.*

She glanced at the man, forcing herself to focus on his face. It was Jean Adaret Benariel.

Isabelle turned again, and this time the world had sped up. When she turned, her dress skirts whirled about her legs, and suddenly she was much taller, hair much longer, and she was looking at the man behind her.

Benariel said nothing, stared at where the dog had been a few moments before. Isabelle realized she was no longer looking up at him and that she was now full-grown, wearing the same gown from today at dinner, as she reached out. But he had not changed. He was exactly as he was then.

"Impossible!" she said, but the truth of her eyes would not be denied. Benariel looked deeply into her eyes. But he seemed unable to recognize her, as if he were still looking at the child and not the woman.

Isabelle awoke, her body heaving from under the covers as she sat shivering in the cool night air. The fire was low and smoldering in the fireplace. The grand bed with its four-poster rails loomed over her in the silence.

He has been here all along, she thought. *Like the Sisters. That was Him.* She lay back in the stillness of the room, staring at the ceiling. Everything was swirling together in one dream.

"It couldn't have been him," she said aloud, as if giving voice to reasonableness would chase away unreasonable truths.

But I saw him, just like—

"No. It was a beautiful dream, from long ago, when I wanted the world to be perfect. There's no way it could be Jean Adaret Benariel. If it were really him, he wouldn't have aged a bit since then. So it can't be. It *can't* be."

It was a long time before sleep found Isabelle that night. She remembered Neci's fear at being discovered that day. What had Neci been afraid of? That she might be discovered talking to Him and not paying attention to Isabelle when the dog attacked? Such an error would mean the death penalty for a governess. But then Isabelle thought about the day she had followed Neci to the game preserve outside Paris, and the darkness inside the ruin, and the voice that had spoken to her.

Perhaps Neci had not been afraid that she would be discovered talking to a man, but that by her actions the existence of this man would be discovered by others.

What a strange thought, she decided, remembering again the voice in the ruins. The voice that now sounded so much like Jean.

She fell asleep to that voice, with a light smile on her lips.

In his room at the top of the tower, Jean Adaret Benariel found no sleep. Finally, he pulled himself from the bed, threw on his heavy wrap, stepped into warm slippers, and paced gently on the floor. He stopped at the window and looked out over the forest.

He could see every tree beyond, and he knew all of them well. He'd outlived some and seen the arrival of others. A precious few had been around when he'd first come to this forest over one thousand years ago. They still stood today.

It is a heavy thing to watch a forest grow and die around you, he thought. He had been told never to leave the Western Wood to live among mortal men. But while the Western Wood was safe and the only place he truly considered home, it was also mightily depressing to look out over the vast expanse of treetops to the inviting meadows and wonder what lay beyond.

He did not belong with mortal men, but neither did he belong locked in a tower of isolation. Something about the royal family tugged at him. They were the most elite of mankind, and still they made him feel like a normal man. He had only known that feeling a few times in his long life.

And Isabelle was compelling. How she tugged at him, requiring his return to the castle in order to live a normal life. He'd wanted that, longed for that, for centuries! But he could never tell her that. He paced back across the room, reason slowly asserting itself again. Sofia was right. He had to remain at the periphery of the world of men, for his own safety. They'd never understand what he could do. What he had been born to do.

Then why did she seem to understand him? Why did she so willingly accept him? Caught between his solitude and his curiosity, he felt unable to move in either direction. There was compulsion and common sense, and he feared a wise man would know which was called for. He might be old, but he still did not consider himself all that wise. But then, who ever did?

Sofia told me to return to the tower, and I have come home at her request. Why then do I want to go back to Paris with this girl?

Go, a voice replied.

It would be disobeying, he said.

Sofia told you to return to the tower, and you have. She didn't tell you not to come back.

Jean leaned against the windowsill, hand to his chin in consideration. *That's bending the rules a little bit, isn't it?*

It all depends on whose rules. You knew sooner or later the day would come when you'd need to live by your own set.

Jean strolled back to the bed and sat. He shivered with chill and then looked at the fire.

The fire was blazing, intuiting his needs. Jean allowed that it was a nice thing to be needed, even if only a little bit. The royals seemed to need—no, require—his presence. A part of him was flattered.

Am I too easily flattered? he thought.

No, you are a man, like any other. You have the same wants, needs, and desires as other men, came the reply. He knew that it was true.

"And still, I am nothing like other men," he said aloud. It was a truth he knew only too well.

The voice did not reply.

Jean lay back in his bed and stared upward, firelight playing on the shadows as his gaze wandered the ceiling beams.

What use am I to the world if, being a man, I do not experience the world of men? What have I to offer? Nothing. What do I learn? Nothing. Is this what I was born for?

And the voice spoke a final time. *No.*

Over her morning toast, Isabelle thought about her dream and tried not to stare at Jean Adaret Benariel. The morning light had washed away most of the mysteries of the night before, but she found that some questions still remained.

Jean seemed to sense her mood. "Is everything all right?" he asked. "You seem very quiet today."

She picked at her bread, considering her words carefully because she would only be able to use them once. "I had a dream last night."

He was looking at his knife and spoon and trying to appear interested in them. "Oh?"

"I am not certain if I've ever told you about this." She put her glass down very gently, very precisely, on the table before her. "Just stop me if you've heard this before.

"I had something happen to me, as a child. In fact, I wouldn't be alive today if it weren't for . . ." She looked up. He was staring at her. "A dog attacked me, and I was saved by a man. Not just any man. This . . . person . . . *banished* the dog with a word. It was a miracle, I think. All my life I have dreamed of this man, wondering if I'd ever meet him again. You see, he changed everything for me on that day. I've never found his equal."

Jean said nothing.

"There's something about you, *Seigneur* Benariel. I'd like to think that you have as much integrity as he did. You *are*—"

She saw him stiffen and quickly added, "—sir—a lot like him."

He seemed to relax and took a sip of water. While he had the cup to his lips, she delivered the *coup de grâce*. "*That* man would come back to the castle with me."

Their gaze met across the long table.

He slowly put the cup down and swallowed. "Naturally, I would never want to disappoint you. But those would be rather large shoes for any man to fill."

"Perhaps. But you see, last night I dreamed again about the dog in the courtyard, only this time you were standing where the man had been when he saved my life. I think it means something. God does not give us these kinds of dreams without a reason. Sometimes He sends them for the dreamer; sometimes He sends them for the ones who do not dream."

"I guess sometimes He does." Benariel shifted uncomfortably in his seat. "I certainly wouldn't want to do anything that would contradict your vision."

"Good," she said as she rose in her chair, pushing her plate away. "We can reach the castle by nightfall if we leave after lunch."

"Or by dusk if we leave now," Jean said, smiling.

Isabelle smiled a bright and sunny smile back at him and dashed up the stairs of the tower.

She ran to her room, proud of herself for cornering him. She'd done what Louis had asked. The mystery was over, and life could continue. Isabelle gathered what little she had come with, then changed out of her light tan dress and back into the riding habit she had worn when she came to the tower. It was cleaned and pressed. Naturally.

Her hand ran over the beautiful fabric of the dresses in the wardrobe. She fingered them carefully as she regarded their fine fabrics. It had been a wonderful visit, despite the odd moments.

There was a knock at her door, and she looked up to find Benariel standing in the doorway. "Are you ready, Princess?"

"Yes," she replied. "I haven't told you how much I enjoyed my visit. Your hospitality has been so grand. I wanted to thank you for it."

He seemed almost chagrined about it. "I wanted you to be comfortable, to have what you needed. You shouldn't have wanted for anything during your stay."

"I hope I didn't inconvenience too badly your need for privacy."

"On the contrary, it has been pleasant having you around. You never infringed upon my solitude. You could be near all the time, and I wouldn't find it tiresome." He looked away after the admission, as if surprised by his own words.

Isabelle blushed. "Well, thank you. Again."

"Shall we?" he offered. Again she noticed his hands were always covered by the gloves he had worn throughout his stay at the castle, whether indoors or out.

"Why do you wear gloves like that?" she asked quietly.

"They are . . . very sensitive."

Sensitive? she thought. "But no one can see your ring, that way."

"Oh, you noticed it?"

"Yes, I like it. It's a lovely cross."

"It's been in my family for a long time."

"I see." She didn't know what else to say. His family matters seemed forbidden.

Suddenly, Jean removed his glove from his right hand, pulled off the ring, and held it out in his bare hand. It shone between his thumb and index finger.

"Would you like it?"

"Would—" she started. "Why?"

He looked at her. "Because you like it."

"But it's your heirloom."

"Trust me, I have others." He pushed it out to her. "Take it, please."

She hesitated, then gently reached for the silver ring and took it from him. It was still warm from his finger, and she suddenly felt comfortable about having it.

She slid it onto her index finger and found that it fit perfectly. She looked back up as he was putting his glove on again.

"*Merci*," she said.

He nodded.

They descended the last stairs, and he looked around the ground floor of the tower as if silently saying good-bye; then he gestured for her to head out the door. She stepped out the heavy wooden door and into the clearing as he gave the door a firm close.

> Everything that steel achieves in war can be won in politics by eloquence.
>
> Demetrius (fourth to third century B.C.)

17

1, février, l'an de notre Seigneur 1240

Pierre Mauclerc had one hand behind his head as he rested on Elizabetta de la Marche's sheets. He looked down at her golden hair, which spilled over his bare chest and shoulders as she rested against the nook of his arm. They were sweaty.

For a moment, Pierre let himself imagine that he had not taken Hugh de la Marche's wife, but that he had taken Princess Isabelle. It made him sigh with satisfaction. Elizabetta looked up.

"I was just thinking the same thing," she said with a grin. She was nothing like Isabelle, from expressions to personality.

"Of course you were," he replied.

"But there is no need to hurry away. Hugh is gone to England for at least a fortnight. We have plenty of time for this."

Pierre just nodded. He would stay here only because of the necessary alliance between his family and de la Marche. That he could pretend he was lying with Isabelle and not Elizabetta was an added bonus.

"I will want more of you in a few," the baron's wife told him. It made Pierre chuckle.

"Your appetite surprises me, *madame*."

"I always get what I want."

"Does that include war with England?" he asked.

"I do whatever it takes. Hugh and I will never forget how much we lost to King Louis when he was a boy. I want all of my land back."

Pierre knew she meant de la Marche land when she said "my," but he also knew who wore the actual pants in the de la Marche family. Hugh was a jealous man, easily ordered around and held emotional hostage by his wife. Elizabetta was cruel and capricious. Nothing like Isabelle. But she had almost the same kind of hair, and that was enough to make their dalliance bearable.

"You'll join us," she said. Just three words, but they would require that Pierre become a traitor to France's king and fight alongside the English.

How succinct, he thought.

"I can't. The Knights Templar and their associates never partake in these kinds of battles. To do so would mean expulsion from their ranks."

"Then join ours. You'll get more than what the Templars pay you." She was turned over on her elbows now, her bare body sliding over his.

"It is dishonorable—not to Louis, but to my own organization. The Templars do a lot for me."

"And I don't?" She kissed him.

When they parted, he said, "Perhaps I can give you sufficient funds to help."

"And what will you require as compensation, when we win?"

Pierre noticed Elizabetta did not say *if* they won. He chuckled and took hold of her, turning her over and pinning her down against the bed. He buried his face in her neck and lost himself in her golden curls. "I will discuss my compensation later."

But it was Isabelle that he wanted, and he would achieve that dream, even if she came to him as a prisoner of war.

⚜ ⚜ ⚜

Norea, the third Sister in the Order of the Rose, backed away from Elizabetta's closed chamber door with utmost caution. She was a graceful figure, taller than Neci but slimmer than Sofia. Her face was aquiline, and her dark cheeks soft as a peach. Today, she was not dressed in the robes that her sisters wore. She was dressed in a plain servant's uniform.

Norea stepped across the hall and slid into another room, where she closed the door, frowning at what she had heard the baron's wife discussing with Pierre.

Within a few moments, Norea had a quill, inkpot, and a piece of parchment in hand and was seated at a nearby desk that overlooked an open window. She could hear pigeons cooing, the edge of a wicker birdcage just in sight from the windowsill.

She stared at the paper and began her letter to Queen Blanche.

✤ ✤ ✤

The rosemary bush in the castle garden had grown steadily since the day Isabelle had walked the courtyard with her sister-in-law Queen Margaret.

Now it was the object of attention from another. Queen Blanche looked down from her sitting-room window and stared at the massive, blooming bush.

Down in the courtyard, an elderly gardener and his new assistant were beginning a little weeding. The young man stopped and looked up at Queen Blanche in the window. She was framed by the archway, her dark hair tumbling down around her shoulders and her raven eyes staring at the lush courtyard foliage.

The old man, Herbert, stopped and looked at his young lieutenant. "*Vite! Allons*, Adam," he prompted.

"Why does she sit like so?" Adam asked.

"She sits like this *du matin. Ne regardez pas.*"

Adam moved away from the castle tower and walked behind the old man, but he kept glancing up at the queen. "What does she do there?"

Herbert shrugged. "The queen, she sits like this every day, from this time until *terce*."

"I am thinking this is a long time to dally," Adam replied.

"She is a queen, *non*? *Madame* can do as *madame* pleases. *Allons!* Get to work now."

Adam started to hoe the ground behind Herbert. He was younger and his back more suited for the work. Herbert was seated on the ground, pulling out the tender shoots of weeds that Adam dislodged.

"But each day there are very important matters, *n'est pas*, Herbert? How does she find this time to linger and stare at *le jardin*? I think queens are busy, *non*?"

"*Mais oui*, sometimes she is so very busy," Herbert replied. "And so every day, despite this, she would still take the time to sit. *Peutêtre* she prays to God."

Adam frowned. "I suppose this could be. I hadn't considered this. *Peutêtre* she takes this time to appreciate the beauty of her land. I would imagine it is so easy to forget what is yours . . . *toutement* . . . when you must tend so very many problems."

"*Oui, c'est vrai*." Herbert continued to pluck away small shoots and roots.

Queen Blanche smiled as the two men moved down the row. She had overheard their conversation. She enjoyed sitting still as a spider in the center of her shining web, thinking. No, "plotting" was really more the word for it, though she disliked the word. It seemed to imply something so menial and vicious.

She glanced again at the letter from Norea that was in her hands. She held the delicate parchment carefully in her lap, as if it were a rose stem.

Norea wrote Blanche quite often. The queen had her do many things outside the castle walls where she could not go. In particular,

Blanche had Norea keeping tabs on a certain family that had always plotted against her own. Hugh de la Marche and his wife Elizabetta were English sympathizers and had spent a great deal of time in England with King Henry after his marriage to a daughter of Provence.

Every week, Norea sent Queen Blanche word about what Elizabetta and her husband Hugh were doing. This week, however, the news that came to Blanche from Norea's hand was most disturbing. She had overheard Elizabetta talking about a siege on France by King Henry himself. And that her husband, Hugh de la Marche, would ride with him. As reward for turning against their country, de la Marche and his wife would be given a great deal of land from what was conquered.

The letter disturbed Blanche. She called for a nearby guard, knowing what had to be done next, knowing it was necessary, but dreading it nonetheless.

When Isabelle and Jean reached the *palais*, she was stopped by one of the front guards, who bowed low and then saluted.

"Princess Isabelle, the queen wishes to see you in her sitting room immediately."

"Very well," Isabelle said, not knowing why or what she had done to encourage an immediate reception into her mother's presence. She turned to Jean, excused herself, and hurried off while he rode to the stable on his horse.

Isabelle climbed the stairs to the Ladies' Quarters, padding quietly down the hall past Queen Margaret's room and toward the large double doors at the end of the hallway. She hadn't had time to change out of her riding attire, or wash face and hands, but with Blanche "immediately" always meant *immediately*. Looking down, she noticed she was still wearing Jean Adaret Benariel's ring. She hastily took it off and put it in a little pocket of her dress, so that she would not be questioned about it.

After allowing a moment to compose herself, she pushed open the tall double doors and stepped inside the receiving room of the queen's personal chambers. She had visited her mother in her quarters less frequently the older she became. It had been several months since she'd seen the inside of the room, but it had not changed at all.

After Isabelle's father died in battle, Queen Blanche had solemnly moved to this room—never before used to entertain anyone, even guests—and had it prepared as a bedchamber and receiving room. It had not changed in its dressings or somber state in over fourteen years, still dressed as if for mourning. Blanche's bedclothes were a rich crimson red with black threading and embroidery. The bed's ornate frame was black mahogany, with matching sitting tables and chairs. The tapestries upon the walls had only the muted colors of red, midnight blue, brown, and dark gold.

It was a sad room, a testament of her love to her former husband; not a woman's room but the room of a widow.

"Mother?" Isabelle spoke quietly. "You sent for me?"

Queen Blanche's voice reached her from the large, arched window on the far side of the room, out of sight behind a wardrobe closet of carved mahogany.

"Close the door, Isabelle."

As she turned to close the large double doors, she nervously wondered if Queen Blanche had disapproved of her and Jean Adaret Benariel traveling to his estate in the Western Wood.

Upon reflection, it did look horrible. One could suppose all kinds of terrible events might have taken place. A woman, alone, following a man who had no family history of honor to claim in defense of good conduct. It was foolish, really, and she didn't understand why she hadn't seen it earlier.

Because, she thought. *Louis had asked me to do it. Does that mean that Louis doesn't even think of me as a woman anymore?*

She closed the door firmly, then turned and walked over to her mother. Like all the other windows in the room, this one was heavily curtained, allowing precious little light to enter the bedchamber. Sunlight would have ruined the somber appearance of the room.

She had to wonder what that meant for her mother, and what her mother could be if she allowed herself to live outside the shadows.

Blanche didn't turn around to look at Isabelle. This was a certain sign of aggravation. Isabelle swallowed, waiting for the barrage of cold insinuations to start.

"I'd like to throw a party for Alphonse," Blanche said.

There was no possible way that her mother could have said those words. "I'm sorry?" Isabelle asked. "What did you . . . ?"

Queen Blanche turned and looked at her daughter's ashen face. "I want to throw a large party for Alphonse—a knighting ceremony—in the Castle of Angers. I want it to happen in half a year. It is time for Alphonse to claim his land in Poitiers. And that means he needs to be knighted. And quickly."

"Mother, why did you ask for me to close the doors? This is surely not a private matter, is it?"

"Yes, it is very private. Not a single courtier with their covetous eyes should hear our conversation today."

"But—"

"There are a great many things you must come to learn, Isabelle," Blanche began. "A member of the clergy or not, you cannot continue to hide from the politics of the world. I bring this to you because I have no other choice.

"Your brother Louis is married to Margaret of Provence. He loves her dearly. Provence is involved in some political dealings with which our family must intervene. If what I am about to say were to travel to Margaret's ears, it would quickly reach her father in Provence, and that would be a terrible state of affairs."

"You think Louis would tell her even against your express orders?" Isabelle asked.

"Isabelle, don't be foolish. You of all people should realize that all my children seem to be constantly doing things against my express instructions."

"Sorry. What about Robert?"

"Robert is completely muddled with the court of Artois. While I know his heart is with our family, his mind is with the dealings of his own province. . . . And that poses another problem, if in dealing with this situation, it means moving against his personal interests.

"Alphonse is simply too busy with the finances. And Joan of Toulouse must know nothing of this. I didn't choose her as a wife for Alphonse because of her tactical abilities.

"That leaves Charles, or you. And as you know, Charles can't be trusted with a single thing. He is a throwback to the great terrors of our past, I'm afraid. And he will have to be overlooked in the line of succession at all costs. He is reckless, angry, and completely off balance." Blanche sighed and seemed lost for a moment in thought. "I should never have made love to your father before his fierce battles— the very battles that ended his life. That was my mistake. Charles is a direct result of the fierceness of your father's temper during that time."

Blanche stood, and Isabelle backed away to let her pass. The queen mother strode into the darkened sitting room.

"So that leaves you, child," Blanche said, and sat at her dressing table. Her hair was still down and unmade, and she began to brush it, a prelude to arranging it for court later in the day.

"Leaves me for what?" Isabelle asked. She sat by her mother and helped put Blanche's hair up from behind.

"A lieutenant, a trusted confidante. I must rely on you now as I have never relied on anyone besides Louis." Blanche looked at Isabelle in the mirror, and Isabelle saw how her mother's face was an oval shape with a dainty pointed chin, just like her own. The resemblance stopped there. Isabelle was like the sun staring into the face of the moon.

"I am about to make you aware of many things kept from you,"

Blanche said. "Having you in the dark in the current situation is unwise. I think sometimes you can handle more than we think. If I had, perhaps, told you the reasons why I wanted you to marry Conrad, for example . . ."

Isabelle stared at the floor, her eyes fixed on Blanche's hem.

"Well, what's done is done," Blanche said, and Isabelle looked up at her mother in the reflection of the mirror. "Conrad was to be our line of defense against the English. Your marriage to the king would have secured an unprecedented alliance between Germany and France. We could have counted on Germany's king to send us anything we needed in a war."

"But why, Mother? Why do we need to be so reliant upon Germany?"

"Because England is stirring."

"But we are sisters now. King Henry has married into Provence. It couldn't be *wise* to attack now."

Blanche chuckled. It was deep and throaty, the quiet laugh of someone older and wiser looking into the face of a novice. "Nothing about England or Henry is wise. He wants the land his fathers held. Richard the Lionheart used to own most of France, you know. His descendant—Henry—wants it back. Marriage is a good prelude to attack, because marriage brings you some claim to the land you want."

Isabelle realized again how Blanche knew pivotal information that no one else seemed to have or care about. Blanche seemed certain that this attack would be coming. "But how do you *know*? I mean, for certain," she asked.

"A little voice tells me these things," Blanche said, and pulled another strand of hair into place.

Isabelle's eyes widened. "You have spies in Henry's court?"

"I prefer to call it 'intelligence,' really—the other word is so negative. And my informant is not in the royal court; my hand cannot stretch quite that far. I can hear the whispers only as far as Poitou, where Hugh de la Marche and his wife Elizabetta live, now."

Isabelle recalled the famous enemy of her infancy. Hugh de la

Marche had been the main force behind the attack on young Louis. Hugh and his allies had wanted another man on the throne and had insisted that a child and his mother could not rule France.

"But the whole ordeal has been over for so long. I was a baby when they last attacked," Isabelle said.

"To keep the peace Hugh was never arrested or charged. He still owns land and has full baronial title."

"Don't you think it odd that they would start all over again now, so long after the last war?"

"Not at all, child. Alliances take years to forge. Many of the worst barons have been overseas with King Henry for many years, forging an alliance with him. Some, like Simon de Montfort, have even inherited English land."

"It really is going to happen, then," Isabelle said sadly.

"Yes."

Isabelle nodded silently for a moment, then looked down. "I . . . didn't know about Germany. I had no idea that these things were so thought-out. I mean, I knew there was some strategy involved, but this . . ." Her words failed her, leaving her with only, "I'm sorry."

"I am giving you a chance to make up for it," Blanche said. "You should be pleased, I suppose. It means you are still a part of this family and that we come first to you."

"What of my vows?"

"The Church has nothing to do with secular affairs, and you will not be placed in opposition to your spiritual obligations. But I need your help on behalf of the entire family. Do I have it?"

Isabelle considered for a long moment, then asked quietly, "What do you want me to do?"

"You will plan Alphonse's knighting ceremony for me. In full, elaborate detail. You must go to all expenses on it, and you must do it in my name. Everything must look as if I am planning the arrangements. You'll meet with Alphonse and Jean Beaumont of the treasury.

Alphonse will insist on something simple, but you will not give him that satisfaction. We must make his knighting ceremony more fabulous, more spectacular, than either Louis' or Robert's."

"And it will be held at Angers," Isabelle said, thinking it through.

"Yes," Blanche replied.

"So, while I am doing this in your name, everyone will think you are preoccupied with the knighting ceremony. Once Alphonse receives his land in Poitiers, he will be directly overseeing the Baron Hugh de la Marche and Simon de Montfort, both of whom are in league with the king of England. This will allow us to keep a closer eye on the two traitors."

"Exactly, and by then, the Castle of Angers will be fully fortified. Louis is overseeing the last of the designs personally, and this is where we hold the celebration for Alphonse. It's in his territory, after all. It will be a show of *authority* on our part. Knighting our royal prince at Angers will show England that *France owns Poitiers*. For that matter, that France owns *all the land* on the coast and southern lands. And we are not to be trifled with."

"I see. And what will you *really* be doing during the preparations for the party?"

"Gathering intelligence. There is now too much at stake to rely on just one person providing information. I must employ others who will listen for me. They will be everywhere, from England to Germany." She looked at Isabelle, and suddenly it seemed to Isabelle that her mother's eyes were very tired. "We have very little time, child. We've hardly enough for your preparations . . . or mine."

"Leave it in my hands." Isabelle rose but did not leave. "Why have you given me this second chance after I failed you with Conrad?"

"We are all allowed one mistake in our life. *Mine* was not trusting that you were capable of knowing everything. I should not have kept things from you. I will never make that mistake again."

That Blanche would make such an admission staggered Isabelle, and she found herself profoundly moved by it.

It reminded her of other days, long ago, when she stood looking at her mother with pride and a love so profound she thought it would shatter her heart. She wanted to tell her mother that, but faltered. It was something inexpressible. Instead, she leaned down and kissed Blanche on her cheek. Caught by surprise, Blanche looked up at her, and Isabelle could see tears in her eyes.

"I will not fail you again, Mother," Isabelle said, and walked out of the dark room a different woman than when she had entered it.

In the darkness, Isabelle watched as Jean Adaret Benariel made his way through the moon-streaked gardens, pacing, evidently lost in thought. She admired his poise and grace from the walkway above. The dew was already forming on leaves and tender plants in the late fall air. He looked at them and didn't make a sound.

Isabelle was about to come down when the sound of footsteps made Jean turn around. It was Sofia. Isabelle froze; even from here she could see from Sofia's expression that she was not happy to see Jean.

"I wasn't expecting you to be here," he said.

"I thought I told you to return to the tower," she replied.

"You did." His tone was soft. He was staring off into the distance.

"Why are you here, then?"

"I have to come back. I can't stay at the tower anymore."

"It is not safe here for you. I've worked hard to protect you. Of all of us, I was instructed by Mother to protect *you* at all costs. Your sisters and I struggle every day to keep you out of harm's way here in the world of mankind lest they see how different we are—"

"You were told to keep me safe, to protect me. But you were not told to lock me in a tower for the rest of my life. And regarding the world of men, they will suspect me just as much if I *don't* come out.

"As much as I know you must protect me, I cannot remain locked away forever," he continued. "If it is my fate to do good, and in so doing to risk being discovered for it, then I will have to take that chance."

"You are the legacy of our family, Jean. You of all of us *cannot* be spared. You must be there at the end! If something were to happen to you—" She was actually flustered. Isabelle had never thought Sofia could be anything but cool and impressive.

"If I am indeed meant to be there at the end, then there is nothing that any power on Earth can do to divert that plan. What I must address is, *Who* will I be when I get there?" He smiled. "You must learn to relinquish responsibility for all of us. Whatever happens to me, it isn't your fault."

She couldn't look at him then; her eyes were angry, reluctant to relinquish that control. When she spoke again, her voice was soft. "The king's trip has been delayed, and I have to leave tomorrow at dawn. I must go with him to Angers, as I have always been by his side."

Jean nodded. "I understand."

"I cannot look after you and him at the same time. You'll be on your own."

"Not at all. Your love will be with me, and mine will be with you."

She nodded silently at that, and they embraced, after which she turned away and left him in the garden, alone.

Still in the dark shadows, Isabelle put Jean's ring back on her index finger, wondering if she should approach or leave, watching Jean Adaret Benariel standing motionless.

Isabelle took a breath, feeling privileged and somehow saddened to have overheard something so private and amazing, then stepped down the walkway into the moonlight. Jean looked over at her.

"Good evening, Princess," he said. His voice was warm, despite the chill in the air.

"Evening, Sir Benariel," she replied, then took a deep breath. "I came to inquire about something, but I was wondering what Sofia wanted. I saw her come up to you just now, as I was making my way down. She never speaks to anyone outside of the queen."

"She wanted to know about me," he said after a moment.

Isabelle nodded, realizing this explanation was both a lie and the truth. She found it more intriguing for that fact. "She's one of my mother's serving women. The Sisters of the Rose are a legend, you know."

"Really?" He seemed polite, but not overly interested, as if he would rather get on to another topic.

"They saved us from death when I was still a baby. I don't remember anything but was often told the stories of their wonderful scheme. It was one of my favorite good-night tales. According to the story, when Louis was eleven years old, my mother learned that her husband, the king, had died on the battlefield. Mother was grief-stricken, but brave. Some of the southern barons commanded that she turn away from the throne and let another man rule France. They had even chosen a relative of my father's ready to assume the crown.

"My mother and Louis were quite literally stuck in Montlheri without even so much as an armed escort, while Simon de Montfort and Hugh de la Marche were ready to march after them with an army if they did not surrender. Even Pierre Mauclerc joined in on their side."

"Mauclerc was against Louis?"

"Yes, though he has since vowed allegiance to France's king. He really had no choice after my brother was anointed. Mauclerc's own lords, the Templars, are friendly to the king of France."

"Ah, he is but a representative to the Templars, then."

"Something like that. He is a petty noble."

"Literally?" He smiled.

"I think so," she replied, speaking the honest truth. She didn't really care for Pierre. "I like the Templars—they are wise and just— but sometimes they employ mere thugs when things go wrong with their monetary transactions. I disdain men like Pierre Mauclerc."

"As do I," he replied, and there was an edge in his voice. "Some things are not meant to be disturbed. Ever."

"What do you mean?" Isabelle asked.

"Nothing," he said, dismissing the thought. "Please continue."

Isabelle walked with Jean a little bit into *le jardin.* "My mother and Louis were penned in at the town of Montlheri until one day a messenger came to her. When she opened the door at his behest, she saw the entire population of Montlheri at the doorstep of the *château,* offering to safely accompany Mother and all of us to Paris—straight to the *palais.*"

"The whole *town* came to her aid?"

"Led by three women dressed in white robes with red roses embroidered on the front. They are the Order of the Rose—the very same women who are still with my mother today."

"It was they who convinced the town to come to your defense?"

"I believe so. It is said that the Order of the Rose was formed to protect those chosen by God. My mother was anointed as queen, and as you know, queens like kings are always chosen by God. The Sisters were there to protect that which God adores. My brother calls them the guardian angels of our family.

"They saved our lives. We owe everything to them." She looked carefully at him then. She could see him hesitating, and deliberating. Carefully. Like a man trapped. She wondered what it must be like to live with a secret so great and terrible as the one that seemed to beat in his chest like a dove trapped in a cage.

"So, you are happy to have them as a part of your household, then?" he asked.

"They would do, and have done, anything for us. And in kind, I and *any* of my siblings—I *know* that my mother—would do *anything* for them." She looked at him and caught his glance with a knowing stare. He looked deeply into her eyes then. "We would gladly come to their aid, or to the aid of anyone they deemed worthy."

Then the moment passed between them, and Jean looked away. "*Anyone* would of course be glad to have such powerful allies on their side. Especially if things ever became difficult."

"We treat our Sisters well," Isabelle said, and shivered slightly in the cold night air, though the cool wind was not to blame. *Why can you not tell me? Can you know so much of me, and my heart, and yet not see that you can trust me?*

"You should not be out at night," Jean said softly. "You will be ill. Come, let's go in by the fire." He motioned to her, and she walked beside him.

"You never told me what you came to see me about," he said.

"I was wondering if you might be able to help me with a task. One that requires complete secrecy. I would appreciate your discretion and your advice."

"I would be honored to help you with anything, Princess." He opened the door of the tower for her, and they went inside.

Before closing the door, he looked back at *le jardin* sitting pristine under the moonlight. Isabelle thought she caught a longing in his eyes.

"Is everything all right?" she asked.

"Yes, I was just thinking."

"About what?"

"About the future, Princess."

"And do you like what you see?"

"I don't quite know yet . . . ," he said, then gently closed the door. They ascended the stairs, their shadows moving along the wall, side by side, never quite touching.

A man's happiness—
To do the things proper to man.
Marcus Aurelius, *The Meditations* (A.D. 167)

18

When Isabelle sat down with Alphonse in the Treasury Room to discuss his knighting ceremony, they were joined by Jean Beaumont, the chancellor, who sat across the table from Isabelle and her brother. Alphonse was adamant about doing everything as inexpensively as possible. But Isabelle had prepared for that by having a private talk an hour earlier with Beaumont.

She looked at her list of preparations. "We'll need one set of plate armor from the blacksmith—"

"Absolutely not!" Alphonse said. "Plate armor is for kings, and it costs the price of at least one hundred sheep!"

"Mother wants plate mail for you," Isabelle replied.

"I'm not even sure that I can support that much weight!"

Isabelle tried not to laugh. Her poor, bookkeeping brother was a dear soul, always caught up in a more-for-less philosophy. He'd learned that tactic from Mother. That so much money would now be expended for his benefit was enough to set his head spinning.

Jean Beaumont stepped in, ever wise and aging, and agreed with Isabelle. He was a tall man, with gray hair, and he carried his authority easily but firmly. "For this occasion, as your queen mother has demanded plate armor, I think that it would be wise to follow her instructions."

"But it's so—"

"Put down one plate armor in the ledger," Isabelle said.

222

Looking pained, Alphonse pushed his spectacles up the bridge of his nose, then ran an ink-splotched hand over his dark locks before scribbling with the quill on the ledger paper. Isabelle looked down and remembered the paper, wondering if the handkerchief she'd given so long ago to the rag-catcher was somehow threaded into this sheet. It would be a fitting irony.

"Good," she said. "Next on the event list: a new coat of mail for Robert and Louis. They must look stunning as well."

"This is madness!" Alphonse cried.

"It is your mother's will," Jean Beaumont said. Even if Isabelle had not coopted him prior to the meeting with a message from Blanche, Beaumont had been through too much with the queen to question her craftiness, even secondhand. If she wanted a grand celebration . . . well then, that was the end of it. Above being entitled to her moments of glory, the queen always knew what she was doing.

Isabelle saw Alphonse crumble while he wrote down the next figure for two more suits of mail. His leg was starting to shake nervously under the great finance table. It was an astonishing amount. Coats of mail were worth sixty sheep apiece.

Isabelle tried not to gawk at it, but simply checked off the next item on the list. "Your *destrier* needs to be a fine breed; a steed of the stablemaster's choosing, not yours. I think Philippe will do a fine job in choosing a mount."

Alphonse muttered as he wrote down the *destrier*, for the cost of twenty oxen. "If we keep going like this, the treasury will be light enough to float along the Seine."

Isabelle suppressed a giggle. "And put down a new sword— nothing cheap either."

"Nothing short of three cows' worth of sword," Jean Beaumont added.

For the first time, Alphonse seemed to straighten a little. There was a faint glimmer in his eye. Something about a sword seemed to resonate with him, as if he was just now getting a glimpse of the moment that would be his alone. It seemed that the cost of that moment had just gotten a little easier to bear.

Isabelle knew Alphonse was imagining his royal entrance wearing full plate armor, riding a new warhorse, his shield gleaming in the sunlight as he walked to the altar, kneeling as a sword of magnificence was crossed over his shoulders in a pure and perfect ceremony.

"Three cows . . . ," he said breathlessly, and flushed a bit. Only he could truly appreciate the value of such an item. Alphonse wrote down the amount. "The sword, I assure you, will be correspondingly treasured."

Old Beaumont was silent, but when he saw the change of heart in Alphonse, he gave a wink across the table to Isabelle.

Isabelle stepped out into *le jardin*, leaving Jean Beaumont to finish going over the treasury columns with Alphonse. She didn't want to be there when they hit the grand total. She was on a spending thrill, and had a royal credit slip for several *gros tournois*, which she would now take down to the marketplace for some linen, wool, silk, and cotton.

Today she would gather all the fine material in Paris seamstress shops. It was all necessary for the banners and table linens of Alphonse's knighting ceremony.

There was still the problem of making all of the festive decorations. She had been wrestling with how to handle all of it, but she didn't want to think about that now, because the idea spoiled her sunny mood. She wanted only to go into town and buy out the entire stock of homespun fabric at the *Grand Pont* market.

"Princess!" came a call from behind her. Isabelle turned and saw Pierre Mauclerc coming toward her. She groaned inwardly at the sight, but she waited, courteously, as he approached.

Isabelle extended her hand, and Pierre knelt to kiss it. He lingered over it for far too long. "It is a pleasure to see you again," he said. "May I accompany you into town? You could use an escort."

"I'm actually going about some personal errands today, *Seigneur* Mauclerc, though I appreciate your concern."

"It isn't safe to go into Paris alone, you know. Don't you get recognized when you walk around openly? If you were in my care, you would be escorted anywhere you pleased."

"But I am in the care of God and the Church. That is care enough for me." Isabelle started to curtsey, a polite signal for him to leave, but Pierre didn't budge.

She was trying to decide what to say next to dissuade him when she saw Claire running down the courtyard.

"Princess!" Claire called out. "I just missed you in the Treasury Room. They said you were going to market." By the time she reached Pierre and Isabelle, Claire was breathless.

"*Oui*, I am. Did you need me for something?"

She seemed hesitant and looked at Pierre. "I wanted to talk to you about something."

"Of course." Isabelle nodded to Pierre and said, "If you'll excuse us, good sir . . ."

Pierre looked upset, but nodded his assent. "Certainly, Princess. Have a lovely day."

Isabelle and Claire strolled down to the castle gates, leaving Pierre behind. Though she said nothing, Isabelle was thankful for the diversion.

"I was talking with some of the women at the seamstress guild," Claire began. "And I told them the story of your kindness, and how I became a free woman because of your generosity."

"Hmm." Isabelle wondered where this was going.

"And well, there are a lot of women there who are in need, and they were asking . . ." She faltered. "Well, they wanted to know . . ."

Isabelle looked up at the skyline and sighed slightly. She had known something like this might happen if word got out.

"I don't have any more jobs for seamstresses—" Then she stopped herself and was struck dumb with delight.

Isabelle clutched Claire's upper arms. "How *many* women?"

"Well, . . . I wasn't going to offer them *all* help, because you know, there are a lot, and uh . . ."

"Out with it, already!"

"All right! There are fifty total!"

Isabelle threw her hands in the air and laughed out loud. She knew Claire had never seen her mistress behaving so crazily before, but she didn't care. She began dancing wildly and kicking up dirt on the cobblestones and then spinning out of control into the grass.

"Fifty women! *Ha!* On any other day, but today! *Fifty women!*" Isabelle couldn't stop laughing. She stared up into the sky, and in her heart, she thanked the Lord.

"Well, honestly, Your Highness, I was thinking about only really giving *ten* of them—"

"No! I want all fifty."

"*What?*" It took a moment before she could accept that her mistress was serious; then Claire burst into giggles. They were like two little girls, grinning and giggling at each other in the middle of the street. Even the palace guards were starting to watch them in fascination. Neither they nor Alphonse could truly understand. Fifty seamstresses meant fifty women able to buy their freedom from prostitution. The joy and the humor of it was almost more than Isabelle could bear.

"Come, I will explain on the way to the market," Isabelle said, and took Claire's hand, pulling her along the road to the *Grand Pont*.

✤ ✤ ✤

Jean finished setting his things into the drawer of the guest room that had been prepared for him and closed it firmly. The palace was a comfortable home away from home, he realized with a smile. Despite the recent admonition from Sofia, he was very glad to be back.

A knock on his door made him turn as Neci poked her head around the open door. "Sofia said you had returned."

He nodded, wondering if this meant trouble too.

Neci just grinned. "I am so glad you're back. And I wanted to say . . ."

Jean smiled in return as she sought the right words.

"I think you've done the right thing. You shouldn't be cooped up in the tower for the rest of your life. It isn't natural."

"Thank you."

They paused, smiling a smile that was a thousand years in the making, and passed in the breadth of a second. Then Jean held out his gloved hands. "I'll have to go about in these, but it's not terribly uncomfortable."

"You'll get used to being around people and will learn when to restrain yourself," Neci replied.

"I can't take any chances. I'm apt to do something without knowing I've done it at all. You've seen it happen."

"Jean, you're a man. You're going to have to learn to live among them. We all have our foibles. But I think I know your heart, and this is where it belongs."

He looked out his chamber window and pointed to the streets of Paris visible in the distance. "Do you know how long I have yearned for a simple view? A window overlooking a town with a quaint little bridge, where I could watch people milling around at market and in the streets?"

Neci smiled. "I do."

"I'll be gone for a while tomorrow, as usual," he said.

"Oh! It's the fifteenth of the month already, isn't it?"

"Yes." He grinned. "But afterward, I'll be back here, and not at the tower."

"Or loitering in that ruin in the game wood?" She chuckled.

"No reason to go there anymore, is there?"

Neci stood, walked over to Jean, then kissed him lightly on the cheek. "I can't tell you how happy I am to see you here. I almost feel like we're regular people."

He nudged her chin up to face him, and considered the gloved hand that touched her face. "Yes, almost," he said.

✤ ✤ ✤

That evening, fifty women of dubious profession but sincere hearts showed up at the palace gates to be admitted into the premises. The astonished guards summoned Isabelle to vouch for them all, and once she had explained the situation, she led them to the middle of the courtyard. Then she realized she had nowhere to put them while they sewed.

She turned to Claire, chagrined, and said in a low voice, "I need to find a place for all of you."

"It's all right. I'll wait with them while you take care of the arrangements," Claire said.

Isabelle hurried off, chastising herself for getting caught up in other preparations and not thinking of this beforehand. She had never actually been in charge of anything in her life, especially of this magnitude and importance, but that didn't stop her from berating herself. As she walked up to the castle, she thought about putting all the women in her own sitting room, but they would be too cramped for comfort.

She sighed. *Where are they all going to go?*

Then her gaze rested on the large stables, with their rows of horse stalls and the hay loft above them.

With a sudden smile, Isabelle ran over to the stables and leaned inside the door. "Philippe?"

"*Ouai!* Is that our princess?" the old man called from the hay loft.

"*Oui, monsieur.* I have a favor to ask of you."

He emerged from the loft, glancing to where the sun was now setting behind the western castle wall. "You're out late."

"I'm still making preparations. I have . . . some women who will be working on decorations. I'm wondering if they can stay evenings in your stables?" Isabelle bit her lip and waited for his reply.

"Well, I suppose it's all right with me. Are they quiet? I don't want the horses disturbed."

"They'll be very quiet. They're sewing."

"Well, make sure they're in the hay loft. And I don't want their lanterns setting the hay on fire."

"*Merci,* Philippe!" Isabelle said. Smiling, she ran off to get the women.

When everyone was settled comfortably in the upper loft, Isabelle climbed down the ladder. The days were getting longer, and the women could make evening work by lantern light. Isabelle was prepared to pay them out of her coffers for the ceremony.

The women worked well and long into the night. Isabelle could see the stables from her attic room, and the lights in the upper loft were alight far into evening dinner. She worried for a few nights that they might start a blaze in the hay, but soon came to learn the practical way about these women and had no fear of their common sense. These were women who lived daily in far more precarious conditions and knew the hazards well. They were good, proud women, capable of beautiful stitching, even by lantern light.

Within just a few short weeks, the banners, sashes, tablecloths, and napkins were all but finished. Even the *sotelties,* ornate table decorations brought on and enjoyed with every course of food, were well under way. Things seemed to be working, however astonishing that seemed to Isabelle at times.

✦ ✦ ✦

In the morning, Isabelle made her way through the city streets she now knew so well. She would personally deliver invitations to the knighting at Angers to the men of the *université*, because while she was in charge of everything, including the guest list, she wanted to ensure that her very favorites were in attendance. Roger Bacon and Albertus Magnus were two of the world's finest scholars, and having them present in Angers would be a delightful show of intellect, an unparalleled and impressive display of culture. Isabelle smiled to herself as she sidestepped an oncoming farmer bringing his cattle into town. A smiling dog trotted alongside his master, keeping the cows in line.

She was passing a carpentry shop just east of rue Garande when she saw a brown-haired man walk from the front of the shop to the back. She stopped so abruptly that she almost tripped over her own hem.

Was that Jean?

No, she told herself. *It couldn't have been.* But in spite of her logic, she waited a moment longer. Sure enough, the brown-haired man walked back out, tall and thin, dressed as a laborer and taking instructions from the shopkeeper. It *was* Jean. But it was impossible. Jean was a nobleman. He didn't work at a carpenter's shop. But she couldn't mistake his eyes, or his gentle nod. He was using a hammer to pound in nails while the old shopkeeper held two boards together.

"What in Heaven is he doing?" she asked herself, skirting along quietly to observe him.

Jean was smiling at the old man. When he finished pounding the nails in, he held up the wooden case they'd just put together. As they talked about it, they ran their fingers along the wood and nodded. She was now close enough to overhear their discussion.

"You don't get a finer grain than this," Jean said.

"Pure, wonderful maple." The old man grinned. "Solid and doesn't bend like the other woods. I love it. Isn't the grain beautiful?"

Jean nodded again and hefted the little case up on his shoulders. "I'll put it out back, for *Seigneur* Hambert to retrieve tomorrow."

"Thank you, Jean," the old man replied, and walked to the front of the shop again. When Jean was gone, Isabelle approached the shopkeeper and quietly addressed him.

"Excuse me, *monsieur*," she said.

The old man looked up, and then his eyes softened in awe. "*Oui, Mademoiselle?*" The old man turned to regard her and then stared at her slack-jawed with recognition. "Oh! It's you!"

She ignored his outburst.

"That man who was just here, working with you."

"Jean," he said.

"Yes, him. Can you tell me about him?"

The old man looked back at the doorway and then to Isabelle. "Well, *mademoiselle*, he comes to help with the carpentry once or twice a month. Works a ten-hour day, goes home with two *tournois* for his pains. Why do you ask? Has he done something wrong?"

"Oh, no. Nothing like that. But I'd like to speak to him, if I could. Privately."

"Oh, certainly, *mademoiselle*. Please, go right ahead." The shopkeeper opened up a little door that led to the storage side of the shop, and Isabelle stepped in.

The back room was dark, with thick curtains over the open windows to keep out the sun. Through an open door to the back alley, she saw Jean putting down some handmade furniture, presumably for patrons to come and pick up.

Isabelle waited, and after a moment, he turned, whisked his hands together happily, and walked back into the darkness. He stopped when he saw Isabelle pull back one of the curtains for a little light.

"Hello, Jean."

He squinted into the light. "Isabelle? What—what are you doing here?"

"I was about to ask you the same question."

"I . . . I come here to work once a month."

"Why?"

"Because it's good, honest work, and it makes me feel good to do it." His words came slow, as if chosen carefully.

She smiled. "You're helping this shopkeeper. That is very admirable. I was amazed to see you here. But I suppose I shouldn't have been. I did much the same when I was younger. Why didn't you tell me you did this?"

"No one knows I do this. You mustn't tell anyone that I'm here."

Of course, she thought. *He is a pious man, and the Bible says that if we do good deeds we are to keep it close to our breasts and not tell anyone we've done them.*

"All right. I'll not say a word, Jean. But may I ask what prompted you to do this?"

He looked at her sadly, a little distantly. "I'm not sure you'd understand. At least, not now, not yet. In time—"

"Then I will wait," Isabelle said. "I am very patient." With that, she left the dark room to his secret motivations.

The old man was still staring at her in awe, and she paused beside him. "By the way, it seems I need a new sewing table and chair. I will need it as soon as possible." She started away again.

"But, Your Highness, that might take a very long time!" he called after her.

She glanced back to the darkened room and smiled. "Then I guess you'll have to use *everyone* you have, then." Isabelle disappeared into the crowds that thronged the streets of the Latin Quarter.

✦ ✦ ✦

The shopkeeper was still staring after Isabelle when Jean walked out of the back. "You must be incredibly special," the old man whispered.

Jean flicked a nervous glance in his direction. "Why do you say that?"

"Heaven's sake . . . *She* talked to you. Do you know who *She* is?"

"I, uh . . ." He cleared his throat. "Who is she?"

"Princess Isabelle," the old shopkeeper said distinctly. Reverently. "She lives up there, in that tower, all alone. Isolated from the rest of the world. She lives above us all, you know. And yet, one day she came here to the Latin Quarter to build that roof over there. See it? Right across the street."

"She built *that*?" Jean asked. "*Herself?*"

The old shopkeeper pointed. "*Ouai*, and I know why she did it too." The shopkeeper gave Jean one of those old, wise-man looks.

"Oh? Do tell me."

"Because she's so special. *Royal* and all. She just wanted to do something ordinary. Be an ordinary person—just once. That's all she ever wanted." He nodded sagely.

Jean looked out into the crowd after Isabelle. But she was long gone.

"Maybe you would have understood after all," he said quietly to the shadows.

Isabelle sat back and admired the way things were going with her little ring of sewing ladies. She looked around at the women, at Claire in particular, and thought how far they had all come. How comfortable they all seemed. How well they worked and how very earnestly they earned their keep. She paid them half of what it would take to hire full-time seamstresses, because these women only needed about two *tournois* a night for their efforts. Up in her attic room, after putting on her nightclothes, she looked through the window and saw the women still sewing by lantern light. She then took an hour to write a letter to King Conrad, and to tell him of her endeavors. She invited him to come to the grand ceremony at Angers. Tomorrow, she would entrust the letter to her favorite messenger, who would deliver it safely into Conrad's hands.

After sealing the letter, she blew out the candle and slipped under her covers. Within a few minutes she was soundly asleep.

Several hours later, she woke with a jolt. She had no idea how much time had passed in the night, only that she had it! *It!* And she knew she must not lose the idea before it had time to cool!

She put on her slippers and threw her dressing robe over her head as she made her way out the door, pausing only to glance once more out the window. The stable was dark now, all the lights of the earnest workers extinguished. The lights of the city were also out now, save the guard towers. It was late, very late, but that didn't matter to Isabelle. She had her purpose now, and there was only one person with whom she could share that purpose.

She went down the stairs to the Gentlemen's Quarters and shuffled up to the door at the end of the hallway. She knocked quietly once, to no answer, and couldn't wait any longer. She didn't want to risk someone hearing her about at this hour, and seeing her at this door.

She put her hand on the latch, depressed it, and went inside the darkened room. Someone stirred in the bed and spoke quietly. "Neci?"

"No, Isabelle."

A startled Jean Adaret Benariel sat up in his bed, pulling the sheets around him. "I—What are you doing here?"

Isabelle closed the door behind her, realizing that her impetuous desire might appear unseemly.

"Oh no, please, I just . . . I know what I want to do, and I had to tell you."

"You had to tell me now?" He rubbed his eyes with one hand.

One bare hand, Isabelle noticed. *No gloves on tonight. No shirt either. The rest covered in sheets.*

Isabelle cleared her throat gently. "Yes. On the way to your tower, you told me I was an intelligent woman and I could figure out what good I wanted to do. You remember the conversation?"

"I think so."

"Well, I've found it! My great wish!" In her passion for the moment she sat down on the floor beside his bed.

Jean leaned over to look down at her face.

"Well, what is it?"

"I want to found a convent. There are men who join monasteries and who help to build cathedrals like Notre Dame. The Brothers of the Bridge have built bridges all over the world. The Cistercians and Franciscans help to educate and build, or to do other chores for the benefit of the secular world. Why not women?"

"A convent . . . a very sound idea."

"Do you really think so? Tell me honestly, because I don't want to do something that is, at heart, destined to fail."

"It would only fail if you didn't believe strongly in it. But I can see tonight, by your face, that you believe quite strongly in it."

He had a point. She had so much as burst into his private quarters where he was peacefully sleeping and woken him up to tell him about her dream. But since he had insisted that she could find that dream if she looked hard enough for it, it was only fitting that he receive the news when she did.

"It came to me tonight, in a dream." Her eyes were bright. They glittered like they'd looked into sacred halls and come away enlightened.

"Then you must pursue it with all your heart," he said, then shivered in the cold night air.

Isabelle grabbed his robe from a nearby peg on the wall and handed it to him. "Here, put this on."

As he took the robe and then slid his arms into its sleeves, Isabelle spoke of her vision. "You see, it wasn't until I realized I needed a place for fifty women that it came to me. I was watching over them as they sewed for a few weeks. They worked so well together, and I realized that what I was doing was helping them and helping my family at the same time, without *considering* my actions beforehand. I just *did* it.

"In my dream, I could see clearly a wide square courtyard and on all four sides, dormitories for the women. In the courtyard was a little garden that was tended daily. And women were at work weaving, sewing, making jewelry and gloves . . . work that kept their hands busy and their minds at peace. They were happy in my vision, with a place to live, food to eat, and good work to do."

Isabelle sat against the bed and leaned an elbow over the straw-filled mattress. "It was like a painting, only better, because it was real and filled with honest grit and intention." Then she looked up at Jean, and noticed him staring at her fondly. "I really think I could do it, if only I could get enough land together."

Jean smiled. "If anyone could, you could."

She smiled back at him then, just as the realization of where she was came home to her, logic and manners finally thundering in now that she had said what she had come to say. She shouldn't be here in his room, alone and unsupervised. He shouldn't allow her to be here, either. Yet he didn't seem the least uncomfortable about it after the initial shock. She wasn't sure what was more disconcerting: that he didn't feel uncomfortable, or that she did not.

She stirred. "I should be going. It's late, and I was rude to wake you."

"I didn't mind." His voice made her stop at the door. He was sitting on the edge of his bed, sheets wrapped around the lower half of his body, robe over his shoulders but unbuttoned down his chest. "Truly. It was an honor."

She blushed. "Thank you for listening to me ramble. I should have waited for morning."

"I didn't mind," he repeated, just the same.

"Good night," she said, and opened the door.

"Good night, Princess."

What lies in our power to do, it lies in our power not to do.

Aristotle, *Nicomachean Ethics* (350 B.C.)

19

13, *juin, l'an de notre Seigneur* 1242

Pierre Mauclerc walked into the dark *bordel*. Within the house of ill repute, men were draped over *chaise longues* or leaning against doorways and walls. Everyone was leaning on or touching something . . . or someone. Women of all sizes and stature were here, smiling at him; some with dark hair, others with fiery red hair, a few with pale blonde hair. None like Isabelle.

Pierre did not touch anything as he made his way through the adjoining rooms. He was looking for the man who had summoned him to this place for business. It made Pierre snort. He stepped over two women lying together upon the floor. Such a place was unhealthy and unkempt. These men knew nothing of the word "restraint." They could not know what it was like to wait a lifetime for one perfect woman.

Unlike these men, Pierre would wait as long as it took to achieve this bliss, only his would be with something nobler, something far greater. His bliss would be named Isabelle. And it would happen, sooner or later.

Pierre heard his name called from a dark corner. There was the man, Edgar, in a corner chair with two French women, one on each leg. It was an ironic sight, since this emissary from England was here to discuss the deaths of many French.

Pierre moved toward them, the moaning and sighing left behind as he entered what appeared to be a more private room.

"I came at your request." Pierre bowed.

"Why does Hugh de la Marche not move his forces as he promised in his last letter?" Edgar asked without greeting or formality. His voice was soft; his eyes were hard.

"I believe that he wishes a signal from King Henry that he will not be left stranded and alone against Louis' forces."

"I'm certain my king will be displeased to know that English land and title was not enough for de la Marche."

"Displeased enough to stop his approach on English shores?"

"King Henry is coming. His ancestral lands beckon, and he is determined to regain the glory of Richard the Lionheart's empire." The emissary leaned forward as one of the girls wrapped her arms around his neck and bit his ear. "There will be bloodshed, with or without Hugh. Henry *is* coming to France, and we will destroy what we have to. Including and especially those who pledge themselves and then do not follow through. Henry has quite a way with the punishment of liars. Tell Hugh this, and perhaps he will move his forces as he was asked."

Pierre bowed to the emissary. "I will work to convince our mutual friend."

"Good," Edgar replied. "Because if I do not see action from your friend, I will come and encourage him in person. And I can be quite persuasive when I need to be."

Pierre bowed again, and then left the room.

✤ ✤ ✤

Like seeds sewn in the hard ground during the spring, Isabelle's careful plans were starting to grow tender shoots. By mid-*juin* of 1242, the family had relocated to the Castle at Angers and it was time for the knighting celebration.

The trip to Angers had been long and difficult, most of the women carried on carts without springs, so that very soon every one knew the road by the pain in their hindquarters. Isabelle had wisely refused to ride in a cart, choosing to ride her favorite steed with a comfortable sidesaddle. Since they carried all their worldly possessions, and since the royals insisted on visiting and resting in each town, the trip took several months.

When the family had arrived at Angers, they marveled at the work completed on the fortress. It was fabulous, including a new outer wall and many reinforcements. More turrets had been added, and the family tower strengthened. The castle was now nearly twice as large as the *palais* at the *île de la Cité*.

In the company of the royal family were two clergymen of high esteem: Bishop Arnaud and Bishop Louvel. They had come expressly on Louis' request, to bless the new fortress and to hallow the ground of Angers' family chapel. As Isabelle was closest to the Church, she was required to guide them to their functions at the chapel itself. She certainly didn't mind. She knew Bishop Arnaud from Notre Dame. Bishop Louvel was an acquaintance from Provence.

Arnaud walked under the pristine arches of the family chapel. "Notre Dame. The family chapel in the *Cité*. And now, Angers. Your brother has spared no expense in his House of God."

Bishop Louvel nodded in agreement and smiled.

"My brother is a most pious king," Isabelle replied. "He believes that we must give back to God all that we have been given in mercy. He is as devoted to the Lord as I am, but the Lord chose Louis to lead people, and so his duties must remain with the secular office."

"Your brother is indeed a most pious king. The first king in many generations to so prominently display his devotion and bond with God."

"I believe he will be well remembered for it," Louvel said.

Isabelle smiled. "I will pass your kind words on to him, and to our mother the queen. It is by her hand that we grew up to be so loyal to God the Father."

Bishop Arnaud returned to the matter at hand. "Ah, so much work yet to be done. We must give this chapel an official sanction. A hallowing as never a family chapel has had. It is truly a beautiful work of God, and it must be given our full attention."

"I am glad you have both come," Isabelle said. "Because even though I hesitate to ask, there is another matter I was hoping you could help with."

Arnaud bowed. "Anything, Your Highness."

"I am looking for land in order to found a convent," she said. "I want nothing grand. Just enough room for roughly fifty women to call their home to God. Do you think you could help me?"

"We must think about what we have to spare," Arnaud said. "Your cause is worthy—I even say that it is divinely inspired."

"It came to me in a vision, Your Grace."

"Certainly your heart is in the right place, Princess," Louvel said. "Let us see if we can find something for you. You are sure you don't mind something small?"

"The head of a pin is small, Your Grace, and yet miracles can still be danced upon it."

✤ ✤ ✤

When the princess had left the chapel, Arnaud's face fell. "I don't know, Brother. Where would we get the permission to give Her Highness as she wishes?"

"That is what troubles me," Louvel said. "The only land we rightly have to give is that which isn't already under some use. And you know what that means. . . ."

"Yes." Arnaud sighed. "Going through the ledgers and seeing who owes us a plot or two and then going about the dirty business of twisting their arms. I hate it."

From behind them, a voice called out, "Good morning, Your Graces!"

Arnaud and Louvel turned and saw Pierre Mauclerc standing behind them. He had a clean and pleasant smile on. They returned the smile, and Pierre bowed low before them.

"I couldn't help but overhear some of that conversation. The Princess Isabelle has been such a good friend my entire life, and when I saw her speaking with you, I had to know what the cause could be. She seeks land?"

Louvel shook his head sadly. "Unfortunately, we don't know what we can honestly do for her."

"I might be able to help with this, as I was recently speaking with a dear friend, Thibault, about this matter," Pierre said with another smile. "But as with all good deeds, would you promise to keep it between us and the Lord?"

✤ ✤ ✤

While Isabelle prepared the outward festivities, Queen Blanche and King Louis were in a deep and secretive discussion within the queen's dark chambers. She had found the one thing that might help them avoid war with England.

"You must pen the edict tonight," she told Louis.

"If all he wants back is a small piece of his family land to avert war, I'll pen the edict now."

As he unrolled the vellum on her writing desk and leaned over it, he asked, "Whence came this information?"

"A double agent," she replied. "And a good and dear friend for years."

"Then you trust her?"

"He will not fail us. His information is always correct."

Just before dipping his quill in the dark pot of ink again, Louis stopped and looked at his mother.

"You went to Thibault the poet?"

She turned and looked out the window and said nothing.

Louis didn't ask any more questions of her that evening, for it was apparent that she had given a great deal of herself for the information her family would require. Thibault loved her, had always loved her since before Louis was even conceived. He had been out of Queen Blanche's royal favor for many years now, but his music was known throughout the land. Thibault sang only of Queen Blanche's beauty. He was a powerful bard, a powerful man, with the information of the world at his breast.

Louis looked down at the vellum and swallowed. Without a word, he signed his name to the edict that would give Hugh de la Marche and his wife, Elizabetta, their family land back in the province of Angers.

On the day of the ceremony, Isabelle eagerly set to work on the heavy task of arranging festive decorations needed for the knighting. Queen Blanche established the daily routine of the household. It was the first time Isabelle had seen her mother for more than a few moments since their talk in her bedchamber. Blanche had spent the months in between steeped in private talks, or traveling to distant towns on the pretext of finding goods for the party—excursions actually designed to meet with sources far from the prying eyes at the *palais*.

Now that they were actually at Angers and Isabelle knew what she had to work with, she quickly put many handmaidens to work hanging sashes from the windows and working on elegant garlands and festive wreaths. Anyone with a free hand helped to prepare tables and food for the festival. Bread was baking, pies were stuffed, and the finest linens and most sumptuous serving dishes of the household were displayed. Great metal bowls, goblets, fine pewter, and silver were all polished to a gleaming brilliance.

Large bonfires were built before the ceremony so that stew pots filled with tender meat could cook. Grills, spits, and bread ovens were put into the fires, and by dusk, there were sausages and hams, smoked and cured, and roasts turning over spits, their thick juices caught in the dripping pans beneath. Large caskets of wine were carted in to stand by every table.

At dusk, hundreds, then thousands of guests poured into the castle gates, filling the courtyard. At Isabelle's request, King Conrad of Germany arrived early, just before the swarm of incoming nobles, and helped her quickly prepare the last of the *sotelties* on the tables. Then, together, they stepped out to greet the crowd.

Conrad looked wonderful. He stood near Isabelle in the receiving line, shaking hands, bowing and smiling. He was still large and fiery, only older now. Conrad had grown into the title of king since Isabelle had last seen him. She realized how impressive he looked tonight, and she smiled. It felt good to have Conrad standing beside her, because anyone who thought there were any hard feelings between them would have to admit that no king would travel from his own country at the behest of a princess unless they were close friends. It was a satisfying moment.

Pierre Mauclerc was also present, and it wasn't long before he had insinuated himself into a familiar circle of people surrounding Louis, Isabelle, and Conrad: the blacksmith, verse maker, stablemaster, brewer, and tutor, alongside the usual close friends and allies who traveled wherever Louis and his family went. The *université* crowd had come all the way from Paris, and Albertus Magnus stood among his flock of students, alongside King Louis and his entourage. They were laughing and talking vibrantly.

Pierre Mauclerc was not an especially welcome addition to this cozy circle, but like any other hanger-on, he was greeted politely. Isabelle wondered if he had the prowess to keep up with the ripping philosophical discourse that the rest of the group enjoyed, though the discussion tonight was not quite so highbrow. The professionals were arguing about who was most important. Of all the king's men, the brewer was winning the argument.

"After all," Robert shouted from a nearby wine keg, "without the brewer, we'd all be sober all the time! What good is that?"

"Not at all," Mort the blacksmith said. "Obviously, the crown of 'Most Important' belongs to me."

"And how do you figure that?" Philippe the stablemaster asked.

The blacksmith smiled his dark grin. "Because none of *you* can even *work* without tools that *I provide* for you."

Hooting, booing, and much merriment accompanied the argument, but they had to agree. They proclaimed Mort the blacksmith "king of the professions" for the night, and Robert gave him a crown of wisteria leaves. The men roared with more laughter as Mort actually put the thing on and danced a little jig.

Pierre barely laughed, spending most of his time looking over at Isabelle with a lovesick face. She thought he looked like a begging dog. Seeing her disdain, Conrad took her hand and led her through the throngs of celebrating courtiers.

"I see you have an admirer in this Pierre Mauclerc," he said with a measure of teasing in his voice.

"Don't *say* that." She frowned. "I should think, as a Knight Templar, he would look elsewhere for his salvation."

Conrad leaned down and spoke into her ear. "I've heard things about the Knights Templar that would make your hair turn white."

"Now that's enough," she said. "I've worked too hard on the arrangements to fret over someone as trivial as Pierre Mauclerc."

At this point, Hugh de la Marche and his wife Elizabetta arrived. They were late, and the receiving line no longer stood at the castle gates to receive them. But that didn't matter, for Hugh was worked into quite a frenzy. He rushed over to where Louis stood among his peers.

"Your Majesty, I wish to address—!"

"I completely agree with you, *monsieur*, and I want to give you this edict, which will restore all the lands in Angers that were once your ancestors'."

There was a mighty pause. The entire assembly of thousands of guests seemed ready to react. Isabelle watched as the hungry courtiers waited for something to happen that would cause a riot of scandalous gossip. A few men and women were vying for good positions to watch the argument between Hugh and Louis; for those who had the most information would be able to tell all the important details to those who were not present or privy to the commotion.

Would there be a brawl? Those courtiers who witnessed it first-hand would be more powerful, and more respected, than the others who'd missed it. And to a courtier, Isabelle knew all too well, the power of that information was everything.

But Hugh had nowhere left to go. He had not expected this turn of events. Isabelle watched carefully, holding her breath, wondering if everything would collapse before her in some unforeseen catastrophe.

"Well, I . . . ," Hugh began.

"Open it. Read aloud if you wish. Tomorrow, this land will be entrusted to the Church in good faith and they shall administer and care for it until it can be fully restored to your family."

Hugh unfurled the sealed document. He did not read out loud, but his eyes grew wide. He looked up at Louis when finished. "Your Majesty would do this?"

"Peace, at all costs, brother." Louis put a hand on Hugh de la Marche's shoulder. Isabelle caught sight of her mother moving slowly, like a careful spider on a delicate web, behind Louis and Hugh. Blanche was watching them both with great, dark eyes.

Hugh exhaled forcibly. "All my lands." He started to chuckle. "All the lands of Angers that were my—my father's!" He didn't know what else to say. He handed the document to Elizabetta, who looked somewhere between consternated and amazed. She pored over the contents of the scroll hungrily.

Hugh embraced his king in a quick gesture of friendship. "I will drink with you, Your Majesty!"

The crowd laughed and applauded. Isabelle noticed she was clapping, and looked at Conrad with an enormous grin. He was looking at her, too. The great German king gave her a wink and a nod. "This is an honorable gesture on Louis' part. It impresses me. The Church as an administrative intermediary is sound."

Ha! We did it! she thought, then looked around, realizing that Jean was not here. He had helped her when she needed him most, and she must thank him for his confidence.

"Come with me, Conrad. I want to introduce you to a good friend. If I can find him." Tugging Conrad's hand, she drew him on, past the group of courtiers playing "King for a Day," past the strolling minstrels, and past the happy dancers. She was looking for Jean Adaret Benariel.

He was hard to find, but eventually she noticed him watching the crowd from a private corner of the garden that everyone else had somehow overlooked.

"*Seigneur* Benariel," she called to him, and saw his expression brighten when he saw her. "I want you to meet my good friend King Conrad, ruler of Germany, son of Frederick the Second."

He smiled, instantly recognizing the name. "*You* are the good friend I've heard so much about."

"But I am," Conrad replied, and they shook hands warmly. Jean's gloved fist was lost in Conrad's enormous pale one.

"I've heard many praises of your good nature, Your Majesty. To hear Isabelle talk, you are a saint among men."

"I am flattered. She is a very good friend of mine. We schooled together when I came to learn French many years ago. She taught me how to be hospitable in French custom." Conrad grinned. "It has made all the difference to me in Germany. They don't know how to take me now!"

Isabelle laughed, but her laughter abruptly halted as someone tapped on her shoulder from behind. She turned to find Pierre Mauclerc standing there, hand extended.

"May I have this dance, Princess Isabelle?" he asked.

"Oh, Pierre, really . . ." She wanted to decline, but it would be very rude. "You know I don't really dance."

"Neither do I, so we may both step on each other's toes," he said, and smiled.

Isabelle hesitated, bit her lip, and then accepted his hand. *One dance will not hurt*, she decided.

As Pierre led her over to the other men and women dancing in a line by the minstrels, Conrad called out loudly, *"Do not dance long! You're a member of the Church now, you know! They frown on that sort of thing!"*

Then the great king of Germany laughed, and Isabelle smiled back at him. Even though Pierre couldn't see, her smile said "thank you" for giving her a good excuse to remove herself after one dance.

As Isabelle let Pierre take her in his arms, he smiled a dark smile. "You are keeping so much from me these days, Princess," he said.

Her heart flew up in her throat. *Does he know what we have been doing?* she thought. *Has the diversion failed so miserably?*

"What do you—"

Then he nodded back the way they had come. "You have yet to introduce me to your new friend."

"Conrad? You know Conrad."

"Non, the other one. The dark one with him. I've never seen him at court before Robert came to the last Christmas feast with him."

"I don't really know much about him," she said. "Only that he's not from around here."

"This is Angers," he said. "None of us are from around here."

"Fancy that," she said.

✤ ✤ ✤

Conrad grunted as he watched Isabelle dancing with Pierre. "I do not like him," he concluded.

"Neither do I," Jean replied.

"I wonder what he plays at, pretending to court a woman of God. Especially being of the Knights Templar, himself."

Jean looked sharply at Conrad. "He's not a full member, is he?"

"Well, he doesn't wear the tabard, but he's one of their financiers. A lower member, I think. Not a very nice man, and probably why he's not been admitted in the higher ranks."

"Too bad. Such behavior would have dire consequences for a true Templar."

Conrad nudged Jean toward the ale barrel. "So tell me, *Seigneur* Benariel, how did you meet Isabelle?"

"I befriended her brother, Robert, a few years ago. He'd been wounded in a hunting accident."

"Ah, so you live with the royal family?"

"For now."

"Lucky. When I lived here, I had a wonderful time. Isabelle is a wonderful companion in her own right." As Conrad picked up a large mug and filled it with ale, Sofia hurried up to Jean and whispered into his ear, then quickly left. Jean frowned as he watched her leave.

"What did Sofia want?" Conrad asked.

"You know Sofia?"

"I remember her well. One of the queen mother's closest aides. There's something mysterious and powerful about that woman, but I suppose that can be said for most of the women in France."

Jean chuckled. "She said we're out of a few supplies and that I should let Isabelle know at the end of her dance."

Conrad nodded. "And a long dance it seems," he said darkly.

"So how is Germany, Your Highness?" Jean asked.

Conrad sighed. "I was just telling Isabelle on my arrival that things have become very difficult lately. My father, as emperor of the Holy Roman Empire, will not stop arguing with Pope Innocent."

"That must make it rather difficult for you."

"I believe my father's empire is destined to fall into disarray from all this fighting. As Germany is part of that empire, it makes me worry. My father . . ." Conrad trailed off, searching for the right foreign words. "When a man receives too much of the world, he becomes insensitive to it. My father is this kind of man," Conrad said sadly.

"You are a wise man, Your Majesty."

"Please, I am Conrad to any friend of Isabelle's."

"Conrad, then." Jean smiled. "Should the Holy Roman Empire fall into your hands soon, I believe you will do it much justice."

Conrad looked at Jean and then smiled at the sincere sentiment. He could see why Isabelle had introduced him to the man. There was something innately gentle and infinitely wise in his bearing.

Then the two returned to watching Isabelle dance with Pierre Mauclerc.

"A long dance, indeed," Jean said.

The leathery man with thin bones and a brittle stare waited for his scouts to return, in a tent pitched in the wood behind the farthest field of the castle. Yasarian's body was slightly bent, like an old bow, and he could no longer sit up straight. Through large, watery eyes he considered his favorite water pipe, which he had carried with him across two continents. As it bubbled and brewed he adjusted the strength of the brew. Finally satisfied, he sucked deeply on the end of the pipe. It made a rattling, gurgling noise in its glass belly. He enjoyed the sound; it helped him concentrate.

It would be no simple task to assassinate the king of France, even a king that was pale and childish. But the Old Man of the Mountain, the Master of Yasarian, could not be disobeyed, however much Yasarian dreaded the task.

Tonight, he would kill this "Louis," the boy king who threatened his Master. Yasarian would destroy the king, and that would satisfy the debt that had been incurred in this place when Nimberu was murdered after stealing a relic from an abbey. This king and his brother had thwarted the Master's plan. There was a price to pay for such actions. One did not slay a minion of the Master. It was not allowed.

Yasarian breathed deeply from the toxic pipe, his emaciated rib cage rising and falling in a deep breath beneath his rags of faded Persian design. The sand-beads had mostly fallen off the wrinkled cloth; his sashes were creased from years of wear. Loosely hung around his neck, on a string of raw leather, was the symbol of the Master: a rune pressed upon a coin-shaped piece of metal. All the students of the Old Man of the Mountain wore these tokens. Yasarian had owned this necklace for as long as he could remember, and he closed his hand around it as he sucked in more vapors from the pipe, holding them in his lungs.

They soothed his troubled soul. Killing a king became a task easier to grasp.

More possible. Less pain.

Less guilt.

Only the Master. Only the Master . . .

There was a noise at the tent's opening. Yasarian turned, expecting to find his two scouts waiting to report. Instead he saw a woman with dark hair, dark eyes, and a white robe with a symbol he recognized from ages past. In years before, it had been the most frightening thing he had ever seen.

Now, tonight, it was to be the last thing he would ever see.

✣ ✣ ✣

Tupare and Minona walked silently through the grass using the sure footfalls they had learned from the Master. The scouts were dark men, with long stringy hair and small inset eyes. They wore black clothes of plain cloth without adornments or anything that might help identify them to their enemies should they be discovered.

When they reached the tent of Yasarian, they relaxed, having made it back to safety. Tupare, the spokesman, entered first, then stopped.

Minona came in behind Tupare, who stood frozen in the middle of the doorway. "Move, will you?" he grumbled. Then he peered past Tupare's shoulder.

Before them stood a pillar of salt, five feet tall. Draped about the top of the cone of salt was the amulet that Yasarian had worn around his neck. The amulet that he never removed, even on the rare occasions when he had to bathe.

Tupare picked up a walking stick from the corner and edged his way, trembling, to the pillar. He picked at the salt lightly, to see if it encased something.

The salt ran at the picking, pouring out over the floor of the tent, collapsing from the neatly formed cone and spilling out into an ever-widening circle on the floor. There was nothing but salt.

Pure, white, glistening salt . . .

The two spies turned and fled into the dark of night.

✣ ✣ ✣

As the festivities continued late into the night, Pierre again asked Isabelle to dance. Before he could finish the sentence, Conrad stepped in and explained that he had already taken the liberty of asking the princess for her next available dance.

Conrad gave an exaggerated bow and led her out onto the floor, where they fumbled through a dance to the minstrel's tune, laughing at themselves all the while.

"You taught me these dances years ago, and I confess I still do not remember them," Conrad said.

"I am just as bad," she said. Then she added, "Thank you for saving me back there with Pierre."

"I should advise you to dance with anyone you can tonight, Princess. It will keep him at arm's length."

"I don't know why he's behaving this way. He's never been this brash before."

"Men are full of strange notions, especially when anyone threatening is around."

"Do you mean, he is threatened by you?" She grinned. "That must make you feel good."

"No, I think he might be upset by your friend, this Sir . . . Jean?"

Isabelle stole a glance in Benariel's direction. He was watching them with a relaxed expression. It was just Jean. Nothing more. Nothing that would threaten anyone.

And yet . . . as they rounded the room with the other dancers, Isabelle looked over at Pierre, who was not looking at her for once. He was glaring across the room, staring at Jean with the kind of anger usually reserved for a hated rival.

"But why?" she asked, more to herself, but Conrad replied.

"Sometimes we see more than is there. Or sometimes we see what others do not yet realize is there," he said. "I hope this does not escalate."

"Escalate? How on earth could it escalate? I'm a member of the Church!"

"And a lovely one." He picked her up by her waist, like the other dancers, and twirled her around, putting her on the floor. They stopped in time for a moment, and then he continued. "Sometimes men disregard logic and boundaries, often pursuing the impossible because it *is* unobtainable. Be careful."

Then he winked in his friendly fashion and smiled at her. She tried to smile back, but her eyes flicked again to where Jean was standing. He was applauding the dance's end as Conrad escorted Isabelle back to him.

Then Conrad took his leave for a few moments, explaining in the German manner that he had to do what Nature intended. When he had gone, the two stood together in awkward silence for several moments.

"You seem to be enjoying yourself immensely," Jean finally said. "I'm glad for that."

"You don't seem to be having a bad time, either," she pointed out.

"I think your plan to show England the family's true intentions was very successful."

"Really?" She was hopeful at his words. "I hope so. Even Hugh de la Marche and his wife Elizabetta were here to pay homage. That is a good sign."

"It is. I believe you've worked a graceful truce. The Church has at least proven itself to be a sound broker for such awkward ancestral squabbles."

Silence returned between them as they watched the minstrels gather together to discuss the next dance. Isabelle's gaze wandered over the crowd, looking for Pierre Mauclerc. She found him slithering along the sidelines, making his way about the crowd and talking to a few gentlemen. She was safe for only a few moments. Isabelle wondered who could provide the next distraction from his advances.

Why not? she thought, and looked to Jean.

"Do you not dance?" she asked.

"Not really."

"You write, garden, philosophize, ride, hunt and forage, read an immense amount of literature, are good with a sword in battle—" She smiled at his surprised expression. "—so I'm told."

"Who told you this?"

"Robert. He said you fenced some on your last hunting expedition."

"Ah, yes. I'm flattered that he thinks I'm good. I'm modest at it, actually."

"But you don't dance."

"I haven't danced in . . ." He thought about it. "Well, in a long time."

Isabelle bit her lip. Pierre was inching nearer, eyes focused on her with that unnerving stare.

She heard Conrad's voice in her mind like a warning: *They are often pursuing the impossible just because it is unobtainable.*

"Would you dance with me, Sir Benariel?" she blurted out.

He looked down at her, surprised, and in his eyes she saw the very question that was shouting in her own mind: *What made her ask that?*

Isabelle felt foolish now. She had backed him into a corner. He couldn't very well say no; she was the princess of France. But then he smiled and extended his gloved hand to her.

She took it, and tingled warmly. She always felt flush whenever they were in proximity, but she tried once again to disregard it. She failed. In an instant, Pierre, Conrad, Alphonse, even the festival . . . all were instantly forgotten.

Jean didn't step on her toes. He didn't misstep, and for that matter, neither did she. The world around them melted into shadows and music and colors as they danced a couple's dance, a slow and stately four-beat step. Their hands were never to part, as per the dance's form.

He was staring at her, and she felt the curious ability of his eyes to reach in and examine her very soul. She wanted to hide how she felt, the way she hid her feelings from herself. But she could not do that and touch his gloved fingers while she stepped close to his body. She wasn't sure she could do anything but stare back into his timeless eyes.

She wanted to pretend she'd asked *Seigneur* Benariel to dance because she was nervous about Pierre. She wanted to believe that

Conrad's warning about unattainable things had more to do with Pierre and less to do with how she envisioned *Seigneur* Benariel and his life. Who He was and why He had chosen her, of all the threatened children in the world, on that fateful day. Why was he here now? Why did he humor her?

She wished for some inane chatter to break the moment that was forming between them, but nothing would come. The tiny tambourine that shook in the background sounded like the frail beat of her heart, shaken and jangling; her temples pounded with a sweet headache, and she forgot to blink. Jean turned her to the side as the music played on, and put his arm around her waist. Isabelle tried to swallow, but found a knot in her throat.

She held his other hand in front of her waist, and they stepped two forward, then three steps back. She looked at the ground and knew he was looking at the top of her head. She could feel his stare, and the crown of her head was warm with a fever as they turned.

She caught another glimpse of his eyes. They were so deep and filled with a gentle wonder. She moved to take his hand and looked down at the gloved fingers wrapped around her own.

The music slowed and then faded. Her breath was shallow. Benariel's hands lingered. They parted slowly. She gazed into his face to find him still looking at her with an expression of soft discovery.

Something was different about him tonight. Something about how he looked at her. She realized that for the first time he looked . . . warm. Alive.

"Why do you glow tonight?" she whispered.

"Because I am happy."

She studied his face. "And why are you happy?"

"Because tonight, this night, I am *inside*," he whispered as though it were a secret. "And so, tonight, are you."

The moment, gentle as a rose petal, was stirred from its dreaming as a voice behind Jean spoke. "May I speak with you?"

In an instant, the moment slipped away as Jean turned to see Sofia behind him.

"Yes, of course," Jean replied.

Then he turned to Isabelle and bowed. "I must take my leave of you now, Princess."

Isabelle smiled kindly, but it was formal. Rehearsed. Nothing out of the ordinary had just happened, she told herself, despite the tremble and shake of her heart. Nothing at all.

"Of course, *Seigneur* Benariel," she said, to her dismay sounding all too much like a princess.

As the two wandered away, Isabelle watched them with a strange pang in her chest, trying to understand what had just happened. She stood in the center of the dancers, unaware that a new song had started, unaware of the figures dancing around her in a circle, unaware that the entire celebration of Alphonse's knighthood was drawing to a close. She followed the figure of Jean until she could no longer see him.

Nothing at all, she told herself again, and wondered if lying was not a sin as long as one lied only to one's own heart.

⚜ ⚜ ⚜

As they left the courtyard for the meadows beyond, Sofia told Jean what had happened. They gathered at the tent's entrance with Neci alongside them.

"Are you sure it was an assassin of the Hungarian Master?" Neci asked, inspecting the tent.

"He was wearing this talisman." Sofia held it up in her fingers, and the other two looked closely at it.

Jean frowned. "This is the second incident."

"It will be the last," Sofia replied.

"How do you know?"

"I have sent a clear message by my actions here. The two scouts have fled the scene. They will return and tell the Old Master what happened. And this one," she said, nudging what was left of the crumbled pillar of salt with her foot, "he knew me. I remembered him from centuries past. The Master knows what we can do. He will not harm King Louis or his family again, knowing that we protect them."

Jean nodded.

"We need to dispose of this before it's discovered tomorrow morning," Neci said. "Quickly, help me with this trunk."

They worked long into the night.

When brothers agree, no fortress is so strong as their common life.

Antisthenes (c. 444–371 B.C.)

20

Isabelle made her way down new castle stairs to a new Great Room. She yawned as she put her hand to the strange oak door and pushed it open. The Castle at Angers was similar to all castles in design: one great tower that the royal family occupied, located in the most guarded section of the keep.

But it was different in its detail. Right turns instead of lefts, uneven cobblestones in places her feet were not used to stepping, doors that gave splinters when rubbed in the usual ways. And inside the Great Room, there was no window seat, like at the *palais* in Paris. Isabelle walked in and sat at her usual spot at the great breakfast table.

No one else was here with her. The festivities of the night before had gone on a very long time. But discipline had taught her body to be up at dawn, despite any lack of sleep. She'd had plenty of experience with sleeplessness and early mornings in her past, from reading good books or worrying over unworthy suitors. It made her chuckle, sitting alone in the Great Room, looking at the morning servants' preparations and all the empty seats.

Footsteps approaching in the hall made Isabelle turn in time to see Robert walk through the low doorway. He grazed his head upon the beam of the door frame.

"Ow!"

Isabelle laughed.

Robert rubbed at his scalp. "Great castle, Louis. Wonderful fortifications. Just let the taller enemies knock themselves silly against your door frames!"

"What are you doing up so early, Enemy of the State?" Isabelle asked, turning and grabbing a piece of bread.

"What do you mean *early*? It's well past working time where I'm from."

"Oh, really? And where is that, exactly? I forget again."

Robert stared at Isabelle as he dropped into his chair. "I'm from Artois, Princess." He played along.

"Really, is it nice there? I've never been."

"Green as emeralds and full of the setting sun at dusk." Robert cast his hand out in a picturesque pose. "And the women!"

"*What* of the women?"

"Oh, such coy, delicate morsels as ever a man laid eyes on. Or other things. But nothing you need know of."

"I gathered that from a lack of invitation."

Robert staggered back, off his bench, across the room, fainting against the wall. "I think I've had an arrow pierce my heart."

Isabelle couldn't help but laugh at his antics, though she was trying to be stoic. "I'm surprised an arrow could strike so small a target."

Robert opened his eyes, and from his place on the floor across the room he said gently, "Do you know what I was doing early this morning while even you were sleeping?"

"Something uncouth?" Isabelle took a sip of water.

"I was making a peace treaty." Robert rose, half crawling like a man wounded, over to her table.

"What do you mean?"

Robert crawled a bit over the table now, getting near Isabelle's face. "You see, I hurt someone very close to me when I left for Angers. I left abruptly, despite her best wishes. I didn't put my faith in her as she had put her faith in me."

Isabelle wanted to look away. It was hard to face his eyes; they were full of honesty, and just behind that truth was a dark sadness.

Robert stretched another inch closer. "So this morning, I was busy making a peace treaty. Between the County of Artois," he pointed first to himself and then her, "and the County of Isabelle."

"Robert, you need no written words or—"

"I know." He smiled and sat back. "Which is why I brought something in common currency. Our very favorite."

What is he talking about? Common currency and all this formality guising his apology . . . Then Isabelle caught a whiff of a familiar scent, and her eyes grew wide. "You didn't!"

Robert grinned as three serving women entered the room carrying plates filled with steaming pancakes.

"Lemon pancakes!" he said.

"Just like when we were children!" Isabelle threw her arms around her brother and kissed his cheek.

After she pulled back he was serious. "Let's eat all we can before the others wake up."

"Precisely my thoughts," she confided to him.

They ate well that morning.

✣ ✣ ✣

Pierre Mauclerc burst into the sitting room at the *château* of Hugh de la Marche just as the lord was sitting down for afternoon meal. At forty-two years de la Marche was a stout man, bearded and gray, with persistent stomach problems. His afternoon meal was no longer the pleasant diversion it had once been, and the only thing he liked less was to be interrupted.

"I just heard King Louis say the most atrocious things about you," Pierre said.

Hugh put down his spoon and frowned. Only a few days ago, he had been satisfied with the show of authority and generosity from King Louis, who had publicly offered to give him back a large parcel of land in exchange for his true homage. The land was plenty for Hugh; it was the land belonging to his father. He had no other real motivation for war.

It had even curtailed Elizabetta's hounding. The gesture had miraculously been enough to keep her from complaining to Hugh after the festivities.

"What did he say?" Hugh asked, his stomach already twitching at the thought of new problems.

"He called you a coward!" Pierre said. "He also said that you were easily bribed into submission and that he intends to keep you chained on a leash like a faithful dog."

Mauclerc was determined to get even with that bride-stealing stranger, Jean Adaret Benariel. He'd devised a way to do that, but it required feeding the fire at de la Marche's hearth first.

"How did you hear this?"

"I was at court with Princess Isabelle. I overheard her speaking with Louis."

"You are in the princess' favor?" Hugh asked, surprised.

"*Oui*, we are quite close. But I feel closer still to you. Which is why you must tell Henry of England to march on Louis. Take what is yours by right of birth. Whatever our problems with Henry, no king of England would treat his subjects as bitterly as Louis has treated us. Louis doesn't deserve to hold the position; he never has. He's proven ineffective for years now. Henry is the wiser king."

Hugh was pacing now, too. "You want me to cause trouble when I have no cause to do so. I have been given back my lands."

"Then you are the coward he claims?"

"I didn't say that!" Hugh's thundering anger shook the wine in his goblet. His fist slammed down on the table.

"Sooner or later it is going to happen. You can either be with

Henry when he marches, or you can be against Henry when he claims victory. I *trust* you, Hugh. I trust you even with my own claims."

"What claims?" Hugh asked.

"Princess Isabelle. I don't want her to come to harm."

"I don't understand. She's a royal—and a member of Louis' family. What do you care if—"

"I want her," Pierre interrupted. "I want her from this war. That's why I've come to you. As your friend. That's why I agreed to help you. Gave you money for it. I knew you would not harm her if you took Louis at Angers."

"I don't understand, I guess."

Pierre stopped walking and looked at Hugh. "I want Isabelle as compensation, for helping fund this campaign. I want her delivered to me as a prisoner of war."

"*That's* what you want?" Hugh asked.

"Yes. We're . . . close. I don't want to see her hurt. She will be grateful for my kindness when all is said and done. You see, I believe she loves me."

"Very kind of you to take mercy on her when she comes from such a terrible family."

"Then you'll march with England? You'll talk with Henry?"

Hugh considered for a moment. "First, I will send an emissary to King Louis."

"What?"

"I want to make sure what you heard was not hearsay. You know how these things can be. The sooth whispers inaccurately and all."

Pierre clenched the back of the chair tightly but kept his wits about him. "Whom do you plan to send?"

"My brother-in-law Roger is visiting." Hugh picked up a large bell and rang it. A moment later a younger man entered the room, with sandy-blond hair.

"Roger, meet Pierre Mauclerc, emissary of the Templars," Hugh said.

They shook hands. Pierre stepped back again.

"Roger, I want to entrust you with an important duty, one I think would make your sister very proud." Hugh walked over to the boy, who shot a nervous glance to Pierre.

"I can do you a service, *monsieur*? You know I would be honored."

"King Louis apparently has said some rather unfortunate things. I want you to go to his court and inquire about them on my behalf."

The boy seemed at a loss for the right words. "Will this earn my knighthood in your service, *Monsieur* Hugh?" he asked. It made Hugh laugh.

"Oh, I suppose. If you do it well enough. We can talk of your knighting when you return."

Roger seemed to buck up at this news. The errand probably didn't seem so dreary if he got something out of his effort, Pierre assumed. Going into the tiger's lair was obviously not something he wanted to do. Pierre understood the feeling: It wasn't something Pierre wanted him to do, either.

Roger bowed low before each man, and then left the room.

"Nice boy, isn't he?" Hugh asked.

Pierre smiled. "Lovely little lad." But he thought to himself, *It's a shame what will have to happen now.*

Pierre allowed a smile as he left Hugh's castle. The baron had always been a proud man, often more concerned with how he was seen than who he was or what he did. His cooperation required only the right nudge and the right words. Pierre's thoughts turned again to Isabelle, and then to the bride-stealing stranger, Benariel. He would deal with them both soon enough.

In the meantime, all that remained was to ensure that Hugh's fire stayed well and truly fed. The Church was growing weary of administrating plots of land for a monarchy with no interest in leaving the land with them. All they would receive for Louis' recent generosity was a pittance bookkeeping fee. De la Marche's land was worth much more than that, and the bishops were already balking. These administrative difficulties were just a few of the problems the Templars were created to help solve, after all. A small talk with the Bishops of Angers and Hugh would learn how little the king's word was worth.

✤ ✤ ✤

Isabelle finished her morning prayers in the family chapel and stood up from the altar. This morning, she had so much to be thankful for. The victory of diplomacy that her brother and mother had won, Jean's companionship as a beloved friend, the safe journey of Conrad from Germany, and for yesterday . . . Robert's sweet gesture of apology. As she turned from the altar, she saw Bishop Arnaud and Bishop Louvel enter. Isabelle smiled.

"Your Graces." Isabelle curtsied low.

"Princess Isabelle, we have just finished our negotiations and are pleased to present you with some land for your splendid convent."

Isabelle, shocked to her core, stared dumbfounded.

"This is what you wanted, isn't it?" Arnaud looked concerned at her reaction.

Isabelle tried to collect her senses. "You—" She cleared her throat. "You have done this great honor for my dream?"

"Why yes, child," Louvel replied. "It was a simple effort on our part."

Isabelle knelt and kissed the ring of Bishop Arnaud and then followed with Bishop Louvel. She could utter no more words. She looked up at them, grateful tears in her eyes.

"Go, child," Arnaud said gently. "We see your pleasure."

Isabelle smiled then, and stood, curtseying once again before leaving the chapel. On her way out the door, she silently thanked the Lord.

✤ ✤ ✤

Later, outside the chapel, Bishop Louvel and Bishop Arnaud waited as Pierre returned with a letter of transfer that would deed Templar land to Princess Isabelle.

"I have written it all out for you," Pierre said. "I'm afraid it's a ridiculously small plot of land. You know the place, I'm sure. Acreage Fifty-seven B, far out from any settlements and next to a lake that mosquitoes love. Now, all you have to do is sign here." Pierre held out the parchment.

"You're such a nice man, Pierre. First you offer to administrate that ridiculous de la Marche mess for us, and now you're giving Isabelle some land anonymously from the Templars."

"Well, what I do I do from the heart, your Grace." Pierre folded his hands over his doublet. "And with deepest love."

"Astonishing. And you say this land is from your own humble commission in service to your Lord?" Louvel asked.

"What is land before love?"

"I will sign this and delay you no further. We shall not speak of your deed to another soul as you requested." Arnaud signed the letter and handed it to Pierre, who bowed and then left at once.

Outside the door of Hugh de la Marche's Angers estate, Pierre Mauclerc held the letter from Bishop Arnaud in his hand. It was the first time he'd ever touched something so powerful. The information in this letter would allow him to change the world.

It was not Pierre Mauclerc's Templar land that was represented on this paper, but some of Hugh de la Marche's family lands taken from plot Fifty-seven B. A little pinching and pulling of acreage; a little fibbing in the eyes of the Lord so as to mask the location; and the landmarks removed and obscured made the details disappear from the eyes of the bishops as they signed a chunk of Hugh's family plot away to the whim of a royal family member. Isabelle's convent would spark the beginning of a great war, a war that Pierre would rescue her from. There would be no need for a convent then.

After folding the letter and hiding it safely inside his shirt, Pierre announced himself and was admitted inside the great estate. Once in the foyer, he could hear distressed voices coming from the Great Room. Pierre made his way to the voices and found Edgar, the emissary from England, talking with Hugh de la Marche. They paused as Pierre entered.

"Greetings, *Monsieurs*."

"*Monsieur* Mauclerc." Edgar bowed. "It is good to see you again."

"Again?" Hugh asked.

"*Seigneur* Edgar told me he would be coming to see you in person if you were not persuaded to ready your troops," Pierre explained.

Hugh de la Marche sat in his receiving *chaise*, something of a cross between a bed and a throne. "It isn't that I have revoked my decision," he said. "I just don't think now is a good time. I have just been given land by King Louis."

"So I heard," Edgar replied. "We're wondering exactly where your loyalties stand."

Before Hugh could respond, a shriek echoed through the *château*. Then, Elizabetta ran into the room, tears streaming down her face, holding a bloody sack.

Pierre found himself strangely fascinated by the scene playing out before him, knowing as he did what she was going to say.

Elizabetta held out the sack in her hands with trembling fingers. "Rog—Rog—" She was still trying to say the name when the sack fell from her fingers. A severed head spilled out onto the floor.

Roger's head, Pierre knew.

Elizabetta tore at the bloody sack. "It's royal—guard's—This is . . . *Louis!*" she screamed and fell to the floor, weeping bitterly. "He killed my *brother!*"

As Hugh knelt down next to the severed and bloody head, Pierre looked up at Edgar. The English emissary regarded him with eyes silently requesting an answer.

It had been difficult to acquire a royal guardsman's bag without leaving any discernible trail of suspicion, but Pierre had managed it. He had also arranged the death of young Roger, on the road to the Castle of Angers, for a small fee. The job was now complete.

"It is a royal guardsman's bag," Hugh whispered, but it was the quiet before the storm. Pierre could see that Hugh was only inches from the edge of unreason. He knew the man could not handle one more piece of bad news, which made this the perfect moment.

"Hugh," he said. His voice, the quality of his tone, made everyone in the room turn and look at him. Even Elizabetta sat up, her face red with tears. "There is something else.

"The land that you recently placed in the care of the Church . . . I believe it was yesterday?" Pierre sighed. "It's come to the attention of my order that your land is no longer with the Church. It's with King Louis. His Majesty received *your* land from the Church today. It was all done to mislead you, and make you look like a fool. You can ask the Church for proof of the transaction, if you wish. Naturally, I thought you should know about it."

"You have never lied to me, Mauclerc. Why should I doubt your word in the face of this?" Hugh stood slowly, his eyes half-mad, as if a force of nature inhabited his hulking frame. Fingers closed around the curling short locks of Roger's lifeless head. He held the head out to the emissary of England. "You tell Henry of England to let fly his wrath. Tell him I await on the southern shore and that not just an army but the very Furies stand behind me."

The sinner sins against himself; the wrongdoer wrongs himself, becoming the worse by his own action.

Marcus Aurelius, *The Meditations* (A.D. 167)

21

Two weeks after the festivities, Louis entered the Great Room of Angers Castle and found Blanche and Isabelle reading with concern a letter that had arrived that morning from England.

Immediately, he knew something was wrong. "What is it?"

Blanche held the letter out for her son. "War," she said. "They demand we turn over Angers or they will take it from us by force."

"Written in English." Isabelle glared. "Insulting, derisive, and aggressive. They plan to march next month."

Robert entered then, followed by Jean Adaret Benariel. Louis handed his brother the letter, and the two men read it together.

"Do we return to Paris?" Robert asked. "Or . . . ?"

"We stay at Angers," Louis said. "We meet them with what force we have. They will not take our land. I reinforced this castle with this possibility in mind."

"How large an army do you expect he'll send?" Robert asked.

"He wouldn't bring all his forces to bear on France. He might be attacked from Scotland if he depleted too many of his resources," Louis replied.

"Unfortunately, our own forces are depleted here," Robert said. "Half our forces have been sent to peacekeep Raymond of Toulouse in the south of France, Louis."

"I know. But this castle will hold. That's why I put in all the work on reinforcements." He paced for a moment, then called to a guard at the door. "Bring me Pierre Mauclerc."

"Why?" Isabelle asked.

"As Robert said, most of my army is still in the south of France dealing with Raymond of Toulouse. I have depleted a good deal of my treasury putting in reinforcements here, and the rest of it on Alphonse's knighting ceremony. If I am to prepare for war, I want a financier at my side."

"But Pierre?" Robert asked.

"He is an emissary to the Knights Templar. Whatever we may think of Pierre, the Templars are a reputable and honest lending establishment."

"Money has never purchased righteousness," Jean said.

They all turned to him. It was the first time he'd spoken since entering the room.

"You're right," Louis said, wondering if his voice sounded as tired as he felt right now. "But it does buy swords. And wars are won by swords, not by righteousness."

"Perhaps," Jean said. "Perhaps not."

The others were unhappy with his decision, Louis could tell. But they didn't understand in the slightest way what this war could really do. They were too young to remember what war had done in the past. But Louis was old enough to remember his father's last commands as king, and his father's most tragic mistake.

War was not taken lightly, as he stood in the looming shadow of his dead father and remembered the past from which he was born.

King Louis VIII had died on the battlefield, leaving his tender family—his own son and heir—estranged and unprotected. He could have planned just a little more, finalized his decisions with one more master plan—even one more thought to safety and his family—and Louis and his mother would not have suffered at Montlheri.

He had only been eleven.

It was a day Louis had never forgotten, and the son of the great king had sworn he'd never let such a fatal mistake happen during his own reign.

The room had long since cleared out, but Robert walked in and stood quietly before Louis as the king looked out the window and considered events.

"Brother?" Louis asked.

Robert walked slowly. "I wish to stand present when you speak with Pierre Mauclerc."

"Why?"

"It is what I want."

Robert was curt, blunt, and said no more. Louis looked at him hard, trying to figure out the unspoken motivation of his brother, when their exchange was interrupted.

The door of the Great Room opened, and Charles came walking in. He was rushing. Robert turned to look at his younger brother.

"I came because we're going to war," Charles said.

"Yes, we are."

"Let me fight." The boy took a step forward. He was still somewhere between a man and a child, awkward but growing powerful of frame.

His older brothers regarded each other in a quick decision. Louis said, "*Non*, Charles."

"But you were fighting barons at my age! You were already commanding great armies!" Charles advanced. "You *must* let me go!"

"Your brother has decided. You're not ready yet," Robert said.

"How do you know?" Charles shouted. "When were you ever involved in any of it, Robert? Just stay out of it!"

"I won't have you speaking to your elders that way," Louis commanded. "I've made my decision. War isn't for angry youths, no matter how appropriate the station may seem."

"Louis, this is the one thing I have ever asked you for. Please!" Charles said. "I've been training my whole life for this! I practice swordplay out in the yard every day, unfailingly! I'm ready—more ready than either of you were when you went into battle!"

"You think you're ready?" Robert advanced on Charles. "You think you know what it is to kill a man? To drive a pickax through his temples, nailing his head to the ground while the soil runs thick with his blood? You know *nothing* of pain and suffering; you know *nothing* of battle and survival. You are a boy, and never forget your place!"

To Louis' surprise, Charles didn't flinch. He didn't cower, cringe, or even grow angry at Robert's rebuke. "I know more about survival than either of you could ever know," he said simply; then he turned and walked from the room.

Prince Charles was in one of the little back alleys in the inner keep of the castle walls. It was a much larger keep than the little *palais* of Paris, and that meant there was more here to explore. The prince came across a lame white cat taking shelter at the end of the alley. There was no outlet here, and no one around for as far as he could see.

No one to see the tears in Charles' eyes as he picked up a rock from the far end of the street.

The cat flinched, seeing him. Charles looked at the rock, thought about his brother's words, and then threw the rock as hard as he could at the cat at the end of the alley. The poor beast yowled in pain and tried to scamper away, but only managed to shuffle helplessly a few inches.

Charles picked up several more rocks, a few scattered bricks, and advanced on the cat. The poor beast had no way to escape his royal torturer.

It made Charles cry, made him feel positively horrible. Tears stained his cheeks while his nose turned red. In his mind he could hear Robert's words.

You think you know what it is to kill a man?

. . . nailing his head to the ground while the soil runs thick with his blood?

You know nothing of pain and suffering!

When Charles was about to deliver the *coup de grâce*, he looked up at the end of the street. He froze, his arm heavy with the brick in his hand, but unable to move.

Jean Adaret Benariel was standing at the far end of the alley, staring at him. How long he had been there, watching, Charles didn't know, but the man must have been watching him for some time. He sniffed angrily and pretended he didn't care. He started to pull back again when the man spoke.

"Why are you throwing rocks at that cat?" Jean asked, approaching. His tone was stern.

"It's going to die anyway. Might as well help it along." Although his eyes were red, his cheeks were soaking wet, and his nose was completely stuffed up, Charles was completely stone-faced.

"It wouldn't die, if you cared about it."

This statement, so simple an idea, made Charles snort. "It's crippled. Caring about it won't make it less crippled."

"Sometimes a very crippled creature can walk straight again, if someone would only stop to care about it."

Charles had raised the large brick up over his head to smash it down on the cat. "Well, this one's about dead."

Then he felt a powerful, bare hand grab his wrist. It pinched down so tightly that Charles cried out in pain and dropped the stone, which landed just inches from the cat's body. The small mass of fur and blood didn't even bother to move.

Charles squirmed and fell to the ground in pain. "Let go!"

Much to his surprise, the fist released him. He looked up to see Jean Adaret Benariel standing directly over him. "If you take care of something, no matter how crippled, it will *always* get better." Jean's tone was cold, almost dangerous.

"I don't care! Hurting it made *me* feel better. No one cares about how I feel inside. They all ignore me—hate me!" At this outburst, Charles felt a great release of hatred and anger; twins that had festered inside his rib cage for years.

Then the young prince reached out and mockingly petted the bloody heap of fur. He would show this man that "loving" something wouldn't do it any good. The little cat was not breathing, was not moving; it did not even react to his touch.

"Pretty kitten, pretty thing. I so love you," he mocked.

Then the dead cat moved and looked up lovingly at Charles.

The young prince bolted upright, his eyes so wide they nearly popped from their sockets. The cat's fur coat was once again shining and luxurious, its eyes big pools of affection that glittered a bright gold. The little animal sat up and walked—perfectly—over to Charles and rubbed fondly against his legs. It did not question or accuse him. It loved him with the same perfect and unwavering love that it would have given had he not picked up the first stone.

Charles grabbed the kitten, broke down, and sobbed, burying his face into its clean fur with utter shame and humility. "I'm sorry," he sobbed. "I'm sorry, I'm sorry, I'm sorry . . ."

When he looked up again, the man was gone.

✧   ✧   ✧

Isabelle had waited all day for the chance to speak privately to Louis, only to hesitate when the room was clear. It had been a very long time since it was just Louis and her alone together, anywhere. The silence was uncomfortable. She wanted to talk to him about her idea for a convent, but had no idea how he would take it, especially in light of what were arguably more pressing concerns. There was a haze of issues swarming about him: England, war, Pierre, Templars, money, Hugh de la Marche . . .

Still, Jean's words were ever present in her mind, reminding her that the idea would only work as long as she had ultimate faith in it. So finally, she spoke up.

"I realize that this isn't the best of times to bring this up, but my conscience demands that I speak with you." She took a deep breath, then said, "I have come across the one thing I truly wish to devote my time to."

She waited for him to respond, waited for him to tell her that this probably wasn't the best time, to come back later or—

"What is your idea?" he asked.

"More than anything else, I want to found a convent. A home for women who have no home, where they can perform public works and do honest labor with their hands."

"Why?" he asked, his blue eyes heavy with the weight of the world.

"Because I want to do something good for the people."

"That's it? In the midst of war preparations, you want me to think about the cost of building a convent so you can *do some good?*"

"I didn't ask you to fund it. And yes, that is why I want to build a convent. I have no ulterior motives."

"What's that supposed to mean?"

"You tell me: You seem to think my reasons are not sound. I can only assume you think I'm doing this for less-than-pious reasons."

"Isabelle, I don't think you're scheming. That's not it at all." Louis stood and strode to the window, but he didn't look out. He seemed only to need distance. "I'm not going to put an official edict or money from the treasury out for a whim. To just 'do good.' I need a better answer than that. If you can provide me one, then I will consider your offer."

"You want my reasons; be prepared to hear them then." Her voice was low at first. "Why would I, the great Isabelle of France, sister of the king, want to build a humble convent?

"Because I gave one woman a new life, and something to live for, in just one minute of my time. If I could do that in one minute, just think of what I could do for women over the course of my entire life.

"I have watched my entire family, rulers of the people, work day in and day out, and not *one* of you has picked a person up from the street and given them something to live for. But I have. At first, I started small, with just one person, creating for her a new world, with only *one simple thought* for her future. That is what I will dedicate my life to, Brother. With or without your blessing. With or without your help."

Isabelle made her way out into the courtyard, paying no attention to where she was going. Everything seemed to be going against her intentions today. Bad enough that there was war coming with England; worse still that Pierre Mauclerc had been drawn into the affair. She hated Pierre. As a member of the Church, she was not supposed to hate anyone, but she couldn't find another word more suiting for the way he made the hair on her arms stand up whenever he was in her presence.

"Forgive me for hating him, Lord, but I do," she murmured. Then she looked up to see Charles walking to the tower courtyard. He was red-faced, his eyes puffy and swollen almost shut, as if he'd been crying.

"Charles?" she asked. But the boy didn't stop. He kept walking past her, trying to hide his face as he went by. He seemed to hiccup a sob as he passed, and then she was staring after him until he walked into the tower and out of sight.

She looked down as something soft began rubbing against her legs. It was an adorable little white cat with a beautiful fur coat and the most golden eyes she'd ever seen. The eyes were ringed with black fur, and it made them pop out almost supernaturally. It seemed happy, but . . . odd.

Then the cat trotted into the family tower, as if looking for someone else to love. Isabelle stared, at a loss.

"Hello, Princess." The voice behind her made her turn.

Jean Adaret Benariel was adjusting a glove, looking relaxed and in reasonable spirits, despite the latest news.

"Hello," she said, and pointed to the doorway. "By any chance, do you know what is the matter with Charles?"

"Why?"

"Well, he was . . . crying. I've never seen him cry." She realized she'd never seen the boy anything but angry before today.

Bells were beginning to ring from the little chapel at the top of one of the towers in Angers Castle, announcing midday meal. She looked to see Jean walking inside the tower too. *He knows more than he says*, she decided. *But when does he not?*

✦　✦　✦

The next day, Pierre Mauclerc arrived at the Castle of Angers and stood in the Great Hall before Louis, who explained the situation with England. Pierre listened, nodded intently, then said, "Truly terrible, Your Majesty. I would have expected England and France to be like siblings. There is so much between you that you share."

"I take it you are referring to the marriages between the king of England and the daughters of Toulouse," Louis replied. "We had hoped to make England family that way, yes. But it didn't quite turn out."

"A shame," Pierre replied. Then, "What can the Knights do for Your Majesty?"

"I would like to take out a loan in order to prepare for war."

Pierre's eyes grew wide. "This is your first loan from the Templars. Your Majesty, honestly, I am quite surprised."

Louis made sure the disdain in his voice was unmistakable. "As am I."

"We will need some sort of collateral," Pierre said casually, looking around the room. The majority of the royal family was present, with Isabelle reading at her customary spot by the window. Pierre looked at her and smiled. She buried her nose in her book.

Louis gestured, and a guard entered with a golden box. "I believe this will suffice," Louis said. The guard walked up to Pierre Mauclerc and opened the golden box. Inside, on a velvet pillow, was the Crown of Thorns.

Pierre found he could not breathe. He went to touch the sacred item and stopped himself quickly, lest he look overwrought with greed.

The pain of parting with his most favored and lovely artifact was apparent on Louis' face. Jean, who stood behind the dais, walked out of the Great Room without saying a word. Louis thought that Isabelle wanted to run after him, but she remained in her seat.

Pierre looked up at Louis with a wide, businesslike smile and said, "I do believe this will suffice. How much does His Majesty have in mind?"

The transaction began.

Once the meeting was over in the Great Room, Isabelle ran out of the hall and into the sunshine. She had to find Jean, but had no idea where to look. She saw no trace of him at the inner keep and made her way to the lower level of the castle, near the stables and the well.

A black horse bolted out of the stable, smashing furiously against the wooden door and bolting across the lower yard at the behest of its rider. Isabelle lurched back to avoid being trampled. As the steed passed, she swore she heard it growling.

That was Jean.

She could sense his fury even at this distance. Running to the stable, she called out for a horse. Within a few moments, Isabelle was in hot pursuit. The wild grasses smashed against her horse's legs and whipped below them. She nudged the beast into a gallop, and they raced over the land toward the black horse pounding ahead of them.

Jean was heading for a plateau in the distance, but Isabelle spied an easier way to reach the same spot he seemed to be aiming for and nudged her horse in the opposite direction. She would meet him at the summit.

It was going to be close, but she could still stop him and . . . and what? She just wanted to know what was happening. Why was he angry? With sheer willpower, she urged her mount up the hill. The poor beast was already exhausted, but she wouldn't stop, wouldn't let up, until she got an answer.

At the crest of the hill, her horse nearly collided with Jean's beast. The black mount neighed loudly and reared up. Jean's eyes were as wild as his mount's. He held steady as the beast beneath him reared back.

Isabelle's horse was also frightened. She held on tightly.

"What do you want?" Jean asked when the horses had calmed.

"Jean, what is the matter?"

"Wha—?" he almost laughed. "What is the *matter*? Do you know what the Crown of Thorns *is*? Do you know what it means and what it stands for? Your brother has just *bartered* the Crown of God for money! Not just any riches, but treasure enough to fund a war. That crown is the very symbol of peace given to mankind for eternity!" Jean shouted. "It represents the pain and suffering of one man who died to prove we must not kill one another!"

"I know," she said quietly, but her words could not soothe his anger.

"How can you possibly know?"

"Because of your distress," she replied.

"Yet you did nothing!"

"What would you have me do? Let the English devour our lands? King Henry will kill all that we love; he would rob us of every last object, including our Crown of Thorns. Do you want such a precious relic in the hands of a man like that? If I'd intervened, had I even a chance of changing the outcome of that meeting, then there would be no help from the Templars and our kingdom would fall to the English. All that we love—all that we are—would be corpses and ash."

"You put your trust in men who cannot be trusted. The Templars are thieves. They have robbed the very House of God—the sacred Temple of Solomon itself. Don't you understand? You have asked the lion to protect you from the jackal!"

"I *do* understand, and you're right. I did nothing. But it is my brother who sold the Crown of Thorns, not me. Why do you raise your voice at me?"

This slowed his fire, and he sat back in the saddle. "I'm sorry I raised my voice. I rode from the castle so that my anger would not fall on the innocent." He was softer now, but his words still burned with an unrelinquished anger. "I am trying to understand why your brother, a pious and wise man, would do such a thing."

"War breeds strange circumstances," she replied. "I can assure you that my brother is in absolute remorse over his decision to part with the Crown."

"You, your family—you all abhor Pierre Mauclerc, and yet you let him . . . touch it. He left with the Crown. I would like to understand how you could let that happen, because my heart tells me it was wrong. If something is wrong, then I don't do it."

"It *was* wrong, on one level. But it will save our people from pain and suffering. The greater good must be weighed against this.

"I like to think I know my brother's heart. Even though he has not shared his thoughts with me in years, I still believe he is the protector of our people. This money will allow him to fight the good fight against Henry, will let him wage war the honorable way—the way that achieves fewest casualties. He made this great personal sacrifice so that hundreds of men may live in a month's time. It's his way."

She stared at Jean, biting back her own anger at defending the brother who had recently questioned her dream. He was looking at his hands, as if he could not look up, frozen with pain. She wondered why this touched him so deeply, more deeply than even she was grieved by it. He seemed personally wounded by its loss somehow. All she could hope was that her explanation would suffice.

"The sun is setting behind you," he finally said. "Will you ride with me?"

Their gaze met, and she realized that the heat of his anger had passed, and a strange residual sadness remained. She remembered the words in Ephesians, which would later make their way to The Rule of St. Benedict: Do not let the sun go down on your anger.

"Of course I will," she replied. They turned their horses and rode silently into the setting sun.

✣   ✣   ✣

The sky was turning from blue to sunset orange as Isabelle and Jean returned from their ride. They were walking up into the courtyard when they passed Princess Joan going out into *le jardin*. Her eyes were wet with tears and her nose red.

"What is the matter?" Isabelle asked.

"They have decided that we must leave tomorrow." Joan sniffed.

"We?"

"The spindle side, we must pack up our belongings and head to the *Cité* where it is safe. It's not safe for the women, Robert said. And Louis agreed. They'll stay here at Angers and defend against the English."

"Oh." Isabelle felt very sorry for Joan. She was a good woman, and she loved Alphonse so much.

"It will be all right," she assured Joan. Joan only nodded and couldn't speak. A hot tear rolled off the crest of her cheek as she kept going past Isabelle. Isabelle watched her run out into the garden, remembering too well needing air herself only recently.

At dinner, the family was quiet, idle hands barely touching their food. Isabelle felt very upset about the war, but she reassured herself with the knowledge that Louis had never lost such an engagement before, and would not start now. She distracted herself by the thought of going back to Paris. She would be able to consult with *Frère* Bacon and the others about the convent. And Bishop Maurice would have ideas as well. She could actually get most of the work done herself, maybe even start it before her brothers returned.

It would be something productive to do, to while away the days while the men . . .

Might be dying down here.

She swallowed dry bread and sat quietly, fully acknowledging that this might be the last dinner with the entire family for several months.

No one spoke. Youngest brother Charles was present, for the first time ever it seemed, and the white cat Isabelle had seen earlier was now perched on the boy's lap, quietly purring and seemingly in love with him. Charles complacently let it relax on his lap. She could not understand how such a sweet cat could stand someone like Charles, but said nothing about it.

When dinner was over, Isabelle made her way up the great winding staircase to add a postscript to her letter. She would let Maurice know she was heading back to the *Cité* so that he could expect a visit in person.

She stopped at the landing that led to the Gentlemen's Quarters. Jean was standing in the hallway, staring out a window at the countryside. He noticed Isabelle.

"Are you going with them?" she asked. It was a simple question that held many more. Are you going into *battle?* She couldn't bring herself to say the word. It seemed too dangerous, too full of the possibility of demise.

"Yes."

"We're leaving in the morning," she replied. He probably knew that. Why did she feel the need to tell him?

"Have a safe journey."

The silence was unwanted, but words wouldn't come for either of them. Isabelle wanted to say that everything would be all right; that her brothers were capable fighters and tacticians; that Robert was the one most fit for war, and that he would save them all.

Instead, she stood there groping for words that sounded naïve and ridiculous.

"Thank you. We will be safe," she said.

She looked at his face and could see there that he knew all the words that would not come to her. He knew and understood her feelings. Even the ones she couldn't show even to herself.

Then he turned and walked into his room, closing the door behind him. Isabelle stared at the door to Jean's quarters for some time, wondering if what he felt was the same strange feeling she had for him. There was something powerful about Jean Adaret Benariel. He didn't seem to need those feelings. He certainly seemed to shrug off consolation. Sometimes he was like a lion: powerful, majestic, and commanding. Especially those times when he was staring into the world beyond a window. A world she could never know or see.

Isabelle went up to her room to pack. On her way, she ran into Charles, who was holding the white cat in his arms. The cat purred and licked his hand. Isabelle couldn't help but comment.

"I see you found a friend here." She smiled.

He looked at her, first ashamed, and then his face softened. "Isabelle, I'm sorry we never knew our father."

It made her heart sink, and yet somehow, she understood everything that made Charles so angry in that one sentence. Only, he didn't seem angry anymore. He just seemed . . .

The cat purred louder and mewed a little bit. It was now staring boldly at Isabelle.

"Me too," she finally said. "Do you have a name for your kitten?"

"His name is Louis," Charles replied, and petted him with such affection it shocked Isabelle. Then the boy walked to his room and shut the door.

✤ ✤ ✤

Elizabetta de la Marche stood outside de la Marche *Château*, her hand up to her brow to fight off the glaring sun. She was staring at her husband's horse's ass. Behind her, the stone structure with its looming tower was a powerful symbol as she shook her fist, screaming, "You're not going to war! You do no good by me! You leave me here as if I were a nun! I won't have it! I am a woman and I need love!"

Norea knew he was too far away to hear her, and even if he cared, he did not turn around. Elizabetta slammed the *château* door shut.

"Well, you deserve it." She was still carrying on as she marched into the front parlor. "You are swine! I should not even be with you. I am fit for a king!"

Norea hurried to complete the last line of her missive to Blanche.

"Norea!" Elizabetta called. "Norea, come at once, we're packing to leave!"

When no immediate response came from her serving woman, Elizabetta opened a side door and found Norea writing something on parchment. Norea looked up fearfully.

"What is this?" Elizabetta snatched the paper and looked at it, paling when she saw to whom the note was addressed.

"Queen Blanche?" she said. "You spy!"

Norea slowly stood and looked around the room for a means of escape. She would have just enough time. Elizabetta would now call for the guards. She could drop out the window if necessary and make it to the stables. Anything was better than discovery—and not just of her role as spy—but discovery of what power lay within her if she were touched or provoked. For the memory of persecution was in her very blood.

The sting of the puncture was severe in her side. Sucking in a wet breath as she turned, Norea saw the bloody dagger in her mistress' hands.

"Guards!" Elizabetta called out. "Come at once!"

Norea grew weak in the knees. She collapsed on the floor in front of Elizabetta. She had underestimated the woman. Not just a schemer and manipulator, but a willing combatant eager for blood.

I should tell Jean . . . The floor came rushing up and the world darkened.

'Tis man's to fight,
but Heaven's to give success.

Homer, the *Iliad* (ninth century B.C.)

22

15, *juillet, l'an de notre Seigneur* 1242

The sky opened, and the rain turned the kingdom to mud. It filled the skies with gray and purple clouds, laced with black intent, and fell upon the soldiers in Louis' army with relentless fervor, with terrible power and a pernicious glee. The soldiers were wet and hungry, chilled to their bones as their horses slogged through fields of mud. Their feet sloshed through puddles and trenches; cold, wet toes slammed against the insides of boots. Their breath hung before them like dragon's breath, withering in the wet, stale air.

It had rained for three straight days before the English were finally seen across the Loire River. The only thing more plentiful than raindrops were the English soldiers. They came down the hills like rain, gathering into rivers and pouring over the valleys, leaving only destruction in their path.

Now, gathered on the other side of the swollen river, they covered the hillside with knights on horses and spearmen. Henry's army was vast, the sheer force of arms arrayed against the French terrifying.

Jean Adaret Benariel was watching the English army and their banners from the open catwalk of Angers Castle. He felt a pair of eyes gazing at him and looked over to see Sofia standing in the doorway of one of the castle's rounded turrets. She would not step out into the rain. Jean walked over and as he came close, realized she was upset.

285

He stepped into the dry room of the turret, and as his eyes adjusted to the light, realized Neci was here too. He nodded at her.

"Blanche has not heard from Norea. She suspects foul play," Sofia said.

"But she always writes once a week," Neci replied.

"I know, but with everything escalating now, there is a chance she may have been captured, or discovered, or . . ."

None of the three said the possibility that she might be dead, but all three realized it was there.

Neci spoke up. "We should go and see."

"I can't leave Louis here by himself," Sofia replied.

"Of course you can." Jean made them both stop. "Louis is a fit king. He's no longer a boy. Norea might be dying. If you don't find out, we may lose her. You can't risk that."

Sofia paced. "He is my charge; I can't just leave him when he's going into war."

"I will be here."

Sofia stared at Jean, and in his face she finally allowed herself to see the truth; that Jean was just as capable, perhaps more capable, than either Sister in this capacity. They said nothing about the moment, but both realized he'd just proven his point from earlier. Jean needed to be in the world of men. This one moment might very well be why he was here in the first place.

"Go for Norea," he said to them both.

The English ranks outnumbered the French legions at least five to one. They were coming for Angers, for Poitou, for southwestern France, the coastal plains; and they were coming for Louis—especially Hugh de la Marche, who walked with English troops across the plains and fields of his homeland, where he had once played as a young boy and later governed as a baron. He'd been publicly humiliated by Louis, made to look the fool. That would now change.

On the fields where he once played pretend games of knights on horseback, fighting dragons for valor and true love, he would now take back his lands and show his peers that he was not a man to be trifled with.

King Henry had come to France, though as was tradition, he led from the rear of his army. Henry had ambitions that matched Hugh de la Marche's own, and had been openly courting the French barons along the coast for the past five years, enticing them with wine, women, and the finest entertainment in the Western world.

As with Hugh, land was the key. Henry wanted his coastal lands back, the lands snatched from his family in the time of Richard the Lionheart. They were due to Henry, by right of marriage, and yet they were kept in the hands of the brat-king, Louis. Henry wanted the barons to rise up in revolt and take the countryside back.

When Hugh de la Marche had told him that the south of France was a perfect place for discord, Henry of England had planted the seeds of rebellion in Raymond of Toulouse. Blanche's own favorite cousin would turn against the Crown and draw half of France's army to the south. A civil war had already been raging in the south for the better part of a year. It was easy to escalate with the funds and resources Henry provided for the southern lord, Raymond.

The king of England was then free to launch a full-scale assault on France—a kingdom with only half an army. It would be an effortless battle for the coastal lands.

Within a few days of the English landing, the first troops sent by Louis had arrived, and the war had begun. The French were always impressive when their backs were to the wall. They smelled death this time, and Hugh felt it wouldn't be too long before England had them firmly in their grasp.

Now, in the distance, on the other side of the Loire, the Castle of

Angers, rightful property of the king of England, stood tall against the clouds. Inside the castle, Louis was governing the French forces. Hugh knew the child would not dare stick himself into the cold rain and come out to fight like a man. Louis was not a large or forceful man. Unlike Hugh, who was brown haired and built like an ox with twice the fur, Louis was a slender blond with a curly-haired, petite manner.

Soon, it would be all over for Louis.

King Henry met with Hugh that night, in the rear of the English camp. Henry had a body that defined a king. He was not overly large, like Hugh, nor petite in build. He was sinewy and rugged, with a face full of hair. He wore the crown with dignity and a deceiving sense of arrogance.

The tent was well appointed, with lavish supplies for a king so far from his homeland. The colors were regal and bright, and pillows covered most of the dry interior. Henry stood alone, his retainers dispatched to allow him a moment's privacy with Hugh. The king held a flagon of wine out for Hugh as he entered.

"Sir Hugh, I do believe that we will take the French tomorrow. They are vastly outnumbered, and Louis shows cowardice. I have not seen him venture out of the castle."

Hugh agreed. "He is a frail boy, Your Majesty. It won't be long."

Henry nodded, but hesitated before continuing. "You don't suppose they have any surprises, do you? I was told Louis has spent a good deal of time in the castle, restoring it."

"No, Your Majesty, as I own lands in blessed England, I swear by my own estates that I have heard nothing about it."

"Well, so far, your intelligence on this matter has been quite thorough. Your wife, Elizabetta, is an extraordinary source of information."

Hugh stiffened and wondered briefly what the comment might

mean about his wife. She had often told him how she was far more worthy of a king than of a humble lord. "Yes, she's been keeping an eye on Angers. We would have heard about anything going on," Hugh replied, though he was still thinking that she'd had more than an eye on Angers. How many men had had how much of her, he still wasn't sure.

"Of course," King Henry replied. He started to turn away, then turned back to Hugh and looked down his long and impassive nose. "I will not worry, then. I doubt the boy will even have the courage to attend the final battle for his own land."

A few hours later, in the Great Room at Angers, Louis paced feverishly. With him were his devoted attendants: Robert, Alphonse, Jean Beaumont, *Seigneur* Joinville, Pierre Raucliffe, and in the corner of the room, quiet as ever, Jean Adaret Benariel.

"Take me out to the men!" Louis ordered.

Beaumont was quick to answer. "Absolutely not, Your Majesty. Your safety is of the utmost importance!"

Louis stepped so close to Beaumont that the man stood back a half step. Though Louis spoke quietly, his eyes were staring straight into Beaumont's own. "I said we are going to the men."

Louis was rarely in this state of passion. It was the first time Beaumont had ever seen him so agitated.

Robert grabbed his thick cloak and handed it to Louis. "I agree. We will go. The king has spoken."

Louis looked at it, then at Robert, and took the cloak without a nod or comment. The king strode out the door and left the entourage behind in wonder.

Beaumont shook his head. "This is the death of the king."

"Nonsense," Robert called out, following Louis out the door. "Let's go."

The others followed, miserably, and when they had left, Jean stood alone in his corner. Taking a map from the table, he followed the others out the door.

Tonight the rain had paused, as if it needed time to replenish its power. The clouds were still heavy, so close to the earth that they could be seen even in the dark of night.

Well ahead of the group, Louis advanced upon the Loire. Ahead of him the lights of the distant English camp glittered and reflected upon the river that stood between the two enemies. The lights danced on the river's surface as if to mock the boy king who stood on the other side.

Suddenly, a spy came out of the shadows and approached Louis, waving a signal flag as he advanced. Robert caught up and pulled his sword.

"Careful, Louis," he said, but the spy sank quietly to his knees. Robert kept his sword out, though he didn't point it at the man.

"Report," Louis said.

"The enemy is strong enough to take Angers tomorrow, even with the castle's reinforcements." Then the man began to weep. "There is no hope."

The group was silent at this news for a long moment, the only sound on the riverbank the man's sobbing and the low moan of the wind.

"Perhaps we should go back inside," Beaumont said at last.

Louis turned to the others. "What would you have me do? Hide like a frightened girl until they knock on my front door?" The ire in his tone was unmistakable.

"Perhaps if they reach the castle they won't be able to take it," Robert suggested. "We have spent so much on its fortification."

Louis pointed across the river. "I can see by their fires that they've only lost a fifth of their force in the battles so far. That's still an enormous amount of men. They will take Angers tomorrow."

"Not necessarily." The voice that spoke up was quiet, surprising them all.

Louis turned, and Jean stepped up from the shadows behind the entourage. The others all looked at him—some with derision because he was not a military man and therefore had no reason to give advice to King Louis.

"Then you think there is hope, tomorrow?" Louis asked.

"Not in the way you are thinking, Sire," Jean replied.

"Beg pardon, Your Majesty, but I hardly think *Seigneur* Benariel is qualified to give you any advice about warfare or strategy," Joinville spoke up, his old frame war-beaten and experienced.

Beaumont added to the sentiment. "*Seigneur* Benariel, you know I do like you, but our families have been advising the king for centuries. You are least in turn here."

"Well, then," the king replied. "What would you have us do, Joinville?"

The old man thought hard, and it made the overgrown eyebrows on his head twitch with the effort. "We should stay fortified in the castle."

"Not an option, according to our eyewitness here," Robert said and sheathed his sword. "I'll not have my brother at risk. The king must be first in all priorities, even in the face of death and surrender."

Louis turned to Beaumont, who didn't wait to be asked.

"We retreat."

Silence hit all the men like a blow to the gut. The words had a sense of wisdom to them. Beaumont didn't stop there.

"In secret, we pull out of the castle and leave a strike force behind to defend the castle while we go for reinforcements."

Robert spoke up. "From where? We can't call our troops back from the south in time, and we can't turn up any more fighting men here in the provinces. We're stuck with what we have. Running will only give the English cause to chase us all the way back to the *Cité*."

"I, for one, would rather die at Angers than die in my own bed in the *Cité*," Joinville said, with an old man's determination. "I wouldn't want the English to get that far. I fear I'd walk the earth a ghost the rest of eternity if I failed to defend our people. We stay here, in the castle, and we defend against the attack tomorrow."

Silence again, while they thought about the grim outcome. The unspoken understanding was that every man here was included in the surrender or defeat except Louis, who was supposed to leave tonight under cover of darkness. All must be willing to die but He Who Leads. Dying in defense of Louis, their king, was expected; it was everything a knight stood for.

Jean said nothing, didn't even look at the other men. It was as if they had never spoken a word. His gaze was fixed on Louis.

Louis turned once again to Jean. "So, Benariel, what say you now?"

"I say we don't retreat. We don't hole ourselves up to certain doom in the castle." His voice was steady and calm. He measured each word like a careful weight.

The others seemed ready to protest, but something about Benariel's voice made them stop.

"Go on," Louis said.

"What I propose is not to be considered lightly. We can win on one condition that you alone can grant, Your Majesty."

Louis tilted his head, and just for a moment, he seemed to look deep into Benariel's thoughts. For that same moment, he looked older, tired . . . but somewhere in his eyes, a flicker of hope burned. "What would you have of me?"

"You must cross the river, tomorrow," Jean said. "Before drummer, horse, or any other soldier sets foot upon the soil. *You* must lead the charge across the river."

The pause as this hit home unsettled each man more than the chill night air.

Joinville was the first to find his voice. "But that is *unheard*-of! No king *leads* the army!"

"He would be exposed to the enemy, right out front, naked and alone!" Beaumont protested.

Louis held up a hand to silence them. The king hadn't taken his eyes off Benariel. When he spoke, his voice was soft. "And that is precisely why it would work. No king would be foolish enough to lead an army into the enemy's assault, unless he was certain of its outcome. More than certain."

Louis turned to the others. "Unless he had every reason to believe he could take back the land from the assailants. To show England who truly owns France. And *who is king*."

Louis turned and began walking back to Angers, his stride determined and unyielding. The men hurried behind him, talking in a quick succession.

"It's death!" Joinville said.

"But it might work—if given enough support," Robert said. "It's a good plan, but it needs some backup. Something to ensure that the enemy feels threatened. A flank attack. Something that looks impressive and unexpected."

Now, Robert was grinning. He always grinned whenever things got dangerous. "Leave it to me," he said. "I can make quite an impressive display when properly motivated."

Jean walked slowly behind, watching the rest of the men. He looked back over his shoulder once before turning around and heading back to the Castle of Angers.

Pierre Mauclerc stood before a high knight of the Templars and showed him the Crown of Thorns. The relic sat in its reliquary on top of a small table in the middle of the Templar headquarters of southern France.

It was a dark castle, in the ownership of *Seigneur* Dunbière, an extremely pious and righteous man. His very presence made Pierre feel like a worm. He wondered if this lord was powerful enough to discern what he was thinking. One never knew with the Templars.

"You got this from King Louis," Dunbière said. "It is genuine and most holy."

"Yes, the Paris chapter allows me to keep it with me. I am highly regarded in Paris."

Dunbière narrowed his eyes. "*Oui*, I can see that."

Pierre cleared his throat. "You haven't told me why you wished to see me, *Seigneur* Dunbière."

"*Non*, I haven't yet." The great Templar waved a hand at the servants, who closed the Crown of Thorns' reliquary. "I'm curious about something."

Dunbière paced slowly with his hands behind his back. "Do you know the Order of the Rose?"

"Queen Blanche's serving women? They call themselves an order, but I always thought they were merely giving themselves an important-sounding title."

"On the contrary, they're both an order and a difficulty I have watched growing on the horizon for some time. They oppose the Crusades in the Holy Land. I believe they sow deceit in the thoughts of the king and queen of France. Deceits about the Templars and other holy orders."

Pierre's eyebrows went up.

"I want you to watch these women, and tell me anything you see that is interesting about them. You are close to the royal family. Closer than any other men we employ."

"I couldn't possibly—"

"I will pay you handsomely for satiating my curiosity about them."

Pierre smiled at that, then bowed. "I am your humble servant, *Seigneur* Dunbière. I live to please your order."

✦ ✦ ✦

King Louis regarded the skies beyond the tower's edge. The moon was a sliver in the sky, the curved edge of a sharp dagger scraping the night on its track across the heavens.

He swallowed. He feared tomorrow. How could Jean stand it? How could any of them stand their ground in the front lines?

Jean has more courage than I do, and the sorry part is, it's my country.

The look in Benariel's eyes was so steady, so unswerving. . . . He would doubtless be there tomorrow, next to his king, if necessary.

I have never been above the law. I have never made an exception for myself. With this truth, Louis knew he would go into battle tomorrow, despite his fear.

Dear Lord, I pray for the strength of Jean Adaret Benariel.

On the dark side of the tower, hidden from the moon, Jean Adaret Benariel saw the last of the servants fleeing into the night. They had been given leave before the battle tomorrow, told to go south and avoid the coming confrontation. Jean put his boot up on the tower ledge and watched the figures dashing out into the fields below: women with huddled children, fathers carrying family belongings; someone's dog was even trotting beside a running child.

He wanted to go with them, and when he realized this, he looked to the heavens, where stars shone like countless pairs of eyes, all looking down with judgment upon his fears.

I do not want to die, Jean thought.

You do not have to stay, the familiar voice replied. *You were not asked to stay, and like those faithful servants, you could leave and they would understand.*

Jean fought against the deep, still voice even though the compulsion to heed it was overwhelming. *I must be the exception. Don't you see that?*

You are still only a man. You can leave.

The knowledge of those three small words ignited his heart. The power of knowing he could set foot into the meadow with the others and leave the battle to someone else made him heady. Jean squeezed his eyes shut.

Father, if you can hear me, I would not *know the things I know, and* *relinquish* all *that I have.* I don't want it!

Make me a rock. Don't let me leave tonight. I beg you to give me the courage *of a mortal king. . . . Please, give me the courage I see in Louis.*

Louis had spent the entire night alone with hard questions and hollow answers. He was long past why and what he had done to deserve this, long past fearing that he would die before the war was won or lost, and past the comfort of prayer. Despite being exhausted from questions, tired of answers that weren't answers at all, one question refused to leave.

What will I tell them?

Louis stared hard at his feet. What could he possibly say that would bolster the men's spirits tomorrow, before they charged? Some of the men would live, but many would die. How could he be worthy of one dying man's thoughts? What words could possibly comfort the wounded and remain worthy of the survivors?

He had none.

He realized that his back was warm, and he turned to face the morning sun that greeted him, that peered over the horizon as if it had disturbed his innermost thoughts.

The morning was beautiful and still. The clouds hung low, but the sun was beneath them, and it stretched golden fingers over all the land, warming it and its inhabitants for only a few moments before it would be lost in the clouds above.

While he couldn't remember the last time he'd seen the sunrise, he knew the feeling of the rising sun well. His hands tingled, his mouth opened, and he breathed in fresh air as his muscles burned in the growing sunlight.

That's when he saw it, just above the tree line at the far end of the castle. He'd almost missed the bird as it tracked the treetops. Louis caught his breath in his throat, and his heart beat faster, for he recognized it immediately.

It was his father's falcon.

It was silent as it flew over the open meadows, the only living thing that was not afraid to cross the open plains alone. The bird of prey flapped strongly a few times and then darted toward the Loire. It flew in a straight line from the castle, across the bridge, until it flew over the English bank. It soared free and unharmed, but most importantly, it soared proudly.

With every pulse of its wings, the bird called out to Louis. Suddenly, he knew why it was here. It was as certain a visitation as the day of his father's death at the battle of Poitou. He had only been eleven, and since then had doubted the virtue of the moment, when his mother refused to believe how his father's white, rare falcon flew to his windowsill at the very hour of his death.

For just a moment, Louis was only eleven years old, and believed his father was trying to say something once again, if only this time he would listen.

Follow me, Son. Louis remembered the words, as he heard them again. *Follow me.*

Louis couldn't take his gaze off of the bird soaring over the English camp, until it finally flew away, completely gone from sight. Then he turned to the stairs that would take him down to his armor.

In the rear of the army, Louis sat on his horse, both stirring anxiously in the cold, gray air. Robert had taken one fourth of the army at Angers to the western ford. Louis had not ordered this, and the lack of men at his flank made him even more unsettled.

At the sound of hooves behind him, he looked back to find Benariel approaching on a black horse. Jean halted the horse beside him, and Louis greeted him with a nod.

Though they sat in silence, Louis was grateful for the company. He wanted to tell Jean about the dawn, and about the falcon. He wanted to tell him how the moment had affected him, but he didn't know where to start or even how to make words out of the feeling inside. He knew Jean would understand, even in the silence.

Finally, Louis spoke. "I didn't sleep last night for thought of what this would mean."

Benariel said nothing.

"If I move to the front of the army, everyone will see me coming, and I will take a stand. Even if I die defending my country . . ." He thought about that for a moment. Never to see Isabelle or Margaret or Blanche again.

"You will not die, Your Majesty."

"How can you be so certain?"

For the first time, Benariel smiled. "If you die, I die, and it is not my time yet."

Then the signal was given, and the regiments were aligned and ready for battle. Joinville, old and haggard in his chain-mail suit, rode back to Louis. Everything about the old veteran was stoic, but Louis noticed that his hand was shaking uncontrollably.

"It's time, Your Majesty," Joinville said.

Louis looked at Jean, then nudged his mount forward. The standing army watched him move through their ranks. Their bodies parted before him and reminded him of how Moses had parted the Red Sea. Men looked into his face with apprehension and confusion.

He didn't stop his mount until he stood before the drummer at the front of the army. The man looked up with a gaping mouth. One of his sticks fell to the ground. Louis looked down at him, and took a breath.

"Are you afraid?" He smiled grimly at the drummer. The man could only nod. "I am, too."

Not one soldier in the small army moved at the king's admission. The silence was broken only by the battering of the wind in the banners.

"And it's all right," he said, looking at the others around him. "Today, you don't have to come with me. I am going over there, alone," he simply said. "But if you do follow me, you will see that it's easy to fly. And you will claim everything that rushes beneath you, and in *that* flight you will never be afraid."

Louis turned his horse quietly and held the feeling of his father's falcon in his heart before plunging wildly across the bridge on a charging horse . . . completely alone.

There was a moment of shocked silence. Then someone shouted, and took his sword from his scabbard. The man ran behind his king. Another man followed. And another. And another. Jean Adaret Benariel spurred his horse into a full gallop, charging across the bridge, gaining on the king. The soldiers raced behind him.

They rattled their shields loudly as the cry rang out, *"Follow Louis!"*

The foot soldiers broke into a dead run, the lieutenants—including Joinville and Beaumont—all leading their regiments across the bridge, this time *behind* their king. Some of the footmen took straight to the river and waded in up to their armpits in order to cross to the other side. Others simply charged out of their ranks, following their king to the bitter end.

On the hill, looking down at the bridge to Angers, Hugh and King Henry sat at the back of their large army. They heard the rallying cry of Louis, but not the words. They saw the army follow him across the bridge.

There was a most unusual moment of tension.

"Is that," King Henry asked, "the King . . . himself, coming across first?"

The shouts of the first ranks of the English were stilled. A mad king was charging at them completely alone and filled with what seemed the wrath of God. They had no idea what to do.

"It . . . uh. It can't be, Your Majesty. I mean, it wouldn't make a bit of sense if—"

"*Get me my sights!*" Henry thundered, less with authority than a quaking fear behind his barking voice.

The sights were fumbled out of an attaché's traveling case. Three men leapt forth to hurriedly unwind the telescoping device from its cloth.

"Orders, sir?" a lieutenant asked the king.

"*My sights!*" he yelled, and snatched the telescope.

He barely had time to look through the device long enough to clearly identify the rider as Louis, when the sound of a French horn was heard to the west.

"It's an ambush!" a lieutenant shouted from amidst the ranks. "Reinforcements coming up the west flank!"

King Henry swung his telescopic device around, and all he caught was the perfect, brilliant white of Prince Robert's glistening teeth.

✤   ✤   ✤

Robert was wearing his kiss-of-death smile as he galloped like God's hand of vengeance toward the "mighty" king of England. His haggard team was charging forward, shouting loudly, after having waded the ford in the middle of the night and creeping up the long coastline until dawn. By all rights, they should have been exhausted, but when King Henry's men shouted in terror at their approach, his unit's energy was unnaturally kindled.

Robert shouted once more for good measure. He let himself get buried in the blood-fury, because in the back of his mind, he knew that if he didn't put on one hell of a good show, he'd be answering to Louis for taking off with one quarter of his brother's forces. And if Louis died, he'd be answering to Blanche, and not just for the use of the army but for the murder of a brother and a king.

Robert spurred his horse again, his nose crinkled in fury as he cried for blood, lunging forward in his saddle and pointing his sword menacingly at the English king who hid behind an enormous army.

❧ ❧ ❧

King Henry panicked—but when he lost his will, he lost it well. The mighty English commander called out orders to his immediate lieutenants. "West flank, attack! South flank, stand your ground and attack!"

The large force moved easily to the west, but the south flank was not moving. The men were restless and afraid.

"*I said stand your ground!*" Henry shouted, causing his horse to rear and trot violently in a circle. He was grateful to be in the rear of the army, for a moment. And he felt the pang of shame at his tailbone. Louis was leading his own men across the bridge.

"He's just a child!" Henry shouted at his men, but more to ease himself.

❧ ❧ ❧

Louis was immediately engulfed in the heat of battle; he waded into the men around him with his sword drawn and slashing heavily. He felt fear and panic rising in his chest, but his own men were not far behind. He had little time to be proud of them, but in the spaces between breaths he knew that he had led a charge against impossible odds, and that his men had not failed him. He wanted to smile, but he was terrified.

As he slashed his sword against a large brute, the English man grasped it in gloved hands and yanked Louis. Louis did not let go of his sword, and as a result, he came toppling off the horse. When he hit the ground, the wind was knocked from his ribs.

The brute was on top of him, raising a sword to the sky in order to slash at him. Louis couldn't move, and found breathing impossible. He stared in horror at the sword coming down at him.

The man over him jerked violently and then slowly slid off and crumpled to the right. Dead.

Louis stared at the dead English soldier for a moment, then looked up. Jean stood over him now, blood on his longsword. The look on the man's face was one that Louis could never forget: hatred, anger, fear, and shame covered Jean like a mask of pain.

The moment passed, and Jean seemed to clear his head. He extended his hand to his good friend.

"Your Majesty!" he shouted over the clashing noise of war. Louis grasped Jean's hand, coughing out air and getting in a clean breath, and Jean pulled his king to his feet.

The moment was over as they were assaulted by a fresh wave of English troops. On the ground now, Louis cut into the men with both hands on his longsword. The sword sunk in between ribs and over soft flesh with sickening slices. Louis realized the only thing keeping him preserved against their blows was the well-made armor he wore. These men were dressed in rags and leather. Any sword could penetrate that. And his did, over and over again.

As the men died before him, their last living sight was the French king.

✦ ✦ ✦

Jean Adaret Benariel had just killed a man. He'd never even so much as scratched a person before today. And that man over Louis . . . it was kill him or watch the king die within a few moments of battle.

Jean had no time to consider his actions. As the tide of battle moved Louis farther away, Jean had to deal with his own attackers. He wanted to shout at them, stop them, as they approached. All they wanted was death. His death or their own; there was no negotiating. His stomach was nauseated, and his neck was cold with sweat.

He killed another man.

And the one behind him raised his sword and struck Jean across the shoulder. He cut that man down.

And the one behind him wheeled and hit Jean in the arm with a heavy mace. Jean stuck the man in the stomach with his sword.

They died too easily. They were untrained civilians with swords, clubs, and maces. Jean grew sick again, knowing he fought people who must have been farmers, blacksmiths, carpenters . . . fishermen. He wanted to scream that this was not their fight—to leave!—to save their lives.

But they just wouldn't stop. They weren't listening. He killed another man.

Robert laughed and stabbed one man while strangling another with his free hand. He moved as if he were something wild and unnatural. The whites of his eyes showed more power than the Devil's. The man in his grasp died, choking.

It didn't bother Robert. Robert had killed hundreds of men in battle. He'd been fighting at the age of nine, even though no one had given him permission.

Killing was what he did best.

Something painful cracked against his back, and he whirled around with a limp, tasting blood where his teeth had smashed into his tongue. He tackled the man in rags behind him, who was wielding a huge hammer.

They went down, a tangle of arms and legs, and Robert squeezed the man's face in his hand while he stuck him through the ribs with his sword. Pain increased his focus for warfare. More pain, more focus.

Robert stood up from the dead man with the hammer, grabbed the man's weapon, and hurled it over the English troops before him.

"*Hugh! I am coming for you!*" he shouted.

Men heard the shout and scattered before him.

❖ ❖ ❖

Louis fought and continued fighting. His legs started to ache; then they stiffened. He walked like an old man who suffered rickets.

He kept going. *This is my war.*

He was wading past the first ranks and into the midranks of trained soldiers.

My men need me. The trained soldiers were good. Their armor was heavier. The blows that came from the English weapons were causing severe bolts of pain now. Louis could scarcely keep his eyes open, and at one point, something leaked into his eye that felt like sweat, stinging and burning. He wiped it away. It was blood.

I must be strong. Another knight charged at him, with a spear. Louis grabbed it and felt his left arm sear with pain. Had he been hit? No, but his muscle refused to move. Damn his weaknesses! He signed too many treaties and didn't use enough weaponry. His arm ached with fire.

I'm here alone. He raised his good right hand and smashed the hilt of the sword down on his attacker's head. The man had lost his helmet somewhere else, and the sword smacked his skull with a deep thud.

He crumpled, his eyes rolled up in his head. Louis realized that he was snarling, his lips pressed back from his teeth and his nose crinkled into raging eyes that could no longer blink for the sweat and blood pouring into them. He hurt, but he kept going. He staggered, but he would not go down. He would not stop.

This is my war.

❖ ❖ ❖

Robert finally spotted Hugh through the thinning crowds of English troops who were actively fleeing the French soldiers. Not wanting his older brother to show him up, Robert waded in and stood right behind Hugh de la Marche. The man was struggling with a weak French lieutenant. The boy was probably no older than sixteen. He had several bruises and cuts, and his face looked like the backside of a branded ox; but there appeared to be no major injuries, just severe fatigue.

Robert waited patiently. He noticed that no other English troops came to test him as he stood calmly behind Hugh. They feared him, he realized.

Just as Hugh pulled back to deliver the lieutenant's death blow, Robert tapped him on the shoulder with his sword's point.

Hugh turned, ready to kill—

He released the already-forgotten lieutenant as he met face-to-face with Prince Robert.

Who was smiling, as always.

✤   ✤   ✤

Hugh and Robert fought like mad dogs before the lieutenant, who could not move from the ground. He watched the two giants battling above and around him. Robert had saved his life, by stepping in, but Robert was fearsome. The lieutenant feared him almost as much as he feared Hugh de la Marche.

Both men held their ground, delivering blow after painful blow for a good length before Robert faltered and took a blow to the arm. He cried out in rage, and both men staggered back as the shock of the wound took hold.

✤   ✤   ✤

It was a deep cut. Hugh's sword had sliced into Robert's chain mail at an unraveling weak spot between the sewn segments. Robert was staggering. The pain and depth of the cut had brought his fatigue to the surface. He had tried to keep it at bay, but the night of travel was beginning to show. Haggardly, Robert raised his sword high and charged, slicing down on Hugh with enormous power in a move that should not have been possible from a man this far into battle.

✤ ✤ ✤

Hugh saw Robert's sword and could not move. He wanted to—he told his muscles and his limbs to get *out* of the way! He could not get them to respond to his request. If he'd had the time, he would have picked up his own legs with his hands, but it was too late. The blade came crashing down on his tired chest.

It didn't cut into his chain mail, but it did knock the wind completely out of him. Hugh felt his breastbone crack, and immediately the swelling of his own tissue crushed against him from the inside.

✤ ✤ ✤

The lieutenant watched as the blow from Robert's sword did its job, and Hugh fell next to him on the ground, croaking while opening and closing his mouth like a fish out of water. The young lad scrambled to get away from the traitorous lord whose gaze was both fixed on him and looking through him.

The lad stood up, crashing into Robert, who turned on him in the frenzy. The lieutenant held up his hands and screamed a high-pitched note of pure panic.

✤ ✤ ✤

Robert stopped his swing in midair when he heard the boy's cry. It took only a second, but he realized he had almost struck one of his own men. A boy, no less.

The young lieutenant looked up at him, shivering with collapse. Robert chuckled, as if he'd accidentally stepped on someone's toe at a court dance. He looked down at the terrified lieutenant, trying to effect a smile that was pleasant, but the boy could only stare at him in morbid fear. Robert wasn't sure if that was a good thing or bad.

Then he realized that he had no time for such thoughts. Robert looked around, wondering why he wasn't getting assailed by a slew of Englishmen. The battlefield had lost the majority of its standing trees. Most of the men were on the ground, either crippled or dead. Others had fled. As Robert assessed the damage, he realized that a whole flank of the English army was fleeing to the west.

"My God, it is a retreat!" Robert was breathless.

Louis swung, and swung again. He couldn't feel his arms anymore. They were past the point of burning, well past anything but an automatic swinging motion. They weren't even effective anymore. The weight of the sword was the only thing in his favor.

He wanted to move faster, wanted to swing with more accuracy, but he felt his arms unable to respond to his requests. They were slowing down. They literally could not move at a normal speed. He felt as if he were swinging through honey, and his sword grew heavier and more erratic in its pattern of movement.

His teeth were clenched so hard his jaw was spasming pain down his neck to his shoulders. He grimaced, sweat poured from his forehead, and he would not stop. *One more swing, one more man, one more swing, one more death. This is my war. Swing! Swing!*

Swing, damn you! Don't fail me!

There were more of them. Not as many now, but there were still more men from the English army ahead of him.

"I will not stop until you all are beaten!" He was surprised that the cry came out loud. His jaw was so sore it felt like he hadn't spoken in five hundred years. His voice was hoarse and cracked midshout.

And again he swung his sword, which seemed to move on its own, his arms just grasping onto it as it pulled him through a tide of bodies.

He kept going, he took wounds, he kept going, he killed more men, he kept going. He kept going. He kept—

Louis collapsed. It shocked him, but his legs buckled beneath him and would not move.

"*No!*" he cried hoarsely. "Get up! *Damn you!* Get up and—*move!* I can't stop!"

He stumbled to his feet, but his legs collapsed again. They would no longer support his weight. This time he fell squarely on his arse. The sword fell from his fingers and he sat in the mud, legs sprawled before him, useless and quivering.

"Nooooo!" He had no voice left for shouting.

Shadows fell over him, and Louis looked up to see ten men standing around him, looking down at him. For a moment he could not tell who they were. His eyesight was blurry; his fatigue made thoughts impossible. Then he saw French colors on their tabards and French symbols on their shields.

"My men." He smiled somehow.

"Protect the king at all costs!" one shouted. They huddled together and fought off anyone who came toward them.

Louis sat in a collapsed heap, listening to clanging metal, tasting blood in his mouth, knowing that mucus ran freely from his nose down to his upper lip, where it hung heavily over the bridge of his skin.

Louis was shaking; his arms were light, and he looked down at them. They were drifting up into the air, on their own. Freed from the weight of his sword, they were floating.

So this is what it's like to fly, he thought.

He wondered if they were losing, or if they were all going to die. He couldn't see a thing from the middle of battle. He could only trust that Beaumont was watching the movements of both armies in his place, and would sound a retreat if necessary.

Louis tried to look around. It seemed quieter now, or was that just his imagination? He found spaces between the legs of the men around him, and peered out, as if from a safe prison.

There were men lying everywhere on the battlefield. Fallen soldiers, moaning in pain, or still as death. Louis lost his balance and fell over into the mud, his elbows digging into the wet soil and his chest covered with cool, wet earth.

That's when he realized Jean was in trouble. He was on the ground, shouting, as he was fiercely attacked by—

"Good God, there are ten men on Jean!" Louis shouted. One of the men turned around to look at him. Louis pointed. "Jean! *Jean!*"

Louis began to crawl through the man's legs in front of him.

"*Non*, Your Majesty!" the man said.

"Save Jean!" Louis screamed. Five men ran to where he pointed.

Jean's attackers were swarming him like angry wasps landing sting after sting. At first, he tried to attack, but now he was on the ground, crying out in pain from every blow that landed on his body. The men surrounded him, and he was starting to black out; the pain was going far, far away, and he was starting to care less about screaming.

Suddenly, the pain was gone. The blows, no matter how far away, had stopped. There was a sense of silence. Jean was afraid to open his eyes. Maybe he was finally dead. Maybe it was a trick.

"Jean," a familiar voice said.

Jean opened his eyes to see Louis' face over his own. Louis looked horrible, bruised and swollen, with a split lip.

Benariel tried to focus on Louis' face. His shoulder was stinging to the bone, and he could feel the flesh exposed beneath his armor. It jostled in the air.

Louis was holding out his hand, from where they sat on the

ground. Benariel grasped it, and the king pulled him upright. They sat together for a moment. Benariel felt as if he was going to be sick.

"Thank you" was all he could manage. It was a whisper.

"It was not your time to die," Louis reminded him hoarsely.

Neither smiled.

✦ ✦ ✦

Louis looked around at the field littered with bodies. It was all over now. Some people were still standing, mostly French, but a few English remained. Louis saw old Joinville first. The veteran knight had fallen to his knees, sobbing and crossing himself over and over again; the tears would not cease as they ran down to the old man's beard.

Louis felt his lower lip quiver and bit it. He still wasn't sure where things stood. Then he heard his brother's shout.

"*French victory!*" Robert's call came from far, far away.

Robert, he realized. Had Robert come in?

Louis found the strength, somehow, to stand again. No one helped him get back on his feet, but as he raised his head up, he saw Robert, hands in the air, grinning like a rictus and standing over the body of Hugh de la Marche.

Was Hugh dead?

"*French victory!*" Robert cried again. "*God, do you hear us? It is a* French *victory, today!*"

A man near Louis, whose leg had been hacked in two, was lying on the ground quietly, dying. When Robert's cry rang out, this man thrust his arm in the air and shouted, "*French victory!*"

He wasn't the only one who called out. Louis realized that all of his men were joining in the call that Robert had started. It was a call of honor and respect. It was a show of loyalty to their king.

"*Victory to the King!*"

"*French victory!*"

"God bless Louis!"

Louis nearly collapsed with overwhelming relief. He looked at Jean, who was also raising his good arm and crying out. Even quiet Jean, singing Louis' praise with head down and wounded arm. Louis swallowed, but nothing went down.

Robert was shouting, throwing his arms in an arc, and yelling *"Victory!"* Joinville could not say a word. The old man held up his arms, but sobbed violently. No words matched the honest tears coursing over his haggard face.

Jean Beaumont, chancellor and advisor, rode on his horse from the back of the ranks. He had been overseeing the battle in Louis' place and was unscathed. He came toward his king now, with a strange look of reverence and respect. He'd always respected Louis, but never had his face openly shown the awe and amazement it held today. Louis realized it and tried to compose himself. The king looked up into his chancellor's face and realized that good news awaited him.

"Today, we won Angers. We defeated the English, who fled west. Because of *you*, my liege, we have won the day and this remains *our* land." Beaumont leaned down a bit, in his saddle, and said quietly, "I will *never* forget this day."

Louis felt himself losing control. Like Joinville, he wanted only to break down and . . . be alone, where only God could see his misery and joy intermingled.

The war was over. Louis closed his eyes, seeking strength, seeking peace.

The shouts still rang out, growing in volume and excitement. Men who were dying were calling his name. Men who were dead would never hear that their lives had bought victory and freedom for France. Louis realized he was looking around at the bodies, at the men around him, and that Beaumont was still quietly waiting for him to give official sanction of the battle.

But Louis couldn't speak.

"Victory to the King!" they shouted

"French victory!"

"God bless Louis!"

Louis numbly started to walk away. His legs moved stiffly; his arms could only swing helplessly at his sides.

"Your Majesty?" He didn't heed Beaumont's question.

"Victory to the King!" they shouted.

Louis moved past Joinville, who was still on his knees. He wanted to put his hand on the old man's head and comfort him. He could not. Louis moved past Jean, who stared up at him as if wanting to say a few words, but Louis could not look at Jean. Louis walked past all the men who lay at his feet.

"God bless Louis!" they shouted.

"Highness! Your Majesty!" Beaumont was still calling from behind, looking toward him in confusion. They were *all* looking at him. Louis could feel their stares, but as much as he wanted to, he could not turn around and *face* them. He could not tell them how he loved them, how proud he was of them, how he knew God was with them right this moment and how—

Louis choked up with tears. He staggered on, without looking back, as they called out his name with painful elation. If Louis so much as waved his hand in their direction, he would crumble.

And no king was ever allowed to crumble before his country.

✤ ✤ ✤

That night, a medic attended to Benariel's wound. Louis didn't want any harm to come to his friend, because Jean had been right. He had shown Louis what it meant to be a king.

More importantly, in the days that followed, Jean Adaret Benariel never once made a point of it. He said nothing, mostly because he was in and out of consciousness. The wound was severe, and Louis found it hard to find the time to thank him. He frowned at the man's ability to be so damned elusive, even when confined to a medical cot.

Finally, on the fourth day, as the army continued to dog the English turn-tails—and as Robert, Beaumont, and Joinville were all finished with dinner and heading to bed—Jean did regain consciousness.

Louis knelt down by his cot. "I wanted to tell you my appreciation for your wise counsel," Louis said. "Don't die on us now. You're needed at my planning table from this day forward."

Jean smiled, his eyes weakly focusing on Louis. "I only meant to keep you and France alive, Majesty. It pleases me to see the end has been met, and that you, my dear friend, are alive and well. I do not believe we will live to see another war together."

"I can give the order to stay in Angers until you are better."

"*Non.*" Jean's eyes were closed now, the word almost indistinct. *Take me home. Take me back to her,* he thought, and said it before collapsing into unconsciousness again. "*Je veux retourner chez moi, je veux la revoir . . .*"

Louis watched as Jean slumped back down into slumber. He was grateful for the words, but for these last few, he wondered why returning home to the *palais*, to "her" as he said it, was so important.

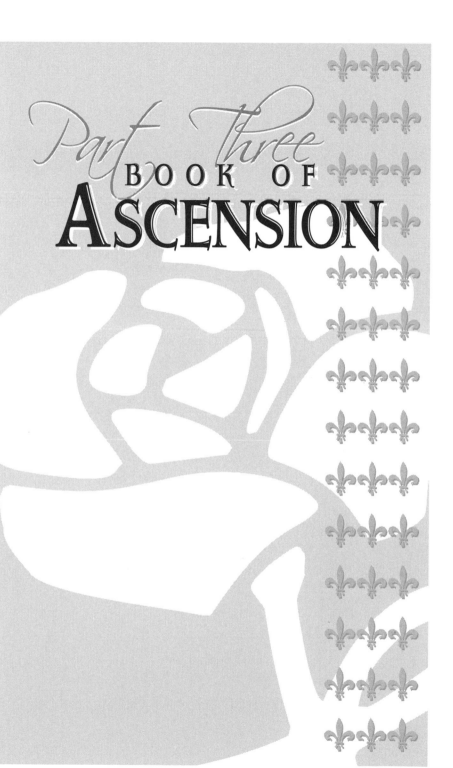

Part Three

BOOK OF

ASCENSION

There is no pain in the wound received in the moment of victory.

Publilius Syrus, *Moral Sayings* (c. 100 B.C.)

23

Norea opened her eyes and saw feet standing on the ground before her. The shoes were Elizabetta de la Marche's slippers and were just peeking out from a full, black gown of velvet. Norea was afraid of being kicked in the face, but didn't have the strength to move. She looked up from the floor feeling the dull ache of the wound in her side.

"Will you speak now?" Elizabetta crossed her arms.

Norea did not reply, simply closed her eyes and put her forehead against the cool stone floor. She had no idea where she was, or what day or time of day it was, only that she had been kept in a dark cellar-style room for what seemed to be a week. She had counted seven days of consciousness.

But Norea had been denied food and water until she would tell Elizabetta everything she knew. She refused to speak, even after days of water deprivation. Elizabetta had finally let her drink, so she did not die. Norea felt her stomach clawing at her insides with the pain of hunger. But she would not tell Elizabetta what she wanted to know. She would not betray her king, her queen, and her Sisters.

"Traitor. I'd kick you, if I didn't have on such lovely slippers." Elizabetta knelt down and picked Norea's head up off the floor by the hair. "I don't want to damage them. But I will damage you, and soon, if you don't speak."

✛   ✛   ✛

The battle had taken its toll, but in a way no one had expected. After the negotiations and reparations, after all the treaties were signed, and French coffers were made rich once more with English gold, Louis and his entourage returned to Paris. The gold would pay the debt to the Knights Templar, and the Crown of Thorns would at last be returned to Louis.

On the road to the *Cité*, Robert kept noticing Louis falling asleep in his saddle.

"Are you tired, Brother? Should we rest?" Robert asked.

"*Non*, I'm fine." Louis turned tired eyes to Robert. "We need to get to the *palais*. I must see to the Crown of Thorns immediately."

"But a few hours of sleep will certainly make the traveling easier," Robert suggested.

"It's an easy road to Paris. I will not rest."

Robert looked at his brother and scowled. It wasn't in Louis' nature to be so tired, and it worried him.

When they stopped for the first evening, Robert made sure his brother rested in the tent provided for him.

"Perhaps I should send for Sofia," Robert said. "You're not well."

"Sofia is chasing down Elizabetta de la Marche," Louis said. "I don't want her taken off that task. It's vital to catch all the traitors to the Crown. This is a cold, that's all. A case of the sniffles."

A young page parted the flaps of the tent and brought in a steaming cup and handed it to Robert. Robert moved the cup around in his hands and handed it to his brother.

"What's this?"

"Broth. Drink it up."

"You will not mention my fatigue to the men. That's an order," Louis said. "Do you understand? I won't have anyone thinking there are repercussions for the risk I took at Angers. I have to be strong for my country, even when I am weak."

Robert only nodded. Being ordered around by his brother made him angry, but he did not show it. Louis had never ordered anything of him in the past. He'd made an absolute point of *not* ordering any of his siblings around like a domineering bully. And part of Robert knew that Louis had a point, no matter how painful a point. It was Louis' job to be strong, to be the leader. If he fell apart, everyone else would too.

The best thing Robert could do for his brother was to be quiet, and to tend to him on the trip as best he could. He couldn't even confide in *Seigneur* Benariel because Jean was being hauled in a cart, sleeping off the grievous injury to his shoulder.

It was late at night, and Elizabetta sat in her *château* at her writing desk, by low candlelight, reading. She had a bowl of cherries next to the book and was eating from the bowl, spitting seeds across the table with thoughts of war and betrayal. Her mind wandered to Pierre.

The last seed flew across the room and landed without a sound. The others had all clattered a little bit as they hit the floor of the bureau. The servants would have had to clean them all up, but the rest of her servants had run away the day Hugh left for war and Elizabetta had taken Norea hostage. Elizabetta sighed.

She looked up, hoping the cherry seed hadn't landed on a curtain that would be stained by the pit, when she saw a figure moving toward her from the shadows of the room.

Elizabetta squinted as she looked at the figure. "Louise, did you return?"

It wasn't her cook Louise, she realized only too late. The face belonging to the woman who approached was a terrifying sight. She wore an expression that Elizabetta had only seen in the illuminated Scriptures, when looking upon the wrath of Michael the Archangel as he came for those who had wronged the Lord.

❧ ❧ ❧

Sofia's shadow stretched over the dark table, dwarfing the woman who sat before her, despite the fact that there was no light behind the Sister to create the impending darkness. As Sofia's shadow engulfed the solitary candle near Elizabetta's elbow, the flame guttered and then went out.

The angel of vengeance had come for Elizabetta de la Marche.

❧ ❧ ❧

Despite his best intentions, each day of traveling seemed to undermine Robert's greatest efforts by worsening Louis' condition. After a fortnight, Robert attempted some conversation that would not irritate his sick brother. "Jean is finally able to walk about."

"You will say nothing to Jean. He will feel horrible that I am sick. I won't hear of it."

"Then let us stop and rest at a tavern for a few weeks, anything, until you are better!"

"No!" Louis' voice rose. "Why don't you understand 'no' when you hear it, Brother?"

"Because I'm looking at a sick man! King or no, you are ill and need attention!"

"If you mention how I look one more time, Robert, I swear I will imprison you for life when we get home. Enough!"

Robert said no more on it. But his usual lively expression had turned into a frown of concern. The ride home was turning into a heavy weight against his heart.

Though he could ride a horse now, *Seigneur* Benariel was also weak and distressed. His wound was very deep, and only after three weeks of continual care did it show signs of improving.

Robert sighed heavily. It was a long ride back to Paris.

✧ ✧ ✧

Norea woke up.

She was still in great pain, and her eyes had trouble focusing, but when she made out the face above her, she was overwhelmed to see it was her sister Neci.

"Norea! Oh, Father, you have spared her!" Neci called to the doorway behind them. "Sofia, come! Norea is awake!"

Norea looked up into her sister's face and saw a mixture of terror and happiness. Then Sofia's face came near as well, next to Neci's.

"I am sorry this happened and we took so long to find you," Sofia said.

Norea sat up and rubbed her aching head. "What happened to Elizabetta?"

"They have hurt you." Sofia touched Norea's wound and it closed instantly at her touch.

"They wanted information—they found me writing a letter to Queen Blanche. Where is Elizabetta?" Norea asked again. "She's not dead, is she?"

"No," Neci reassured her.

"But she is in our custody," Sofia replied. She had a sharp tone. "And she will be that way as long as necessary to take her before the king."

Neci helped Norea to stand. "Come, we go to Paris."

"The war?" Norea asked.

"We won the war." Neci smiled at her sister. "You are very weak. I want you to sleep. We have a cart ready for you."

Norea only nodded.

✧ ✧ ✧

Pierre Mauclerc shook with rage when he heard that the English army had been defeated and Hugh de la Marche had been taken into custody. It had taken years to get this campaign off the ground, and now it had all come crumbling down because of a trick. Damn Louis!

He'd been so damn careful to set everything up in such a way that it would avoid failure. It all seemed a loss, now. Would Hugh tell the king about Pierre's involvement? He couldn't be sure, but if Robert found out about it, that would be the end of Pierre's life. He'd have to flee the country or face beheading. Pierre knew one person who would give him some idea of Hugh's predisposition for squealing, but when two days' riding brought him to *Château* de la Marche, no one was there. No servants, no animals, no mistress. Elizabetta was nowhere to be found. She was either captured and brought with Hugh, or she'd fled to England for sanctuary. Pierre mounted his horse and took to the fields. He would find Edgar, the English emissary, and ask him what had happened.

Despite his ragged look, the king was greeted by all of Paris in a shower of cheers and applause. Minstrels were playing on every corner, and grain was thrown into the air upon his return to the *Cité*. Word had spread of his charge at Angers, and now he was the hero of France.

Louis waved, smiled, and looked at the crowd with hollow, dark eyes. He felt he had completely withered away to one small sinew, ready to snap at any moment.

When Louis finally escaped behind the gates of the *palais*, away from the throngs of people, he collapsed on top of his war steed. Robert raced over to catch him before he could strike the ground and hefted him over his shoulder, rushing him up the steps of the castle tower.

"Let me pass!" Robert shouted. "Give me room!"

Blanche trailed behind him, Margaret and Joan running after.

"Go to the birthing room, Robert," Blanche said, her voice trembling.

Robert took the tower stairs two at a time as Alphonse and Charles came running.

Robert made it to the Ladies' Quarters and walked heavily to the third door on the left. Blanche opened the door, and he carried Louis into the darkened room.

"Call for a physician!" Robert shouted.

"Yes, immediately!" Alphonse replied, and ran from the room.

"He's fevered!" Blanche said as Robert put Louis down into the large bed. Joan let the bed curtains down so that Louis would be warm. A servant started a fire in the fireplace.

The physician, Theodore of Montpellier, came to Louis within the hour. He felt Louis' forehead with his hand, touched two fingers to the soft side of Louis' wrist, and waited patiently. He asked everyone to leave except Queen Blanche, and suggested the man's clothes be removed for an examination.

Alphonse and Robert had to carry Margaret out of Louis' chamber, shrieking and sobbing, since Queen Blanche was ordered to remove her son's clothes in privacy.

"He's my husband!" she shrieked. "Let me in!"

Robert held her fast, and Alphonse shut the door. Alphonse was often irate about Margaret's sniveling tone. They quarreled about it frequently. But today Alphonse had snapped, reaching a threshold that even his gentle disposition could not avoid.

"Silence, woman!" he shouted. The exclamation made Robert look over at him in shock. Margaret instantly stopped and shrank to the floor, gasping with emotion.

"Your true love is at death's door, and here you yell as if you're the one dying. What is the *matter* with you?"

Margaret huddled down by Robert's feet. She could say nothing, but it was obvious that she felt utterly alone against a family she had always felt separated from.

Shaking, Alphonse shrank down to his normal, mousy self as he looked at Robert, who said nothing. Neither brother consoled the queen.

It was clear to everyone in the family why Margaret never sat by Louis or was called upon as queen.

It was just not clear to Margaret.

Shortly after the awkward silence, the door opened and the doctor stepped out. Margaret rose, looking like a foal trying to stand inside the constraints of her skirts, and then dashed into Louis' room.

The doctor spoke to Robert as the blur that was Margaret darted past him. "I have monitored his symptoms, but the analysis will come when I test his urine. À *demain*," he bid them good-bye, and then turned to leave.

"Oh, and consequently," the doctor said, remembering, "I want you to watch over him round the clock. Feed him nothing but water if he wakes."

"Until tomorrow, then," Robert replied, and nodded.

Theodore of Montpellier walked down the hall, showing himself out. Robert watched after him. Montpellier was a part of the *université* and an institution revered all over Europe for its knowledge of diseases and cures. Theodore was the family's trusted advisor on all things medical. He had been called for Margaret's first birth, when the midwives had tried their best to stop her hemorrhaging. Louis had called for him, even though birthing was not a time or place for men.

The midwives had failed, but Theodore, with Margaret unconscious upon the sheets, had managed to stop her bleeding and ultimately save her life.

Blanche was looking at Louis, and Robert could see she was imagining that her son would die before her very eyes.

Alphonse walked into the room and held his wife's hand solemnly.

"We will keep watch over him," Robert said to the others as he walked over to his mother and put his arm around her. She leaned against him, grateful for his support. He felt in charge now that Louis was so ill. "Alphonse: you'll be here in the morning. Margaret: in the afternoon. Mother in the evening, and I will take the midnight watch."

Margaret looked up then, her face streaked with tears and her nose red and stuffy. "Where is Isabelle?"

"She went to *Petit Pont*," Blanche said, not moving her head from Robert's shoulder.

"She's going to be stuck in the city for a while. The people are swarming the streets," Alphonse said.

"I hope she is all right," Joan said.

Alphonse nodded in agreement and held his wife close. "To spare Robert the trouble at this time, I will preside over the English bounty. I will call for Pierre Mauclerc and the Knights Templar today in Louis' name. We must bring the Crown of Thorns back home immediately. Perhaps that will help rouse Louis. I will see to the arrangements."

Robert nodded at Alphonse's decision, knowing that it was not just the settling of accounts that his good brother worried about, but the lack of a very potent form of spiritual salvation. The Crown had never been outside the family since its inception to the chapel. Alphonse was correct, perhaps; if it was returned within a few days, Louis might pull out of this malady. Perhaps.

Woman is man's confusion.
Vincent of Beauvais, *Speculum Majus* (thirteenth century)

24

2, septembre, l'an de notre Seigneur 1242

The streets were so thronged with people, there seemed no end to the masses for as far as Isabelle could see. Her visit to the *université* had proved fruitful. She received a book of medicine well favored among the elite, called the *Secretum Secretorum*. It was an Arabic compendium of medical and moral advice, newly translated into Latin. She had been talking with Albertus Magnus about new plans for acquiring convent land when the town had turned into an uproar.

Since her return to Paris, she had been going round and round with the Church about land issues, money, and investment in her convent project. She had then turned her attention to the *université*, a group of more open-minded and less political friends, in the hope that they might help her more than the Church.

Then news of Louis' arrival had turned everything into an uproar. As soon as the good tidings came, she ran from *Petit Pont*. She had to get to the *palais*, to see them, to see that Jean . . .

Is he all right? Is he with them? She'd done everything in her power *not* to think about him, or anything about the war, because it was just too difficult to imagine the terrible outcome. But now . . .

It was so frustrating! She had to get home—she had to know if he was all right!

She had been walking for an hour, and she'd only managed to get as far as rue Garande, where her infamous roofing job had taken place a few years ago. As she neared Jacques' shop and home, she looked up at the roof that she'd managed to tack on completely by hand. It was still sturdy and beautiful. It hadn't really faded over the years despite some of the weather.

Then, as her gaze made its way over the roof, she froze. Perched upon the roof itself, staring down at her like a gargoyle from his lofty perch, was none other than Jean Adaret Benariel.

She blinked. Her mouth dropped open, and everything in the world dissolved. There were no people here at all; the world held only . . .

"*Jean!*"

He heard her shout, and smiled at her. She didn't have time to think, couldn't even breathe because he was *alive!* He was *here!*

. . . Somehow.

She rushed over to the building, pushing past the crowded villagers. When she reached the side, she saw a ladder going up to the roof.

She climbed the ladder as if she had a pair of wings and was able to fly up rather than step, and when Jean offered his gloved hand to her she grabbed it and then threw herself against him, burying her face against his chest in relief.

Jean Adaret Benariel stood in amazement. His gloved hands paused before gently resting against Isabelle's back. She held him tightly. He was still in a great amount of pain, but it seemed today that all the pain endured was worth this one moment. He didn't know what to do, just held her as if she were delicate blown glass. He tried not to think about how it made him feel, to have her in his arms. He closed his eyes; wanted to put his cheek against her hair, but held himself in check. He kept his eyes closed and let the moment wash over him.

❖ ❖ ❖

Isabelle realized she'd just done something completely impetuous. And now Jean was touching her back as if confused and uncomfortable about her forward behavior.

What made me do this? she thought as she stepped back awkwardly and tried to catch her breath. She could smell him; the smell of sweet, ancient roses lingered around him. It was an antiquarian scent that made her somewhat dizzy.

She groped for words that would explain her behavior before finally settling on, "You're alive!"

He nodded, watching her with a curious expression.

"I wasn't sure I'd ever see you again," she said, then gave up trying to explain. It was very embarrassing how he stared at her so. "Is everyone well?" she asked, realizing she'd been just as worried about the others. "Louis? Robert? . . ."

Was she just as worried about the others? Yes, of course. She'd been worried all along. That's why she was so glad to see Jean Adaret Benariel. She loved him as much as her brothers. Naturally.

"Let me take you to the castle," he replied with a small smile, and then turned, looking down at the street thronged to immobility by the crowds.

"It appears we're stuck." She laughed. He moved across the rooftop, very calmly, surveying the area.

"At least, being stuck, we are on a very firm, very wonderful roof," he replied.

She knew he was not saying it lightly, or absently. Isabelle could see that he knew the story behind this roof.

"*Oui,*" she whispered, and looked away, embarrassed.

Jean pointed across the rooftops. "The rooftops are all interconnected in this district; we need only walk across them."

She was not looking forward to the adventure. "It's dangerous. Not all the roofs in this area are as secure as this one. And most are made from straw, not tile."

"I promise you, Princess, I will not let you fall," he said, and somehow, she believed him.

He bent down and took the book she had dropped when she ran into his arms. Then he walked over to one roof that adjoined this one and looked back at her. "Come on, then."

She hesitated and smoothed her skirts. "I'm in a dress. I can't."

"I won't let anything happen to you," he said again. Then he added, "You can get through across the rooftops in a quarter of an hour."

She picked up her skirts and moved over to the second roof.

Jean smiled and kept going ahead of her, dropping from one roof, and stepping up to another. Isabelle followed. They made good time. Within a quarter of an hour, as promised, they reached the end of the island of town homes. At this end, there was a ladder waiting. It seemed too fortuitous.

"Did you put this here?" she asked Jean.

He looked at it. "No, but the watchmen did."

She tilted her head, and he elaborated. "The watchmen make routine checks over the rooftops to make sure there are no brawls or stampedes going on in the city."

Jean started down the ladder. Isabelle looked after him, amazed at how much he knew that she had never been aware of in all her time in Paris. Then she followed him.

Once on the ground, they made their way through back alleys until they reached the *Petit Pont* bridge. It would take them over to the *île de la Cité*. The bridge was also mired in civilians all celebrating shoulder to shoulder with one another. It would take an hour at least to go across.

Rue de St. Jacques seemed to be miles away. Crossing the bridge was going to take forever and the Quays were on the other side of the *île de la Cité*. Jean was walking down the sloped embankment to the river.

Isabelle followed, carefully treading down the steep slope to the river's edge, where a little rowboat was roped to the shore. She saw it and just laughed.

It was an incredulous noise, and Jean turned around with the boat rope in hand.

"Why do you laugh, Princess?"

"I don't believe it," she replied. "You brought us a boat."

"There's nothing unusual about a little forethought, Your Highness."

After all this time, she never understood why he still called her "Your Highness" and "Princess."

"Jean." She was hushed, and he looked into her eyes. "It's Isabelle. You're so dear to me. You've helped me, humored me . . ." She thought about it. "Taken me across rooftops and in boats to secret me home quickly, and yet you won't call me by my familiar."

He was staring at the rope. "Are we not friends?" she asked.

"Yes, we are friends."

"Good." She was pleasantly curt as she slipped into the boat. He slipped in beside her. Isabelle watched him pull in the rope and pick up the oars. They pushed off from the bank and started to row to the other side.

Today the Seine was calm and easy. As they pushed off from the bank, Isabelle looked around at the river. Under the *Grand* and *Petit Ponts*, the boat water mills were pounding away with large wet wheels. They were slowly being replaced by water mills attached to the sides of the bridge, though, as those were more powerful and had ramps for water to rise up and fall down on the wheels, turning them much faster than the currents of the wide river could make the others turn.

She looked up at the *Petit Pont* as they passed near it, and saw to her amazement that inside windows she could see a myriad of activities going on. The rag-catcher was walking carefully along the narrow catwalk behind all the shops, avoiding the crowds. *Well, that's one way I can get across in a hurry*, she thought. Then her common sense spoke up: *If you want to risk dying from the fall*, she thought.

Inside one of the windows, a physician was holding up a urine jar to the sunlight and looking at its contents. At another window she could hear the clanging of a smith at work on metal, and she saw the sparks flying out of the window as well as inside with every pound.

Smoke curled up from the bridges and the city beyond. There was traffic on the river. Boats were bringing wine casks and firewood to the city gates, where they were being inspected.

Jean rowed, and Isabelle thought, *He knows how to row well.*

"What else do you know how to do?" she asked.

"Oh, much, much more," he replied. It was a massive understatement, she could tell.

It intrigued her, but everything about Jean intrigued her. Today, she wondered how he could stand to be locked in a tower. And how had he learned so much if he was there all that time?

"We're here," Jean said. The boat had reached the opposite shore, and Isabelle hadn't even realized it.

Isabelle stepped onto dry land. Jean secured the rowboat and started up the bank.

"My . . . book?" she asked.

"Oh, of course." He pulled the book from his bag, then handed it to her.

She took it and felt a tingle move across her arms. Jean let go and turned.

"Allow me to accompany you to the castle," he said, but his tone was sad.

Shortly upon her arrival, Isabelle learned of Louis' collapse. Jean had not told her about the trouble that her brother was in, feeling it more appropriate that she hear it from Robert. After she had spent some time sitting beside Louis in the sick room, and pointing out certain herbs and balms that should be applied to his forehead and neck by Margaret, she left the room.

Margaret had calmed upon having something productive to do. Isabelle had at least found something to keep Louis' wife occupied so that she would not be wailing when Louis needed much rest.

Isabelle gently closed the door on the sad lovers. Louis had slept the entire time she was bedside. Isabelle sighed to herself as the door snicked shut. She'd been elated just a few hours before, walking above the streets of Paris with Jean.

It was obvious to her now that he had been searching for her in the city, and why he had taken care to speed her to the castle quickly. But he had said nothing to her about her brother's condition. She bit her lip and continued down the stairs past the Gentlemen's Quarters.

She heard a faint gasp. Someone was in quiet pain.

Isabelle looked up. The floor was completely deserted, but the door of the common room, the one that led to the bath, was opened a crack. There was a faint rustling from inside the room. Concerned, Isabelle made her way to the room and peeked in.

She caught the last glimpse of a figure walking past her narrow band of view, his white linen undershirt stained with bright blood. She knocked.

"Yes?" It was Jean's voice.

"May I come in?"

The door creaked as her hand slid around the side of the wood and grasped the edge.

"Just a . . . Let me just . . ."

She looked around the door's edge and found him fumbling weakly with an overcoat.

"You're wounded," she said. She moved through the doorway to where Jean sat on a low, wooden bench.

One sleeve of his jacket rested against his good arm, and the other sleeve was still behind his back. A wound spread across the soft spot between his chest and shoulder, and his linen shirt was stained dark red above the skin.

"Why didn't you tell me about this?" she asked.

"About what?" He put his head back against the wall and closed his eyes, his body heavy with fatigue.

"That you were wounded." She knelt down before him when he didn't answer and inspected his shirt. "You shouldn't have been climbing ladders and rowing me across a river with a wound like this."

"I had to see you safely to the castle. There wasn't a lot of time and no other choice." He opened his eyes and watched her, surprised by her attentions.

"It's completely torn open again. It might get infected at this rate. We can't risk that—not right now." She looked around the room. "If you are not careful, you will wind up like Louis. Why do you men never take care of yourselves? You leave it up to us to nag you. Women don't like to nag, but you leave us no choice." She scowled at him and nudged his jacket off. He was shy about her touching his clothing, seemed to wince at her insistence.

"Perhaps men like the attention," he suggested.

"Your shirt is sticking to your wound."

"Put your finger upon it."

Isabelle hesitated with her hand just inches from his skin. She could almost feel the warmth radiating out from the wound and didn't particularly want to touch it. Yet there was also a part of her that wanted very much to tend it. She tried not to think about it, but it was there, just under the surface. The conflict made her hesitate.

"Don't worry," he said gently.

She pressed her finger down until she could feel the opening of his wound beneath it.

"Move it slowly around," he said, then inhaled sharply as she started.

"Oh—I'm sorry!"

"No, we're almost done."

"There." She opened her eyes and knelt back a little. The wound seemed to close slightly under the pressure of her touch.

"Can you help me lift off the shirt?" he asked.

"Yes, of course."

She gently removed his shirt cuff from around his hand, and then slid the soft sleeve over his elbow as he pushed his arm out the bottom of the shirt. He helped pull the shirt over his head.

"Thank you," he said, and cast the shirt on the bench beside him.

"I should go and get bandages."

"I have some." He pointed over to a little knapsack on the door-knob of a cupboard.

She went over to it, took the sack down, and opened it up to retrieve the bandages.

"I can do it," he insisted.

"No, I will help you." She unrolled some of the bandages. "Why didn't you take care of this?"

"I did. I had the wound bandaged and it was nearly healed, but . . ."

She pressed a bandage to his soft spot, and he winced and looked at the floor. "But you opened it again when you came for me."

"Yes," he replied.

She continued wrapping. "I wish you had said something about Louis when you came to get me."

"You would have been upset, without anything to do but worry, and I would have caused you unnecessary suffering." He looked at her face, and she continued to stare at the bandages she sealed closed.

She didn't answer him, because there was no reply necessary. There was something about how he said it that made her understand. She was touched, and didn't know what more to add to his explanation.

"I'll take my leave now," she said.

✤ ✤ ✤

As Isabelle left, she stopped in the hall and left the door open. Jean heard a voice he recognized as belonging to Pierre Mauclerc.

"Are you here about the return of the Crown of Thorns?" Isabelle asked.

"*Non*," he replied. "Not exactly. I'm making sure you didn't need any consoling."

"Why would I need consoling?"

"I heard that Jean Adaret Benariel was grievously injured during the battle, by many men. I knew he was a friend of yours."

"Jean is just fine, *Seigneur* Mauclerc. *Merci*." Her voice sounded irate.

"Ah. Well," Mauclerc said, sounding slightly dismayed. "I'm so very glad to hear that." He obviously wasn't, Jean could tell as he glared at the door.

Jean realized something, deep inside, and his anger began to grow.

There are things you suspect, things you know, and things you can prove.

He suspected Pierre Mauclerc for being interested in his particular well-being, for being absent at the battle of his king, and for the seven large and sinister men who'd attempted to kill him during the battle of Angers. Suspecting him led to no form of proof, however.

Footsteps receded down the hall as Pierre Mauclerc walked out, but not before Jean moved into the hallway.

The force of Jean's stare made Pierre turn on the stairs.

"*Seigneur* Benariel!" Pierre smiled.

Jean didn't say a word, just stared at him.

"Can I do something for you?" Pierre asked.

Like a lion watching prey, Jean simply stared.

"Well, I'm very glad to see you're alive." Pierre waved a bit, smiled, and then left.

Jean stared intently at where Mauclerc had been standing until a beam against the ceiling cracked with a loud *pop!*

Knowing sorrow well, I learn the way to succor the distressed.

Virgil, *The Aeneid* (30–19 B.C.)

25

The family was gathered in Queen Blanche's darkened sitting room. They'd come at the queen's command, to discuss Louis' condition.

"Louis is unable to attend to matters of state. His son is a mere child, and his wife is stricken with grief. I ruled in his place when he was only a child," Blanche said. "And today I will take up his burden again."

"Mother, I do not mean to disagree," Alphonse said. "But shouldn't we declare an official period of prayer and supplication for him? Shouldn't the Church at least be alerted to pray for him?"

"No, we must appear strong. The sake of the realm depends on our unity. It must look as if nothing has happened to weaken France," Blanche replied.

"But Louis is dying," Isabelle spoke up.

"Don't say that!" Margaret started to cry. "He isn't dying! I won't let it happen!"

"I agree with Isabelle," Alphonse said. "I think we must make peace for his soul somehow—if not publicly, then we must pray or mourn in the house. It feels wrong to just go about our business." Joan sat beside her husband, silently nodding, but soothing Margaret on the back.

Queen Blanche pulled open the drawer of the sitting room table where she sat. From inside the drawer, Blanche withdrew an old and weathered piece of paper. She held it as carefully as a dried rose petal.

"This is the last thing your father wrote to me, just before he went to the battle that killed him. In this letter he told me that whatever happened to him, I must be strong. I must raise my son to become a king and never falter in his father's name. He told me, here, 'The world expects us to go on.'"

Blanche stared for several moments at the words written on the letter. "My son is dying. And the world expects us to go on."

Isabelle said, "Then we will go on, Mother." Then she rose and showed the family out of Blanche's sitting room, leaving her mother alone.

When Blanche heard the door close, she stared at herself in the mirror and clenched the letter tightly in her hand. Her husband's words echoed in her ears. They grew louder, whirling into the sounds of warfare and strife, painful cries of grief and agony; they pummeled against her temples with such ferocity that she could no longer stand it.

Queen Blanche ripped all the bottles, combs, jewels, and material from her sitting room table. Vials exploded in shards against the wall from the force of the impact. Material fluttered like fallen birds and landed limp against the floor. Metal clashed against hard, stained wood.

Then the world was silent.

Queen Blanche looked at the letter in her hand. She had loved her husband. She loved her son. She opened the door of her barren sitting room table and replaced its priceless contents. The letter disappeared from view as she closed the drawer quietly once more.

The Order of the Rose returned to the *palais* a day after Louis' collapse and unsuccessful medical treatment by Theodore. The three sisters made their way with quiet dignity to the gates of the castle. Jean stood at his tower window and saw them approaching. He was apprehensive, but he felt a great sense of relief at seeing Norea with his two other sisters. As soon as they dismounted their horses at the stable, Jean blew out the candle on his bed stand and made his way down the stairs from his room.

Within a few moments, his three sisters walked through the sitting room door.

"Jean!" Neci cried, and ran to kiss and hold him. "Oh, look at you —you are wounded!" She had noticed him wince as she held him fast.

Jean only nodded quietly in acknowledgment. He looked over at Norea, who had some cuts and bruises on her face. His heart skipped a beat as he walked over to her. Without a word, he held his sister close.

Norea held him tightly in return with her head against his chest.

"We brought Elizabetta to the dungeon," Sofia said without a greeting. "Hugh de la Marche was most pleased to see his wife, for some odd reason."

"They had a fight," Norea replied, leaning back from Jean's embrace. "That's when she discovered me and . . ."

Neci approached her. "It's all over now." She rubbed Norea's shoulder. Norea took her sister's hand against her shoulder and patted it gently.

Jean sat down, exhausted.

Sofia walked up to him. "I just heard about Louis, from Blanche. It's dysentery. He's dying. Why didn't you take care of him?" The other sisters seemed surprised at her directness.

Jean looked at Sofia with a bit of surprise. "At first, I didn't know he was ill. No one did."

"They can't hide something like that from one of us."

"Is that so?" Jean asked irately, and thought about Isabelle and all that she was capable of.

"I left him in your care, and you failed me."

"On the journey back from war, I was mostly unconscious or too weak to move," Jean explained. This took Sofia by surprise. "I was recovering from my own wounds. You know I must suffer what wounds I sustain, yet you didn't even bother to ask about my own injuries."

Neci interrupted. "Jean, I know you are wounded. It's all right."

She came over and sat next to him, and looked up at her older sister. "It's just that Louis has been in our care since he was just a child. We've come too far with him for it to end like this."

"We must do something," Norea agreed.

"You're too weak, Norea. You *must* rest."

"It's all in vain," Sofia replied. "The king is so wasted away, if one of us tries to save him, we may not survive."

"I will go to him tonight," Jean said.

"You could die," Norea replied.

"I know," he replied.

"You might survive," Sofia thought aloud. "You have always been . . . stronger than us." She paced quietly. "But the king is so close to death, I don't know what the outcome would truly be."

"The outcome is irrelevant. The king must live, and that is all there is to it. I will go to him tonight."

Jean left. Neci stared after him, her eyes brimming with tears.

❧ ❧ ❧

As Norea passed Pierre Mauclerc in the hallway on her way to bed, he recognized her immediately as the serving woman in Elizabetta's *château*. Only she was wearing a white robe with a red embroidered rose . . . just like the other Sisters of the Order of the Rose.

Pierre realized that Norea must have been the one Edgar had told him about—the spy in Elizabetta's *château*. Very clever to roost as a serving woman while spying for Queen Blanche. The English emissary, Edgar, had also told Pierre that Elizabetta and Hugh de la Marche had been captured, but could shed no light on whether or not they would talk about Mauclerc's involvement.

Pierre's only recourse was to see if they'd told the king. He decided the only way to do that was to come straight to the castle as if nothing had happened.

It appeared that Hugh had not squealed. The royals and their company treated Pierre no differently now than before the war. And this was certainly an interesting development, this Norea being a part of the Sisters. It was all good information for his own order, the Templars. He would let *Seigneur* Dunbière know about it immediately. For a fee, of course.

⚜ ⚜ ⚜

Queen Blanche was surprised to see Isabelle attend court in the Great Room for the punishment of Hugh de la Marche. It was a look that Isabelle had not seen often across her mother's face, but she recognized it for what it was.

"Why?" Blanche asked. "You've never come to such a meeting before."

"Since Louis can't be present for his punishment, I thought more than one family member should be here as a show of unity and authority." Isabelle sat on the bed-turned-throne next to her mother.

Before Blanche could reply, Hugh de la Marche was shown into the room. He was chained, shackled, and filthy, and he appeared to have suffered injuries incurred after his capture. Isabelle looked on him without pity. He had been responsible for the start of war; he had given Louis the dysentery he might die from. He deserved punishment.

Blanche spoke first. "We have decided upon your sentence, Hugh de la Marche. When once We were forgiving of your crimes against Our family, We know now you are not worthy of forgiveness."

Hugh would not look at her. He said nothing, only stared at the floor before him.

"You will be executed by dawn."

His face betrayed no expression, no emotion. Finished with him, Queen Blanche motioned to the guards to pull him away. But Isabelle interrupted.

"Why?" she asked. It was directed not at Blanche, but at Hugh.

It was the simplest sentence—only one word—but it made Hugh look at her. "Because you killed my brother-in-law and took my lands after pretending to give me my heritage back. Because you were dis honorable, hiding behind the Church. And I would do it all over again, only this time I would find a way to purge this country of your dishonest blood."

Isabelle stood. "What are you talking about?"

"Don't be so grand and all-assuming, Princess. You stole my land. The Church took the land from me, and presented it to your family for use as a convent for your little holy dream. I checked with them. It was the most disgusting thing anyone could do in the name of God. I assure you that we will meet in the future, together in hell."

Blanche looked at her daughter. Isabelle reached for the cushions in order to stop the world from spinning. "The Church . . . that was *your* land?"

The pain on Isabelle's face, the look of betrayal, could not be mis-read. It stopped everyone in the room. The moment was long and cold. Isabelle felt as if her stomach were shrinking. Blanche must have realized that such a revelation was not fitting for the eyes of a prisoner.

"Take him below," she ordered the guards. They moved to haul Hugh from the room. He had no other words, it seemed. But neither did Isabelle.

When they were alone, Blanche held out her hand to her daughter. "My dear girl, are you all right?"

Isabelle sat hard, missed the cushions of the seat and landed against the floor. She didn't even notice.

"No, Mother," she whispered. "I started a war."

✤ ✤ ✤

A choir of boys echoed in the hallowed halls of Notre Dame as the large doors at the end of the church were opened in the middle of Mass. The volume of the choir lessened, the children noticing the disturbance as the congregation turned around. Bishop Arnaud was at the altar, and he shielded his eyes from the glare of the sun streaming into the dark cathedral. The last of the singing halted.

Two guards stood at the opened doors as, from the light, Princess Isabelle appeared. She walked out of the blinding sunlight and down the long, dark path toward the altar. When she reached the sacred dais, she knelt down silently before it. She put her steepled fingers to her lips. They were moving in a silent prayer; her eyes were closed.

No one said a word.

Bishop Arnaud watched Isabelle rise from her knees, pulling a scroll he recognized from her skirts. She held the scroll out. He didn't take it, but he stared at her with a look that told Isabelle he did not understand this royal intrusion.

"I just prayed to the Father, the Son, and the Holy Spirit," she said as if to explain. "I am hoping that I will redeem myself before them today in a place where they cannot help but watch my actions. Do you see this scroll, Your Grace?"

"Yes, Princess?"

"This is the land of the Church. You gave it to me for the founding of my convent."

Arnaud stood taller in his red robes. Isabelle could see he looked at her with strange concern. She didn't care what it meant; she didn't care if he knew or didn't know what he'd done one day many months before.

"I revoke the claim to this land in the name of God the Father." Isabelle dropped the scroll on the cold, gray stone of Notre Dame's floor. Arnaud's gaze followed it to the floor, where he saw Isabelle's boot raise up and then come smashing down on the royal seal of the Church. The red wax smashed to pieces beneath the hard sole of her boot. The holy insignia was marred beyond recognition.

Arnaud gasped.

"The only thing that will come bubbling up from this land is the blood of the men who died from the war it started."

Isabelle turned, and walked from the dark cathedral, back into the light streaming in from outside. She did not close the doors of Notre Dame on the way out.

✤ ✤ ✤

Neci approached Jean's room and knocked softly. As she opened the door, Jean turned to regard her.

"What is it?" he asked.

"I know you're going to Louis soon, but let me prepare him for you," she said, stepping inside. "He's not in good condition. I will clean up his person."

Jean nodded, staring at his hands. He had removed his gloves. "Things are a lot different than the last time you came to see me, aren't they?" He held up his hands, gloveless and vulnerable, between them. "Not so many things hung in the balance. I didn't know coming here would mean risking such a failure."

Neci rushed over to him then, and held him fast. "I'm sorry it's come to this. I wanted you to be happy here."

"I have been happier here than anywhere else," he replied, stroking her hair. "Don't worry. I will be all right."

✤ ✤ ✤

Robert had nodded off, sitting over Louis' bed. It was late. The door cracked open behind his sleeping frame. Neci, youngest sister of the Order of the Rose, crept into the room.

She was dressed in her regular white robe with red rose embroidery on the front, and her hair was pulled back in three ties cascading down her back. She put a hand on Robert's shoulder and gently roused him.

He sat up, immediately overwhelmed with the guilt of having fallen asleep on duty. Robert looked up and saw Neci, not Margaret or Blanche, standing over him. She smiled down at him with a gentle and yet somehow sad face.

"I guess I drifted off," he whispered.

"It's understandable, Your Highness. This is not your usual hour. It's very good of you to take the hardest watch."

Robert nodded, and shifted in his seat, trying to wake up.

"Please, go rest. I will watch for you until morning," she said.

Robert looked up at her, and his face betrayed the gratitude he felt deep in his very bones. His bones were grateful because they had started aching from sitting up all night in this chair, instead of being in his warm bed. The change in his sleep schedule had been very difficult. It was a kind gesture.

He looked into Neci's eyes. If ever a grateful man could look so wholly at a woman with innocent pleasure, this was the very portrait of it.

"Go on," she urged in a whisper. "I'll rouse you after eight hours."

"Thank you." He stood, stretched his cramping legs, then turned to look at her once more. "And please wake me if he worsens or wakes." The "wakes" was nothing more than a dying hope, for it was long past possible for Louis to come out of his state. Theodore the physician had said Louis was now on his last days.

But Neci didn't flinch in the face of this hopeless request. "I will have someone rouse you should his condition change either way. Go now, and sleep."

Robert nodded and left the room. Just before the door clicked shut, he saw Neci sit beside Louis' bed.

✢ ✢ ✢

The angel was close. Her wings flapped against the wind and made Louis' hair stir. He opened his eyes. The angel was surrounded by a bright light, just as it had been described in Holy Scripture. She was the most beautiful thing he had ever seen.

This celestial form was very close now, radiant. Her graceful hands reached out for his pale, sickly ones. He could not lift them to her; he could not move. He was so tired. So tired of fighting. He just wanted sleep.

"It is time to bring you back, my king," the angel said. Her face was hard to make out, because she was so radiant, but he thought he saw her smile. It was ethereal, melancholy, and the most beautiful smile he'd ever known. He felt the angel clasp her hands over his. They were so warm, like stepping up to a hearth after being out in the snow.

Louis felt his body began to pink, felt her body against his now, warm and delightful. Firm, soft, unlike any other body he'd ever known. Was this Margaret? Was this angel who pressed herself against him really his wife? Was it a fever dream?

A rosy glow spread between them. He could feel himself breathing now, could feel the angel's breath against his lips. Her face was so close. He could almost make it out. Did he know her? She looked like someone he couldn't recall. . . . She was beautiful.

She was so beautiful. . . .

Shaking lips touched his own. Did angels kiss? He couldn't remember. But he kissed her back. When he opened his mouth, a hot vortex of air flew in against his tongue. His eyes opened wide, and he felt tears tumble from his eyes. He felt the angel's lips against his own.

Such sweet lips. Such a breath of air. He sucked in another gulp, and it was sweet and revitalizing. Louis opened his eyes. He wanted to see her again. The angel was growing dim. The angel was dark now, receding into shadows that were swallowing her. Swallowing up the angel and leaving him cold, alone . . .

Louis stretched out a hand and touched the face before him.

Neci looked haggard and tired, tired beyond the ability of his words to describe.

She tried to smile, the best she could effect.

Louis was crying. "Neci?" It was barely a whisper from his lips.

Her hands still gripped his own.

"Neci, did you . . . ?" He tried to think. He was warm, as if in a drunken stupor. "Did you just kiss . . . ?"

Abruptly, she staggered back and released his hands. Louis saw white robes against ashen flesh, her dark eyes. It was all that was left of Neci. It was as though everything about her that was alive had flowed into him.

Louis' lips moved again: *Why?* But no voice or whisper could come out. Just the lips moving in silence.

"Because . . . we . . . love you."

❧   ❧   ❧

With the last of her energy, Neci staggered to the door of the king's sick-chamber. With a groan, she pushed open the door and tumbled out into the hall.

A serving girl shrieked as Neci fell into her, causing her to drop all the linen she was carrying. Then, realizing that Neci was in great pain and distress, the young girl knelt down and held the woman in her arms.

There was a moment of panic as the seconds ticked by, and then with her last gasp, Neci breathed, "Wake the family, the king . . ."

That is all the youngest Sister of the Rose could manage. She collapsed in the serving girl's arms. The young girl shrieked.

❧   ❧   ❧

Isabelle was praying when she heard the commotion from downstairs in the tower. She feared the worst, but finished her prayer—a vigil that had been going all night long. Then she stood and grabbed her dressing robe.

By the last few stairs, she could already hear Margaret and Blanche shouting. She thought they were arguing at first, but then the shouts sounded more frantic.

She flew down the hallway. The third door on the left, Louis' sickroom door, was wide open. There was a crowd of servants in the hallway and hardly space to make her way through to his room, but when she elbowed in, she saw her brother Robert, Sofia, Blanche, and Margaret inside.

She heard Margaret's voice, again something between grief and happiness. *"Oh! Louis!"*

Isabelle stopped at the door. There was Louis, sitting up in bed, holding Margaret, who was sobbing against his shoulder.

He looked . . . perfectly fine. Blanche was on the other side of the bed, kneeling, her dark head bowed and her forehead touched lightly against her steepled fingers. Her lips were moving in a silent prayer.

Louis looked up and saw Isabelle standing in the doorway. Their eyes met. And for a moment, Isabelle knew something unbelievable had just occurred.

As if she were nine years old again, she padded over to the bed and remembered the feeling on the day long ago when she had asked him to marry her. She knew Louis was remembering it too; she could see it in his eyes. He looked at his sister.

"Louis, I thought . . ."

She trailed off, for it was apparent that the statement had probably been uttered by everyone in the room. He was sitting healthy before all of them, when hours before he'd been at death's door.

"I am better now," he said in a thin voice, not completely recovered but obviously well.

"How . . . ?" she asked.

"I don't know, really. I woke up, and Neci . . ." He trailed off.

"That's all I know." He looked confused, as if he had more to say, then simply looked sad.

Isabelle looked around the room, then back out into the hall. "Neci?"

"It's a miracle," the queen mother whispered.

"Neci?" she called again, her stomach dropping, and she left the room to go back into the hallway. The hall was still thronged with servants, and not one would answer her.

Something was horribly wrong, and she couldn't understand until . . .

. . . She saw the body behind the throng of servants, past Louis' sickroom on the other side of the hall. The white robe, the red flower on the center, embroidered in thread, the pale neck and the dark hair . . .

The dark hair of her beloved Neci.

"Neci!" she cried.

She quickly fell to her knees and scrambled over to Neci's lifeless body. Isabelle wanted to wake her up, wanted to make everything all right. How could Louis be alive, and Neci be dead? Neci and her sisters had been the strongest part of the whole family. A life without them wouldn't be the same.

It couldn't happen.

Jean appeared beside her, holding Neci in his arms, and his face was a mixture of pain, regret, anguish, and shame. Isabelle saw his face as he looked into her eyes, and she couldn't hold back the pain any longer. She burst into tears, grabbing at Neci's body and hugging it to her face.

"*God*, what have you done? No, no, no!" Her cries were half tears, half growls of absolute pain. She cried for Neci, for herself, and most of all, she cried for Jean. He could not release his anguish in front of the others. Not here, not where the courtiers, priests, servants, and hangers-on would all see it. But she would cry for him, because she knew that Neci was his sister, and now Neci was dead.

The pain was horrible, choking and suffocating her. She wouldn't let go of Neci as a retinue of priests came to take the body to the

church, where there would be a wake, and where the final arrangements for burial would be performed.

Jean was looking into Louis' room now with a blank stare. The
family was still huddled together, thankfully receiving attention from
their healthy king.

Isabelle turned to him, still full of sobs and unable to speak clearly.
"I'm going . . . to pray at the family chapel. Come with me."

Isabelle returned to Louis' chamber, realizing one more sin yet to be
absolved. "Brother, promise me you will hold off on Hugh's execution
until I return from the chapel. There is something I must tell you."

"I will hold his execution until we speak." Louis looked at her face,
tear-stained and puffy, and his expression was one of abject sorrow.

"Thank you." Isabelle sniffled against the sleeve of her dress. She
touched Jean's arm and walked out with him.

✤ ✤ ✤

Once they reached the road outside, Isabelle realized that she must tell
Jean what she knew: that he was Neci's brother.

"Jean." She turned to him. "I haven't been sure how to say this,
because I haven't been certain that it was the right time, or the right thing
for me to know. But since this has happened, I'm going to tell you . . ."

His gaze grew more panicked as she kept talking, but she continued. "I know you're Sofia's brother."

He was hoarse, and angry tears broke out in his eyes as he stopped
in the road and wouldn't walk any farther. "How?"

"I accidentally overheard your conversation when you first came
back to our castle. When Sofia asked you why you had disobeyed her
and come back from the tower. The day you thought she had already
left with Louis. I *know* it was not something I was meant to overhear,"
she said, and felt him turn cold beside her. She risked a sidelong
glance, and the look in his eyes made her shrink back.

"I debated telling you for two years," she added, but he was speeding up, walking briskly to get away from her. She ran to catch up with him; tears were starting to stream down her cheeks again.

"Jean, *please* don't walk away!" Isabelle was sobbing through the cry.

"It would have been much better had you never told me that you knew about this."

"I thought so too, until today. You were miserable in there, and I knew that if I didn't give you a chance to get to the chapel to grieve, you would die of pain. I am your *friend*. I . . ." She faltered, losing her voice again to tears. "I *care* about you, Jean."

He was staring off at the trees, crying silently, as if he couldn't believe the sentiment.

"I will never—even under duress—tell anyone what I know. I swear it."

"I'm afraid for my family." He shook uncontrollably. "See what has happened to us."

"I understand that fear."

"You can't understand," he said; then he stopped. Head bowed, he replied simply, "No, I know you do. I don't know how you could know, but you do. And you always have."

"I always will," she said, and she held one of his knotted, gloved hands to her chest.

Jean looked at the ground, and tears dropped from his long lashes and hit his chest. He said two hoarse words, but they were more than words. They were a vow.

"Thank you."

We are all equal in the presence of death.

Publilius Syrus, *Moral Sayings* (c. 100 B.C.)

26

Louis was kneeling in prayer at the altar of the family chapel when Isabelle came into the room. It was late afternoon, and she was so very tired. But she'd had to come here and make peace with her circumstances. Isabelle knelt down beside her brother, put her fingers up to her lips, and stared straight ahead.

"What did you pray for?" she asked.

"The strength to understand my enemies," he replied.

Isabelle closed her eyes. After a few moments she opened them again, still staring at the figure of Christ on the cross before them.

"What did you pray for?" he asked.

"Oh, the same."

"I see" was his only reply.

"Do you think that God is capable of forgiving us for *everything* we've ever done?"

"I believe He can."

"Even if we didn't know that we'd done it, but our offense still caused great injury? Do you think . . . that He could forgive us that?"

Louis paused before saying, "I think so."

"Then I must ask God to forgive me. Each day, I will ask Him to forgive me. For the rest of my life."

"What did you do?"

"I started a war," she replied.

Neither brother nor sister looked away from the figure on the cross. "Isabelle, you couldn't possibly have—"

351

"No, I did. I didn't know it, but . . . I gave Hugh his reasons for striking at you."

"Is this why you went to Notre Dame the other day?"

"You know about that?" she asked.

"I know of everything that happens in my realm," he replied. Isabelle realized her brother sounded older today. Wiser, perhaps. "I also knew it was only a matter of time before you came to tell me why you did what you did."

"Then you know about the Church land I returned." She put her hands against her lips again as she spoke. "You can't kill Hugh. He fought against you because we took more of his land. It was reasonable cause to fight."

"You didn't know," he replied.

"It doesn't matter if I knew. It was wrong. Call it an oversight, call it what you will, it killed hundreds of innocent men, it nearly killed my brother, and it has caused much pain and suffering. Louis, I can never atone for that. But I can spare Hugh's life."

Without looking over at her, Louis rose from his prayers. "Meet me in the Great Room."

Louis left the room, and Isabelle's eyes closed, her forehead collapsed against the palms of her hands, and she sat shaking for many minutes.

Hugh de la Marche sat across from his wife in their cell in the darkness beneath Paris. She had done nothing but complain for the duration.

"You are such a wretch," she said, not for the first time.

"Elizabetta, be silent. I will hear no more." Hugh was to be executed today, and although he was certain it was far past dawn, he anticipated that the axe would soon be against his neck. For what Queen Blanche decreed was never reversed.

"You!" Elizabetta nearly screamed. "Hugh, you are a petty, vindictive, sniveling man. The only reason I ever stayed with you was because of your ability to make my name great. But you can't even live up to that. Instead we sit here, rotting away in the dungeon of a snot-nosed king— for how long? You can't even barter your freedom! You filthy—"

"I said enough!" he shouted.

"Do you realize I could get out of here right now? I could leave you behind in one gesture? I can have any man I want! I could take any of those guards in there, right now, in front of you. That would teach you never to raise your voice to me!"

"Elizabetta, *I* would take one of those guards at the moment! If someone's going to be riding my *arse*, then I'd like it to be someone who's *enjoying* himself!"

Before she could reply, a guard stepped over to the door. Hugh looked up in time to see the guard smile darkly, pry open the lock, and point to him to come out.

✦ ✦ ✦

Isabelle and Louis watched as Hugh was dragged in from the dungeons. He looked upon his king with contempt.

"Wanted to see me before I was decapitated?" Hugh asked.

"Hugh, why did you strike at me after I gave you land at Alphonse's knighting ceremony? I treated you as kin."

Hugh laughed at the irony. "You're still playing the role of injured hero, I see. You *stole my land from me!* And if that wasn't insult enough, you killed my brother-in-law when he came as a protected emissary to your court."

Louis had not heard this before, and Isabelle had not remembered what he'd said until now. "I killed your brother-in-law? Who was this emissary, for I do not remember him."

"Don't lie to me," Hugh said.

"I have no reason to lie." Louis was calm in reply.

"Then you are trying to save face now that the ugly truth is out." Hugh shook his head.

"Save face with who? Guards do not care about lies or honesty, Hugh. But I do. Who was this emissary?"

"His name was Roger of Artois."

"Isabelle?" Louis didn't even have to ask. Isabelle walked over to the large book on the shelf and pulled it down. She thumbed through the pages, then looked at Louis and shook her head.

"We have no record of his arrival at court," Louis said.

"Of course not—you could have killed him on the road! Your royal guards did it!"

Louis shook his head. "I did no such thing."

Hugh was so outraged, he walked up to the king and spit in his face. Isabelle slammed the book down on the table, and Hugh looked over at her. There was a stunned moment as Louis wiped the spittle away.

"I know your anger, and I know you think I did this. But I did not. Nor did I know about the land the Church gave to Isabelle."

"I have since revoked the claim to that land," Isabelle said, returning to Louis' side.

"And as king, I have asked that it be returned to your family, as a reparation. You can see proof of that, when you arrive at Notre Dame."

Hugh looked at Louis, who produced a key from his garments and unlocked Hugh's shackles. Then Louis handed the key to Hugh.

"Your freedom."

The two watched as Hugh rubbed his wrists and tried to discern what was happening. Isabelle could see him still trying to grasp his anger and not fathoming what had just happened: How could Louis have unlocked him and set him free? Louis couldn't possibly have defeated him in battle, captured him, and let him suffer in prison if the end result was simply to set him free. Isabelle could almost hear the thoughts in Hugh's mind.

"Your . . ." Hugh tried to say. Was it a trick?

He looked at his hands holding the key to his freedom. "Your Majesty, I—I don't understand."

"You are free to go," Louis said simply. "I understand your rage over the death of your brother-in-law. I would be filled with fury if my brother was murdered. And naturally, I would direct it at whatever man I thought was the guilty assassin." Louis leaned in. "Go and find his killer."

Hugh obviously had no idea what to do. The man sank to his knees. He seemed stunned, yet again, with all the wind taken from his sails. He was unable to move.

"Oh. And We *will* be conducting a thorough inquiry into the matter of your brother-in-law," Louis added. "I don't know if We'll ever find who did this, but at least with an inquiry, We have a hope of dissuading any individuals who strike at your family. And mine." Louis rose. "You are free to go."

"Your Majesty." Hugh bowed, sitting there upon his knees in wonder.

Jean stepped inside the room that he had occupied for months at the castle. Today, he would be leaving. As he opened drawers and emptied their contents into a saddlebag, he realized how very little he had in the way of personal items.

He regarded the bag in his gloved hands with a sense of detachment, then slung it over his shoulder. He was remembering the day he'd put his gloved fingers to Neci's chin and regarded them, realizing at that moment how very close to the real world he had been.

Too close. He squeezed his eyes shut in pain. When he opened them again, he took one last look at his room before leaving.

Pierre Mauclerc had a double interest in the royal family these days. Not only had he insisted on keeping the Crown of Thorns until Louis was well enough to ask for it back, but he had sent word to the Templars about the miraculous recovery of the king and the mysterious death of the serving woman named Neci.

The Templars had replied, asking Pierre to keep a close eye on the Sisters and anyone who came and went in consultation with them. Pierre did as instructed, glad for any money that could be earned. At first he thought the whole fascination with the Order of the Rose was a ridiculous curiosity. Now, it was beginning to worry him. He was seeing things recently that he didn't want to believe. Strange forces that he was starting to wish he wasn't a part of—money or not.

Pierre was holding the Crown as insurance, but also as a charm against what he was investigating for the Templars. If this Order of the Rose got any more peculiar, he was going to bow out of further investigations. Something about those women, Sofia in particular, made his skin crawl.

Isabelle had needed some time alone, despite her best intentions. The death of Neci had been very hard on her. She had been particularly fond of Neci, since the time she was very young. . . . That odd day in the courtyard had brought them closer together, somehow. It wouldn't have seemed they were close to an outsider, but it was unspoken love.

Now, Neci was gone. They had put her body in a stone mausoleum, at Sofia's instruction, and had rolled a giant stone door closed over the entrance. The tomb was beautifully carved and exquisite in detail. Sofia had overseen all the arrangements for Neci, and it was from their own funds that the tomb was erected. The Order of the Rose would not take offers of charity from Blanche and Louis. At first, this upset the king and queen mother, but Sofia explained that while the gesture was kind and appreciated, it was not the Sisters' way.

There was no public ceremony for Neci. A very private one was held with Blanche, Louis, Robert, and Isabelle present. Sofia and Norea, of course, had arranged everything and were standing at the head of the great sarcophagus as it was taken into the vault. As they sealed the tomb shut, Isabelle wept.

✦ ✦ ✦

Jean stood with his two remaining sisters. Sofia was motionless, but Norea was slowly stroking the stone that had been rolled in front of Neci's great tomb.

"It's getting late," Sofia said. "We should be going."

Norea slowly let her hands slip down the stone until she no longer touched the smooth carvings. She walked away with her head down, unable to look up from grief.

Sofia started to join her, and then realized Jean was not with them. "Jean?" she asked.

"Go on," he replied.

"You will be missed at court."

"So will Neci." His voice was bitter. Sofia had no answer for the comment, and both Norea and she left him alone with his grief. That is exactly what Jean had wanted, because now he would right the situation, even at the cost of his own happiness. Or at the cost of his own life, if it came to it.

Jean approached the mighty stone that sealed the tomb shut. He touched it lightly with both hands, and he spoke to the stone as if to a sleeping child.

"Open," he urged in a whisper.

Be not forgetful to entertain strangers: for thereby some have entertained angels unawares.

Hebrews 13:1–2

27

20, *octobre, l'an de notre Seigneur* 1242

The grief of Neci's passing struck deep at the entire royal court. Where there was once merriment and laughter, the sounds of children and minstrels, there was nothing but sad silence. The family waited without speech as noblemen came to profess their claims before king and court. Louis' recommendations were brief, his edicts even shorter.

God moves in mysterious ways, Isabelle considered one day, when the silence of her family was enough to drive her mad. This was the day that God had given the royal family of France a new voice. His name was Thomas Aquinas.

The young man strolled into the Great Room of the royal family and slowly made his way to the great dais where Louis and Blanche sat. He bowed low, his portly frame threatening to fold over from the shift in weight. He was dressed demurely, in dark cottons and suede.

"Great king and majesty, Louis the Pious. I come before you a humble lord from Aquino, and ask your permission to examine the *université* so that I might discern if I can study here in Paris with your good people."

"*Oui*, you have my blessing, good sir." Louis seemed almost nonchalant.

Thomas Aquinas stood back up and stared around at all those assembled. His eyes slowly took in Louis, Blanche, Isabelle, and

Charles, who was also present. Then Aquinas looked at Louis and spoke. "You have suffered a loss recently; I can tell by your grieving faces. Have I come at a bad time?"

Louis shifted uneasily in his chair. "What is your name again, good sir? For any who looks so kindly upon my family's grief is friend to me."

"Thomas Aquinas." He bowed again, "Your Majesty."

"I am not familiar with your home estate."

"Aquino is near Naples, in Italy, Your Majesty."

"Ah, you're Italian. You have traveled a long way, then."

"I hear the *université* is well worth any travel. That it contains the books all men seek."

"That is true," Isabelle spoke up, closing the book on her lap.

"You are familiar with the *université?*" he asked.

"I go there every week at the minimum."

"Our Princess Isabelle is a scholar and recent honorary member of the Franciscan Order," Louis said.

At this, Aquinas' eyes grew large and appreciative, and he bowed his head reverently to Isabelle. "It is an honor to make your acquaintance. As a young boy, I studied at Monte Cassino, the monastery. I have a passion for theology. Doubtless, we share an appreciation for the divine word."

"Perhaps you would be so kind as to show *Seigneur* Aquinas to the *université* today, Isabelle?" Louis suggested.

Isabelle nodded quietly. "I would be honored to take you on a personal tour. Come, as my guest." She gestured to the door. Aquinas turned back to Louis and Blanche and bowed once again before them.

"I thank Your Majesties for your hospitality. I promise you it will never be forgotten."

The sentiment was received with a simple nod, neither Blanche nor Louis having the heart yet to effect a smile. *Seigneur* Aquinas followed Isabelle out of the Great Room.

When they were in the main courtyard of the castle, he inquired, "What has happened to your family?"

"A recent death of a beloved member at court."

"Ah, that is a shame. Is there any comfort I might offer in this time of grief?"

"*Non*, but your sentiment is appreciated."

"Perhaps this is not a good time for a tour. I understand if you'd rather wait for a few weeks."

"It's quite all right. There is sadness and grief, *oui*, but there is also a need to move on with life. Would that my family could give this tour and not I. . . . They are more in need of that lesson."

"You sound tired, Princess."

It was an astute observation, and very candid. "You like to speak your mind, don't you, *Seigneur* Aquinas?"

"Does it bother you?"

"Not in the slightest. It has measurably impressed my brother Louis, however. He would not have opened up to you in the royal court had you not assessed the situation."

"I did not speak my mind to gain your brother's favor. I realized I was intruding upon his melancholy."

"I see. You have a directness of purpose that I have not discovered in the nobility of France. I do wonder if the upbringing of children is different in Italy."

"Not overly. But I was raised at Monte Cassino. There the monks taught me to be honest, straightforward, and alert to the sensitivities of others. I try to apply it to everyday life."

"Well, I find your view most refreshing. I'm really the only one in the family who does pretty much the same thing you do."

"Is that why you joined the Franciscans?"

"*Oui*," she said, and hesitated. "I want to do good for people. I don't like politics and didn't care to marry into another royal household. I've seen enough oddities in my own family. I don't want to inherit a whole new set."

"I quite understand," he said, and chuckled. "I'm considering joining a religious order myself. Of course, my parents objected when I first told them what I was considering. They locked me in a tower for years. I was only recently released to come here."

Isabelle stopped and stared at Aquinas, who walked a few paces and then realized she was not following with him. He turned around.

"They *locked* you away?"

"They were dissatisfied with my decision and thought it might help to change my mind."

Isabelle walked up to him, and they continued on their way. "And I thought my family was bad," she realized aloud. "But you didn't falter."

Aquinas smiled an old smile on a young face. "No, I didn't."

They said little after that, until they reached the streets of Paris and the Latin Quarter. There, Isabelle showed him the campus of the *université*. Bacon, Albertus, Guillaume, and Petrus were in the library, as usual, studying. They were delighted to see Isabelle, who introduced them to Thomas Aquinas. He immediately entered their discussion about the teachings of Aristotle. Isabelle saw that Aquinas knew a great deal of scholarly information, some of which even she and the rest of the men had not had access to in the *université*.

Aquinas revealed that he had studied at Naples as a young man, up until the time his parents had locked him away for wanting to join the Dominican order.

"So what brings you here?" Bacon asked.

"This *université* and a personal quest," Aquinas replied.

"Ooh, what quest?" Guillaume begged to know.

"I cannot say any more than that. It is personal. But I will tell you this," Aquinas said, leaning in so that Isabelle and the men felt inclined to do the same. Aquinas lowered his voice. "I am chasing a mystery here in France. I am here to solve a divine dilemma."

"A dilemma posed by man for God, or a dilemma posed by God for man?" Bacon asked, smiling.

"Yes," Aquinas said, returning the smile.

The men's faces split into grins of appreciation. Even Guillaume gave a wink as he chuckled.

"Your secret is safe with us," Petrus told Aquinas, patting him on the shoulder. Then he turned to speak with Isabelle. "And how are things at the castle, *madame?*"

"Ah, they are sad. That is why I'm here. Sometimes I can only grieve so much."

"I understand. Would you care to see what I am working on?" He indicated another room where a little gadget hung in suspension from twine rope.

"Of course, you know it fascinates me."

"We call it a pendulum." Petrus took Isabelle by the arm and began explaining.

✤ ✤ ✤

They spent hours in the *université* before Isabelle realized it was dusk and time to head back. When she went looking for Thomas Aquinas, she found him having a debate about Averroës with Albertus Magnus, still in the same spot she had left him.

"I must away," she told Aquinas. "It was a pleasure."

"Oh! The day is gone!" Albertus shouted immediately with embarrassment. "And I have kept your lovely guest all day long to myself!"

"I was delighted by it." Aquinas grinned at both of them. "I will come again tomorrow, and you shall see what I mean by the Naples accounts. I will bring what little I have from my travel here. The rest is at home in my library."

"*Oui*, bring it! For I don't believe you!" They laughed at one another's persistence. Isabelle walked outside with Aquinas.

"*Merci*, Princess, for that lovely tour."

"You're quite welcome," she said, and sighed. Leaving the *univer-*

sité was in some way automatically oppressive. Now she felt an odd weight coming back home again.

"Why so solemn again? Just a few moments ago your spirits were soaring."

"Just not looking forward to going back to the castle, I suppose."

"Ah," he said. "I do believe you are as much a prisoner of your family as I was of mine. Except that your prison is more subversive."

Isabelle looked at him, shocked for a moment; then the words sank in. She closed her mouth and walked along in silence. His words were right, but coming from a mouth so young they were almost brash.

"How old are you, *Seigneur* Aquinas?"

"I am seventeen years old."

"As am I."

"Why do you ask?"

"I just wondered where you get your wise observations."

"Do you not sit and contemplate things? Ask questions of Nature and all its workings?"

"Sometimes," she said. "I am not a philosopher, though."

"Of course you are. The more you ask why, or how, the more you learn about yourself and the world. Then, one day, you learn so much that you realize you know absolutely nothing whatsoever. All you have are a great many questions. Then you realize suddenly you are a philosopher, and your reputation goes up in smoke!"

Isabelle laughed as she thought about this and posed her own question to the universe. *I wonder where Jean is right now, why he's away, why he left without telling any of us.*

But Aquinas was right: The answers did not come easily, and the few that did come were too angering to think about.

He left us because he doesn't truly care about any of us, she thought. *And we're easily forgotten, easily left behind. He's probably taken for the tower again and could not possibly care less how we feel about it, or what it looks like now that he's missing.*

"Whatever you're thinking about right now," Aquinas said, chuckling. "I sure wouldn't want to be it."

Isabelle heard him, was about to protest but then realized her brow was so furrowed into a knot that she had to work to unfurrow it. Realizing how ridiculous she felt and looked, she broke into a short laugh. Thomas joined her and the two walked on in companionable silence for the rest of the trip back to the castle.

That very night, Louis came to Isabelle's attic room. She was not sleeping. Instead, she sat at the window overlooking the country below the tall tower. The gentle knock on her door disturbed her considerations, and she turned to see Louis come into her room, closing the door again behind him.

"I have to speak with you," he said.

"All right," she replied gently, surprised but pleased that he had chosen to come and speak with her, and not someone else.

"Something has happened to me, Sister. And I don't know what it is, but something fills me with guilt and a need to set things right again." He sat heavily on her bed.

His tone and his manner intrigued her. "What is it, Louis?"

"The night that I almost died," he replied. "Does it not strike anyone else but me the least bit strange that Neci died that night? But I didn't?"

"I don't think anyone wants to make the connection between the two for fear of what it might mean."

"Then you have also been thinking about it?"

She nodded.

"Did you ever believe in the legends, at all?" he asked. "The ones about how the sisters have certain . . . abilities . . . are certain chosen ones, or . . ." He trailed off, unable to find the right word.

She found it for him. "Guardian angels?"

"Yes, exactly."

"I have had my own strange experiences with them," she replied. "Everyone has. You know Mother won't speak of them in front of us for any reason."

"Isabelle, I am going mad, but I must say what is on my mind." He seemed as confused and dislocated as Isabelle had been on the day she had heard the voice in the monastic ruin of the game woods. "I believe that Neci saved my life."

Her face softened into a sweet expression of concern, for this was the same line of thought she had already taken. Neci had done something to bring Louis back from death, but couldn't save herself in turn. Something powerful.

"Am I mad?" he pleaded.

"*Non.*" She took his hand. "No, you're not, Louis."

"If I . . . took away her life . . . ," he uttered, his voice starting to break and the pain clear on his face.

The pause was a long one.

"Then I must be worthy of it," he finished.

His statement hit Isabelle like an arrow through her heart. He must be *worthy* of it; as if he had not sacrificed and been a *good* king all his life.

Isabelle had once told him that he was only going through the motions and never truly sacrificing for the good of his people. She had said these things to him so long ago, yet they had stuck in his mind, only to come out now, when it was the worst possible time for him to remember them.

It hurt Isabelle deeply to see her bitter statements come back at her like this.

"If Neci's life was *given* to you, it was because you had already *earned* it," Isabelle said. "You have done a great deal of good for our people. You are the greatest king that has ever lived. Our people sing your praises more than any other. All you need to do is listen to be assured. What Neci did was necessary to save you, for if you were not alive we would surely fall to the English or the southern lords."

"Being king has nothing to do with it." He shifted uncomfortably. "I'm going to tell you something no one has ever known. I kept it a secret for years. I was not the heir apparent, Isabelle. I had an older brother, Philip."

Isabelle's eyes widened.

"He was destined to be king, but he died in the cradle. And so I was born to fill his place."

Isabelle was silent, only now comprehending something that must have plagued her brother for years.

"Do you have any idea what it is like to be born under the shadow of someone who might have been king but for God's intervention? I spent the better part of my life wondering if God killed Philip to make way for me."

"No, Louis—"

"And if not that, then did Father *really* love me? Or was I instant insurance as the heir presumptive turned heir apparent, one security that was only created on a night of grief?"

Isabelle could not speak at this; the words were almost blasphemous, though she could not say exactly why they made her feel horrible. Perhaps it was hearing from her strongest sibling and the king of France that he'd lived with shameful doubts; perhaps it was this that caused her to feel the sickness sitting in the pit of her stomach.

But Louis' face had somehow relaxed, as if the weight of that confession was gone, now that it had been admitted openly.

"I thought I'd overcome that terrible shadow on the eve of the battle of Angers," he said. "Do you remember Father's favorite falcon?"

"The white one Mother forbid you to speak of," she replied.

"I saw it again, before I went into battle. I saw the snow white feathers as it flew, and then I realized I was right where God and Father had intended for me to be. Father came to me twice, when I needed him most in my life. Father sent that bird to guide me." He smiled. The words were easier now, and he seemed strong again. Isabelle watched with a strange fascination.

"Then what is troubling you tonight?" she asked.

"I used to look in the mirror before I went to bed, and I would ask myself: If I am a perfect king, and I do all that the Lord asks of me, *then* will He spare me? Will I avoid Philip's punishment? Can I make my kingdom strong with faith and supplication, and in so doing, can I ever make Father proud? For the first time in my life, even as I lay dying, I didn't *have* to ask those questions anymore. The battle of Angers had proven it." He laughed at this. "You see, I had to prove to *myself* that I was a rightful and just king, and I could have gone to Heaven satisfied by my efforts."

Isabelle said nothing.

"Then Neci died," he continued, "and I realized it doesn't matter that I am king. That is not a good enough reason for Neci to have died. She must have died for something worthy of *me*. Not just for the title of king. And now *I* must even the scales, as Louis, not as king." He touched his chest once, lightly. Then he looked at Isabelle, as if she could understand.

"I know how you feel." She sighed. She thought of her luck with the convent and how poorly it was all going.

"It appears the responsibility is my burden to bear alone," he said.

"We all have to go our own way, even when others don't understand us," she said.

"That's why I have decided to take up the cross," he said.

"Crusade?!" Isabelle hadn't thought he would be *that* drastic! Crusades were an absolute warrant of death. If the Saracens didn't kill invading Christian armies, then they died by plague or bandits. No Crusade had gone well since the first capture of Jerusalem. Isabelle's heart was beating rapidly.

Louis only seemed perplexed at her outburst. "I'm going to the Holy Land, to make up for this and to set the scales right."

"You just got over an illness, and you might get sick again. You could die in another battle!"

"I must do it. It's the only thing that will set my mind at peace."

Isabelle frowned. She didn't like it at all.

"Surely you can understand having only one course of action that makes you feel as if you're doing something right? If I take up the cross, I will have earned Neci's gift of life. I will show that I didn't take her gesture lightly, and that after coming back, I chose to do something with my existence."

"Not that Jerusalem isn't a glorious place, but honestly, Louis—if things weren't going well there, Baldwin would be there and not in Constantinople. It will take more than one man to change that."

"If you're right, then like Neci, I will die defending what is right. Emperor Baldwin needs our help against the Saracens, to win back Jerusalem. He is emperor in name only. No one is giving him aid. But, I have proven myself in battle. I will be all right."

"But what about France?"

"I will not forsake our people. I will take care of matters at home first, and then Crusade." He got up from the bed, went toward the door, then smiled sadly at her. "Isabelle, I *must* go to the Holy Land. Just thinking about it makes me feel better about what happened to Neci. I never want to forget that I've been given a second chance."

She nodded.

"Thank you for letting me confide in you. I knew of all people you would understand what happened and not judge me mad."

"You know I would never judge you at all, Louis."

"You know, there's something I wanted to tell you. It was the one thing I hadn't confessed before dying, and I knew I should have told you long ago. Do you remember the day you told me about the lord extorting money from his servants to grind their grain . . . ?" He hesitated, and Isabelle nodded, wincing. "I had the lord in question killed for extortion. As an example to the rest. I never told you that, but . . . you should know that I did hear you that day."

With that, he left the room.

Alone again, Isabelle looked out the window. It seemed all the secrets of the world had piled on top of her head. Her shoulders sagged, and the weight of everyone's words were heavy. She was tired, but not sleepy. It would be a very long time before she found sleep.

Put not your trust in princes.

Psalms 146:3

28

In the morning, Isabelle descended the tower stairs to the Great Room for breakfast bread. Louis was finally present at the table again, while there was a vacant seat where Jean had once been.

Isabelle took her seat, next to the place Jean would sit and where Conrad used to sit, so very long ago. Breakfast bread was broken and passed around. Blanche was the first to break the awkward silence.

"Louis, I cannot condone this action."

"I took up the cross this morning, Mother. I cannot retract my vow because you disagree."

"You cannot do this!" Blanche was furious, and would not eat. "You are not fit for travel, after nearly dying from dysentery. I will not agree to it, Louis."

"It is not your will that I seek. It is God's will, and you will not go against God's will." He was calm, quiet, and impressive. Isabelle had never seen him so resolute. He seemed to be at absolute peace today.

Just then, a messenger came in with a parcel and bowed low before the seated king. He was French, but carried a small letter sealed in an envelope of German colors.

"Rise and report," Louis said gently.

"A letter, from His Majesty King Conrad the Fourth of Germany to our Isabelle, princess of France."

"By all means, deliver it to Her Royal Highness, and *merci*." The messenger walked over to the side of the table where Isabelle sat. He bowed low and extended the letter to Isabelle.

370

She took it kindly. "Thank you, *monsieur*."

It wasn't the only time Conrad had written; he had sent a letter to Isabelle about once a month, in her own native tongue, and kept her updated about the events of his life. She would write in return and tell him about the small daily activities of her own keeping. The correspondence was a healthy and thriving friendship between the two countries, and it had even succeeded in softening the blow Germany had taken when Isabelle refused to marry the king.

Isabelle wanted to save the letter for after breakfast. She put it in her lap. Blanche, however, did not approve.

"Open it, child. I suspect this is news that affects us all if it was delivered so ceremoniously."

Isabelle pulled the envelope from its place, reading the contents.

Her expression changed measurably into surprise, then concern.

"'Matters are growing worse with Germany. It now appears an invader is coming after Europe, from the east. A Tartar master has invaded Henry of Poland. His name is unknown to them but he is an heir of the legendary Genghis Khan. Emperor Frederick has plans to fight a war with him soon.'"

"How much of a threat does he pose?" Louis asked.

"Clearly Conrad wanted to make me aware of it, in case these Tartars should take over Germany. He believes his father's military is strong enough to keep the man at bay, but it may prove difficult. This Tartar master may have some kind of sorcery on his side. Eastern countries breed strange wizards."

"Well, good of him to tell us." Blanche was staring at the seat that had once held Conrad's frame. It was empty this morning. Jean Adaret Benariel was not present in his place.

Isabelle felt her mother's stare and knew the impending question was next.

"Have you heard anything more from Jean?"

Isabelle lied. "Yes, he told me that he still had some matters of estate to take care of at his tower, but that he would return eventually. Now that Louis is better, he thought he should make a swift job of it."

Blanche didn't take her eyes off the seat. "Odd of him not to tell us all."

"He chose to tell me because you were all very busy with Louis' recovery."

The queen mother nodded, but said no more. Louis broke the silence.

"I'm sending some scouts to eastern France and Germany for our own edification. I'd like some firsthand accounts of this Tartar leader who has chosen to take up arms against the emperor of Germany." Finished with his bread, Louis stood and started to leave the table, then paused at the door.

"Isabelle, when you write back, please tell Conrad that I send my sincere gratitude for news of this kind. It's good to get an advance warning from our neighbors. Wish him well for me, and tell him not to hesitate to let us know if things go poorly. We can provide some measure of support."

"Of course," Isabelle replied.

"Where are you going, Louis?" Blanche asked.

"I'm going to Pierre Mauclerc." He was grim. Determined. He was a king in full form today. "I want my Crown of Thorns back."

Louis walked out, and Blanche raised her eyebrows at Isabelle, who foresaw a monstrous clash of wills. She knew who was going to win, though. Blanche winked with a snicker. Both knew Louis, both knew Mauclerc, and they suspected they would hear the yelping all the way from Mauclerc's country residence.

There was a gentle knocking at the door as Thomas Aquinas entered. He bowed low before the queen mother and her daughter.

"Hello, *Seigneur* Aquinas," Isabelle said.

"Your Highness, Your Majesty," he said to each. "I was wondering if you'd like to accompany me to the *université* today, Princess. I am going to show Albertus Magnus my documents from Naples."

"I wish I could, *Seigneur* Aquinas, but I have made some other arrangements today. Perhaps I can meet you down there in a day or two?"

"I would be honored, Your Highness." He bowed once more. "Good day, ladies, I take my leave of you."

⚜   ⚜   ⚜

Aquinas rounded the corner of the great outer courtyard, deep in thought, and nearly collided with a man standing there.

"I'm terribly sorry," Aquinas said. "I didn't even see you."

"The error was mine," the man said, and extended a hand. "My name is Pierre Mauclerc."

"Oh, I have heard of you!" Aquinas shook his hand merrily. "You work for the Knights Templar, do you not?"

"Why, yes. How astute an observation. Are you heading into town?"

"*Oui*, I'd been hoping Princess Isabelle would accompany me but—"

"Isabelle? We are the best of friends, you know."

"Really? I had no idea."

Mauclerc nodded. "I will walk with you to the city. I was going myself, anyway."

"She is a most beautiful and enchanting woman, isn't she?"

"Yes, quite. In fact, we dined last night at my *château*," Pierre said. "I see."

"I'm on my way to the Templar's facility here in Paris, now."

"Then we are well met," Aquinas said. "There are a few things that the Templars might be able to help me with."

"What is that?"

"Well, I'm here on a private mission." Thomas Aquinas looked around a little furtively. "Something I haven't even told the king and queen."

Pierre put an arm around the stout fellow. "And what would that be?"

"Well, if you promise you won't share it with anyone but the Templars, I will tell you. Can you ask them some questions for me?"

"Of course," Mauclerc said as they walked away from the castle, Pierre's arm around Thomas in a very friendly fashion. "I can even win you an audience with the grand masters. . . ."

❖ ❖ ❖

Isabelle received another letter at noon that day. It was from Bishop Maurice. He had gone through great pains to beseech Archbishop Stephen Tempier to hear her plea for convent lands. The auspicious meeting was to take place in a fortnight. Isabelle caught her breath and could scarcely believe the news. She was thrilled. It was possible— just possible—that this would be the final meeting and the convent land would at last be secured.

Through all the trials of war, finances, moving from Angers back to Paris, and dealing with the frustrations of Jean's secrets, she had *still* managed to keep this dream alive. It was breathtaking. She needed to share it with someone, but Jean was nowhere to be found.

Isabelle showed the letter to her mother. She was proud of it. Blanche was measurably impressed.

"You've actually managed to get the ear of the archbishop," she said. "I am stunned."

Isabelle swelled with pride.

Blanche continued. "I haven't said anything because I wanted to see just how far you'd get on your own. But I am very proud of what you've accomplished here. I'm not sure I say that enough to you, Isabelle. But this does make me most proud."

"Thank you, Mother. You have no idea what that means to me." Isabelle stuffed the letter in her pocket and ran up the stairs to her attic room.

❖ ❖ ❖

It was the middle of the afternoon when two regimental soldiers dressed in full chain mail pounded on the door of Pierre Mauclerc's residence. The door opened, and Pierre looked out at a squad of about a dozen soldiers. Behind them stood the king, on his favorite steed.

"Your Majesty." Pierre was shocked, and half dressed. He fumbled with his buckle.

Louis got straight to the point. "I want the Crown, Mauclerc. Now."

"I . . . You owe interest on the principal we loaned you."

"I owe no such thing as interest. You never stated that this 'interest' would be applied to my loan against me. I believe that such things must be stated up front in a verbal *or* written contract. I've come for the collateral you have in your *château*. My men will take it by force if necessary."

Pierre was angry that his residence had been disturbed at a most inopportune time. He had no intention of giving over the Crown of Thorns in this particular state. He wanted to make a big show of its return, wanted to proceed up the great avenue to the castle for all to see his generosity and might.

It was the least he could ask for, through the Templars. "I will return it to you tomorrow, I promise, in a great ceremony that so honors Your Majesty."

"*Non*, you will hand it over now."

The soldiers began to move past Pierre, knocking him out of the way. The armed men poured into his *château*.

"No!" Pierre shouted. "No, you can't go in there! *Stop!*"

The soldiers started to ransack his *château*. Within a few moments there was a feminine shout from the back room. A naked woman, clutching a blanket around her body, came running out of the *château*. Louis saw her, and noted that she was young, probably in her teens. She also had golden hair. When she saw the king of France at the door, she fell to her knees, weeping.

"*Une . . . survenante, Pierre?*" the king asked, implying the girl was quite an unexpected guest.

"Please, Your Majesty, please . . ." was all she could say, repeatedly.

"She is my cousin," Pierre replied. It was true at least. The problem was how apparent was what he and this cousin had been up to in the house.

A guard came out, carrying the Crown of Thorns without the pillow beneath it. "I found this, sir, *on* the bed. I can't find the box or the pillow."

Louis was thoroughly outraged. He dismounted. "You swine!" he roared. His voice turned into the voice of his father, the thunder of a lion. Pierre Mauclerc remembered the authority of that voice well.

Mauclerc started to run, but Louis grabbed him by his hair. "*You blasphemer!*"

Pierre howled as his hair was clenched in the fist of the king. The woman on the ground cried out too.

"Your Majesty! I am sorry! It is truly not what it appears! I was merely showing the girl the Crown! Please don't tell the Knights Templar! It will forever ruin them!" Pierre cried out as Louis threw him to the ground at the feet of the soldiers.

"You will take him with us, to prison. I will decide his punishment when I am rational. For now, I would pull my own sword and kill him in God's name." Louis' chest was heaving; his face was a mask of anger and shock. He had always known Pierre was a scoundrel but never that his private transgressions were so vile and corrupted.

The guards carted Pierre away, and Louis returned to the castle, shaken and angry, but with his Crown of Thorns intact.

Isabelle found she no longer had the patience to wait for Jean to return to the castle if and when he decided the time was right.

Isabelle would go after him herself. After all, there could only be one logical place for him to retreat: his tower in the Western Wood. After writing a return letter to Conrad, imparting all the information she had received at the table that morning, she gathered traveling materials and put pants on beneath her traveling skirt.

She took her horse from the stables and rode into the countryside. When she was finally well away from the castle, she dismounted and took off the riding dress. Travel was difficult enough in the dress of a woman, and the forest she was going to enter was not kind to delicate clothing. The pants were a wiser choice.

By midday, galloping at a good pace over the meadows, she reached the Western Wood. It looked more bleak and foreboding than it ever had, if that was possible. She had remembered a particular landmark near the entrance of the wood that Jean had taken her through. It was an upturned stump with its roots exposed and twisted, pointing away from the forest and looking like a sinister pipe organ grasping out at the happy meadow. Just to the left of it would be the break in the thorny briars. She searched an hour and finally came upon it.

Isabelle found the break, just as before, and led her mount into the wood. The beast neighed loudly, unsettled by the place. Oddly, the horse had not done this when they came with Jean. Isabelle patted his neck and soothed him.

"I know, old fellow. This place makes me tremble too."

As they traveled into the darkness, she found no wide and easy road. Had she missed it?

No, the road had once been directly in front of the break in the tree line, not more than fifty hands in. And yet, there was no road here today. This was not a place to become lost. She felt the cold hand of fear cover her heart, and she tried in vain to make the feeling go away.

She looked back and found the tree line was now well behind them, shrouded in darkness.

Turning back, she nudged her horse. "We go on."

It was an order, given to herself as much as to her horse, in a gentle though shaking voice.

The horse started to walk, carefully picking his way through brambles. They traveled in what seemed to be a northerly direction, as best she could tell. The brambles and branches were getting tighter, scratching them both.

She came to another wall of brambles, with only a narrow path cutting into them. Too small for a horse.

She dismounted her steed and patted him carefully, then tied his reins to a nearby branch that had twisted and writhed up from a low-growing tree.

She soothed him, for his eyes had white fear ringing their gentle brown orbs. "I will be back soon, I promise. Stay here; eat what you can. It won't be long now."

She took her necessaries off the saddle and slung them over her shoulder. Then, with great trepidation, she entered the bramble opening and started down the narrow path on her own.

This is madness, she thought. *There was a road here. I know it. I was on it.*

The more she thought about it, the more it frightened her. It was not natural. Roads did not simply disappear without a trace.

The tunnel of brambles was narrowing down on her, and it seemed that dusk was settling in. Her cheeks, hands, and neck were scratched, and soon she was exhausted, ready to turn back. Her body ached; her feet were sore and stiff. She wanted to break down in tears. It was agonizing, and yet she *refused* to go back. She would not let Jean, his wood, or his mysterious tower win. She *would* find him, and as the Heavenly Host was her witness, she would *bring him back*.

She lost all sense of logic the longer she walked in the haunted wood. She knew now, the wood must be protecting him. But she wouldn't surrender to it.

She started battling the thorns in front of her, swatting them angrily out of the way.

As she brushed a thorny limb back it abruptly snapped and fell to the ground. Others fell all around her, as if in surrender.

Behind them was a clearing.

And in the clearing was the Tower of Benariel.

There was no joy in finding it; it was more a flood of relief. Tears washed over her scratched cheeks, and she let them sting her new wounds with their cleansing salt. She didn't care. She had found Him.

Isabelle stumbled out of the thorny underbrush into the clearing. She walked past the wonderful rosebush, but did not stop this time to admire the lovely roses. They were in full bloom, despite it being past their season.

Of course they're in bloom, she thought. *When aren't they?*

She walked on to the door and pushed her body against it with the last of her effort. Even the door resisted her, and opened slowly, unlike when Jean had shown her in the last time. She pushed harder, urging it open inch by slow inch as she groaned loudly.

Inside, there was a fire going in the fireplace, the flames dancing high in the hearth. The light reflected on the books that were shelved around its mantel, illuminating the stacks upon stacks going up into the darkness of the ceiling. There was a chair pulled close to the fire, with a hand resting on the arm of it. The large chair-back was too high to make out the person within. But she knew she'd found him.

It only took a moment to realize she was wrong.

Neci got up from the chair and whirled around to face the intruder at the door.

Isabelle stared at Neci.

Neci stared at Isabelle.

The same horror was reflected on both their faces. They struggled for words.

"How did—?" Isabelle asked.

"How did—?" Neci asked at the same moment.

Then Jean's footsteps came shuffling down the stairs. Out of the corner of her eye, Isabelle saw him stop on the very last step before the ground floor. But she couldn't take her eyes off Neci.

Neci!

There was too much here, too fast, after too long an ordeal. She felt faint, as though her head were floating upward, her body made of air, her veins filled with foam.

Neci's face—alive somehow—was the last thing Isabelle remembered before the blackness set in.

Fate has terrible power.
You cannot escape it by wealth or war.
No fort will keep it out, no ships outrun it.

Sophocles, Antigone (442–41 B.C.)

29

When Isabelle opened her eyes, she was lying on the very bed where her brother Robert had been kept alive inside the Tower of Benariel. She sat up, remembering where she was, and when she rested her hands on the side of the bed, she realized that they were no longer covered in scratches or cuts. They were perfectly clean and smooth, without scabs or scars. She sat and examined them for a minute before realizing that Jean was sitting in a chair near the bed. When he saw her get up, he put down the book he had been reading.

"Welcome back," he said, but his voice was grim.

Isabelle put her hands down quickly and looked at him. "Where is Neci?" she asked.

"I bade her leave, so that we could talk alone," he replied.

"She's not dead."

"No," he replied. "She is quite alive."

"How . . . ?"

He shook his head.

"*How?*" she asked, firmly this time.

Jean considered honestly for a moment before replying. "I don't know. That is the truth. I went to her tomb, went inside, and found her lying there, cold and still. I touched her cheeks with both my bare hands and kissed her brow."

Isabelle realized that Jean was not wearing his gloves.

"When I pulled back, she took a breath and opened her eyes, as if from a deep sleep."

"You did it," Isabelle whispered in awe.

"I don't know exactly how it happens," he said, half-irate and explaining it away. "But I couldn't let Neci leave her tomb alive in front of other people, so we came back to the tower under cover of darkness. While Paris slept, we ran here, to where no one could accuse us of . . ." He found it hard to continue; the words would not come from his mouth.

Isabelle suspected that he meant witchcraft, devil's work, or pagan inspiration—any ill-meaning term of ignorance. She knew better. She knew Jean.

He settled on a few choice words. "It would have been better if you had not come here."

"People are beginning to note your absence from the royal court."

"It is not your duty to look after me," he said, his voice betraying a sense of ire. "I don't know why you insist on it."

"Because you are my friend. As I care for my family, I also feel a sense of obligation to you. It's the same for Robert or Louis."

"That sense of obligation is getting you into trouble. If you insist on prying into my affairs, you will find things I cannot protect you from, try as I may." He stood up and put the book back on a shelf.

"Protect me from what?"

"From the truth. There are aspects of my family that even I don't understand. I can't ask you or anyone else to understand if I don't."

"You're wrong about that. It's about *accepting* what you don't understand. I *accept* you the way you are. I don't need to understand it."

He paced the little alcove, not meeting her gaze.

"But you will not let me," she continued. "Though I try my best, you will not let me in."

"I *can't*. If I let you in, it will damn you to a life you wouldn't want." He turned and walked into another room. She pushed herself out of bed and followed, refusing to let it go.

"The last time I was here, you wanted *me* to tell you how I felt about you, to implore you personally to return. So I took a personal interest in you. Now you don't want me to have *any* interest in you. Am I to forget the best parts of our friendship because miracles haunt your family?"

She slammed a table with her fist, forcing Jean to face her. "Yes! Neci is back from the grave. I don't know how you did it—maybe that's because I am young, or a woman, or mortal. But Jean, do you *really* think me so fearful that I cannot see past these miracles to *who you are* and *love* you for that?"

The silence following her declaration hit them like arrows. It was out now.

"You wouldn't be able to do that forever," he said quietly.

"I believe you've insulted my integrity."

"No, Isabelle. I mean you wouldn't be able to love, like, or hate me . . . *forever.*"

"I know you have been here since the beginning. You were the one who saved me from that rabid dog as a little girl. I was no older than nine years old at the time. You were *there*, in the gardens. And I know it was you in the ruin, telling me all about my future when I followed Neci out of town. You have always been there for me. You have all guarded my family and this land. All of it.

"And it doesn't matter, because I *know* all about it. I *lived* in it! Don't you see? I know it *all.*"

Still he refused to meet her gaze. "You can't know it all, Isabelle, because not even I know it all. There are some things left a mystery on purpose. I don't know why I am here, or what I am meant to do . . . or when I am meant to do it!

"All I know is that I am meant to be alone, because as much as I want to," he said, his voice hoarse, "I can't keep my friends forever. Even friends pass on; things change; life evolves."

"But not you," she said. "You remain constant."

"Yes, *I* remain." He stopped behind a table, holding himself back from walking over to her, grasping the chair like a drowning man clings to driftwood.

She saw it in his eyes and walked up to him until they were only inches apart.

"They *are* miracles, aren't they?"

His eyes were sad. "You could call them miracles. That you see them as such is kind. But others would not." He reached out then and held his hand between them, stopping himself from touching her. "You should go now."

"I'm not leaving without you."

"Isabelle, it will only get worse if I stay among people. I can't go back."

"My family will protect you, and more importantly, you will have me. I will be there for you. No matter what. You *must* come back. If I mean anything to you at all, you will come back. We will try again, this time with no secrets."

He watched her with eyes that she was sure wanted to believe her, to believe *in* her.

"Come back for one fortnight. Let the family know you are well. We'll talk about the alternatives after we get back."

He studied her for a long time before finally nodding.

"I will return for a fortnight, but then I will have to withdraw from your world. I can't stay, not with what's happened, not now."

I will work on the fortnight part, she thought to herself, *but at least this is a start.*

"You work your own miracles, Princess," he said. "Let us go."

✤ ✤ ✤

When Isabelle stepped out into the courtyard, in front of Jean, she saw her horse standing there chewing quietly on some stray grass. She also saw Neci bending over the rosebush in the center of the courtyard and tending to the gentle flowers and stems at her fingertips.

When their eyes met, Neci said, "Isabelle, I—"

"It's all right," Isabelle said. "Jean has told me. You are alive, and that is all that matters to me."

In the space of a few seconds, the two women grasped each other in a tight embrace. Isabelle breathed in the scent of her friend's hair. "I thought I'd never see you again," she said, a tear escaping.

When they parted, Neci said, "I cannot go back to Paris."

Isabelle understood. "I will come to see you often. I just can't— It's so hard to believe—and I am so happy." Isabelle kissed Neci firmly on the cheek, then realized that Jean was standing behind them.

"You're going back, aren't you?" Neci asked him.

"For a while. They are concerned that I am not present at court." Jean moved toward another horse at the far end of the courtyard.

Neci took the moment and held Isabelle's arm. "Take very good care of him," she warned. "He is suffering for many things that are not his fault."

Isabelle nodded. "I know. I mean to help him. You will see."

When Pierre finally received a letter from the Templars, brought for him where he sat in the depths of prison, he read it and grimaced. They would not stir themselves from nearby Villeneuve du Temple and come to his aid. The letter told him that he had acted profanely in their name, with a most sacred relic of the Holy Church, and as such he was subject to whatever punishment Louis decided was appropriate. They would not give him the sanctuary he desired.

He wondered briefly why Isabelle had not come down to see him, or why she had not pleaded with her brother to let him out of prison.

Perhaps because she does not love you, he thought.

Pierre hung his head and cried out bitterly.

"She must love me!" he shouted. But the dungeon was isolated; there was no one to hear him. "She must love me! I love her! Why can she not love me back? Why can't she be *mine*?"

The force of his anger made the last word sound like a vicious snarl instead of a word. He knew why Isabelle had forsaken him in his hour of need.

Jean Adaret Benariel.

She wanted him more than she wanted Pierre. He had been severed forever from Isabelle by that bastard. Pierre tore up the letter from the Templars and slammed his head against the wrought-iron bars of his prison cell.

"No!" he cried pitifully.

Louis sat alone in the Great Room, replaying the events that had led up to this moment. He had just transferred Hugh de la Marche and his wife Elizabetta into house arrest where his men would watch over them for the rest of their lives. He couldn't bring himself to kill them. Neci's eyes were staring at him every day now in his thoughts, watching him from wherever she was . . . begging him to do the right thing at every turn, because she had sacrificed herself to keep him alive.

He wondered what Neci would have thought of him abusing Pierre Mauclerc the other day, and winced at the thought. He had acted poorly.

A guard stepped into the room. "Your Majesty, there is a young woman here to see you."

"Show her in," Louis said. Anyone who wished to visit the king and had the means and spirit to do so was permitted within his audience.

When the woman entered, her footsteps echoed in the Great Room until she stopped before the dais.

He immediately recognized her as the lovely young woman who had been at Pierre Mauclerc's the day Louis had taken back the Crown of Thorns. He looked at her, but his face didn't look kindly.

Her beautiful little face was round and rosy, with big green eyes and little curled tendrils of golden hair that fell against her forehead. She was wide-eyed and terrified to be in the royal presence. She was dressed in a blush-pink gown of modest fabrics, and her hands were trembling.

The girl dropped to her knees, then prostrated herself before Louis.

"Oh, please, great and wise majesty, king of France and hero of our people. I know my lord, Pierre Mauclerc, has been terribly wrong—I realize it was unwise to show me the Crown of Thorns—but I beseech you to have mercy on him for my sake. He is my benefactor, and without him, I am lost."

Louis saw her body trembling. In truth, despite his threats, he knew he couldn't kill Pierre, no matter how much the man had offended him. Lordly politics aside, he knew Neci would not approve. And now this girl was actually repenting before him as if he were the pope.

"I feel responsible for his imprisonment," she continued. "I ask that I be placed in the cell and he be set free. It was all my idea, Your Majesty."

"I will not kill your patron, *mademoiselle*," he said gently.

She looked up then, sitting back on her knees in her lovely gown. "Oh, merciful majesty! You are kind and just!"

"However, We have decided to inform his authority, the Knights Templar, that he has acted grievously against Our person as well as in their own name. I imagine it will remove him from their ranks. He is not worthy of the Knights Templar."

"*Oui*, Your Majesty."

"One more thing, *mademoiselle*," he said, and she looked up at him, at his command. "You would do well to find better company. My mother often warned me as I am about to warn you. 'I would rather see you dead at my feet than guilty of a mortal sin.'"

The young girl nodded sadly.

"You would do well to listen to the queen mother's words, child,"
he said.

She broke into sobs of sadness. A long, heaving, shameful moan
racked her small frame, and she hid her eyes.

"Go now, and when We are ready, We will send *Seigneur* Mauclerc
back to his home."

"*Merci*, Majesty," she said, barely able to get the words out. Then
she knelt once more and kissed the hem of his robe and backed out the
door, her head hung low.

When she had left, Louis sighed with the weight of authority. He
would release Pierre Mauclerc from the dungeons of the castle on the
following Sunday. He had decided to be merciful, but he was in no
particular hurry to demonstrate it.

✠ ✠ ✠

Aquinas hurried to catch up with Isabelle in the long hallway of the
palais. The castle walls echoed with his heavy footfalls.

"Princess!" he called, smiling. "So glad to have found you."

Her smile in return was a bit distracted. Her brother Robert had
just arrived that morning for a brief visit. He'd heard that Louis had
transferred Hugh de la Marche and Elizabetta to house arrest and that
Pierre Mauclerc was in custody. She knew he would want to know why.

Isabelle was also thinking of a way to make Jean Adaret Benariel stay
despite his insistence. They had been back less than a day, and already she
could see a readiness to depart in the darkness of his eyes. He was aching
to leave the castle, despite all she had done to tempt him to stay.

"Albertus Magnus has asked me to become his student!" Aquinas
said cheerily.

Isabelle understood the magnitude of that news and grinned from
ear to ear, despite her situation. "*Seigneur* Aquinas, that is so wonderful! You couldn't ask for a greater honor!"

"I have you to thank for it. You are very good to a simple nobleman who really has no lineage to speak for him. You have given me so much."

"You have a gift for words, *Seigneur* Aquinas. That is all that I needed to see, and more than enough reason to have helped you. I merely opened the door of opportunity. You had to step through it."

"How can I thank you?" he asked. "Your family was in grief, and you still took the time to introduce me to your peers and vouch for my character."

Isabelle shook her head. "I don't require thanks."

"I must! You cannot leave me with a burden of guilt this great."

She considered his words, then smiled. "You could tell me what this secret investigation of yours is." She gave him a sidelong stare.

"I . . ." He seemed uncomfortable. "I don't know if this is—"

"*Non*, I'm sorry. My curiosity was rude—"

"No, I can tell you." He spoke softly. "But you must promise not to utter a word of it to the men at the *université*. I want the dissertation all to myself."

"I promise. Not a word."

"Good. Is there somewhere private where we can discuss it?"

"The family chapel is always empty this time of day," she said, indicating the staircase in front of them. He gestured for her to precede him, and they ascended.

"I really don't think Bacon or Petrus or the others would ever steal your idea," Isabelle said as they entered the chapel, with its white walls and few wooden pews where the family and close courtiers sat for services in the early-morning hours. The small room echoed with their discussion and was, as Isabelle had indicated, entirely empty.

"Forgive me, I didn't mean to indicate anything bad about your friends," he said quickly. "It is the way I work; I tell no one about my work until it's finished and written out entirely—edits and all. Please do not be offended."

"I'm not. I see how that can be a good practice." She motioned for them to sit at a pew where she could keep an eye on the hallway. The chapel had no door, just an open archway.

"I have been looking into an interesting mystery in the Holy Church," he said. "You may or may not be able to help me with it yourself."

"Me?" she asked, surprised.

"You see, there is a crisis in the Holy Church—has been for years now—about the bones of the Saint Mary Magdalene."

"Why?" she asked. "Everyone knows they're here in France."

"They're also in Byzantine Constantinople."

"No, they're here in—" She stopped short. "Oh! I see the crisis now."

"Quite." He nodded. "Now, I have seen some documents at Naples, by Averroës, that indicate that Mary Magdalene might not have stayed in the Holy Land after the crucifixion, but there is another legend—"

"Our legend of France," she burst in.

"Which contradicts the papal decree that Mary Magdalene lived her remaining years out in Constantinople and was buried there when she died. There are actual remains to prove it, I'm told, though I have not traveled to see them. The Church 'officially' sanctions those. Then the French rumors sprang up. I'm curious, Princess, what do you believe? Do you think Mary of Magdalene came to France to live after Christ died?"

Isabelle put a hand on Thomas' leg as she saw a figure move past the door. Aquinas turned his head, and both saw Sofia walking by the open doorway; she slowly turned her head, and her eyes stared directly at the two of them. She didn't turn her face away when they looked at her, but continued to stare at them and then walked very slowly, deliberately, past the open door and out of sight.

A chill swept over Isabelle. "I believe we should go and talk about this somewhere else," she said.

"What is it?" Aquinas asked.

"Let's go."

"Why?" he asked as she stood up.

"It looks like someone wants to use the chapel." They walked out the door and into the hallway. It was completely deserted. Isabelle got another shiver.

"Who was that who walked by?" Aquinas asked.

Isabelle looked around nervously. "One of Mother's serving women. Let's go to the courtyard for some air, shall we?"

Aquinas followed along. Isabelle didn't see Sofia after that, even when they went outside into *le jardin*. But the look in Sofia's eyes—something strangely unnatural about her stare, almost threatening—was still seared into Isabelle's thoughts.

She tried hard to just brush it past. *Sofia just wanted to use the chapel at a time she didn't suspect anyone would be there, and we were infringing on her given time and territory. That's all.*

Isabelle almost believed it. She turned to Thomas Aquinas and said, "So, there appears to be some confusion as to authenticity, then. Which legend, which account of Mary Magdalene is accurate."

"Exactly. I came across your version of the Magdalene story while looking through the Naples' archives of Averroës," Aquinas replied.

"Interesting," Isabelle said, and shrugged. "Well, the myth is based in the county of Toulouse, right here in France. The county claims they have the Magdalene remains and that they have always possessed them. Joan could probably tell you everything about it. She's very good about the history and legends."

"Joan?" he asked.

"Oh, sorry. Joan of Toulouse is wife to my brother, Alphonse. She's probably the one who knows the most about it."

"Would you introduce us?" he asked.

"Of course," she said.

✤ ✤ ✤

Robert paced around the Great Room in a fury. "You let him go?"

Louis sighed. "There was no reason to detain him. He didn't act against the royal family. He was just careless and blasphemous with a holy object."

Robert threw up his hands in exasperation. "Louis, you are most pious. This isn't like you!"

"Why do you want to see him killed?" Louis asked.

"You can't just let him go around doing these kinds of things," Robert said. "He's dangerous!"

"Do you have proof that he's acted against us, and not that he's simply acted in a way that the majority of men act . . . which is to say, immoral?"

Robert could not tell him about that day long ago, with the Holy Nail of France and saving Pierre as his throat was being slit, knowing all the while that he was a stupid traitor. He'd sworn before Pierre that any harm from Pierre against the royal family would be dealt with in blood. But Louis let Pierre walk freely with other respectable noblemen. This put Robert in a bind.

"All I can say is that he shouldn't have been released."

"That isn't good enough, Brother," Louis said. "I'm sorry. The Church does not kill for these kinds of transgressions, and neither should I."

Robert stormed out of the room.

✤ ✤ ✤

The Orchard was the pet name given to the little grove of miniature trees that Louis and his family had set up in the courtyard just past the family garden.

Isabelle and Aquinas came across Joan making a necklace of daisies with her youngest daughter in her lap. Joan looked up at them from the grass and smiled in her bright, sunny way.

"Hello, Isabelle," she said. "And who is this?"

"Princess Joan, please meet my good friend, and future scholar of the *université*, Thomas Aquinas," Isabelle said.

"I would stand and curtsey, good sir, but I fear I have become a mountain for my young one to climb upon." She extended her hand, and Thomas Aquinas bent low and kissed it gently.

"An honor to meet you, Princess," he replied.

"I wanted to let Aquinas meet you, as he is interested in the region of Toulouse for some research he is doing."

"Oh, how delightful!" Joan smiled again. "What about Toulouse interests you?"

"Your religious relics and histories," Thomas said as he sat on the grass beside her.

Isabelle looked up and around. Something still stirred her into a sense of unease. When she looked into the shadows of the castle's inner wall, not far from where she'd stood as a young girl when the rabid dog came to attack her, she saw Jean near the wall, nearly hidden by a tall hedge. She realized only slowly that Aquinas was speaking beside her.

"Not only did Mary come here, but she brought another man with her to teach the locals from the Bible. And she had children too—"

"Children!" Joan gasped loudly. "No! Let me tell you what has been passed down to me by my own parents!"

Seeing that they were deep in discussion and that she would not be missed, Isabelle stepped away and headed over to where Jean was standing alone.

He was looking at Aquinas as she approached. "Jean?"

"Hello, Isabelle." He didn't turn around.

"Is everything all right?"

"Yes, and no." He sighed.

"What is it?"

"Something is coming. It has upset my mood today." He looked down with that penetrating, gut-wrenching stare.

"I think you are looking for reasons to try and leave us again."

"I don't wish to leave you," he said simply.

"Then we should try and enjoy ourselves. Let's allow things to be just as they are meant to be, all right?"

He looked at her with such affection that she was unable to move or look away. "Let's enjoy what time we do spend together," she quietly whispered.

He moved closer to her, took her hand in his gloved fingers, and bent down to smell her hair. "I'm so sorry," he whispered. "So sorry . . ."

"Isabelle!" Joan's voice broke the moment between them. Isabelle released Jean's hand from her own, and he stepped back as she waved to Joan and Aquinas on the grass.

"Tell Jean not to be such a hermit." Joan laughed. "Get you hence and talk to our guest!"

Isabelle smiled at them and turned back around to Jean.

"Come and meet Thomas Aquinas," she said.

"No," he said. "Not today."

"Please, Jean. For me. It will look bad now if you don't come. You have been requested. I promise we won't stay with them long. We can spend the afternoon together, can't we?"

He nodded, and they crossed *le jardin* together. Isabelle smiled, despite her troubled thoughts. What had he been apologizing for?

✤　✤　✤

Isabelle was good about changing his mind. Jean wondered how she did it. The mortal woman before him was a call to all his desires. If he wanted solitude, somehow her contact drove away his need for loneliness. If he wanted companionship, her company was never tiresome or detrimental. As much as he kept from her, she allowed him to do it. And as much as he'd let slip and shown her the extent of his power, she'd accepted it. How could he have found such happiness only to be forced to abandon it?

Her discretion was their only saving grace, for if she had ever collapsed in the face of the emotions shared between them, there would be no redemption for either one of them. But a part of him didn't care how far he fell; it would be worth it, for just one touch, one moment . . . to be joined with her.

It was so hard for him not to give in. And so, he extended his gloved hand and said hello to Thomas.

Blessed are they which are persecuted for righteousness' sake: for theirs is the kingdom of Heaven.

Matthew 5:10

30

Isabelle was furious. Louis would not attend the meeting with Archbishop Stephen Tempier in half an hour even after she'd begged him to go with her. These were to be the final, critical negotiations for her convent. She had the name: the Bonne Clares, named in part for Bernard of Clairvaux but also for Claire, her first seamstress and friend. She also had friends at the *université*, scholars and Franciscan friars, who were drawing up a charter for new members despite the lack of land. She had everything but the land itself.

"And I am not giving up my family lands for it," she insisted to Louis. He had shrugged. "If I don't use those lands, someone else in the family should have them. They are royal lands and by nature of joining the Church I have abdicated them. It would be hypocritical to use them."

Louis, on the other hand, saw no blasphemy in using land that would otherwise have gone to a husband. It would go to a convent for God, which in his mind was a much better use. "Is it not the same as being married to God that you give your lands to God?"

"They are *royal lands*. They belong to our descendants. Besides, the Church of Paris has plenty of land, and all I require is a small corner of earth for my women. It isn't a lot to ask."

She had been determined to pursue the argument further, but something had "come up," and Louis had proclaimed himself unable to go with Isabelle to the meeting with the archbishop of Paris. If something had indeed come up, that would be one thing, but Isabelle was certain that he'd just said that to get out of it. He liked the archbishop and didn't want to press the matter with him in an attempt to have him accede Church land to Isabelle. Politics favored good intentions yet again.

Now, as she stood in the foyer preparing to leave, she tried to put her arguments in a row, but her anger washed over all the logic and made them mockeries.

"Isabelle?" a gentle voice behind her inquired.

She turned and saw Jean approach behind her. "Hello, Jean," she said, trying not to sound exasperated.

"Is something wrong?"

"Louis has backed out of an appointment to see the Archbishop Stephen Tempier about land for my convent. I wanted him there as a show of support from my family, but apparently he didn't feel it necessary to be there for me."

She realized she'd let it all tumble out and then bit her lip in embarrassment. She began to apologize, but Jean stepped in. "No need to excuse your anger. I understand. Can I accompany you instead?"

"Are you sure? I fear it's going to be a very nasty debate. Maurice is in favor of my idea, but the archbishop of Paris despises women, or the idea of convents, or both, or something. I don't know, but he's just horrid."

"Then let's go together," Jean said quietly, but with something behind his eyes that suggested authority. "That way, there will be at least one pleasant memory from the journey."

✦ ✦ ✦

They reached the cathedral of Notre Dame a little late, but Jean had insisted they not hurry. He spoke calmly to her, about things like the weather and the book she was reading. She had finally begun to relax as they entered the great, dark cathedral. Her thoughts, a jumble earlier, were clearer now.

Inside, Archbishop Stephen Tempier and the archbishop of Notre Dame, Maurice, were waiting for them. They stood talking casually at the junction of the two wings. Isabelle curtsied low before them both, and Jean bowed slightly.

"Thank you for seeing me, Your Grace," Isabelle said.

"A pleasure, Your Highness." Maurice looked on, smiling as Stephen Tempier continued. "And who is this?"

"Jean Adaret Benariel," Isabelle said. "A friend of the royal family."

"Good afternoon, Your Grace," Jean said. "I understand that Isabelle has requested some land for a convent from your great and expansive Church of Paris."

The archbishop blinked at his straightforwardness. "*Oui*, I was just getting to that. You see, for matters involving the delicate balance of important, resourceful land, we are unable to grant you the land you requested, Princess."

Isabelle paled a bit.

"Surely, there isn't an *earthly* problem the Church can't overcome?" Jean asked.

"Well, we do have to be careful what we honor with actual land from the Church itself. When we lose land, we lose resources—"

"You mean money?" Jean clarified.

"I—I beg your pardon?"

"The archbishop of the Church withholds land from a woman who wants to create a convent, because the convent might not be as profitable to him as land that's tilled by serfs."

Maurice was growing red. "This is outrageous. You should not talk to a man of God like that!"

Jean just smiled at the comment.

Isabelle took hold of Jean's sleeve. "Let's go. We'll come back another—"

"No, I think that I've discovered the problem here. I want to remind you, Archbishop, that 'It is easier for a camel to go through the eye of a needle than for a rich man to enter the kingdom of God.' Clearly, you have forgotten this lesson. But you can still repent if you start to atone for it now."

"Don't you start quoting the Bible to me, young man! I've been reading the Bible longer than you've been alive!"

"With all due respect, I doubt that," Jean replied. He seemed in fine form, his eyes sparkling. The bishops were growing angrier at his insolence.

"Jean, please—!" Isabelle said. Maurice looked up abruptly.

"Did you just use his personal name, Your Highness?" he asked.

"Yes. Oh, no—see, we're good friends—No, it isn't like that, Your Grace, honestly!" She glanced at Archbishop Tempier as well, but he was oblivious to her distress, his furious attention focused fully on Jean.

"Don't you stand there and tell me what I already know! You called the House of God a *bank*!"

"If you're not a *bank*, you can give Princess Isabelle what she requires. Surely a tiny plot of land won't disrupt your own amenities," Jean said.

"We came here with a decision on behalf of the princess, and *you*, *Seigneur* Benariel, have no right to enter into these negotiations!"

Jean was still calm. "I have every right, as her friend, to make sure that she is not slighted by the very institution she so faithfully upholds."

"*Get out of my church!*" the archbishop shouted, pushing Jean toward the door. Isabelle scrambled to keep up with them.

"*Out!*" Maurice was fuming now, almost purple with anger. "*Out and don't come back!*"

Jean took Isabelle by the arm as they moved out the door. "'No one can serve two masters,'" he said over his shoulder. "'For either he will hate the one and love the other, or he will be devoted to the one and despise the other.' You cannot serve both God and money."

"*Out!*" The two priests' cries sounded like furious bells of Notre Dame.

There was a moment of silence, as they stood on the steps alone, and then Isabelle looked at Jean in outrage. "*That* was *helping* me?"

"You don't want anything to do with them anyway," he said, disgusted.

"I don't know what came over you in there, Jean, but now you've made things worse for me."

"Listen," he said, but she was walking away. "They should have given you that land. They're making money off that land, and that's why they won't give it to you. They want you to add your own land to theirs so that they have even *more* profit. They expected you to bend to their pressures."

"Well, I wasn't planning on giving in, but I wasn't planning on starting a *war* with the Church, either!"

"I'm sorry," he said, and stopped. "I might have overstepped my bounds as a friend, but I cannot abide men like that. And I can't just let them ruin your future."

"You protect me too much, Jean." She sighed, but she couldn't really be mad at him. She didn't like the archbishop either. But Maurice was another matter. She'd looked bad in front of Maurice, and he was a good friend.

"I just don't know where I'm going to get the land now. All the doors have just been slammed shut before me."

"No, not all," he said, and they walked on. "If you ask for it, you will receive it. You must keep asking."

"Yes, but who?"

"That answer will come to you in time. There are never any dead ends, not really. If a door shuts before you, just knock on it, and it will open again. Trust me." He smiled at her.

Despite it all, despite what terrible thing had just happened . . . she smiled back. She had pulled him from his retreat precisely because she trusted him and valued his advice. It would hardly be polite to change her mind now.

✤ ✤ ✤

"But, I saw him with her at the church. They were kicked out the front steps!"

Pierre Mauclerc waved a dismissive hand at his informant, Theodore, and said, "Isabelle would never get tossed out of Notre Dame. I have to go; there's no time for your report." He looked at the open door of his estate to the field beyond.

"But it was Jean Adaret Benariel with her, and you *told* me to—"

"I'm late for an important meeting. I hear you. But you have brought me absolutely no information on the Order of the Rose. *That* is your mission of primary importance, not watching Isabelle and Jean. Those two are everywhere together; it's easy enough for me to observe them. The *Sisters*, do you hear? I want information *on the order*! Now, off with you!" Pierre clasped his cloak around his shoulders, grabbed his sword, and before he had turned to the door, Theodore was gone.

Mauclerc nearly collided with the young woman entering his estate. Her blonde hair cascading down in ringlets made him stop for a moment. *Isabelle!*

He'd almost said the name, but realized no . . . it was not Isabelle, it was his cousin, Therese. She held a wooden box with a lid.

"What are you doing here?" he asked, noticing her large eyes, as if his presence had surprised her.

"I—came for my things. I'm leaving you," she said, ducking past him.

Pierre Mauclerc grabbed her arm; the box in her hands fell to the floor.

"Let *go* of me," she cried.

"*Why?*"

"Because I would rather die than be caught in a mortal sin again," she said, and stuck out her chin. "And since you won't heed my warnings and stop scheming, I'm leaving."

Pierre recognized the sentiment. This was Louis' doing, or perhaps the words had reached Therese from Queen Blanche. He knew them well: They were the queen mother's favorite motto.

"I'm not scheming; it's work," he said.

"I don't know the details, Pierre. I don't want to. It would only give you a reason to keep me here against my will. But I see by your late-night meetings and your . . . special friends . . . who come to visit you, that whatever it is, it isn't benign, and I won't be a part of it anymore. I'm going home to *mon père.*"

As Pierre tightened his grasp on her arm, she added, "Don't, because Father's already expecting me. He knows to come looking for me if I don't show up within the hour."

"You *don't* trust me, evidently." Pierre was actually hurt. He'd been fond of Therese, despite the girl's youth, or maybe upon reflection it was because of it. But now he saw an aging disdain in her eyes as she regarded him.

"What does *ton père* think of me now?" he asked. It was like rubbing salt in his own wound, but something deep within him *had* to know.

"He said you were once a good man. Ambitious, but still kind. After your incarceration, he told me that you are no longer kind; you have kept your ambition and replaced kindness with stupidity."

Pierre let go of Therese's arm and slapped her. The girl's hand flew to her stinging cheek. On an exhale, she stood taller, and her disdain grew into a full-fledged hate. Pierre couldn't look at her anymore, and he angrily left the room, late for his appointment.

✤ ✤ ✤

"You wanted to see me, *Seigneur* Dunbière?" Pierre Mauclerc asked as he stood in the dark receiving room of the Villeneuve du Temple outside Paris. Dunbière had traveled to the Templar's main headquarters in Paris from his southern estate in order to speak directly with Mauclerc.

Pierre had arrived late, and he did not rise from kneeling before the great Templar lord.

"Yes, and you would do well to acknowledge now that this meeting never happened," Dunbière said as he walked into the grand foyer from the shadows of the adjoining hallway. Pierre was kneeling over a Crusade cross etched in fiery gold on the floor tiles.

"*Oui*, Sir. I will keep our meeting completely confidential," Pierre replied.

"Rise," Dunbière said. Pierre stood, and Dunbière continued. "You have been cast out of the Templar order, but you have not finished my task. I cannot risk asking another to do what you have started. At this juncture it would be very unwise."

"You refer to the Order of the Rose?"

"Yes, and no." Dunbière motioned as he turned to walk into the dark hall beyond the foyer. "Follow, *Seigneur* Mauclerc."

Pierre followed the lord into another dark room at the end of the hall. The walls of the room were covered in fantastic ancient tapestries and scrolls. Pierre could not discern the language of many of them, but a very few were in Latin, others looked Greek, and most of them were in strange scrawling print that could have been Hebrew, Aramaic, or Arabic. They all depicted holy scenes from the Old Testament or from Jesus' teachings.

"Your collection is most impressive, *Seigneur* Dunbière," Pierre said as he strolled around the room.

"It all comes from the Temple in Jerusalem."

Pierre stopped abruptly at this statement. *"The* Temple?" he asked.

"Upon the first capture of Jerusalem on the Great Crusade many years ago now, our order uncovered many interesting discoveries in the Temple. We have kept the majority for ourselves because others are unworthy of properly protecting them. These were passed down to me from my ancestors; we have all been Templar lords."

"I . . . see." Pierre felt awkward discussing the Templar activities. It seemed tantamount to theft to take holy objects from the Temple in Jerusalem. There was no more sacred place in all the civilized world, and here he was staring at artifacts removed from that holy presence for display in some kind of trophy room in Paris. It made him some-what sick to his stomach.

"I'm not exactly sure what to say, Sir," Pierre said.

"I show you these relics only to enforce my claim to information." Dunbière came close to Mauclerc and spoke confidentially. "We dis-covered many things at Jerusalem, Mauclerc: a great many secrets that must never be divulged to the common man, and a few secrets that not even the Holy Church of Rome should know about."

Pierre nodded. He didn't like how close and confidential *Seigneur* Dunbière was getting.

"We have spent several long years tracking certain . . . relics. Cer-tain . . . legends. There are some things we must still know. There are legends in France that must be proven to our order and then fully delved."

"You speak of the Order of the Rose," Pierre realized. "Who are these women?"

"The Order of the Rose is very old; it has lived under many names, many centuries, and in many countries."

"How much of a threat could they possibly represent to the Tem-plars?" Pierre asked. "I've never heard of them outside France."

"Nor would you have. You are not one thousand years old, for one thing. The Templars first came across them as a reference while in

Jerusalem at the Temple. We tracked them here, to France. At first, we couldn't locate them, so we made our headquarters in Paris, and waited. We have been waiting a very long time."

"The First Crusade was over a hundred years ago," Pierre said.

"It was precisely *l'an de notre Seigneur . . .* 1099. We were led by Raymond of St. Gilles, count of Toulouse, who was clad as a penitent and a pilgrim. The armies first sighted Jerusalem on the seventh of *juin*, and after a fearful five-week siege, the city of Jerusalem fell on the fifteenth of *juillet*," Dunbière said, as if he had been there himself.

"One hundred and fifty years is a very long time to wait for information on an order of women," Pierre said.

"They are *not* what you think they are. They are the one holy secret we cannot penetrate and examine. We must know about them. They already know about us. It's dangerous."

"If you can tell me more about them, I can help you. I want to help you."

"At current you are unemployed and in royal disfavor. It behooves you to help me, doesn't it?" Dunbière said and smiled a thin, cruel smile.

Pierre sighed. "Perhaps if there are others I can track, it will be easier. I am not as able to access the royal palace as I once was. And lately, I've seen far too much of its dungeons for my own pleasure. I'd like to stay clear of it."

"Of course," the lord replied. "They have a tower to the north, deep in the heart of the Western Wood. We have finally learned of its whereabouts, but none of us have been able to go there. And you certainly couldn't reach it. The wood is well guarded."

Pierre scoffed at this until he realized Dunbière was staring at him with scorn.

"Where might I find other *members* of the order?" Mauclerc asked.

"Go to the tomb of the one who died recently," Dunbière said. "Her name was Neci. Anyone outside the royals who comes to grieve for her is probably part of the Order of the Rose. This is the first time we've ever heard of the death of one of their members. Now that I think of it, her tomb itself may be worthy of further investigation."

"I will do so, *mon Seigneur*," Mauclerc said as he bowed again.

"Make sure you report back to me immediately, and share your information with no one. *I* will be the one to inform my superiors of any worthy news. It will be *my* credit, and you will be well paid."

"Yes, Sir." Pierre stood and turned to leave.

"One more thing," Dunbière said. "There are others who seek to unravel this mystery. You must speak to no one about it. The fate of my order lies in your filthy hands."

"As you wish." Pierre left the lord in his dark room filled with arcane secrets and unnatural suspicions.

✤ ✤ ✤

Isabelle knocked softly at Bishop Maurice's rectory door. The gentle voice of her friend on the other side said, "Come in, Son."

When she opened the door, she saw Maurice at his sparse desk, writing on some vellum. He put his quill down, and there was a moment of uncomfortable silence.

"I came to apologize to you," Isabelle said.

Maurice rose and gestured for her to walk with him. He never let her stay within the walls of the rectory for too long. Women were not permitted inside, but as a princess, she could come and go as she pleased. It never seemed to disturb him, even today.

"Walk with me," he said as they left the building and headed out into the daylight. It was a cloudy, pensive day, matching both their moods.

"I came to clear up any misunderstanding that happened at Notre Dame," Isabelle continued.

Maurice grunted and said nothing. They kept walking. She was at a loss for words that would change his feelings, and she could tell he had been deeply wounded by that exchange.

"My friend, *Seigneur* Benariel, is a plain-speaking man. And I will say from the very start that I don't think he was out of bounds for saying what he did to the archbishop." She took another deep breath and continued as Maurice's face displayed surprise at her comments. "I don't think it would be difficult to give me a small plot of land for my women. But I see we're past negotiations now. In fact, we've entered into the silence of enemies."

Maurice nodded, and Isabelle finally put her hand on his arm in an attempt to draw him out. The old priest regarded her.

"I don't want to be your enemy, Maurice. I didn't mean for the discussion to escalate like that. You have given me so much, and it was not my intention to ever hurt you. I feel as if you are my only father, since I never knew mine, and I can't have you kept in silence and hatred," she said. "Will you forgive me?"

As the words came out, Maurice gave in and took her hands in his large, rough ones, patting her hands as he replied. "Child, I could never hate you, and I do forgive you. There's something you should know."

Isabelle was first relieved and then felt the pang of fear in her stomach at his last statement.

"I'm retiring to a monastery at the end of this month," he continued. "Because your friend Jean, he was right. I was so angry at what he'd said, but after you left and I had time to contemplate what had happened, I realized . . . the Church is no longer what God intended it to be. I read over Scripture that night," he said, and Isabelle nodded. "Jesus came to the temple and tossed out the money lenders. Well, I cannot toss out the lenders of the Holy Church of Rome. And I can no longer in good conscience be a part of it, now that I know it. So I am leaving for Clairvaux."

"You're joining the Cistercians? They're so strict," Isabelle said.

"I can no longer tolerate the worldly offenses around me. It's not that what happened the other day made me want to leave the Church proper; it's that over the years, I've been slowly moving toward this decision, and what happened with your friend was the final sign for me to pack up and retire."

"I will miss you if you go to Clairvaux."

"As I will miss you, but we can send letters to keep us together while apart," he said, and she nodded sadly. "This is what God says I must do."

All Isabelle could do was stare at the ground. She still felt somehow responsible for this turn of events. Maurice pulled her chin up so they were looking one another in the eye. "I want you to tell Jean Adaret Benariel that he has opened this old man's eyes to God."

Isabelle was surprised, but she saw something in Maurice that had been absent in the years she had known him. There was a light in his eyes—a faith shining behind the pupils that had not been there before.

"I will tell him. I know he will understand." They embraced to say good-bye.

✦ ✦ ✦

Thomas Aquinas strolled through the streets of the Latin Quarter, happily buying pastries, vellum, and some more ink during the waning afternoon light. As he paid the attendant at the booth he saw Pierre Mauclerc walk by.

When they saw one another, there was a moment plain to Aquinas that both had wished they had *not* seen each other. Now Aquinas would have the discomfort of talking to someone he had once enjoyed, but who had been thrown in Louis' dungeons for lewd and unacceptable behavior with a holy relic. Thomas held a sigh in check.

Pierre nodded in greeting, seemingly distracted. Aquinas wanted to simply nod also and just keep walking, but he knew how rude that would be. So instead, he said, "*Bonjour*, Pierre. Out for some air today?"

Oh, he wanted to kick himself for that! It probably wasn't the best phrase to use with someone freshly released from prison. *Damn my*

*wandering philosopher's mind! I have learned to speak it openly, and it is both
a blessing and the foulest curse!*

"Good afternoon, *Seigneur* Aquinas. I am getting a bit of sunlight
today."

Aquinas nodded in extreme discomfort. Pierre seemed very reluctant to speak to him. Thomas wanted to make up for his embarrassing
faux pas. Blessedly, he landed on a solid topic. "I wanted to thank you,
personally, for introducing me to the Templars." Pierre seemed to react
to his comment, so he continued. "I learned very valuable information.
Your help to me was a blessing on that day."

Pierre nodded quietly and seemed lost in thought, possibly even
angry. "Thank you," he finally said.

"I was just out buying some supplies," Thomas said, and
shrugged. "Isabelle is expecting more ink, and I've picked her and
myself up a bundle of it."

"Isabelle must be writing quite a lot lately, to be in dire need of
ink," Pierre said, finally meeting Thomas' gaze.

"Oh, yes, what with the Church being so demeaning and all, you
know."

Pierre obviously didn't. "Oh, no, naturally you wouldn't have heard
—You were in the—" Thomas said as he blundered out of another *faux
pas*. "Well, there was quite a scrap over at Notre Dame the other day.
The archbishop refused to give the princess land, and so Jean Adaret
Benariel gave him a good reprimand for his shortsightedness."

"Benariel?"

"It seems he'd come back to town just in time to help Isabelle with
the meeting. Such a good thing to do, considering he'd been occupied
elsewhere for so long."

"How long?" Pierre asked.

"Oh, at least three weeks," Thomas replied.

"That's odd, considering he'd never strayed far from the royal
palace since his arrival."

But Pierre's comment was lost to Aquinas. "Jean even quoted Scripture at the archbishop, and apparently the holy man was driven to such a frenzy he had to go and have a lie-down before he burst his temples with anger." Aquinas laughed. "I wish I'd been there to see that!"

"As do I," Pierre said bitterly. "Good day, *Seigneur* Aquinas."

"Can't I at least buy you a drink to thank you?" Aquinas felt bad for Pierre's predicament. He watched as the man considered his request, then nodded in agreement.

"Let's go, then," Aquinas said as he gestured to a nearby tavern. "I will tell you a bit about my visit to the Templars."

Robert walked among the blooming flowers of the *palais* garden thinking about Neci and her passing. He had never really known her in all the years she had been an attendant of his mother's circle. But he remembered in particular the time he and Neci had traveled together in order to retrieve the Holy Nail from a Saracen assassin.

That quest had shown him very little about Neci beyond what he already knew, and at the time he'd still been fearful of the Sisters despite their kindness; so there was no reason for him to want to learn more about her.

He looked down at the note in his hand. Neci's handwriting carefully danced across the pale yellow sheet. He'd already read it seven times since finding it tucked away in his top bureau drawer that morning, but his gaze glanced over the words again, this time without seeing them.

Neci had left him a parting note, written before she died. The first line, the one her lyric voice spoke in his mind's ear, said, *Dearest Robert, You were always my secret favorite.*

As you were mine, he realized. *And I should have known you better.* There had been something different about Neci that he'd always figured was simply an approachability that her sisters didn't share. But now, holding her letter in his hand, he realized it wasn't that she was more approachable. It was that he had always wanted to approach her.

It was too late for such a revelation. His jaw set firmly as he read Neci's letter again.

> Take care of your brothers. Louis will need you on the road to Antioch. Watch over Isabelle for me, because she is the sort who needs a watchful eye without a single touch of redirection. She is your salvation, Robert, and the glue that holds the royal family together. No one else ever saw this, but I pass on what small knowledge I have. Make sure Charles is knighted before too long, for he is the one destined to give your family a great future, and he will find something your country has long since lost. Most of all, take care of yourself, and I will see you again, beyond the end of Time.

"They were most kind to me," Aquinas said over his tankard of wine. The tavern was a cozy place where Pierre and Thomas had been a few times before, discussing palace news and politics. Thomas had taken him there today as a show of old faith.

"Your lords are so very thoughtful and benevolent," Aquinas continued. "I'd always heard odd things about the Templars from others in Italy, but you know, I see their true merit after our meeting."

"*Oui*, I'm certain." Pierre downed his drink and stared at the bar.

"Another drink for *Monsieur* Mauclerc," Aquinas called to the tavernkeep. Then he said, "The Templars told me something of great importance to the Magdalene mystery. They had proof that Mary Magdalene not only came to France; she came with three daughters and one son. I was shown an ancient, surviving scroll from one French priest named Maximinus. He came with Mary and founded a chapel at Villa Lata, now called St. Maximin—after him, obviously. It is located near a cave where she reputedly died, near a hill known as La Sainte-Baume for the Dominicans—my order," he added proudly. "Anyway, I *saw* the scroll and can vouch for its authenticity."

Pierre only nodded. He didn't seem particularly interested in

Thomas' research into Saint Magdalene. But that was for the best, because Thomas might have become too excited by heated interest in his research. And he really had no intention of telling Pierre the really important information the Templars had given him, though it might have slipped out if he wasn't careful.

Aquinas had discovered that Magdalene's children might still survive. The Templars had been vague at best, and they could have meant that there were simply surviving descendants, but Aquinas had other thoughts on the matter. He was now following his own theory of who the children were and where they might still be living. It was so arcane, so mysterious, that the whole matter was simply breathtaking for him. He tried not to even think about it openly himself.

"I know you . . . ," a voice said, and the conversation was interrupted by a man behind them who put a hand on Thomas' shoulder and turned him around.

Thomas regarded a man past his prime, with a red nose and crooked teeth, dressed in courtly attire and wearing a ridiculously fashionable hat on his head. He seemed vaguely familiar, but Thomas couldn't place him at first.

"You're Thomas Aquinas," the drunk man said.

"Am I?" Thomas answered with a twinkle.

This made the drunk think for a few moments, and then he shook his head dramatically. "Yes, you are."

"If you say that I am, then I must be what you say," Thomas replied. "For if you have given me a name, then I suddenly fall within your sphere of influence."

The drunk man blinked and stood very still for a moment and then laughed. "*Ouai!* They *said* you were a philosophicker."

"Did they also say you are *drunk*?" Aquinas was sporting with him. "Or do you go by some other name?"

"I'm not drunk; I'm Thomas de Brabant."

Suddenly, Aquinas remembered him. This one had always been

hanging about the palace with many other assorted courtiers, always either at the royal family's great chamber or the room just next to it. He was what polite society termed a "courtier" but what really amounted to a hanger-on. And if memory served, Thomas de Brabant was an extremely bitter hanger on, which would explain the drinking.

"Perhaps then, I can buy you a drink and you can—"

"I want to ask you . . . ," Brabant said.

"What?"

"I want to ask you . . . something." He spoke through muddled thoughts. "And . . . I forget now."

"How about a drink then?" Thomas urged, hoping to get the man distracted enough to move on and leave Pierre and him alone.

"Aquinas, *you* show up a few weeks ago, at the court of the king, and suddenly, you've got the king's ear. You're with the royal family and attend every family function." It appeared that Brabant had remembered what he'd come to say, and Aquinas shifted uncomfortably in his seat as Pierre Mauclerc turned to look at them.

"Now, I like you. Honestly, I do," Brabant said. "But I want to know how you did it, in just a few weeks' time. And, and that *Jean* fellow. Jean Benariel, him. How'd he do it? *He* shows up out of the blue, and immediately gets the ear of the king, the queen, his brother the prince, and he is awfully fond of Isabelle, isn't he? In fact—"

"Why don't you go get another drink?" Aquinas tried to cut him off.

"I don't *want* a drink. I want to tell you this, because it's *bothering* me. I've been a courtier for *fifteen years*," Brabant said, and poked Aquinas in the chest with his finger. "In all that time, I've had— what?—five minutes with His Majesty the king. I've never even *had* a chance to talk to Princess Isabelle, and . . . you and . . . this *Jean* fellow, you're not only in with the royals, but you get to talk to those Sisters! *Oh! And those Sisters!* They're—"

"Well, it's a long explanation, and this really isn't the place for it," Aquinas started to reply, but oddly enough, Pierre butted in.

"You mean the Order of the Rose? They are rather reclusive, aren't they?"

"Re—" Brabant said, laughing. "Reclusive! I once tried to talk to one of them, and the room turned *ice cold* for fifteen minutes!"

Aquinas was in quite a bit of distress; people were beginning to notice Brabant's voice as it grew louder. The last thing Thomas wanted was for some hanger-on to make a scene about Jean or Isabelle, and most especially in front of Pierre.

"*No one* talks to the Sisters, but *Jean* talks to the Sisters! *No one* walks with Isabelle, but *Jean* walks with Isabelle. *Jean* can do *anything*, can't he?"

Thomas started to escort Brabant to the door as he kept getting louder. "You know, it's not just me! Other courtiers see him meeting with the order at odd hours, and in strange places. He was even holding the one that died—that Neci girl—in his arms the morning of the murd . . . her death. He was there, before Isabelle made him leave the body and *walk* with *her*."

Pierre's eyes grew large at this news. Thomas had reached the door with Brabant and opened it. "I think it's time you were leaving, Thomas," he said.

"I'm not done!" Brabant said, and held onto the door frame like a dying man. "You ever *see* those two together, the princess and Jean? You'd think she'd been *bewitched* by him. They're always doting on one another, even though she's supposed to be a virgin and a member of the Church."

Thomas was prying the man's fingers off the doorway. "*Non! Non, Seigneur* Aquinas, I'm saying this because I *have* to *ask* you!"

"What?" Thomas nearly shrieked. The man wouldn't go *away*!

Brabant held onto Thomas' shirt, sliding down, unable to stand straight any longer. "How did he *do* it? How do *you* and *Jean* do that? I must know how to bewitch the royal family. Don't you see I have to know?"

He was sliding toward unconsciousness, and Aquinas helped lower him gently to the ground, then patted his own sweaty brow with a handkerchief. *Good Lord!*

"Quite drunk," Thomas said, clearing his throat apologetically while he stood up over the body of Brabant.

Pierre had walked over to the door as well, his eyes glittering as they focused on something far away. "Quite," he replied absently.

Thomas had left abruptly after the drunkard's outpouring of venom against Jean Adaret Benariel. The poor young philosopher was extremely uncomfortable with what had been said, but Pierre understood Brabant's sentiments entirely. Pierre knew how it felt to be cut off from something he most desperately wanted. He could empathize with hating Jean. After all, he wasn't so fond of the man who'd stolen Isabelle, either.

But the tavern excursion in general had provided some most intriguing insight on a number of levels. As Pierre stepped out into the streets of Paris, he considered the entire discussion. Thomas Aquinas had been asking the Templars about Mary Magdalene and her remains. He remembered when Thomas had first come to Paris and confided all the mysterious information in him. Most of it had come out at this very bar, as a matter of fact. Pierre chuckled at that.

Aquinas' Templar information had made Pierre realize a few odd coincidences in his own Templar fact-gathering. So, there were three daughters of Mary Magdalene. There were also three sisters of the Order of the Rose. Both were biblical mysteries tied to the Holy Land, and both were arcane secrets that the Templars themselves had been unable to unlock after years of research and observation.

Seigneur Dunbière had said that others would be looking into the mystery and that Pierre should use the utmost caution in guarding the secrets he'd been let in on.

Thomas Aquinas had said that Jean had come all the way back to help Isabelle at Notre Dame the other day, after having spent three weeks away—*occupied elsewhere*. Occupied with what?

Thanks to fate's intervention and a drunken courtier with a love of gossip, Pierre had the beginnings of an idea. Quietly, he let it grow in his mind as he walked down the street.

After a few moments, he realized what it was! He'd been so foolish to overlook it. As Dunbière had said, there *was* one other person investigating this mystery—discreetly getting in before anyone else could get the chance—and he had been right there in front of Pierre the entire time.

Jean Adaret Benariel.

This explained why Jean had mysteriously appeared and insinuated himself into the royal circle. Why he had ingratiated himself with Princess Isabelle, stealing her away from Pierre and using her to get closer to the real target: the Order of the Rose.

Benariel is out to learn the same secrets! He's out to steal the discovery—from me and the Templars!

Pierre stopped at this realization, and found himself moving in a slow circle.

Well, Jean won't get the chance to steal from me twice! Pierre might have realized what was actually happening late in the game, but he wasn't about to give up the hunt.

I will do the Templars a favor and at the same time, rid myself of the competition. He already knew exactly how to get rid of Jean Adaret Benariel. The drunkard in the tavern had given him the best idea. Coupled with Aquinas telling him about the Church fiasco, he finally had the means to nail Jean once and for all.

I will strike at his reputation. I will tear down his credibility. First of all, it was a great offense to speak against the Holy Church, and secondly, the drunk courtier had claimed that Jean had *bewitched* the royal family. Pierre had heard the allegation and realized the full extent of the accusation. He'd been drunk, and "bewitched" had obviously been a throwaway term. But not for Pierre. "Bewitching" was a perfectly helpful term when taken absolutely seriously.

All it would require were a few more charges, trumped up by Pierre himself—the truth never mattered in these things—and Jean would have to undergo a criminal trial for the accusation of witchcraft.

If Jean was found guilty, anything from a swift fine to execution was the outcome. They probably wouldn't kill him, but Pierre let himself fantasize about it for a little while anyway. If not death, then the accusation and trial would forever mar the bastard. Even if Jean was acquitted, his reputation would be tarnished forever and he would no longer be in royal favor or admitted to the royal court.

No more royal favor, then no more access to the Order of the Rose. Even better, there would be no more access to Isabelle. Pierre smiled and headed toward the royal graveyard. He only had one more thing to attend to today, and that was looking over Neci's tomb.

Beware of the man of one book.

St. Thomas Aquinas (1225–74)

31

"You'll be interested to know that I ran into Pierre Mauclerc while fetching us both some ink," Aquinas told Isabelle as he set down the package in front of her.

Isabelle sat at her desk in her sitting room, and Aquinas pulled up a stool to have a seat before her.

"Why would I be interested?" she asked, cutting the flax rope on the package with a small knife.

"Well, he was your friend before the situation with the Crown of Thorns," he replied.

"He was *not*," she said, and the knife popped the rope apart with a solid movement of her hand.

"But he said that you were the very best of friends." Thomas scratched his nose; he was starting to get a sinking feeling in the pit of his stomach.

Isabelle set down the knife and frowned. "That was a lie," she said, shaking her head angrily. "I don't like Pierre Mauclerc."

"He must like you, then."

"*Oui*," she replied with a scowl. "He has liked me a great *deal* since I was born. He 'likes' me for my lands and my status at the royal court. He is deluded and a fool. Even when I joined the Church, he kept asking after me at court as if he could still marry me or hold me as property. I try and avoid him. You would do well to do so yourself."

"I'm sorry, Isabelle. I didn't know he was such a man and fear I've upset you," Thomas replied. He thought of everything he'd told Pierre in the tavern, and what the drunkard had said of Isabelle and Jean. If Pierre felt unrequited affection for Isabelle then the tavern scene had more implications than what he had first realized.

Thomas did not feel right telling Isabelle about the drunkard. He knew how such moments were only hurtful to those in positions of popularity and how very helpless people were against them. You couldn't truly imprison someone for slander without making yourself look insecure and inadequate to others around you. So the pain of such accusations could only be held and never relinquished.

Aquinas tried to feel better about keeping it to himself, thinking how he was shielding Isabelle from unnecessary pain, but it was difficult to put the courtier's slurred accusations down as regrettable statements that an idiot had made while intoxicated.

"No, it's all right," she replied kindly. "You can't be expected to know the intricacies of my family or our history with the nobles at court. You couldn't possibly have known. Now that you do, however, you'll be more careful."

"Of course I will," Aquinas said as he stood. He took Isabelle's hand in his and kissed it gently. The gesture hid the worry in his eyes.

"You're leaving?"

"This was only one of my errands today. I'm still looking into a few things that the Templars have been kind enough to share with me." Thomas wanted to move on to something that would make him feel better. This conversation had left him with a plaguing distaste he wanted to forget in lieu of more rewarding and enlightening discoveries.

"That is quite an accomplishment in itself," Isabelle said, and smiled. "The Templars never share anything with anyone. They are quite secretive that way."

"I gather I have impressed them favorably, for they are magnanimously helping me with my mystery," he said, smiling back at her. "Anyway, I have one last bit of research to do, and it requires what's left of daylight. Please, hold my ink until I return to the castle tonight?"

"Of course. See you at dinner," Isabelle said, and released his hand. Aquinas left happier than he had been a few moments before, but he still felt as if trouble was nagging along at his heels. He shrugged and made his way out of the castle toward the cathedral, in search of clues about the children of Magdalene.

✤　✤　✤

Pierre walked the streets of Paris.

Three sisters, three daughters, three members of the Order of the Rose. Sofia, Norea, and Neci.

Now that I think of it, Seigneur Dunbière had said, *her tomb itself may be worthy of further investigation.*

Dunbière had also made a point of saying they were *not* what Pierre had expected. Pierre saw the royal cemetery nearer now, as he closed in on his final destination for the day.

"But there was a son, Aquinas had said. If there is Sofia, Neci, and Norea, who then is the one man?" Pierre frowned as he thought aloud. *Seigneur* Dunbière had not said anything about a man in the Order of the Rose.

I had not asked him about any men, though, he thought. Pierre had arrogantly assumed the order was all female. But if there was one man who might be a part of it, he'd have to find out who it was before anyone else—even Dunbière—could find him out. If he could learn who the man, the son of Magdalene, really was, he might win considerable favor with the Templars again. And *that* could get him reinstated, perhaps to a greater position of power than before. Pierre smiled at that.

As long as Jean doesn't find out who the brother of the order is before I do. Pierre's smile faded as the thought came to mind. *I'll have to move quickly so that even if Jean does know who the brother is, he'll never be able to act on it.*

In the shadow of the cemetery, Pierre looked at the tombstones of the great kings and their families before settling himself in front of Neci's tomb. He marveled at it for a moment.

I have been the loser against Benariel since the day he arrived at the palais. He has stolen my love. Only a master manipulator would have snatched Isabelle so completely from me. He deserves all the pain that he will get.

Benariel, he thought, *I finally have you.*

But first, Neci's tomb, Pierre thought as he stepped into the chapel to find a bishop.

⚜ ⚜ ⚜

"What do you *mean* it's empty?" the bishop asked.

"The body is missing from her tomb." Pierre stepped back out into the sunlight and beckoned for the elderly man to follow him.

They stood in the dark stone cell and stared at the slab of granite where Neci's decaying body should have been resting. There was no trace of the body, clothing, or any disturbance. There were no windows and no other openings for the body to have been dragged through. Only the rolling, carved door at the entrance could let anyone in or out.

"Has the tomb been sealed this entire time?" Pierre asked.

"As far as I know, *mon Seigneur*. We were instructed never to go inside."

"Have you seen anyone around the tomb?"

"No, sir, no one at all. Well, only the groundskeeper. He tends to the plants and bushes around it."

"Call him in," Pierre said.

The bishop left to fetch the groundskeeper as Pierre put a hand to his beard and stroked it in thought. This was certainly the kind of development that would interest Dunbière. But it was also slightly disturbing. Why would someone remove a corpse from a tomb?

The groundskeeper shuffled in. He was an elderly man with missing teeth and a crooked nose. "Sir? You wanted to see me?" he asked. The bishop came in behind him.

"What is your name?" Pierre asked.

"François."

"Have you seen the body that was entombed here?" Pierre asked, pointing to the empty slab.

"*Non, monsieur*," he replied. Then he looked again and realized aloud. "It's missing, *monsieur*!"

"Someone must have taken it out," Pierre said. "Have you seen anyone around the tomb?"

The groundskeeper thought for a while. Pierre pulled out a purse of money and jingled it heavily before the man. It obviously helped the groundskeeper to think, even though he couldn't take his eyes off it.

"There was a gentleman come here late in the afternoon of the day she were buried," the groundskeeper said. Behind him, Thomas Aquinas walked into the open doorway and overheard the conversation. "He came to the door, and I saw him pull off a pair of gloves, and put his bare hands against the carvings. I was called away at that moment, to take down some branches and weeds around *Mademoiselle* Hadebeau's tombstone. One of her relatives asked me to. That's all I know, sir. No one else has come near since that day."

Pierre nodded, then said to Aquinas, "What are you doing here?"

"What are *you* doing here, Mauclerc?"

The tension of silence hung among every member of the room. When the shock had subsided, Pierre was the first to speak.

"I am conducting an inquiry into Benariel's involvement with diabolic spirits," he said, and the others gasped. "It is exactly as I feared. Neci's body is *missing*. Stolen, because it would show evidence of murder. Perhaps poison. She was too young to simply die of natural causes. Surely you've all heard the rumors?"

No one could speak, and Pierre kept going. "I believe Jean is responsible for Neci's death, and also responsible for my misfortune and imprisonment. Most importantly, I believe he's responsible for Isabelle's bewitched infatuation with him. I can't undo what this witch has done to destroy my life—but I *can* save Isabelle from him, before she suffers a fall from grace in the House of God!"

"That's a lie!" Thomas said under his breath; then he spoke louder. "It's not true! And you know it!"

"Now, if you'll excuse me," Pierre said as he moved out of the tomb, "I must bring this matter before the king himself. And bishop, you mark my words. This woman Neci was murdered by a man in league with evil spirits. I mean to see him brought to justice."

Pierre walked away as Thomas called desperately after him, "Don't *do* this, Mauclerc!"

But Pierre didn't turn at his words. Thomas looked back at the horrified bishop.

"It isn't true," he tried to explain. "Mauclerc and I just came from a tavern where a courtier was spreading evil rumors and—this isn't *true*, do you hear? Do you—" Thomas looked into the tomb again and saw the empty slab where Neci's body should have been. There was absolutely nothing he could say that would refute such a strong statement of mystic or malevolent intervention.

For the first time in his life, Thomas Aquinas ran without stopping; he ran as hard as he could, despite his weight and his habit of food slowing him down. He had to reach the *palais* before Pierre Mauclerc. He had to warn Jean Adaret Benariel and Isabelle and stop the terror he had set in motion.

After morning meal with her mother and Robert, Isabelle received another letter from Conrad. The invader from the east, the son of Genghis Khan, had been defeated by Conrad's father Frederick and had retreated east. However, he had sad news to report of his father's misbehavior. The papal state of Rome and Frederick of Germany were arguing about succession and the rightful power of the Holy Roman Empire. Conrad wrote openly of his dislike for his father's actions against the pope, and he could see that the emperor was alienating himself from Rome and other civilized nations.

It was Robert's last day at the *palais* before heading back to Artois. Isabelle showed the letter to her mother, who agreed that Frederick's recent attacks against the pope had excommunicated the entire royal German family from the Catholic faith and caused a stir among the Western nations.

"There is nothing one can do when one's father is mad," Blanche said resolutely.

"I know." Isabelle thought. "I often wonder if I'd have been excommunicated, too. It may be best that I never went to Germany."

"I am inclined to agree, for once," said Blanche. It surprised Isabelle, but it was the truth, stated simply. "Although, mind you . . . hindsight has the benefit of always being perfect."

Robert leaned over and tugged on Isabelle's golden hair. She looked over at him and smiled. "How is the convent going? I have not had time to ask, since I've been playing grown-up."

"It's going poorly and wonderfully at the same time. I have everything I need, including members. I'm just missing the land to put everything down on."

"Why don't you just give it up and try something else? There are plenty of other things you can do for God," Robert said.

"Because I believe that this is my calling. And I know it's been difficult, but I'm not giving it up yet. I *know* I can put women without homes to good labor and help the community the way the Brothers of the Bridge or other monasteries have helped with public works. I know I'll be good at this."

Robert winked at Blanche.

"Remember when I had those women in to make the sashes and decorations for Alphonse's knighting ceremony?" she asked, and Robert focused on his sister again. "It occurred to me then what a wonderful idea it would be to have a group of women who could help in the ways of textiles, writing, reading, education, gardening . . . anything."

Isabelle's face was flush from just talking about her dream, and Robert regarded her with a crooked grin. "What does the archbishop say to your passion?"

"He says I can use land from my dowry, but it's not what I want."

"Why?" Blanche asked. "You're never getting married."

"We don't know that yet."

Blanche raised her eyebrows at Robert, who looked just as surprised. The doors to the Great Room burst open, and Pierre Mauclerc appeared in the doorway.

Queen Blanche stood up, outraged. "Mauclerc!"

"How dare you come into the presence of the royal family in this manner!" Robert shouted.

Pierre bowed and went down on one knee. "I am sorry, Your Majesties," he said. "But I have come to give testimony against a member of your court who has been dabbling in most dangerous black arcana."

"What nonsense is this?" Blanche asked.

"Since my exile from the Knights Templar, I have been looking into the reasons for my peculiar behavior on the day Louis came to snatch the most beloved Crown of Thorns from my home. I believe I have been under the spell of a witch, or warlock, Your Majesty."

Blanche was taken aback measurably by this. It was not a claim to be taken lightly. Cries of witch or warlock tended to put the whole country into an uproar because of the sensationalism even though they were much more common than cries of heresy or blasphemy. When someone came with an accusation against a witch, it was to be considered with the same manner and custom as a mundane case in court, but the popular pressure was enormous and contributed to hysteria.

"Come now, Pierre, you don't mean—" she began.

"I believe that Jean Adaret Benariel—this man who has no history, no family to speak of, and who speaks only vaguely of his lands—has made me act in profane ways. He's recently made my favorite cousin Therese turn against me. She may even join the clergy, believing that I am a devil. He has taken me from the holiest of jobs with the Knights Templar and left me destitute. And most terribly, he consorts with your daughter Isabelle in unholy ways. I have proof today that he uses his magic openly!"

"*I object to this!*" Isabelle shouted over him, but all froze at the utterance of Pierre's last statement.

"*Seigneur* Mauclerc, do not come into Our home and soil the repu-tation of France's great friend." Queen Blanche stretched herself tall and stood like a true regent.

"Jean Adaret Benariel is a very good man who saved my life in a hunting accident," Robert said.

"And he helped Louis win the battle of Angers. Do not come into this court unless you have proof of witchcraft, or I will hang you in the square for all to see the punishment of a liar." Blanche's voice was cool as ice.

"I have proof, Your Majesty. Proof enough to pale your skin," he said.

Then he pointed at Isabelle. "I'm sure *she* knows exactly of what I speak," he continued. He was unaware that Jean Adaret Benariel had walked into the room behind him.

"First, there is the damning evidence that he blasphemed the arch-bishop of France, using the Holy Bible against the man. Even the devil may use Scripture to his own ends, as Jean did that day in the sacred halls of Notre Dame. But even more terrifying is the fact that the body of Neci is *missing* from its *tomb*," Pierre continued. "I witnessed its absence in the presence of the bishop himself! Not only did *I* witness it, but *Seigneur* Thomas Aquinas was with me. He is my witness!"

"*Seigneur* Benariel has stolen the body of one of your own aides to use her remains in his black arts, casting spells that he uses against you and to hurt anyone whom you deal with! You are all under his spell, don't you see?"

He was so vicious, so angry and vile, that Isabelle raised her hand completely without thought and struck him squarely on the face. She was not as cool as her mother, for her father's hot temper now raced through her veins.

As Pierre was recovering from the blow that was even now leaving a surprising red welt on his cheek, Isabelle spat, "You have *no right*! You've been salivating over my hand in marriage since the time I was born! You have coveted Our family's position and wanted to be a part of it! That is why you say these things. These are not accusations— there is no proof—it is nothing but *jealousy* on your part.

"And I will not have it! You will not soil the reputation of my friend. *I will not have it in my presence!*"

As she pulled back her hand to hit him again, Jean's voice called out behind them. "Isabelle, no!"

She stopped, caught off guard, and her hand collapsed to her side as she looked at Jean.

Pierre whirled when he heard the voice. "What spell have you put over the royal family? What have you done with the body of their aide?"

Jean just stared at him with a flat expression.

"Whatever you have done, you will need more than witchcraft to save you! When I'm through you'll be burned through to the pits of hell!"

Then Mauclerc stormed out of the room. As he left, he bumped into Thomas Aquinas, who had just entered, huffing and puffing.

Robert spoke. "He is wrong, Jean. I know he is angry that Louis imprisoned him and then told the Knights Templar of his actions, so that they removed him from their ranks."

"Do not listen to him," Isabelle implored. "He is nothing!"

Jean only looked at her sadly.

In his eyes she saw everything was confirmed. She saw what he had meant when he told her about retreating from her world. She understood what he had been apologizing for that day in the garden when she'd urged him to meet Thomas Aquinas.

Jean Adaret Benariel looked away then, and left without saying a word.

Thomas Aquinas fell to his knees as Jean walked by. "Please, *Seigneur* Benariel," he said in anguish. "It is all my fault. Please, listen. We can set this to rights, I swear by my family name and my faith—"

Jean kept going, not heeding any of the words. He walked into the hall and slowly descended the palace stairs.

"Jean!" Isabelle cried out.

Thomas Aquinas sat against the door frame and heaved breaths, face white as a ghost, eyes wide with fear and his face clammy with sweat. He looked at his hands and saw they were shaking. "Oh, great and merciful God, what have I done?"

Blanche walked up and looked at her daughter carefully. Isabelle, aware of her presence and not caring what thoughts might race through her mind, gave her the benefit of the doubt. "We must stop Mauclerc from slandering Jean, or we will lose Jean forever, Mother."

"You're too late," Aquinas said. "Mauclerc's already told the bishop at Notre Dame. After the outburst I witnessed, I believe they will not only take the charge seriously, they will enjoy doing so."

Robert broke through all of them and strode out of the room.

"No," Isabelle said without a voice, and sank down, suddenly inches smaller, her body wilted with grief.

Blanche looked out the door. "My guess is that he has been rooting around for some kind of scapegoat to blame since we let him out of jail."

Blanche reached for her cloak and headed out of the Great Room. "I will go to the tomb myself to see this alleged empty crypt. That should put this to an end."

Knowing what Blanche would find, knowing it would damn Jean, knowing it was a lie she could never disprove without revealing Jean, Isabelle burst out of the room in tears.

Jean, she thought. *Jean!*

✤ ✤ ✤

Sofia was sitting in the Queen's Chambers, quietly looking out the window of the dark room, when Jean entered the room without knocking. The oldest sister looked up at him, understanding immediately what his intrusion meant, before he even spoke.

"It's happened again," he said. "We have to leave."

Sofia stood slowly. "We should never have stopped at Montlheri. We should have left the queen and her family to their end, and continued east to the Holy Land as planned."

"You showed this family compassion. You acted out of mercy." Jean stepped closer. "Don't remove what was once freely given."

"I never should have let us stay this long," she replied.

"We each stayed for our own reasons, Sister."

"We can no longer stay, despite those reasons." Sofia's voice was hard. "I know it pains you." Jean turned away, unable to face his sister in light of the truth. But her last words surprised him. "It pains me, as well, Brother."

The future struggles that it may not become the past.

Publilius Syrus, *Moral Sayings* (c. 100 B.C.)

32

Upon her arrival at Neci's tomb, Blanche discovered that the bishop had indeed been informed, and although he said one should act cautiously in heeding such accusations, he did have a gleam of suspicion in his eyes. Blanche saw it as plain as day, and knew from her own experience that the fervor would not die down but only grow.

The bishop had made a great deal of pointing out how the groundskeeper had seen a man resembling Jean put his bare hands to the tomb after removing a pair of mysterious gloves, and how coincidental it seemed that the groundskeeper had been asked away at the very moment of something suspicious going on. Blanche could only nod and hold a sigh inside where it would not be observed. For all she suspected, Pierre himself could have dragged Neci's corpse out of the tomb and hidden it to make false allegations. But it didn't matter. It had already gone too far.

In any accusations of witchcraft, she had learned as queen, the accuser generally pointed to one action of the accused. Something as benign as a display of ultimate grief could be twisted into malicious intent. Pierre's accusations had been carefully considered and well witnessed.

And it was also no secret that Jean Adaret Benariel had spoken in anger with Archbishop Stephen Tempier at Notre Dame. Speaking out against the Church would no doubt be used as the final indictment against him, if none of the other charges were strong enough to damn Jean's innocence.

In the company of her escorts, Blanche resignedly left the royal cemetery after pausing to pray. It was nearly dusk as she rode through the field toward the *palais*. She had much to think about—much that she hadn't thought about before, but had always accepted on blind faith.

In the distance, she saw someone approaching from the castle. She recognized the silhouette instantly. It was Sofia. She told her escort to wait as she rode up to where Sofia stood alone, already suspecting what she was about to hear.

"We must leave you, *madame*," Sofia said, confirming Blanche's worst fears. Her voice sounded as resolute and even-toned as ever, but Blanche, well accustomed to it, also heard true sadness disguised in it.

"Is it because of Jean?"

Sofia nodded.

"I thought as much. Though you never spoke of it, never even addressed him in my presence, I felt the bond between you, saw it in the way you looked at him."

"How—?"

Blanche raised an eyebrow at Sofia. "I have been a mother as long as I have been queen of France. I know many things, and certainly I know a family when I see one. If there's one thing I know, by God, it's the ways of a family. Any family."

"Majesty, I—"

"Do not apologize, Sofia. There is no need, and we have known each other too long, trusted and loved each other too well, for apologies. We all have our secrets. I was content to allow you yours. It is surely not the first."

"It was always my hope that none of them would ever cause you distress," Sofia said. "Now that it has, we cannot stay. The danger is too great."

Blanche sat, silent for a moment, considering the sky. "Can you at least tell me why?" she asked.

"To do that would only subject you to greater danger," Sofia said. "As I have loved you and served you, I cannot do that. The only way to protect you is to leave."

The silence returned between them.

"Did you know that my great grandmother Queen Eleanor of Aquitaine brought me to France when I was just twelve years old?" Blanche asked at last.

"Yes."

"She told me many wise things. Many things to beware, to heed, and to accept. But most of all, she taught me that faith manages. And that faith in one's destiny will bring you to a happy end." Blanche looked at Sofia then, and their gaze met.

"I believe in you, Sofia. No matter what or who Jean really is to you. Or what happened to Neci. No matter what your source of power. You have always been kind to my family, since the day we most desperately needed your power."

"I stopped in Montlheri because I too have always believed in you, Your Majesty," Sofia replied softly. "Being in your court for two decades has been well worth the halt of our journeys."

Blanche nodded to herself. "I suppose I always knew it would come to this, one day."

"The world is not ready for us yet," Sofia replied. "One day, but not today. We have left France many times in the past, to roam from land to land, until our time comes." She smiled thinly. "It will be a long time from now."

"We have done much with France, don't you think?"

"More is yet to come, and we cannot be here to guide you. But in truth, my queen, you no longer need our guidance."

Blanche smiled, and turned her attention back to the sky. The sun was gone now. Soon it would be night. She would not ask where the sisters would go, or what they would do next. She didn't need to know.

"I will never forget your help. One day, when I am finally able to retire to the blessed life of a convent, I will chronicle all that you have done for me," Blanche said quietly. "God speed."

"God speed," Sofia said softly.

Blanche waited as Sofia turned, continuing on her way through the fields almost as if gliding through them, her white robe gradually disappearing into the shadows.

✤ ✤ ✤

When Pierre returned to his *château*, happier than he had been a few hours before, he was abruptly stopped at knifepoint. Standing before him was the dark and impressive *Seigneur* Dunbière.

"What have you done?" the lord uttered.

"What?" Pierre immediately panicked, and the dagger in Dunbière's hand pressed closer to his breastbone.

"What have you *done?*" This time Dunbière shouted the last word, and Pierre realized that he was about to die without knowing exactly why.

"I just returned from the *palais*," Pierre tried to explain. "I was making sure that my investigation was not compromised by the one you told me was investigating the order."

He was backing up, trying to get away from the dagger's point that Dunbière kept thrusting at him; with every step back Dunbière came forward menacingly.

"You have destroyed over a century of careful work—and the trap was almost sprung! You idiot, you have threatened the very existence of the Templars!"

Then Dunbière lunged. Pierre did his best to avoid the blade. "You can't kill me! I have friends in the royal court who will avenge me!"

Dunbière halted at this just as the door was kicked in violently and swung against the stone wall behind it, nearly shattering with the force of the impact.

Prince Robert stood in the doorway, sunlight streaming in behind him. His longsword drawn, scabbard thrown to the ground, he pointed the blade at Mauclerc. "This man is mine to kill. Get out," he told Dunbière.

Dunbière looked at Pierre, looked back at Robert, and then smiled. "I'll leave you to your royal protection," he said, and walked out the back door.

"I should have done this the first time I caught you," Robert said. He was smiling that goddamned smile.

"You can't touch me," Pierre said. He had time to draw his own sword now. "You swore an oath that you wouldn't touch me if I stayed away from your family. I've harmed no one who is related to you—in fact, I've saved you from a curse!"

They went at each other viciously: no armor, no elite fencing; just two men determined to live, determined that he would kill the other one.

Pierre was unaccustomed to fighting, and he found it difficult to fend Robert off. Within a few moments of the battle, he took a cut to the face. It infuriated him. In the heated frenzy, he knocked over chairs, then threw them. A chair hit Robert as he pulled up an arm to deflect it. Pierre took the opportunity and lashed at Robert with his sword, cutting into his thigh.

It was a good wound, but Robert didn't stop smiling, even at the impact. Pierre felt the blood rush from his head. Robert still came against him, smiling, still strong. Pierre skittered back, and fell over a low bench behind him.

His legs were over the bench. Robert swung for them, barely missing as Pierre pulled back at the last possible moment. But Robert's sword was cutting into the wood so deeply that great welts formed in the wood grain and splinters flew at the impact.

Pierre thrust as Robert tugged at his sword, now wedged deeply into the bench. Robert couldn't pull out in time and put one hand up, stopping Pierre's blade with his bare fingers. Robert's red blood ran down Pierre's blade to the hilt.

When Pierre looked up, Robert was smiling. He punched Pierre in the face and sent him flying back.

"It was *Jean*. I did it . . . for Isabelle . . . Jean, I went for *Jean*!" Pierre gasped as he crumpled to the floor.

"You're a liar!" Pierre rolled over and stared up at Robert. The prince stood over him with his own sword at his throat. "You said you would not harm me as long as I didn't act against your family."

Robert came down on Pierre, right at his heart, and stabbed deeply till he felt the floor on the other side of the body with the tip of his sword. He gave the *coup de grâce* with his damning smile as he watched Pierre expire beneath him.

Just before the last light left Mauclerc's eyes, Robert stopped smiling. "You never bothered to ask, or I would have clarified," he said, his face slack. "Jean *is* family."

Lord Dunbière rushed down dark alleys, avoiding main streets on his way to the wharf, where he would catch the last ship sailing for Greece. A figure stepped from the shadows. It was a figure that on any other day he would have prayed to God himself to get a glimpse of, but today, the old Templar only went ashen.

Jean spoke quietly. "We will be coming for Jerusalem. And for what belongs to us, not to grave-robbing orders like yours."

Dunbière, realizing in Jean's words that he would not be killed today, could afford the luxury of being smug. "We stand at an impasse in France. We've made it too dangerous for you to stay here, so now all you can do is resort to threats."

Jean turned, and without a breadth of thought, he looked back over his left shoulder. "Threats are mere wishes. But this I promise: Two generations hence, France will also be too dangerous for you. And unlike my family, you will *all* perish."

Then he walked away into the shadows.

✤ ✤ ✤

It was shortly after ten o'clock at night when Thomas Aquinas finally checked Notre Dame for any sign of Princess Isabelle. He had a hunch, after searching all day in places she might be lurking, that she had come to the Great Cathedral. He followed his intuition and found Isabelle lying on a long pew in the dark, her cloak wrapped about her shoulders and legs to keep warm.

"What are you doing here?" he whispered to her.

She looked up then, her cheeks streaked with tears. "Jean?" she asked hopefully, then saw who it was. She struggled to get up. "*Seigneur* Aquinas—"

"Thomas, please." He sat down next to her.

She only nodded. It was all she had energy for.

"How long have you been here?"

"I have been praying here since this afternoon. I thought if anyone could help, it would be Our Lady the Blessed Virgin. She would right the wrongs and protect Jean."

Isabelle rested her arms on the pew before her and laid her head on her forearms.

"My dearest friend, it's cold now. You'll catch a chill and become sick. Come back to the castle."

"I'm not finished praying. I know I can make a difference. I know I can set things right." She started to weep again.

"Why do you do this to yourself?"

"Don't you see?" She raised her head. Tears, hot and streaming, soaked her cheeks once more. "I am the reason he is distressed. I told him to come back. Pierre hates him because he is close to me. Pierre has won!"

"No, Isabelle. It's not your fault. You questioned the natural order of things. You *seek* answers. You live and in so doing, let others around you truly experience life. You did nothing wrong in drawing him out as you did with all around you."

Isabelle wiped her eyes and tried to straighten the hair that had fallen out of its casings.

"It's *him*, isn't it?" Aquinas asked. "He is the one. He seems to attract this. There is something about him that draws people, interest, and lightning in equal measure. Why—"

"I can't tell you anything, Thomas. Would that I could tell you everything and get it all off my chest. But I promised." She stared at him then, with her red-rimmed eyes and running red nose.

"You don't have to say a thing, Isabelle. Not a word. We are friends, are we not?"

"Yes." She nodded.

"And the Lord works in mysterious ways, does He not?"

"Yes." She choked on a sob.

"He will not let harm come to Jean. He knows, above all, what must happen, and not even your prayers can change that. What must happen, must happen. But there is a reason for everything, Isabelle. That I know."

She sobbed again, her hands on the back of the pew with her head resting against them. Thomas Aquinas sat for a very long time by his friend until she could not cry anymore. How late it must have been, he had no idea. He didn't feel tired, oddly enough.

"I have heard that the Order of the Rose and Jean are leaving soon. I will be leaving for Naples in the morning myself. Do you know where your friends might be going?" he asked her.

"I don't know. I would imagine . . . east. That's just a guess."

Thomas nodded. "If it is within my power, I will watch over them, if they come through Italy. I have many friends, contacts, discreet people. I will be a silent guardian. They will never know I'm there."

She looked at him hopefully. "You would do this for Jean?"

"I would do it for both of you. None will even know I'm watching, save you and I."

She sat back against the pew and just stared ahead at the nave of the chapel. After several long minutes of both grief and relief, she finally spoke. "I cannot see the good in any of this, though I have been trying." She sniffed.

"It is said that we are all in a constant state of becoming. Every being has potential, but whether we realize that potential is another matter. I believe we come to God for this. Or, sometimes, God comes to us.

"It is a happy accident," he continued. "That I was curious at all about the relics of the Saint Mary, for I wanted to reconcile the Magdalene with my own faith. I have stumbled upon enlightenment, if only in part."

"It doesn't frighten you?"

"On the contrary, if the Holy Spirit does indeed reside with us, walking to and fro on the earth until the end of days, perhaps in the form of your friend Jean and his sisters, it can only confirm my faith in God." Aquinas leaned over. "There are very few of us truly ever touched by Him. You have been touched, Isabelle. Touched by the Hand."

"And still, I fail to see."

"That only requires time. And all that we are given in life is time," he replied. They sat at the altar until just before dawn.

The fog glided along the nooks and crannies of the green valleys. The blades of meadow grass, wet with dew, glittered like strands covered in silver. From the door of the castle, heading over the crest of the hill, footprints marked the silver lining on the grass. The tracks led to the stables.

Draped in a black cape, with a black wool gown beneath, strands of golden hair escaping from the hood of her cloak, Isabelle followed the tracks in the grass. She stepped into the dry stable, out of the cold weather. At the back, Jean Adaret Benariel was saddling up his mount.

Her voice broke the stillness of dawn. "You would leave without telling me?"

He stopped, but did not look back at her. "I held this moment off as long as I could."

"My family would protect your honor."

"And in so doing, soil their own reputation. No, I must go."

"Jean, they will die down; these things always come to nothing, and everyone forgets. You don't have to leave."

"Even if you were right, there would come a day when . . . they wouldn't know what to do with me."

This truth hung between them.

He finished packing all his bags tight against the saddle, and they stood there, unmoving in the darkness before the dawn. Today, she noticed, he wore no gloves. It was the first time in a while that she'd seen his hands freely unrestrained, gripping the reins of his mount.

"Then I will wait for you," she said, her eyes filling with tears. She didn't know what else to say; she couldn't imagine the void in her life without him.

"Don't do that. Live your life, Isabelle. It would make me very happy. I give you the Tower of Benariel; it is your land to keep." He walked over to her and said, "And I need you to do me a favor with it."

"What favor?" she asked.

"Look after my roses. Make sure they never come to harm. They are very special to me, and alas, I cannot take them with me on my journey. And I believe you will find some other use for the land around it."

She nodded and knew he spoke of her long-held dream of a convent. She could look after his roses, yes. "Where will you go?"

"East, to the Holy Land. We were heading there when we came across your family at Montlheri." He looked above her head and focused on something far in the distance. "You still have the rest of your life ahead of you." Then he looked down at her, and his eyes were kind.

She wanted to speak, but no words came. Only grief.

"And I see a great many things that you will do, if you just let yourself do them, dearest Isabelle." Then he came near without hesitation and put his bare hands gently on her face. His palms were warm. This time, despite her immense sadness, she realized that the strange warmth and tingling sensation was not her own, but came from his very hands. She gazed deeply into his eyes.

A flash came to her, and suddenly she was staring up at a man with long brown hair, lashed to a great pole, hanging limply, a nest of thorny vines about his head, a gash at his side and his arms stretched wide. She staggered back, feeling the weight in her stomach, and upon looking down, saw not herself but another woman's body, pregnant and swollen under plain coarse robes. At her feet were a scattering of bloodred roses.

"*Tetelestai*," he whispered. "It is finished."

The woman below sobbed.

Then suddenly, the world went dark. The wind screamed and the dust burned and the sky opened. The last breath of the man above her was the sound of the world, the sound of pain, the sound of hope, the sound of renewal. It scoured the earth, and the sun hid itself behind clouds, behind shame, behind blood.

It is finished. . . .

It is finished.

Isabelle wept, and when she looked back up again, she met Jean's eyes. She was back in the calm and quiet stable. The horses stamped a bit behind them, as if they had felt the charge that momentarily passed between the two people.

"What was that?" She was breathless.

"A soul memory," he replied quietly. "I leave you with a gift. . . ." He bent down, closed his eyes, and touched his lips to hers, pressing them gently against her mouth. It was like a whisper, and closing her eyes, she felt the rush of wind in her ears. She felt his breath, sweet and warm against her lips, skin against tender skin. A rush of heat filled her mouth and tingled down the back of her throat. Her body flushed, ran hot.

Finally, they parted, and her eyes opened to find him looking at her, his eyes bright with sadness as well. Then his warm hands let go of their soft embrace on her face, and he backed away.

They walked outside in the cold air together, his hand on the reins of his mount. She felt the residual warmth of his hands on her cheeks and wanted it to remain forever. But already it was fading, though her lips still tingled and her ears were hot and flush.

He mounted his horse, reins in hand, and took one final look at Isabelle standing in the doorway. "I think I finally realize how impossible it is for me to leave you. And I know now that I must have loved you. Always."

Then he turned his mount and headed away.

A soul memory, she thought as she watched him ride away. *He did not say it. He did not say the words, did not say the rest of it.*

But she knew. Knew it as she would never again know anything in her life.

A soul memory.
Of his father.

Live not as though there were a thousand years ahead of you. Fate is at your elbow; make yourself good while life and power are still yours.

Marcus Aurelius, *The Meditations* (A.D. 167)

Afterword

As Isabelle knelt down to pull a few stubborn weeds from the base of the rosebush, her back twinged. She was getting older; the seasons were shifting with more permanence against her bones. She stood upright and sighed.

Above her, the Tower of Benariel stretched into the afternoon sky. The clouds were turning lovely shades of pink and lemon, with a hint of violet crowning the evening's eminence. The clouds took notice of her gaze and moved slightly, as if responding to the breath of her sigh. It was one of countless sunsets that she had seen in a lifetime, but every sunset in the Western Wood was handsome, a moment of such exquisite natural beauty as to compel even the most devout monk or cloistered nun to dream fantasies unending.

Her tired eyes wrinkled at the edges as she let a smile escape.

I miss him.

Somewhere, somehow, Isabelle could feel the connection of his thoughts like a wind against her face. She imagined Jean was standing elsewhere, at the edge of the earth perhaps, looking up at the sky like this, wondering about her at the same moment that her thoughts had turned to him.

The sky was gilding now, a deep rich gold over the rippling clouds. Isabelle looked down and noticed that one of the five open roses on the bush had lost a few petals. It was dying, making way for a new bud farther down the branch. Isabelle reached out and gently stroked the full, red blossom. Beneath the whisper of her fingers, the velvet petals stretched and refreshed into a completely healthy bloom.

Jean's gift.

She looked deeply at the vibrant rose and thought, *I could not be there for you, Louis, when you fell ill on your Crusade. I wanted to travel to you, but I wouldn't last the journey. There is nothing to be done but to wait out the rest of our earthly sentences, Brother.*

It struck her heart and made her wince. She looked up with the eyes of an old woman and wondered where the years had gone, and how they could have gone so quickly.

The Sisters of the convent she had built on Jean's land had named Isabelle's little garden "Le Jardin de la Rose." Anything planted here in the small plot of land just outside the tower grew tall and straight. Isabelle had even bought a lemon tree from a merchant in Paris who'd brought the trees up from southern Italy. Everyone had said that it would not grow in this ground, this climate. But Isabelle knew better.

It was King Conrad's idea that she buy a lemon tree. His last dear letter had indicated things were again going poorly for Germany. He had been given papal excommunication, and they had even elected an antiking to rival his own regency. The letter told her of all the grave circumstances, and then had insisted she must try a lemon tree in her garden. But that was dear Conrad. She had written back and told him he could seek refuge in France if need be. He was a good man, and she supported him to the end.

She'd taken the small cutting home to the tower and planted it on the far edge of the garden in its own plot, surrounded by a small willow fence. The tree had thrived, even through the rainy months of *février* and *mars*. The sisters called it a miracle.

It probably was, she thought, looking at the tree now heavy with large, sunny lemons. She could just make out their tart, fresh scent from across the little enclosure. They were ready to be harvested.

Tomorrow, she decided, as she had decided each day of the seven preceding days. There was something delicious about a lemon tree with its lemons hanging low on branches heavy with their weight. It was a satisfying sight, and it meant the convent, the grounds, the world were all bountiful. She didn't want to deprive herself yet of that lovely image, wrapped around one tree and its yield of fruit. It would wait another day.

The clean scent mingled with another, coming from inside the tower. Isabelle pulled up the last stubborn weed at the base of the rose-bush and closed her eyes. She put her chin up and inhaled slowly. The smell of baking bread mingled with the lemons. Sister Angelina was making loaves out of wheat from the far field again. The smell was mouth-watering.

Isabelle heard a laugh: a memory of a laugh she had not heard for many years. It was Robert, with his robust smile and bright white teeth that flashed beneath a black, slick beard and mustache. She could hear him, and with her eyes closed, she could see him, young and hearty, racing into the Great Room just ahead of a tiny nine-year-old girl. She knew the girl; it was herself, racing her older brother into the Great Room for . . .

What were we striving for? She stopped, her eyes closed. Her mind followed the children. *Ah yes, lemon pancakes, my favorite.*

I will fight you for the last! she heard Robert challenge.

A duel then! she had said in reply. *Was that truly me? It was so long ago*, mais oui, *I was feisty and aggressive once upon a time.*

She had won, too, she remembered. *And I didn't share a whit with him.*

Isabelle chuckled to herself and opened her eyes. She was looking once more at the lemon tree. "You were always so quick to battle, Robert. Even then, I knew one day you would die in battle." She spoke to the shadows, which remained silent. "A product of your insatiable need to be at the forefront. Your reckless hotheadedness no one would curb, not even Mother, God rest her soul. You were destined to die young and on the battlefield for Louis."

The door to the tower opened, and a woman dressed in a dark habit came out to the garden. Isabelle saw her approaching. "At least, dear brother, I still have your laugh."

"Princess Isabelle, are you all right? I saw you from the door and thought you had not moved in a great while."

Isabelle had to smile. "I am remembering, again, *Bonne* Clare."

Claire, a much older woman these days, looked at her long-cherished princess with an expression so kind, and so respectful, that the royal turned her head in modesty to look around the garden once more.

"I have a letter here for you, from Thomas Aquinas," Claire said at last.

"Thomas!" Isabelle's old eyes sparkled happily. "Oh, please let me see."

Claire passed over the letter and smiled. "It's getting late. What would you like for dinner tonight, Your Highness?"

Isabelle looked at Claire for a long moment; then her gaze softened into a delightful memory. The lines in her face had smoothed out, nearly disappearing at the thought.

"I would like lemon pancakes tonight."

"I do think we have a recipe for lemon pancakes, Your Highness."

Isabelle's eyes focused on Claire with the look of a hopeful young child. "You think we can have lemon pancakes, really?"

"I assure you. I will need to take a few lemons from the tree, though."

"Then let's do that. And tomorrow we will harvest the whole tree." Isabelle smiled.

"Very well, Your Highness. I'll get things prepared." Claire walked over to the tree and selected three of the most plump and vibrant lemons on the lower branches.

Isabelle opened the letter from her dear old friend Thomas

Aquinas. At last report, he was en route to Paris to see her. But the letter was not about his trip.

Dearest Isabelle,

I have found Him. I have at last known beauty and peace. And I can do no more. Such secrets have been revealed to me that all I have written now appears to be of little value.

Your friend,
Thomas Aquinas

Claire turned as Isabelle put the letter down on her lap and closed her eyes with pain and joy intermingled. With the lemons hefted into her apron, the younger Sister walked back to the door of the tower, then paused, looking back.

"Your Highness?" Claire called.

Isabelle opened her eyes, bright with unreleased tears.

"Sewing laid out as usual for you tonight?" Claire asked.

"*Non,* tonight I think I'll write."

"Write, *madame?*" Claire was surprised. It was definitely not one of Isabelle's customary habits to write in the evenings. The candlelight was rarely sufficient to the needs of her eyes these days.

"Yes." Isabelle paused. "I want to write. Set my table, parchment, and quill for me by a large taper, will you? I'm going to write."

"About what?" Claire asked.

"Roses," Isabelle said, but she was looking at the sky, not at her garden. "The memory of roses . . ."

The End

Codicil

BEING, ONE HOPES, A SELECTION OF THOUGHTS ON FAITH, FACTS, DREAMS AND THE POINTS AT WHICH THEY INTERSECT

I wish I could properly explain how this book came to be, but in truth I don't really know how to do that. Ask any writer how he got from point A to point B in the story, and sometimes you'll get a concrete response: a particular bit of information, research, or structure that solved the story problem. Most times, though, the answer is simply, "That's where the story chose to go." Which is appropriate, since this book is about faith. I have learned to put all my faith in the process of creating words, because the writing always knows what it is doing. The only real truth is in the writing.

That is, however, a fairly poor answer to the question, "Where did this book come from?" So I'll do my best to reconstruct the scene of the crime by showing the trail of my footsteps through the facts involved.

Within my small writing nook is an entire corner dedicated to the textbooks, biographies, and historical records of France. These documents were the starting point for this novel at a time when I began my original plan: to write about an order of knights made entirely of women. But as I dove into those great historical essays and pored over ancient letters, I discovered a world of mysticism and belief that today's world can no longer comprehend.

Among the many books on my shelf are *Holy Blood, Holy Grail*, a modern treatise on the possible outcome of the life of Christ; and *The Hour of Our Death*, a huge book concerning the nature of cemeteries throughout the centuries, including the importance of saints' relics, that I once had the displeasure to read in college. The saints' relics that the royal family encountered in this book were accurately portrayed as an important part of medieval life. Much infighting and bargaining was taking place with saints' relics at this time, with churches, abbeys, and monasteries fighting over who had the best relics and who thus merited the most tourism from pilgrims. (In one account, a member of one church visiting a competing one that featured a hand as its sacred relic bent over to kiss the ring on said hand in order to bite off the finger and return it to his own church as their newly acquired sacred relic.)

Secret Societies is an invaluable resource on the Templars and the Old Man of the Mountain, who was also known as the Hungarian Master. He was also discussed in Joinville's primary source materials as well as in a variety of history texts. (You'd think they could come up with a more imaginative name, especially since I had to write about it with a straight face, but there it is. He was an old man, he lived in a mountain, and that's how they named him. Happily, I did not have to refer to the king as The Guy with the Big Hat in the Castle.)

The assassination attempt was described as it happened, and the Old Man makes another appearance later in Louis' life, during his Crusade. Probably still upset about the name thing, I suppose.

Folklore of Women is a rare, out-of-print volume given to me by a dear friend, full of wonderful, old-fashioned anecdotes that I drew upon for the telling of this tale. *The Medieval Calendar Year* is a great resource to keep the calendar events of this book accurate.

Medieval and Early Renaissance Medicine is a textbook from a college course where I learned about the medical procedures once used to help victims of dysentery, which Louis contracted after his war. This book also discusses the processes of a kind of medicine very foreign to us now, such as divination with a urine jar (a practice now found only in certain fraternities). I even found a chance to put the urine examiner in the city as Isabelle looks upon the bridge from her boat across the river.

The Medieval Garden, The Medieval Reader, Chivalry, and *The History of the Knights Templars* were all incredibly useful. Pierre Mauclerc's name appears in documents in a generalized but suspicious way, so I stretched him the most and made him into an emissary for the Templars.

The Templars themselves were destroyed by Louis IX's grandson only two generations later, when the tension between the French monarchy and the Templars reached their highest point.

Cathedral, Forge and Waterwheel is an excellent source book from which I learned the process of building the great cathedrals, including Notre Dame, which was being built during Isabelle's lifetime and took several lifetimes to complete.

Women in the Middle Ages taught me a great deal about the reality of life for women in this time, and how they found the strength to live more progressive lives by joining the Church. Queen Blanche was a queen to rival Eleanor of Aquitaine or Queen Elizabeth I, and it is recorded in historical texts that Eleanor had chaperoned Blanche as a young girl when she came to marry Louis VIII.

The Knight in History, Life in a Medieval Castle, Life in a Medieval Village, Life in a Medieval City, and *Clothes of the Medieval World* were all very helpful in the reconstruction of medieval Paris, its festivals and ambience. Sadly, the *palais* referred to in this book no longer stands. France's kings built greater palaces in later years, and the old *palais* became obsolete and vanished.

Daily Life in Medieval Times was an indispensable book for describing the most inane and important details of life for Isabelle and her family. It was the source of many fascinating tidbits, such as the rag-catcher who winds his way throughout this book. *A Place Apart*, a book about the monastic life written in contemporary times, provides a glimpse into the timeless regime of monks and nuns, a life that has not changed over the centuries.

The Rule of St. Benedict contains my favorite rule of the monastic orders, the one that Jean Adaret Benariel quotes when he suggests that Isabelle and he ride into the sunset so the sun would not set on his anger.

Joinville and Villehardoun: Chronicles of the Crusades is one of the most influential primary sources of information for the book apart from my textbooks on history, from which I created a meticulous time-line. Its scope provided the backdrop for all the characters, including Hugh de la Marche and his wife, Pierre Mauclerc, and many others who truly existed in history. I did, however, exercise poetic license in giving them each a distinctive character.

Several other university textbooks are still kicking around on my bookshelves, and I was able to pull from them quotes from such luminaries as Thomas Aquinas. (Thomas admittedly did not visit Paris so early, but I wanted to fit him in, and I'm reasonably sure he didn't mind the trip, being in prison at the time. And who wouldn't want an occasional night out on the town?) It also provided a wonderful picture of the *université* at Paris, with Bacon and all the other historical figures who resided there before they became . . . well, historical figures.

The only personages created whole cloth were the women of the Order of the Rose and, of course, Jean Adaret Benariel. For this, I turned my attention to the Internet, which is the best source for rumors, speculations, sightings of the miraculous, and obscure recipes. I had already read, in *Holy Blood, Holy Grail*, that Magdalene might have been the Beloved Disciple of Christ and was possibly married to him. Other books have delved into their actual relationship, but I was curious about their family and their childrens' lives, wondering if the children stood to inherit the world in their father's absence. I then discovered an even more fascinating legend stemming from the south of

France, in Toulouse, that Magdalene went to France after Christ's death and that her remains were said to rest there. (It was, after all, a long voyage, and the woman doubtless needed a nap.)

According to accounts from the time, Princess Isabelle really did found a convent, which was extraordinary for a woman at that time, and later she and Louis were both sainted upon their deaths, unusual even by contemporary standards. It is not too far a stretch to believe that something great must have touched their lives in order for others to preserve them in the memory of the Church for eternity. Perhaps it took the form of an alliance with a holy order that few had ever heard of: namely, the Order of the Rose.

When that thought occurred, dovetailing as it did with my original plan for the novel (Old joke: How do you make God laugh? Tell him your plans) suddenly the novel took a sharp turn. Instead of delving into the world of an order of women knights, it became a backstage account of the real reasons behind so many of the major historical events of France. Why were certain battles fought, why were other castles built, what lay behind the demise of the Templars at French hands, and why were the king and princess sainted?

Was it because they had been touched by something or someone who would change their lives forever?

On such questions are novels born. Including the one you now hold in your hands.

This story came to an end at a time before the lives of the family of France had come to their own conclusions because to do otherwise would have required a book that could only be raised by forklift. But for those curious to know what happened next . . . While the youngest royal brother, Charles, does not get much time to shine in this novel, he later ruled over Anjou. It was he who found and protected the alleged bones of Mary Magdalene in southern France. Louis' Crusade was the pinnacle of his life, but the reader did not get the chance to venture forth with him.

Isabelle's convent had finally been founded when the book ends. What happened next, the tapestry of events, is so rich and fascinating, it could only continue beyond the pages into another book. And perhaps one day it will.

The only character not discovered through the course of reading was Jean Adaret Benariel. I'm horrified to admit this because it sounds so cliché, but I must confess that this one came to me in a dream one night.

I had already written about his sisters in the Order of the Rose: Sofia, Neci, and Norea—names chosen for their resonance with legends and Middle Eastern origins. They had sworn their allegiance to Blanche of Castile, and everything was going just fine when suddenly Jean was thrust into the middle of the storyline by something as inconsequential as a dream. I had never anticipated his presence, but once I woke from the dream, I knew the novel had changed course and that the vision I had been following originally would have to be abandoned for the writing's vision.

In my dream, he left Isabelle a pearl comb.

In my novel, he left her an undying rose.

And he left me the final key to this mysterious tale.

Jean became a touchstone for everything. He was the son of the Son of God, heir to this world and the next. I surrendered my own ideas about this story and just started writing down what came to me. As a wise woman once said, writing is not about thinking something up, it's about getting something down. I have great faith in that process.

The Crown Rose is the result of faith in things I cannot see or explain but know in my heart to be present, even if only in dreams.

FIONA AVERY is a writer working in Los Angeles, California. Her work ranges from prose to screenwriting, with everything in between. Previous television credits include work on *Babylon 5*, *Crusade*, and *Earth: Final Conflict*. In 2001, her short story "Luring the Tiger Out of the Mountains" earned an honorable mention in *The Year's Best Science Fiction*, published by St. Martin's Press. Avery has been in the Bestselling Top Ten Comics with works such as the Eisner-winning *Amazing Spiderman*, *Rogue: Icons*, *Peter Parker: Spiderman*, *Tomb Raider*, *Witchblade*, and *X-Men*. *Witchblade: Obakemono*, her first graphic novel, sold at number 2 on the GN charts for July 2002. The foremost news magazine in the industry, *Wizard Magazine*, has listed Fiona Avery in its exclusive Top Ten Creators list. Her original property, a comic book called *No Honor* was recently optioned by Platinum Studios and is in development as a feature film. You can visit her online at www.fionaavery.com.

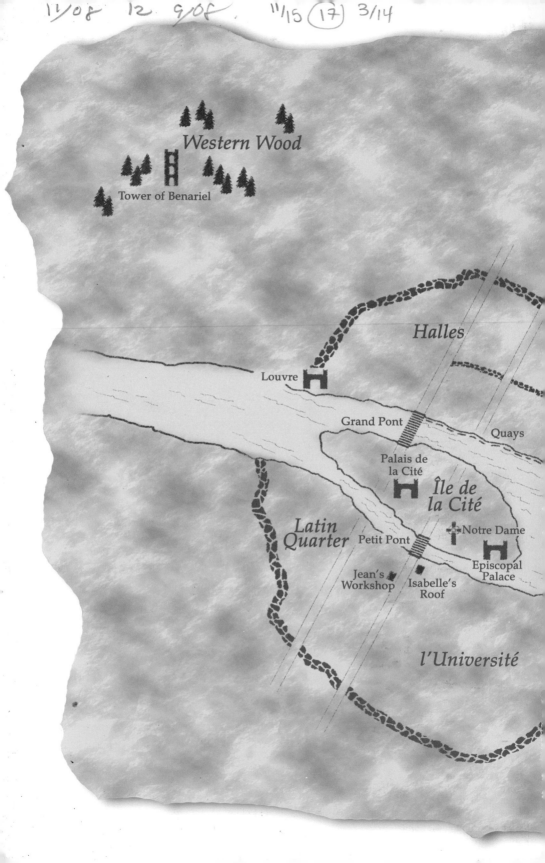

Western Wood

Tower of Benariel

Halles

Louvre

Grand Pont

Quays

Palais de
la Cité

Île de
la Cité

Latin
Quarter   Petit Pont

Notre Dame

Episcopal
Palace

Jean's
Workshop   Isabelle's
Roof

l'Université